D1461097

*read*iscover...

BooksMusic**Film**
Family history
FaxingGames**Chil**

Please return or renew
avoid fines. It may be ren_
in person. Please quote th_

Honey

Honey

A novel

ARNOLD WESKER

Scribner

First published in Great Britain by Scribner, 2005
An imprint of Simon & Schuster UK Ltd
A Viacom Company

1 3 5 7 9 10 8 6 4 2

Simon & Schuster UK Ltd
Africa House
9804   64–78 Kingsway
London WC2B 6AH

www.simonsays.co.uk

Simon & Schuster Australia
Sydney

A CIP catalogue record for this book is available from the British Library

Hardback ISBN: 0-7432-6855-5
EAN: 9780743268554
Trade Paperback ISBN: 0-7432-7606-X
EAN: 9780743276061

Typeset in Bembo by M Rules
Printed and bound in Great Britain by
The Bath Press, Bath

To
Rose Tremain and Richard Holmes
who kept a guiding eye on me

With love and admiration

Gratitude

Attempting to write a first novel at this late age (seventy-two) induces all manner of terrors. With so much good writing around how dare one? Yet, with a little help from those close to me, I dared, and I wish to acknowledge and offer gratitude for their help.

First to my wife, Dusty, for looking after me, enabling me to concentrate on writing freed from domestic chores.

To my assistant, Jan Morris, to whom I dictated from a written manuscript, who not only typed all these words into the computer but encouraged me along the way.

To my friend Sylvia Parker, who pointed to typos, bad grammar, clumsy sentence structure, tautologies and sheets of poor writing, angering me in the process but persisting till I conceded she was right.

To the instigator of it all, my agent, Christopher Sinclair-Stevenson, who, after reading one page, urged me on when I was not sure I had a talent for prose.

To Tim Binding, my editor at Simon & Schuster, who commissioned the novel on the basis of the first sixty pages or so, and who, when it was finished, perceptively identified the irrelevant and superfluous.

Finally to Neville Schulman OBE from whose inspirational book 'Some Like It Cold – Arctic and Antarctic Adventures' he graciously allowed me to plunder.

For the notice I didn't take of some of my readers' comments I am entirely responsible.

If there is to be a 'next one' I know it will benefit from all I have learnt this time round.

AUTHOR'S NOTE

Honey is about the heroine, Beatie Bryant, of my play *Roots*, the second play in *The Wesker Trilogy* (so named by The Royal Court Theatre, where the plays began, not by me).

It is a play about 'self-discovery', ending with Beatie finding her own voice instead of quoting her boyfriend, Ronnie Kahn, all the time. I was frequently asked what happened to Beatie after she found her own voice, what did she do with it? For years I contemplated writing a novel that explored her life after the final curtain.

The moment came, but I found myself ignoring the period. I'm not sure I understand why but I brought her life forward from the sixties to the late eighties. I suppose I have the right to play around with chronology this way and I offer this note simply to avoid those, who might be familiar with the play, writing to me saying I got the years mixed up.

Let everyone speak. Even the dead.

CONTENTS

1

He said

He said:

'When you get too old, as I am, you look. I'm sorry, young woman. Rude of me. I've finished my morning coffee. I'm going.'

I told him I didn't mind. 'Men always look,' I said. 'I'm beautiful.' That made him smile. I saw the young man he once was, and thought – the streets are full of young men trapped in old men's bodies.

'Ah,' he said, 'now,' he said, 'there are many people would hear you say that and think, "What a vain young woman." Not me. I loved it: *Men always look. I'm beautiful!*" Ha!' He smiled again. I saw mischief in his eyes. He reminded me of someone I once knew. His smile became a laugh. Infectious. It made me laugh with him. 'It's the way you said it,' he explained, 'I heard the way you said it. Not a boast. A statement of fact – *"I'm beautiful."* And you are, young woman, you are. Which of course is why I looked. I hope,' he added, 'you were not offended by the way I looked.' I said no, I wasn't. 'It wasn't a lecherous look?' he asked. I said no again, only this time with a slight pause. 'Well,' he said, 'yes, it

was. If we're going to be honest, you and me, it was. A little lecherous. But there, what can I do? I'm old, you're young . . .'

He broke off, rose, shouldered his backpack and offered his
hand. 'It was very kind of you to allow me to talk to you.' And
then he said something I shall never forget. 'The world,' he said,
'is divided between people who are immediate and those who
are hard work. You, my dear young woman, are immediate.
And when I'm gone see if you can think of dividing the world
like that.' We shook hands and I watched him walk away. He
was not stooped, or slow. He strode as though on a hike across
plains. Impressive. But, I thought, if he continues carrying a
backpack on his shoulder he will strain his spine, which will lay
him flat.

Two things he said that were strangely phrased: '*If we're going to
be honest, you and me*' as if we had a future together; and, '*Very kind
of you to allow me to talk to you.*' '*Allow*' him? Did I? Did others not?
Did he have a history of being told to shut up? He left a strong
presence. I took it home with me. The world, I found myself
thinking, is divided between those who sparkle and those who are
dull. I have been thinking about him ever since.

I have also been looking at myself in the mirror. I *am* beautiful. It is true. But only my face. I'm not elegant. My body is
not long and slim; lumpy, actually. Fleshy, Rubenesque. I have
the kind of body men want either to bite into or fall asleep
upon. I can be caressed but they don't seem to know that.
Besides, I say to myself in the mirror, have you forgotten, Beatie
Bryant, that real beauty combines intelligence and character
with physical shape, and that intelligence and character come
through the eyes? And are not your eyes intelligent and full of
interesting character?

I scrutinise myself intently. I feel good about myself. I feel
whole, complete. Not fulfilled yet, by a long way, but – the parts
are there, in place, they seem to fit, belong to one another. I have
no fear of fragmentation, mostly the centre holds. Sorry, Mr Yeats,
it just does.

It is a most peculiar thing to scrutinise yourself in the mirror. At first you merely see someone looking at you. Yes, you know it's you, nothing special, but if you stare at yourself long and hard, if you *scrutinise* – then it's different; you become embarrassed, make a face, stick out your tongue, which makes you smile. You see the smile, which leads you to *think* about the smile. Is it an attractive smile? A supercilious smile? Do you smile tightly, with a touch of meanness, a begrudging I'm-doing-you-a-favour smile? Self-questioning leads to further self-examination: you're looking at your face being thoughtful about your smile. Is that what you look like when you're thoughtful? Did the old man find that look interesting? I wonder. *I* would be attracted to such a thoughtful face. Your face changes again, no longer thoughtful but vain. You're looking at your face being vain about your face looking attractive while your face is being thoughtful. Yet another person emerges. She's sad, this other person. Vanity has saddened her. Which is the moment you turn away. Though not completely. You look again as if to make sure you're still there. You are. Reassured, you turn again. But not for the last time. There's always that one last look. And then you've had enough.

Thus do young women of twenty-five fresh out of college, who have not yet discovered what to do with their one-and-only life, pass idle moments. And thinking about idle moments brought me back to that old man. What did he do? I had not asked. There he had been, full of his sixty years, sitting at a table in Shepherd Market alongside mine, and I'd not asked him about himself. How did he earn a living? How had he filled all those years? I would never know. All I know is that when I sat down he was at the tail end of a conversation with a man who had bumps on his face talking about bees and honey, only he seemed not to be listening too intently, and the man with bumps on his face got up abruptly and left, after which he ordered another coffee and, having asked the waitress if there was any honey, and after she had rather sullenly brought him a small pot, he had spooned it all into his coffee. W*as* sixty – old? And what made me think he *was* sixty?

Off he'd gone with his shoulder bag, striding like a young man who could have been less than sixty, and I knew nothing about him.

2

I should have stayed

I should have stayed and talked with her. Lingered a little. Why do I always feel this need to be decisive? Why is decisiveness more admired than reflection? Miriam was decisive, my pauses to reflect irritated her. *She* moved with purpose, *I* lingered with second thoughts. 'On the other hand,' I would always say. 'You and your *other hand*,' she would chide. But that's me – anxious about the other person, the other view, the other need. Everyone has other needs. She seemed not to care about others' needs. 'I'm the needy one,' she would say, 'and *I'm* your responsibility.' I understood. To begin with. Now? Ah, now – Miriam! Will I ever confront the truth about Miriam?

Bloody backpack! Why do I fill it with so many things? I'm like a woman lost without a bag in my hand to carry this and that, a book I might want to read, space for things I might want to buy, a present I might see for a future someone, something catches your eye and you think I know who that will be good for – Christmas time, birthday time, visiting time.

Why are you having this conversation with yourself? You *know* why your backpack is heavy. You're rehearsing your body for a trek; your poor body for a long, arduous trek in Antarctica. There's fat must fall away and muscles to be found and toned.

And Barney. I'm visiting him. I can't visit him and not take him something. You can't call on people empty-handed. But what does he need? Barney was always difficult to buy for because he didn't ever seem without. He was a 'never without' person.

In what state will I find him? Last time I found him full of Proust. At last he was reading Proust. He'd marked up passages to read to me. Listen to this! You must hear this! Proust Proust Proust! Barney was inventing the wheel.

Still, nothing wrong with inventing the wheel. So what if we discover something we didn't know hundreds of others had discovered before us? We still had to work it out for ourselves. Like when I conceived of automatic gears. I was hitchhiking, a teenager, hitching a lift, and there was silence in the car. I didn't know what to say, and the driver didn't know what to ask after 'Come far?' And as we drove through built-up areas I watched him change gear again and again till finally I said, 'You'd think it would be easy to invent gears that change automatically as you increase or decrease speed.'

'They've been invented,' he smiled.

I told Barney I'd read Proust and to stop reading to me. You've forgotten, he said, everybody forgets what they read. Do I let him invent the wheel? What will he invent this afternoon, I wonder? I'm worried. No I'm not. I'm more anxious. Barney is old. Old before he needs to be. His daughter Tamara sent him a card saying: 'Why are you having another birthday? Weren't you old enough last year?' He was! He was seventy. Witty daughter. His other daughter, Natasha, thinking he was a lonely widower, sent him a card with a photo of a naked woman in which she wrote 'Try and be happy, old man.'

Barney is eleven years older than I am. In what state will I find him, and what can I buy him?

3

Who *did* he remind her of?

Who *did* he remind her of? That mischief in his eyes, that infectious laugh, that confident stride? Two faces in her memory swam over each other and matched. Ronnie! Of course, Ronnie Kahn, her young, eccentric, ever-optimistic lover who, like her, had come from a working-class background: hers rural, his urban Jewish. Ronnie Kahn, a nonstop crackerjack of ideas, knowledge and appetites. The Hackney lad had electrified and changed her life as literature and cinema had changed and electrified his. He had handed it on as though duty-bound by an ancient pact he felt driven to honour. She had not instantly made the connection because there had been lovers since Ronnie, and because she'd gone through five years of intense education, was preoccupied with getting a job, and the Ronnie she had known was young while the man in Shepherd Market was old.

Ronnie. Her mother had thought he was a gypsy when Beatie showed her photographs of him.

'He's dark. Like gypsies he's dark.'

'He's Jewish, Mother.'

'Jewish? Ent never met a Jew before. Where d'yew find him?'

'In the kitchen, the Dell Hotel, Mother, Norwich, Mother, where I'm a waitress, Mother.' She was impatient as teenage daughters frequently are with their mothers.

'He a chef, then?' Her mother loved her youngest and indulged her shortcomings.

'No, a kitchen porter.'

'Thaas a bit lowly, Beatie. Can't you do no better'n that?'

'He ent never gonna *remain* a kitchen porter, Mother.'

'Oh?'

'He's gonna be a writer.'

'Oh? He ent ambitious to be a chef, then?' The working class perpetuated itself by limiting its children's horizons.

'Christ, Mother!'

'Well, why *ent* he planning to be a chef, then?' Mother Bryant was known in the family to drive home her point ignoring reasonable alternatives offered.

'Cos a writer is better.'

'More money being a chef.' Her mother seemed the reasonable one now.

'Not if he's successful.' And the daughter the fantasist.

'A writer?'

'Yeap.'

'Clever, then?'

'Yeap.'

Did Ronnie ever become one, Beatie wondered? She had not seen his name around. Her studies in English literature stopped after the later, dense novels of D. H. Lawrence, but she read beyond that for her pleasure. His name had not leapt out of the decade's hopefuls.

Ronnie. How can one have loved so intensely and then – nothing?

No one in the Norwich Hotel could understand what Ronnie was doing there. He spoke what sounded like the King's English; his topics of conversation were notches above those of normal kitchen staff; and the daughters of the manager flirted with him.

When interviewing him for the job of kitchen porter the manager had asked had he absconded from his public school or something? He was a man confused when the parts didn't fit, yet kindly enough to take on the strange youngster.

Beatie couldn't do enough to win the effervescent Londoner's attentions, offering to do his washing, bring up food and drink to his room – they 'lived in', she at one end of the attic passage, he at the other, in small attic rooms. He had soon rearranged his, placing a small table to work on in front of his window, and gluing art postcards on the walls – Miro, Klee, Modigliani, Dufy, Mondrian – wild and colourful moderns she'd never seen before. Dufy became one of her favourites. They made love as often as they could between working, going out to events and his writing. He wouldn't let her anywhere near him when the muse struck no matter how plaintively she knocked on his door begging to come in promising to be quiet.

'I'll read a book and you won't know I'm there.'

He was adamant. 'No!' She was too sunny, too restless, a distraction. Which pleased her a little. Sometimes he read to her what he had written; but what, in those days, did she know of structure, plot, characterisation or the jargon of literary analysis? She simply luxuriated as in a soft bath to the musicality of his voice.

She had never felt so alive as in those first months of them being lovers. He had taken her to exhibitions of paintings and ceramics, foreign films, touring opera groups and concerts, enchanting her with conversation, making her feel clever beyond dreams. She developed a taste for objects and colour and the vibrancy of startling juxtapositions. He encouraged her to regard architecture in a different way – urged her to look up and register how differently each house, each building was shaped and decorated; she began to look at people with a curiosity she didn't know she possessed, at the shapes of their faces, amazed how various they were; she heard music in the way people spoke, in street noises. The hive of human activity buzzed around her as

though before meeting him she had walked deaf through mists.
But above all she was, and would forever remain, grateful to
Ronnie Kahn for introducing her to music. She was finally to
become passionate about literature but it was music that drew her
through all the emotions of joy, sadness, the birth of things, the
ending of things. For the experience of music she blessed the
Hackney boy, and for his love, which transmogrified her passive
life into a life lived at an intense level, an intensity that was to
help her through university.

With the passing of the months he drew away saying this was an
impossible relationship that couldn't work. Besides, he needed to
be in London. Publishers were in London; literary magazines
proliferated in London; there were pubs in London, and cafes
where the like-minded gathered. What if an editor wanted to
discuss something he had written? She followed him there, an act
of great courage since Norwich had been the largest city known
to her. He worked as a trainee pastry chef in a restaurant on
Lower Regent Street called the Hungaria run by a Hungarian
called Louis Vechi, a man known to his uncle – the only successful member of his family, who helped everyone in it, including,
now, Ronnie, for whom he had found the job. Beatie plied the
only profession she knew – waitressing, in the National Hotel in
Bloomsbury, living in, of course.

Then came that fateful tea party. She had returned home for a
short holiday at the end of which Ronnie was due to arrive to
meet the family, who had been driven mad by Beatie talking
about how Ronnie say this and Ronnie think that. They had
been assembled by the formidable Mother Bryant to high tea
from a table sagging with sandwiches, sausage rolls, scones, homemade blackcurrant and gooseberry jams – Mother Bryant's hedges
and bushes were heavy with fruit – clotted cream, fruit cakes,
bowls of crisps and nuts and, as a centrepiece, the biggest trifle
ever made in Christendom set in a huge glass bowl normally used
for fruit. He hadn't turned up. The last post brought a letter
instead:

My dear Beatie. It wouldn't really work would it? My ideas about handing on a new kind of life are quite useless and romantic if I'm really honest. If I were a healthy human being it might have been all right but most of us intellectuals are pretty sick and neurotic – as you have often observed – and we couldn't build a new world even if we were given the reins of government – not yet any rate. I don't blame you for being stubborn, I don't blame you for ignoring every suggestion I ever made – I only blame myself for encouraging you to believe we could make a go of it and now a week of your not being here has given me the cowardly chance to think about it . . .

Beatie had been mortified, ashamed, wrenched apart – she thought she would never ever be able to put the parts together again. The lover she had been lauding to the skies had dropped with heavy feet of clay to earth. Her mother was furious. Everything Beatie had claimed for him echoed hollow. Mother Bryant spoke for them all.

'I prepared all this food, I'd've treated him as my own son if he'd come but he hevn't! We got a whole family gathering specially to greet him, all on us, look, but he heven't come, and we're made to sit here like bloody fools.' She was hurt. They had all been hurt. The boy to whom Beatie had given herself utterly had insulted her family and shamed her. Her mother was not going to let her off lightly.

'All this time she've bin home she've bin tellin' me I didn't do this for her and I didn't do that for her and I heven't understood half what she've said. She talk about being part of the family but she've never lived at home since she've left school, look. Then she go away from here an' fill her head wi high-class squit and it turn out she don't understand any on it herself. It turn out she do just the same things she say I do.' She poked her daughter and spoke loudly into her face. 'Well, am I right, gal? I'm right, ent I? The apple don't fall far from the tree. When you tell me I was stubborn, what you mean was that he told you *you* was stubborn. Right? When you tell me I don't understand, you mean *you* don't

understand isn't it? When you tell me I make no effort you mean
you don't make no effort. Well, what you blaming me for?
Blaming me all the time! I haven't bin responsible for you since
you left home – you bin on your own, look.' By this time Mother
Bryant was feeling she had gone too far for too long; she sensed
reproachful looks coming from the others in the room. Apology
crept into her voice, though not for long. 'She think I like it, she
do! Thinks I like it being cooped up in this house all day. Well,
I'm telling you, my gal – I don't! There! And if I had a chance to
be away working somewhere the whole lot on yers could go to
hell – the lot on yers!'

Beatie, despite her shame, felt sympathy for her mother. But
she was her mother's daughter made with the same strengths and
a certain defiance.

'You're right, Mother, the apple don't fall far from the tree. I'm
like you, stubborn, empty, wi' no tools for livin'. I got no roots in
nothin'. The world's bin growin' for five thousand years and we
haven't noticed it. We don't know what we are nor where we
come from. Something's cut us off from the beginning. No roots!
And it don't bother us, neither.'

But it did bother Beatie. Profoundly. Resolve seeded itself
within her head and heart. Ronnie's collapse of faith in her potential unleashed her bravery. Her spirit heaved one hundred and
eighty degrees to take a different direction in life. She stopped
quoting her lover's words, stopped thinking her lover's thoughts,
found her own voice and took a college called St Hilda's in
Oxford by storm. Well, not quite.

There was nothing stormy or whirlwind about the painful,
plodding progress she made on her return to education. O levels
with teenagers who seemed light years away from her now that
she had Handel, Beethoven and Stravinsky, Steinbeck,
Hemingway and Dylan Thomas in her basket of the world's good-
ies. Nor were A levels a sweet and easy ascent. She was every day
amazed to discover a capacity for discipline, concentration, assim-
ilation and organisation. She had returned to Norwich, found

work and a flat, set up her classes, arranged her rooms, her work-space, her time, and put together her days like a patient bricklayer. The wall would go up, the spirit would find courage. She discovered reserves of determination like reserves of oil. There they soared! Into the air! She had not known such reserves existed. Ronnie had, even though he hadn't followed through. He would have been proud of her. She was indebted. Without him the parts of life would have assembled misshapen. Now she came through the gates of St Hilda's ready to face all and everyone.

But here was a perplexing thing. For long periods she would forget him and then a day would come when it seemed he was at her side, whispering in her ear, guiding her; or she would dream about him, and his presence would linger for days. Now, just now she wished he were there, to touch him, to look into those mischievous eyes. He wasn't. She hoped he had not done anything foolish, was still alive. Perhaps he had gone to the States. He often said he might have felt more at home in pulsating New York than deprecating London where Schadenfreude ravaged talent and bowed the heads of hopefuls. Or had he become one of Cyril Connolly's enemies of promise having written a novel she had somehow missed? Had there been no other, nor the promise of one? The thought made her sad. She felt a heart-aching sense of loss. She knew nothing remained the same and that all things must pass, but the inexorability of life's drive towards its end did not make the ending of it easier to bear.

How *can* one have loved so intensely and then – nothing?

4

Manfred Snowman took the Underground

Manfred Snowman took the Underground, Piccadilly Line from Green Park direct to Finsbury Park, bought his friend a pot plant and boarded the W7 bus to Heathville Road in Crouch End where he found Barney tense.

'You look awful.' Manfred was tender but blunt. 'What's making you look awful?'

'I'm choking.'

'Open windows. Loosen your tie.'

'It won't help.'

'Let's go for a walk.'

'I'll go for a walk but it's not fresh air I need though what makes us think we'll get fresh air in these streets I don't know.'

'We'll walk along the old railway track,' Manfred said. 'No cars.'

'It's still London,' his old friend countered. 'But I'm telling you, it's not the absence of fresh air that's choking me.'

'What's choking you, then?'

'Age. Age is choking me.'

'Stop talking nonsense. You can't choke on age.'

'I wake up some mornings and I can't breathe. I feel the years clogging my throat.'

'You choke on fish bones not on years.' Manfred knew when he had to be stern.

'Oh, you're so clever.' Barney's tone was scathing. 'What's this pot plant?' he asked as though it was the last thing in the world he wanted in his flat.

'A blue hydrangea. It says on the ticket, look! Hydrangea. Blue.' Manfred attempted to gauge his friend's mood. 'Perhaps I should take it back. Plants eat up oxygen. You need all the oxygen you can get if you're choking.'

'Jokes! He's always making jokes! You English! Everything has to be laughed at.'

'And you're not English?'

'You were born here. I came over when I was four.'

'Big difference!'

'Four years? Yes! Difference enough.'

They were silent a while.

'The world is divided,' said Barney, 'between those who are good at being young and those who are good at being old.'

'And you were only good at being young, I suppose?' Manfred knew his friend too well.

'Right!'

'Madness! Everybody is only good at being young. Tell me anybody who's good at being old.' The friends fell silent again. This game of 'the world is divided' was one they had played since the early fifties, each trying to outdo the other in succinct observation.

'Well,' asked Barney, 'you haven't got one for me?'

'I've got one, I've got one,' Manfred assured him.

'I'm waiting.'

The point of their little game was to name a division in life that would identify a recognisable truth. Like a Haiku attempting to encapsulate wisdom in three lines.

Not an absolute truth – they agreed there were only a few of those in life. 'Primary truths,' they called them. They knew they could only deal in 'secondary truths,' of which there were many about the same theme: love, death, loss, ageing . . . They often lamented that they had never kept a list of their divisions.

'The world,' said Manfred, 'is divided between those who think about risks and those who take them.'

'And you take them!'

'Not as many as I'd like.'

'What are you talking about? You're always taking them. Everyone admires you for it.'

Manfred let it pass. Climbing mountains and trekking across snowy wastes seemed like a risk before the assault took place, but not afterwards. Like pain, contemplating it was more distressing than the experience of it. And when pain had been lived through it was soon forgotten. He didn't want to get into all that with his friend. His friend's fear of the years concerned him more.

Manfred looked around the flat, a pot plant was the right gift to have bought a 'never without' person. The only problem was where to place it. This flat, in a converted Edwardian house, was spacious but not as spacious as the Victorian house he had to leave when Tina, his wife, died. Everywhere was cluttered. Books on the floor as well as on makeshift bookshelves; box files, envelope files, bronze nudes (he was a collector of), patterned jugs, unpacked boxes of God knows what, too many armchairs, coffee tables, stacks of CDs, columns of LPs, prints and paintings not only hanging too closely on walls but leaning against walls waiting for space to be found. In the lounge dominating all was a massive carved desk strewn with gadgets and a huge electric typewriter – Barney developed headaches looking at a computer screen – typing paper at the ready. He was a music critic. Bernard Perl that had been Bernard Perlmutter, writing for the *Daily Telegraph*.

Barney tried to explain.

'It began with a dream of dying. Two or three weeks ago. It

woke me up at five in the morning, a dream so terrifying that I was frightened to go back to sleep in case I entered it again.'

'Describe it.'

'I'm not sure I can. I'm part of a film, lying on my back moving forward feet-first through a narrow space, like the inside of a cigarette packet. Confined. But I'm not me. I'm an actress in a film about being in this narrow, confined space. And I arrive at a point where I think I'm free, safe, "on land". But I'm not. I've arrived instead on a tiny island with a car wreck on it, and I have to remain in the narrow space. What's confusing is that I'm lying on my back in this cramped condition both experiencing this tunnel nightmare *and* watching it happen. Until I can't take it anymore. It was so oppressive that I forced myself to wake up, and I lay there in bed in a state of terror in case I fell asleep and re-entered the dream. I felt that if I did I'd never wake up again.' Barney paused, drifting out of focus, reliving the nightmare.

'And then?' Manfred asked.

'I had to get out of bed. *Had* to. I could feel panic coming on, and had to get out of bed and start typing the dream as though by typing it I'd get it out of my system. But I couldn't. I needed more, something else. Daylight. I needed daylight to come. I felt trapped by the dark. It was – I don't know – tightening around me. The dark was tightening like a noose around me. I looked out of the window in search of light. There was no daylight yet, only the light of street lamps. This is what dying is like, I thought, trapped in a process about which you can do nothing. And then came another craving – I needed more than daylight, I needed the day to *begin*. I needed to go through a day of living, of being with people, of getting caught up in the ordinary details of life, anything to shake off this sensation of being trapped by death. I was overcome by a feeling that I'd never again be able to fall asleep on my own, that I'd never shake off this feeling of entrapment. Perhaps I wouldn't ever be able to be alone again. I've had other dreams of being close to death but nothing like this. Nothing! I felt shaken like never before.'

Manfred watched Barney move in and out of his terror. There was more to the dream. He waited. Barney continued:

'And then I dozed and the fear eased, but not before I had another sensation – of having a nervous breakdown, going mad. Not that I did, but I seemed to understand how it could happen, how one could – could – I don't know – lose control of one's mind. Lose grip.'

'And that was it?'

'That was it. Nothing's been the same since. Even though it wasn't a dream about ageing it made me conscious of the years. They were choking me, the years were like a rope getting tighter and tighter, choking me. Time! Like a noose! And now I can't get rid of it, the noose.' He looked up as though a noose might be hanging from the ceiling. 'The years! They don't pass, the years. They just tighten.'

Manfred was distressed by his friend's dream and the state of mind it had induced. He was a dreamer himself and had also experienced vivid and frightening nocturnal journeys. The mood of some had even lingered for days. But only days. Nothing had so affected him that it pervaded the rest of his life. Except Miriam. And soon he would have to face the truth about Miriam.

Of course, Barney had lost Tina. Her absence, Manfred thought, must be contributing to this sense of the years closing in upon him. She had been a consuming presence. Not an intellect but a powerhouse of action. A doer. An initiator of adventures. A solver of problems. An unending basket of appetites and opinions. A bulldozing spirit that permitted no excuse for inaction, accepted no alibi for failure, left no room for doubt. Oh, you could have your faith-doubts, your political-doubts, your doubts about the meaning of life – she took none of that seriously. 'Life *has* no meaning,' she declared, 'only purpose.' And to enable purpose to be fulfilled she permitted no self-doubt. 'Of course you can do it, what do you mean you *can't* do it?' And whatever 'it' was she would support. Tina was an anchor to his life and a safe haven for their friends. And she was a vibrant laugher. When a spirit like that dies the floodgates open and all that was waiting to cave in, collapse, does so.

With Tina gone Barney's frightening dream made sense. Manfred understood.

'Come,' he said, 'time for that walk along the old railway line.'

5

Beatie – we must explain more –

Beatie – we must explain more – had not spent all that many moments in idleness before her mirror. It is just that few women are ever satisfied with what they see reflected back of themselves. Breasts too large, not large enough; bum sticks out, too flabby, too flat, too hanging, too wide; neck too long; ears like wings; top lip thin; thighs like tree trunks; look at that ribcage! Where's my waist gone? And, Jesus Christ! My upper half is out of proportion to my lower half. Nothing, nothing, nothing fits!

But sometimes it does. Sometimes mirrors are reassuring, what you're looking at is pleasing. This time Beatie was pleased.

Her pleasure, however, was not taking her onwards and up to her purpose in life. After all, you can wake up singing one morning not knowing why, nor what to do after the song is sung. No matter, she thought, I can be pleased that I'm not a malcontent. A malcontent? What made her think about not being a malcontent? Where did thoughts about malcontents come from? She reached back over the day and remembered: when the old man (who might not have been as old as she surmised) carrying his backpack in a way to strain his spine, had walked out of sight, a woman had taken his place.

There was about this woman, something arresting. (Beatie was to find herself frequently gazing at women's faces, driven to guess, to build their lives from what she saw in them.) She was in her late forties, black hair, Mediterranean complexion, distraught intense eyes. That woman, thought Beatie, is saturated with discontent. Then the waitress approached and asked, rather abruptly: 'Yes?' and a moment occurred, one of those little epiphanies that mosaically make up a life. The waitress was tall, elegant and beautiful. Her next few words, 'Do you want anything with your coffee?' revealed a German accent. They also revealed in their tone a stern and haughty melody that said: 'This is not what I'm made for.' More, the melody said: 'I will *never* find what I am made for.' And in that melody Beatie understood – it was the waitress who was saturated with discontent. She looked more closely at the Mediterranean woman. Her eyes, she could now see, were not distraught but simply had lost the habit of smiling. She was not a malcontent, she was unhappy. The waitress was the malcontent. The epiphany taught Beatie how understanding states of mind – as with the assessment of quality – can best be made by comparison. Stroke two cloths between your fingers and, just by comparison, your touch will know the finer.

The nature of discontent had, during the time taken by the Mediterranean woman to drink her coffee and dip her croissant, made itself known to Beatie. She walked away from her mirror thankful not to be like the elegant, discontented, pouting young German maiden.

But then reflex turned her to give that one last glance and she saw the mirror rather than herself – tall, cracked, screwed to a cracked bathroom wall in a small apartment despairing with cracks. Where she lived was revealing itself for the first time, or she was seeing it for the first time. There it was, surrounding her, depressing her, diminishing her with its mediocrity – two styleless rooms above a Greek restaurant in north London constantly assaulted by smells that were obese, gone off, too much of a good thing, or a bad thing, rather: overstewed vine leaves, saturated fried onions, stale fat, hints of burnt lamb offerings wafting and disturbing what little clean air remained in the polluted suburb.

Everything about the apartment was stale; dusty curtains, stained furniture, peeling veneered cupboards that were ugly when they were new – she could imagine their owners' pride when the wardrobe and sideboard arrived from a dreary shop cluttered with ugly furniture spilling out onto the pavement. One change she insisted upon – her own sheets. A proud and spotlessly clean mother, who had accumulated more than she needed in her lifetime, and needed even less with her four children gone, bequeathed her beloved Beatie clean, stern sheets with not one corner threadbare.

It was a long way from her Oxford digs, her lovely, homely, tiny but cosy abode for two years after a year in a St Hilda's house. Beatie Bryant, daughter of a pig-keeper for a huge Norfolk estate south of Norwich, after a loose life waitressing in that city's hotels, slithering with lewd waiters and smooth-tongued travelling salesmen, had met a young man who loved her, taught her, opened horizons for her and then fled her, terrified of what he had unleashed.

She had lived through that, and had cleaved through sixth-form college with high grade 'A's followed by a place at St Hilda's on the Cherwell where she studied what too many study for and achieve: a degree in English literature that would, if she was not careful, take her down false avenues overcrowded with eager, throbbing-with-potential young women crazed by all that might and might not, may and may not, could or could not work for them in that great, big, interestingly full-of-everything-and-every-one-world ahead.

Yet here she was – in a slummy appartment having persuaded herself that this first move into London was temporary. And it would be. Nothing would keep her swimming in these evil smells. She would find a job and flee to the centre and ever thereafter not have one thing in her life that was not of beauty.

6

Manfred and Barney had their walk

Manfred and Barney had their walk along the muddy and dog-shitty old railway line talking and talking and talking. That was their friendship. They had known each other for nearly half a century, had met and parted, met and parted, sometimes in anger, sometimes because their work took them off to earn pennies or see sights or both. Between the comings and goings there were these meetings of heated exchange as though all their life there had been only one long conversation that they were picking up where it had left off last time they were together. That's what their friendship seemed like to them – an unbroken duologue.

'It didn't happen,' said Manfred, referring to something they had spoken about last time.

'Why not?' asked his friend, knowing exactly what it was.

'The house was too large.'

'It would be. Designed by da Vinci, what did you expect?'

'And Tuscany, my favourite place of all places, is finally too far away.'

'A farm labourer's cottage Mr da Vinci would not have built for himself.'

'Underground to Heathrow, Heathrow to Rome, car from Rome a hundred miles to San Gimignano . . . on, off, up, down. I'm too old.'

'Stupid is what you are.'

'Stupid I'm not.' Manfred didn't really need to defend himself.

'Illogical, then.' Barney wasn't going to let him go.

'Sometimes that,' Manfred conceded. 'So?'

'Do you love the place?'

'I'm passionate about it, you know that.'

'So go back and find a smaller house.'

'I'm used to space by now.'

'A smaller house with big rooms.'

'You're right.'

'They don't have to be as large as da Vinci needed.'

'Right.'

'Da Vinci was a painter, you're a . . .'

'Don't say it!' Manfred snapped.

'Why not?'

'I don't like the sound of it.'

'You should be used to it by now.'

'Besides – it no longer applies.'

'It still applies. You haven't sold yet.'

'How do you know?'

'Because it would be in all the papers, that's how I know.' They walked on in silence wondering who was right, who wrong. 'And,' Barney couldn't resist, 'I would have had Miriam on the phone.'

'You'd think there'd be a "Railway Walk Committee" to clean this place up,' Manfred grumbled, evasively.

'There *is* such a committee,' said Barney. 'They had one meeting and unanimously decided to keep it wild.'

'How are the girls?' Manfred asked.

'Thank God for the girls,' his friend replied. Adding: 'The world is divided between parents blessed with their children and those cursed with them.'

'And you're blessed.'

'Mostly.'

'What are they doing?'

'Do they tell me?'

'They must tell you something.'

'After their mother died they rang every day. Sometimes twice a day. But you know what time does, it softens the pain, reduces concern and makes short distances seem longer. The girls have busy lives. They know their father can look after himself.'

Manfred was not satisfied. 'Tamara – what's she doing?'

'Researching documentaries for the BBC.'

'It's a good job.'

'She's capable of better,' said the proud, dissatisfied father.

'"Better" she'll get. The BBC is a good beginning.'

'Only it's not a beginning. Ever since she left college some years ago she's been dilettanting here and dilettanting there. P.A. to him and P.A. to her, a theatre company, a film company, a writer's agency. She doesn't settle.'

'She's searching,' consoled Manfred. 'And Natasha?'

'It's not easy being a twin.'

'I know,' said Manfred, 'my father was one. But not all twins suffer the same problems.'

'She's shacked up with a musician who's younger than her.'

'A musician? Then you should be happy – music in the family! The violin? The piano? Cello, perhaps?' Jews can only imagine their children as classical musicians.

'Guitar,' said Barney.

'Great concertos written for guitars,' Manfred consoled.

'Chords and strumming. In a pop group.' After a pause. 'Clubs and pubs.'

Manfred said nothing. Both understood the significance of such details. The elderly men trudged on through troughs of hardened mud and potholes, ducking under overgrown black-berry brambles threatening to scratch their faces, side-stepping the dog shit they might carry on their soles into the house. Foxes had been spotted there, a badger or two, squirrels, rabbits, a bewildered hare, but mostly birds – the thrush, the yellowhammer, bright-breasted robins, the blackbird, the boring pigeon, an occasional gull, straying inland in the hope of securing a better living for his family. Sparrows, of course. Where would London be without sparrows!

'What are you going to do about Miriam?' Barney asked.

'I don't want to talk about Miriam.'

Barney knew better than to press even though talking about Manfred's nightmare might have distracted him from his own.

'I've been thinking,' said Manfred after they had leapt, not as young men do – further than is needed – but as old men do who pretend they are still young and don't quite make it over soggy puddles.

'I should hope so,' said Barney who, being the older of the two, had even more not quite made it and was looking for tufts of grass on which to scrape off the clinging sod.

'Why are you bothering?' his amused companion asked. 'There are lots more to hop, skip and jump over, only perhaps next time you should hold my hand.'

'Or perhaps you should pick me up in your arms and carry me! Jokes!'

They walked on in comfortable silence.

'You were thinking,' Barney reminded his distracted friend.

'I was thinking about conversations.'

'Our conversations?'

'No, conversations in general.'

'*Prompted* by our conversations, then?' Barney asked.

Barney was secretly proud that he'd come from nowhere, had made himself an authority on music and could hold his own on the subject in the highest of intellectual companies. In fact, as he had grown older, he sometimes discovered himself so flattered to be addressed by some of the brightest minds in the land, in whose company he frequently found himself because of their passion for music, that he barely paid attention to what they were saying to him. They're talking to me, *me*! he thought when he should have been listening. Me, who came from Stepney London streets and bypassed university, me! His pleasure in Manfred's company was due in no small part to the weight of what they conversed about. No wonder he thought that Manfred was about to talk of them.

'No, not prompted by *our* conversations but by another I'll tell you about in a moment. For now, think about this,' he went on. 'What is it we're doing when we're engaged in conversation? When we're listening to someone talk to us what precisely is taking place?'

Barney answered instantly. 'Someone is talking and someone is listening. Simple!'

'Not so simple,' Manfred said slowly. 'When we're listening to someone talk to us we're doing five things. Within a split second *five* things. We're listening to words, we're understanding those words – making sense of their meaning—'

His old friend interrupted him, instantly enthralled. 'Is that two or three things?'

'Two: listening and understanding. Then we *consider*, we *think* about the meaning of what we've understood.'

'Listening, understanding, considering. That's three.' Barney, childlike, was eager to show he was keeping up.

'Fourth – we're formulating a response. Vaguely. Not coherently. Not sharply. But vaguely. The sharpness and the coherence come when we begin to *articulate* that response.'

'For you, maybe,' said Barney who had always found it difficult to marshal his thoughts anywhere but on paper. 'For you, not me! *You* can be sharp and coherent and articulate. I have to scribble notes on paper, like a jigsaw, and then pull the parts together. And the fifth?'

'Here's the wild card,' said Manfred. 'The fifth is – linking.'

'Linking?' Barney was thrown. 'Linking?'

'You listen, you understand, you consider, you respond – and all that is fine, as it should be, that's how ideas are exchanged in conversation. But the problem I find – and this is what limits me as a conversationalist and also, I don't mind admitting, makes me a slow reader – the problem is that when someone says something interesting or I read something that's resonant, my mind shoots off to something else which may or may not be relevant to the meaning of what was said. Linking is taking place.'

'Some people call it a grasshopper mind,' Barney quipped.

'You want to be serious or not?'

'Aha! He wants to be serious now.'

'I'll talk about the weather if you like.' Manfred had become spiky.

'What you really mean,' it was Barney's turn to become spiky, 'is that you're getting old and you're experiencing difficulty focusing.'

'It's not because I'm getting old,' Manfred protested, 'I've *always* been like that. Everything sparks off everything. That's why I go on my expeditions. Long treks and remote places focus my mind.'

'Yes, yes, of course.' Barney's tone was sarcastic. 'Dangerous animals and unpredictable elements do indeed focus the mind.' The truth was that Barney was a little envious of the physical challenges with which Manfred had confronted himself in these last years. 'So what was the conversation that prompted these thoughts about conversations?'

They were coming to one of the many exits from the disused railway line, narrow alleys leading back into clean streets, and they mutually agreed to cease their muddy tramp *thorough bush thorough briar*.

'I was having a coffee in Shepherd Market—'

Barney interrupted him. 'What on earth were you doing in Shepherd Market?'

'I like Shepherd Market. Reminds me of Paris.'

7

What was I doing in Shepherd Market anyway?

What was I doing in Shepherd Market anyway? I neither live there nor live near there. Whores hang out there. I could have been picked up. No, I couldn't. I don't look whorish. Or do I? *Do* I? I'm not going back to the mirror to check. Truth be told the whores these days don't look whorish either. Not sure I like the word 'whore'. On the other hand 'prostitute' sounds clinical. 'And may I ask your profession, Miss . . . er . . .?' 'Prostitute, my profession is prostitution!' Or what about 'harlot'? No! Shades of *Fanny Hill*, Hogarth and flouncing petticoats. Prefer 'whore'. More gutsy. More honest. 'I'm a whore, sir, a whore.'

What must it feel like to be a whore, I wonder? I once met an actress who had to play one, and thought she needed the experience, though why an actress needs to experience what she performs I don't know. Isn't that why she's an actress – because she possesses the skill to *imagine* what it's like to be someone else? I mean what happens when she lands the role of Lady Macbeth? Anyway, this actress, a petite little thing she was, surprisingly badly dressed, tells me she persuades a male friend to procure a client for her, stipulating that he's to make no outrageous demands. I remember details – which were fascinating: and *where* she told me – on a train travelling to Liverpool Street Station (she'd been for an audition to the Norwich Playhouse). I was an eager listener because, I'm ashamed to confess, the notion of doing it for money excited me. Oh, not seriously, it's just that I feel I should be open to all experience. Careful, Beatie. Stop preparing sophistries for future mistakes. And remember, the Aids scare renders loose living a gamble for fools. Still, the telling of it excited me. But why did she tell *me*? We were strangers. Perhaps that's why; we were never to meet again. We could tell each other anything.

The encounter is set up. She describes her attempt to dress as she imagines a whore would – a high-class whore that is, she's playing an expensive high-class whore – black stockings, matching knickers, suspenders and high-heeled shoes she's bought specially, and, being unused to such heights, wobbles unsteadily on; and pays to be made up by a beautician so that she looks a knock-out even to herself. In fact, she tells me, she's so subtly coloured that when she finally puts on a loose-hanging black dress and looks in the mirror she is auto-eroticised. This isn't going to turn out right, she thinks to herself. She fears she's going to become excited, involved, when all she wants is to be entered and paid. She merely wants to know what it's like to part her legs to a stranger, help him come and take money for it. She's playing a seller of sex not a salesgirl. She just wants to know what it feels like to be the other side of the counter, the fence, the big divide between the acceptable and the unacceptable.

As I'm remembering, or trying to remember, I'm thinking – how could she ever have known how to dress when now she was so tastelessly dressed, not dressed like an actress at all? It wasn't because she wore jeans and a nondescript pink-washed T-shirt and worn flat shoes and a grubby denim jacket, it was because everything about her was shabby and kitschy. On the other hand how are actresses *supposed* to be dressed? What if, like most actresses, she was impecunious? But even impecunious actresses hint at flair, a touch of taste picked up from the costume designers they've worked with. This actress seemed never to have been near *any*one with taste, let alone rubbed shoulders with a theatre costume designer. And she couldn't string words together. The story as I tell it is more to do with *my* powers of narration than hers. She couldn't name the parts of things; a simple part like lobes of ears or cuticles in nails or pleats in skirts. But she was well spoken. She wasn't a 'cor-blimey girl' or an upper-class girl speaking 'cor-blimey' in order to assert her allegiance to the working class; she was – I don't know – she was un-puttable-together. Still, her story being about whores was compulsive listening.

'He was a shy man,' she began. Her male friend had procured not one of his own friends but the friend of a friend, a lecturer in the history of art specialising in mosaics – the putting together of fragments to make a whole. 'Shy and not handsome. In fact,' she said, 'he was what some would call ugly. But you know us women – who some find ugly we find appealing. And he appealed. He was shy and slow in his movements but his eyes were on fire. I couldn't stop looking at his eyes. They belonged to a youth let into an ancient tomb expecting to find the world's treasure trove. And that made me wonder,' she was an astute little lady, this little actress, 'was I his first whore?' She relished the word. Whore. Swinging on the 'or'. Whooooor!

'I asked him: "Is this your first time?" "With a . . ." he couldn't say the word, I had to laugh, "First time . . . buying it, yes." This really put me ill at ease,' she said, 'at a disadvantage, in fact. A more experienced client would have made his wishes known but now *I* had to help *him*, I had to be the experienced one wheedling from him what those wishes were. I had to ask again: "Is there something special, some special way, some – request?" I realised, crikey!' (She actually did say 'crikey'.) 'I don't really possess the language for trading in sex. I began to stumble and stutter all over the place and asked him: "Do you want to – er – enter? In

front? Behind? Or would you like me to – er – take you in my –
er – go down?"

'Well' she exclaimed, 'what a tizz we *both* were in, and his
reply,' she told me, 'threw me into even more of a tizz.' It was
mesmerising to watch her acting out the tizz – hands up and
down as though there were hot coals in front of her to be picked
up. She continued in the kind of prurient detail that embarrassed – especially as she was telling her tale in loud whispers. He
had just wanted to look, and she became aroused. 'He knelt at the
foot of the bed and gazed back enjoying just the sight of me
offering nothing but promise. That was his pleasure, for the
moment, the promise of things.'

Her story began to worry me. I was held, absorbed, I could see
clearly everything she described but – I don't know – it was *too*
clear. I wondered: was this the story from the play she had performed rather than the *preparation* for the performance? Even so,
I continued giving her my wrapt, credulous attention.

'I know I blushed. I was wet. I was responding. It was not what
whores were supposed to do. When he'd gazed and touched
enough he stood up, reached for my hands and swivelled me half-
circle so that I was on my back with my head at the end of the bed
and my feet to the wall. I felt his face over mine. He was going to
kiss me. That's not allowed – that much I knew about whores –
no kissing, no touching of lips. Lips were for emotions, emotions
were no part of whoredom; the orgasm on the other hand was
mere sensation – permitted. I clenched my lips. "I know," he
said, "kissing's not allowed." "I thought I was your first?" I think
I scolded him. "I was warned," he explained.'

And here's the strangest part of her story, or rather the telling of
it: she rushed through to the end in thirty seconds.

'That was it. He undressed me, caressed me, got between my
legs, sucked me to orgasm, left seventy-five pounds on my bed,
said thank you and left without satisfying himself. Isn't that
weird? Long, drawn-out opening then bim, bang, wallop and
done! Over! Gone! I felt used. Or rather I began by feeling loved

and *ended* feeling used. And I couldn't use the "used" part to play the whore, which is perhaps what whores feel, because he'd left me confused. I hadn't brought him to climax, which is what whores are supposed to do, aren't they? I was left with absolutely no idea how to play her, and ended up quarrelling with the director and the cast and had the most miserable time in my career to date.'

Perhaps she could see my growing scepticism and felt driven to reach the end sooner than planned. We exchanged telephone numbers as the train drew in to Liverpool Street Station, and parted with promises to meet and eat together sometime soon but that was two years ago and I've never seen her anywhere since, neither on stage nor screen and certainly not on the train from Norwich to London.

You know what, Beatie? You were taken in. I'm suddenly realising, you're like a stupid Candide, meandering through life adrift and gullible – she probably had no such experience. She probably wasn't even an actress. You should have guessed from the way she was dressed and her kitschy jewellery that she wasn't an actress. She probably tells that story to any chance encounter, like the ancient mariner who stoppeth one of three. Why would she do it? Or does she invent a different story every time? Would they all be about sexual experiences or would some be about being robbed, involved in a plane crash, surviving cancer, winning the lottery and spending it all in a year, and so on. Fantasy after fantasy as soon as she found a gullible soul such as you, Beatie Bryant. Are you going to be gullible all your life? The world is divided into: those who tell and those who listen; those who need to lie and those who need to believe; those of guile and those of gullibility. You should be neither, Miss Bryant, though I fear for you, you seem to have a propensity for the one rather than the other. Be careful, Missy, you've only just begun this life. Hold on or you'll fall apart.

And you still haven't answered the question – why were you in Shepherd Market?

I was there because it's a part of London that is Paris where I once spent a long, cheap, romantic weekend with Ronnie. I had a need. While I have no job I have these little moods and needs. I can't account for everything in my life.

8

I was worried about Barney

I was worried about Barney. He had jumped over puddles, more or less, and had seemed eager to talk about the nature of conversation and how 'linking' was for me a distracting element in conversation. But I felt all the time it was an effort for him to walk, jump *and* converse. That dream seemed to be lurking behind everything he did and said. He could smile, cut and thrust, but my friend was a frightened friend. 'Time like a noose,' he had said, 'I can't get rid of it.'

And I can't help. I can't take Barney on one of my treks, he's too old. And even if he wasn't I don't think trekking to the cold poles is an undiscovered part of his hankering. He's in the middle of writing a book, besides. So how *does* one get rid of such a sensation? Normally one doesn't have to, it fades. It may linger longer than normal but, no matter how disturbing the dream, it slinks out of the system sooner or later.

Not Barney's system, it seems.

It was a long way home but an easier walk – no puddles to challenge us.

'So,' said Barney once we'd got into a stride – well, hardly a stride; I strode, Barney galumphed. 'So,' he galumphed, 'you wanted to imagine you were in Paris and you had yourself a tea in Shepherd Market.'

'A coffee.'

'And?'

I related to my friend, who loved gossip and tales of any kind no matter what mental state he was in, how a man with bumps on his face had sat down near me and begun bending my ear about bees and hives and how honey kept him young. I knew that, I told him, as I was a bit of a honey addict myself. He said he had wondered what had kept me looking young. I had been looking at the bumps on his face in that way one stares sometimes too long, and thus rudely, at a neighbour's blemish, and he said:

'You're looking at the bumps on my face, aren't you?' I apologised. He assured me it was all right and informed me that he was a beekeeper, amateur not professional, not for selling to shops but just for his pleasure and to have gifts of home-produced honey to give to his friends.

'I must say I was intrigued,' I admitted to Barney.

'Who wouldn't be!' he replied. 'But what's bees and honey got to do with your theories about attention spans?'

I went on to explain how the man with bumps on his face had enthused lyrically about the colours of the honeycomb, and how there were 60,000 bees in an ordinary hive with only one female, the queen, and how the drones are the large ones but lazy and stupid, and the worker bees not only do all the work but take nothing for it, they simply provided the service of pollination. He got me worked up (despite that he was a rather dreary raconteur) so that I began imagining myself living in Tuscany keeping bees and supplying Harrods with honey. In the background he droned on about bees having a different colour sense from humans – they see red and black as the same but have a penchant for blue, blue/green, and yellow. Humans can distinguish sixty colours, he informed me, still astonished by this fact, but bees can see only four – the fourth being ultraviolet. Much else tried to make its way from him to me, long passages of which I didn't register.

'It's such things about people that confuses me,' I said to Barney. 'Here they are, many many many with interesting and original things to pass on to us passing them on in such dreary tones that they pass us by. In one ear out the other.'

'Like poets reading,' said Barney who often complained to me about the 'poetry and chamber music' sessions he sometimes had to attend. 'Have you noticed? Poets intone like priests preach, sepulchrally.'

'Is there such a word?'

'Believe me, there is – sepulchrally, as though every poem was about death. Or they deliver each line as though handed it by the Greek muse herself.' Barney could be wicked – fear of dying or no fear of dying. Now he challenged me. 'That wasn't an example of linking. Your mind wandered to beekeeping in Tuscany because your neighbour with bumps on his face was boring.'

He was right. Barney never let me get away with anything. Well, he was almost right. Linking *had* taken place but it had degenerated into mind drifting. And then I found myself talking about her.

'The bumpy man could see I'd lost interest, and then came this young woman whose attractiveness drew me to stare at her which made him get up abruptly and leave.'

'Which made you feel guilty,' said Barney.

'Of course.'

'As always.'

'And so I called out my thanks as he left saying he'd made me want to take up beekeeping. And do you know what he did? He didn't turn round but just pushed his arm behind him and stuck two fingers up at me. I can't tell you how that upset me. Not because *he* had told me to fuck off but because *I* had been rude. I hate being rude. To anybody. Hate it!'

'This young woman,' asked Barney bringing me back to some-one who, truth be told, interested us more.

What could I tell him? We'd hardly spoken. There are just some encounters that are fleeting and memorable. I told him about two such. One was in New York. A client who'd been a model was now tired of the catwalk and imagined herself an actress. She was auditioning for a film and wanted me there as moral support. I'm your accountant, I told her, not your therapist. She didn't want her therapist, she wanted *me*. I was flattered.

There was a woman in my hotel who I kept meeting in the lift. She was a redhead. Well-dressed as an executive might be with deep brown eyes, and a powerful stillness that brooked no nonsense. Fearless is the word. Here is a woman who would not flirt her way to the top, I thought. The first meeting was just between two residents in a lift on their way down. The second time, going down again, we smiled in recognition. The third time, on the way up, there was more in the smile than a smile. Not an intense mutual attraction, not a clutching-of-the-heart moment, more a sort of curiosity moment, as though hadn't we met before. We hadn't but there was a spark, a kindred-spirit spark. A kindred-sprit-deep-brown-eyed spark.

The fourth time the lift was very packed and we were forced to stand close to each other. Those are bizarre moments those lift moments. A group of people stand silently side by side moving, stopping, moving, stopping. I said to her: 'At such moments I always feel like saying, "We are gathered together, dearly beloved".' I could feel everyone else in the lift stiffen with embarrassment. She just smiled, wanted to say something, I could see, but had to get out.

The fifth time was not in the lift but at the front desk. She was paying her bill, leaving. When we saw each other a smile leapt from us both. 'Going home?' I asked. 'No,' she replied, 'going on.' There was no hesitation between the two of us. We reached to one another and kissed goodbye on the lips. Not a peck, not the kiss of strangers; a lingering kiss, a lover's kiss. I wished her bon voyage, and left at once, but not before we had each registered great sadness knowing we would never meet again, and that we would regret the wasted opportunity.

The second encounter was of a completely different order. I was looking for a piece of jewellery for Miriam's birthday – I used to buy her jewellery as often as I could, a Jewish hangover from the pogrom days when jewellery was the one possession our grandparents could pick up and easily run with. Miriam's pogrom turned out to be me, and she had easily packed up her gifts and run, which is when I began training for long treks to the cold poles. And in this shop was a stunning, elegant woman who spoke with an Italian accent. She was trying on rings. There was one she kept returning to but rejecting because it was too expensive for her – ribbed gold with a heavy wedge of tiny crystals that sparkled like diamonds. It was cleverly wrought. The cost lay in the painstaking craftsmanship.

Everything about this woman – she must have been in her mid-forties – was appealing. She was dressed in a suede jacket and skirt with a beige blouse, and revealed a sweet nature as she shared her financial difficulties with the sales lady in a low, mellifluous voice, a touch gravelly. Graciousness pervaded her manner. She was captivating. As she turned to leave I asked her please not to protest but I had a strong urge to purchase this ring for her that she so loved and would she indulge the impulsiveness of a stranger who would be gone in an instant. I moved swiftly – laid the money on the counter, took her hand, kissed the back of it and left without buying the gift I'd come for. I calculated that the elegant Italian would be paralysed by surprise, even too embarrassed to protest, and I would be out of her reach, out of her life before she could ask questions. The only concern in my mind was that every movement I made, every word uttered, and the tone in which I uttered it had to let her know unequivocally that I was not making a crude pass or harbouring the slightest expectation.

It worked. Well, I would like to think it worked and that the gesture would remain in her memory a romantic gesture, even a mysterious one, from a man who appeared out of nowhere and disappeared into nowhere. For my part I was gratified to have found myself capable of the impulse, for who does not want just one such moment of breathtaking, fantastic, altruistic, dumbfounding, mysterious generosity in their life. Just one.

Barney didn't believe me.

'You made up those stories to distract me. I know you. Just because I like stories.' I assured him they had happened. 'And you had a similar encounter with this young woman?' he asked.

'No.'

'So?'

'There's little I can tell you. She was in her mid-twenties, I'd guess. And she spoke with the hint of a rural dialect though I couldn't detect which one.'

'There are only two,' said Barney. 'North and south.' It was his weakness to possess a weak wit. I told him not to be silly.

'Don't tell me not to be silly,' he replied, testily.

'Don't be silly and I won't tell you not to be silly.' I let Barney get away with nothing as he lets me get away with nothing.

Something else was in the air, however, for this was not a silly man. I thought I saw him on the verge of tears.

'Barney?' I wanted to know. He didn't reply. 'Is that dream still with you?' I pressed.

'Tell me about the young woman in Shepherd Market.' He was avoiding my questioning.

'Is it your book?' I pressed on. 'Have you got a block with your book?'

Barney's book was his only book. He'd been working on it for a dozen years or so, the biography of a little-known Italian composer, Giovanni Marcantonio, who lived a short life between 1583 and 1610 and who Barney thought was the precursor of the innovative Mozart, a neglected genius and an artist who suffered dismissal by posterity for having no learning – the absence of which, so Barney's research uncovered, was of no concern to Giovanni's contemporaries who recognised his musical genius, ignored his lack of education and applauded and rewarded his

short life. After his death came the opportunity for envious enemies to bury him and consign his sheets either to the fire or the
dusty corners of universities and churches where Barney, having
been tipped off in a bar in Macerata by a drunk and rather stupid
lecturer in ethics, found them. In Giovanni's life Barney had
found the mirror to his own – dismissal for having no formal education. There was only one difference – and it was major: Barney
was not a musical genius. He had aspired to be; in his galumphing
youth he had composed music he hoped would lead him to be. It
didn't happen. He became a music critic instead, retaining sufficient generosity of spirit to attempt rescuing Giovanni
Marcantonio – a musician to whom it did happen – from obscurity. Barney had decided he would live the life he craved,
vicariously.

'The girl, the girl,' he insisted, 'the girl in Shepherd Market.'

'Nothing much to tell. She was blonde, green-eyed and plump
and looked as though she had just landed on the planet.
Everything seemed a surprise to her. She looked around as though
she was seeing everything for the first time. Innocent. Innocent
but clever. She may have been seeing things for the first time but
she seemed capable of seeing through them, too. She seemed surprised both pleasantly and incredulously. Her looks asked how
could there be both loveliness and ugliness in the world, cleverness
and stupidity, honesty and sham.'

'I can see she made an impression,' said Barney, a touch sarcas-
tically.

'Made an impression and made me feel my age.'

'You didn't talk to her?'

'A few words. I was staring so hard that I had to apologise. I
said: 'Sorry, rude of me. I've finished my coffee. I'm going.''

'And you left, just like that?'

'Not quite. No! No no no! It was her response that made me
see her for the kind of woman she was. Listen to this, it bowled
me over. She said she didn't mind me looking. "Men always
look," she said. "I'm beautiful." I could have eaten her. Such

sweetness, such innocence. "You are, young woman," I said, 'you are.' And then I confessed: "It was a lecherous look, wasn't it?" She didn't deny it, she just smiled. I said I hoped she wasn't offended. "But there," I said, "what can I do? I'm old, you're young." She smiled and I left.'

'And you will never see her again.' Barney shared my loss.

'Just as I will never see youth again,' I said. My story had saddened me. It was my turn to be consoled. Barney rose to the occasion.

'But you will see mountain peaks and the South Pole,' he reminded me, referring to my plans to climb Kilimanjaro and Mount Kenya, and to cross Antarctica. 'Not many young ones do that.'

9

And I didn't get the jobs!

And I didn't get the jobs!

That's how my weekend began: two interviews on Friday morning before taking the train home to Norfolk. Odd interviews. People are odd. Or at least people given the task of interviewing you are odd. They pull their lives round them like a heavy coat on a cold day. Every time they meet someone it's a cold day. Their heads sink into their shoulders as though you've come to do them harm rather than seek employment, to take from them rather than give. And those antipathies! Those looks and that body language crying out, 'Not for me! Not for me!' Tones, eyes, movements – 'Not for me! Not for me! Hurry up and go!' That was the first interview, anyway.

I had seen both ads in the *Guardian*: assistant to the book buyer for a chain of bookshops, and assistant to the editor of a publishing house. Why do I go for jobs to do with books? Every gal with a degree in English looks for a job in publishing or television or journalism. And why, even, did I take a degree in English? Politics, philosophy, economics – PPE, or history, why not them? With economics I could have gone into industry, property, bought and sold houses, worked my way up to tycoonery. That's what I really enjoy, at least the idea of it anyway – transforming derelict houses into little palaces. Well, not palaces, of course, but – to make order out of chaos, to make beautiful what was ugly, to change, to transform, rebuild, surprise, get the parts right. And here I was in an office so spare and chilly confronting a man who obviously liked nothing about me from the moment I entered. With tight-lipped courtesy he asked me to sit.

What was it about me? I saw him freeze as soon as I came through the door. Freeze, bristle, stiffen, stifle the cry 'Not for me!' I tried to see myself as he was seeing me, hear myself as he was hearing me. But I had hardly spoken. Simply knocked on the door, entered when a weak voice looking for pity cried, 'Come in,' stretched out my hand to shake his and said merely: 'Beatie Bryant. Thank you for seeing me, Mr Creighton.' What, in those few seconds and a handful of words could have been communicated that sent shivers through his huge frame? And huge he was, a mountain of a man whose head seemed too far away from objects for them to make an impact on him.

Ah! *That's* what he saw, a young woman who looked at him and thought: here is a mountain of a man whose head seems too far away from objects for them to make an impact on him. Or was it my handshake? I remember now – I offered my hand to be shaken before he had offered his, and he took it as though it shouldn't have been offered at all. Or was it my confident tone of voice? God knows where *that* comes from since I'm so lacking in confidence about everything. But I recognise it in myself – this unearned confidence. It's worrying. Since I've not yet done anything with my life to earn confidence does it come over as cockiness? He asked a few questions. My answers were mono-syllabic.

'I have others I must see, you understand,' he said with his face half turned away. I told him I did, rose, smiled, offered my hand again and left after five minutes. There! A handshake, some dozen or so words and I've lost a job. I would probably have spent my time dusting books anyway. Still, not the most propitious start of a career.

That was the 11 o'clock appointment, time for a coffee before the second one, an interview at number 20 Fitzroy Square. 12.30 sharp. I calculated I would be called in at 12.45 leaving fifteen minutes for the interview because of course at 1 p.m. he or she would have a lunch date. I didn't know if it would be a he or she. I was rung up and told to be there at 12.30 to meet Lindsey? Lindsay? On paper I would have known: 'e' for a woman, 'a' for a man. I was interviewed by an 'e' – Lindsey Shackleton.

Lindsey Shackleton was a senior editor of Solomon King Publishers who were the result of John King Publishers, old and established (1852), buying up Michael Solomon Publishers, who had insisted on one condition before selling – that Solomon came before King (1958). Miss Shackleton explained.

'Michael,' she was on familiar terms with him, 'had built up the most dynamic list of writers between the sixties and eighties, and—'

'Why sell a dynamic list of writers?' I interrupted. Mistake.

'He had grown tired of writers' egos,' she said sternly as though I was a writer with an ego, 'and couldn't wait to get out.'

'And also,' I said, compounding my mistake with a touch of humour I had not yet earned the right to indulge in, 'King Solomon might have raised eyebrows.' Queen Lindsey was not amused.

'It would have been King *and* Solomon and I'm quite sure Michael would have seen that before anyone.' I suspected he'd been a pushy publisher (he would have needed to be to acquire such a list in so short a time) and had wanted his name up there ahead of everyone else. 'I also think, having a great feeling for language, that he thought the syllables fell better that way.' She offered me one of those smiles in which the mouth widens but the eyes remain fixed. It was a story she had related many times, no doubt, so I forgave her. I could not, however, forgive what followed.

She spoke with her teeth clenched as though were she to

open her mouth her heart, God forbid, would open too. It was Msssss (I hate that) Shackleton who had prompted the image of a person drawing their life around them for protection though why she needed to protect herself from poor-inno-cent-just-out-of-college-unemployed-and-broke me I don't know. What sort of threat could she see in me? I had no ambition to become a senior editor. This wasn't New York and I wasn't the girl in the lift you had to be nice to in case she became the head of the company. This was little old London where the cut and thrust of business was more gentlemanly, surely; where you knew the importance of being civil to your employees in order to get the best out of them, surely; where the old help the young, surely?

'You were a mature student?' she asked.

'I don't know about mature,' I tried modesty in an attempt to mitigate my misplaced humour, 'but I was certainly older than my peers.' I also tried smiling but it seemed to worry her that I smiled with my eyes.

'You smile a lot,' she observed apropos of nothing that seemed relevant to me.

'It's a weakness.' I smiled again.

'I need an assistant who's a superb organiser,' she informed me in a way that left no doubt she thought I wasn't.

'I keep my bedroom tidy.' I couldn't resist it. Do I have a death wish?

'You don't strike me as a serious young woman.' She was going out on a limb now, testing my tolerance for rudeness.

'I'm very serious,' I replied, 'but I try to avoid being pompous. And I do tend to laugh a lot, it's true, but that doesn't mean I'm not responsible and hard-working and reliable and . . .'

'Are you intelligent?'

'I don't know how to answer that.'

'Yes or no. Simple.'

'Would you expect me to say 'no'?'

'You were a waitress before you went back to education?'

'Yes.'

'Did you read books as a waitress?'

'No. I had boyfriends and went dancing.'

'What made you go back to education?'

'I met someone.'

'Who read books?'

'And listened to music, and talked about paintings and opened my eyes and gave me a vocabulary.'

'How sweet.' Her teeth were very clenched now. 'Do you know anything about books?' she asked.

'What do you mean – how they're priced? Sold? Remaindered?'

'No, no, no!' she slammed at me, and drew a deep breath through those bloody clenched teeth. I tried again when in fact my instinct was to stand up, say, 'Thank you and goodbye,' and walk out.

'How they're printed, manufactured?'

'Yes, that!' She picked up a book from a stack that seemed a heavy breath away from toppling over, opened it and pointed to the inside cover – a reproduction of an old map of islands somewhere in the Atlantic. 'Do you know what these are called?' I imagined she was pointing to the maps.

'Maps?' I suggested not really understanding why she was asking such a simple question.

'Endpapers!' she spat out contemptuously. 'Printed ends in fact.' Contempt through clenched teeth is distressing to experience. I was distressed. On the verge of tears, in fact. I watched her watching me and realised she was hoping I would burst into tears, which of course determined me not to. 'And have you read any of our authors?' she asked as though playing her trump card. I named some. 'Because,' she said, 'we have some of the best contemporary giants in our stable.' I wasn't sure how that could be since she mixed her metaphors, but I thought it would help me recover my composure if I went for the full lie.

'It's one of the reasons why I leapt to apply for this post.'

'You and thirty-seven others,' she warned, adding like a full stop, 'the *best* contemporary giants.'

Because she had protected herself by damaging me she could now afford to unwrap her 'coat' and draw herself up like – like – like what? It came to me – of course, like one of the giants in her stable. Of course! Her strength lay in what she represented. Her glory was not her own, it was reflected. Was this true of all intermediaries – producers, directors, publishers, conductors, agents? Do they all mistake themselves for those on whose behalf they mediate? A novelist confronting this demon publisher, awaiting judgement, would not be a novelist standing before just *any* woman, he would be confronting someone through whom *many* novelists had passed. This dreadful woman may not be a writer but behind her, intimidatingly, are the names of *all* the writers she's published, those 'contemporary giants'. Her importance is composed of the literary achievements of men and women who come together in her and make the poor young novelist feel he's nothing compared to their combined glory.

It must be the same in all the arts. The young painter doesn't feel he's intruding on the time of merely the gallery owner, but of the gallery owner *who has hung masters.* The young dramatist insisting his play be performed as he conceives it isn't arguing merely with directors and actors, he's arguing with directors and actors *who have interpreted (and reflect) the glory of those dramatists posterity has already crowned.* The poor individual artist must cower before the collective. The solitary supplicant is overshadowed by the thunderous might of the already acclaimed who are unaware that their combined talents are being exploited to intimidate a potential young colleague. Why were these thoughts familiar? Why was I thinking them and feeling I had read them elsewhere? I had to wait to find out.

Until then I had to endure the final venom of this vituperative hag who probably hated my plump good looks. Why? What was the gain? Surely this was not the way to conduct an interview – for either of us. I take some of the blame – she may have been rude and haughty but I was too playful. Perhaps neither of us wanted the other from the start – not her me nor me the job. Why not? I like being around books. I like the feel and promise of them. So why this death wish?

These were her final words:

'You will not,' she said, 'amount to very much.' She won. I burst into tears. As she had wanted.

'Why,' I asked between heaves and sobs, 'do you say such things? We're complete strangers. You know nothing about me. I'm young, you're old. I'm in need, you can help. You have a powerbase, I'm a beggar at the gate. You have a responsi*bility* to help. You don't want to give me a job, fine. That's your right. I can take that. But this rudeness? I don't understand it. This destructiveness? This . . .'

She didn't let me finish. 'You enter a room with the air of one who imagines everyone in it is an idiot.'

'How do you deduce such a thing?' I cried. 'What did I say? What did I do?'

'I have an instinct about people as I do about books, which are like people – you trust them or you don't; you believe them or you don't; they come at you stridently or they offer themselves gently.'

I blew my nose into a handkerchief and tried to talk at the same time. 'And I was strident?' I asked. '*Strident?*' Or rather I *tried* to ask. The word 'strident' splashed into my handkerchief and was lost. I gave up stood up and turned to go. 'Thank you,' was all I could say, though I must admit, begrudgingly admit, that my mind was still sufficiently alert to appreciate her observation that books were like people – you believed them or you didn't. 'I will remember that,' I told her.

Was the interview a learning curve? Must I mend my ways and lose my cockiness? Am I cocky? How can I be cocky? I've nothing to thrust and wave around saying, 'Look at me.' No protuberance cries out, 'I'm here! Here I am!' My breasts? Those are there, for sure. No avoiding Beatie Bryant's breasts, but I don't thrust them, there's merely a cleavage. *What*, therefore? What, what, what had upset her? And him? Both my interviewers! '*You enter a room with the air of one who imagines everyone in it is an idiot.*' Do I? Do I really? I must think about that. Reflect on it. Take myself apart. Inspect the parts, as with a car, clean this scrape that, grease this renew that!

Before catching the train from Liverpool Street I had to return home and shower. I was smelly from distress. And I went looking for what it was had reminded me of this confusion of personas – the publisher mistaking herself for the writer she published. It was in a special magazine, an old one, one of those I pick up from times past whenever I stumble across them in the boxes outside secondhand bookshops. I soon found it. A magazine called *Armageddon*, Vol. 10 Summer issue, 1897, an essay that has since become famous from frequent anthologising by the eminent – though young at the time – critic Dr Ronald Skewer: 'Who Lasts, Who Falls?'

> Beware of they who glow with the talent of giants whom posterity has hallowed with time, who speak with the authority of earlier tongues, who cudgel you with genius their blinkered sensibilities would have failed to recognise had they been contemporaries. They are poor things of reflected glory who will whip you into place with glee if you but once engage their minds, flatteringly deluding them they possess intelligence.

Good old Skewer. He lasted. Went on to assemble and defend twenty-five so-called 'minor' writers in a seminal volume entitled *In Praise of Pale Genius* – a reference to the scathing, mean-minded and slim volume *Giants and Pale Reflections* by Paul Rempton, the stern and feared Cambridge don who dismissed every writer bar a top ten he considered the literary greats. Skewer argued that here-and-there literary gems added up to a superb necklace the British nation should be proud to wear round its neck. He despised charts, league tables, top tens and the notion of 'favourites'. His colleagues skipped smugly between the safe major names in world literature while Skewer preferred to rummage in dusty corners blowing away cobwebs to reveal scintillating one-offs. He lasted but lived too long, saddened by the gloomy opening days of World War Two.

Why, I wondered, hadn't I put his lines into my 'quotes book'? Or had I? I reached for it to check; always a dangerous thing to do as I have difficulty not pausing to reread all the wonderful wisdom I've recorded from here, there and everywhere. It's a huge, partly leather-bound book of alphabetically divided pages, and so I assume was originally intended as an address book. I must get it dated one day. It has the feel and look of turn of the century, perhaps earlier. Dickensian, I've often thought. I couldn't resist buying it for a few pounds in a junk shop, with its conveniently spaced pages into which I could file my cherished gems by author. I looked up 'S' – Skewer. Not there. I wrote him in at once and then, as I feared, glanced at other quotes, always a joy because I forget what I've entered, and I encounter those perceptive minds all over again.

Don't you think men overrate the necessity for humouring everybody's nonsense, till they get despised by the very fools they humour? *George Eliot*

It is wrong of women to receive us with pouting, querulous and shrinking looks that quell us even as they kindle us. The daughter-in-law of Pythagoras said that a woman who goes to bed with a man ought to lay aside her modesty with her skirt and put it on again with her petticoat. *Montaigne*

All the sins of men I esteem as their disease, not their nature. *Ruskin*

Children who weep at the death of the first chicken they see killed laugh at the death of the second. *Voltaire*

Be more humane when you speak against fanaticism, anger
not the fanatics; they are delirious invalids, who would assault
their physicians. Let us make their ways more gentle, not aggra-
vate them.

Voltaire again. And one of my favourites that I can't attribute so
it's there under 'C' for Chinese.

A Chinese sage of the distant past was once asked by his disciples what he would do first if he were given power to set right
the affairs of the country. He answered: 'I should certainly see
to it that language was used correctly.' The disciples looked perplexed. 'Surely,' they said, 'this is a trivial matter. Why should
you deem it so important?' The Master replied: 'If language is
not used correctly then what is said is not what is meant. If
what is said is not what is meant then what ought to be done
remains undone. If this remains undone morals and art will be
corrupted. If morals and art are corrupted justice will go astray.
If justice goes astray the people will stand about in helpless
confusion.'

Some of the pages have loose scraps in them covered with quotes
I keep meaning to enter into the book. Uncharacteristic of me
to have neglected such a task, organised as I am, anal, some
would say, but there it is – I'm not perfect. Still, as Ruskin
observes:

All things are literally better, lovelier, and more beloved for the
imperfections which have been divinely appointed, that the
law of human life may be effort, and the law of human judgement, mercy.

Something nags at me. Why for Christ's sake didn't I know that
they were called 'endpapers'? That really shook me. I vowed, as I
sat seething and shivering before the Witch of Fitzroy Square, that

I would find out and name every part of a book. But there was more. I can't identify it. I felt a vague sense of having moved on a step, like a fire crackling before bursting into flame. I was not feeling it physically but – I don't know. I felt on the verge of something, the approach of an idea, a milling around in my head. I was being prepared, slowly stirred, like disturbed water. I feel it now as I write, a thickening, a taking shape. My imagery is all over the place but that teeth-clenched harridan had ruffled my feathers. (Another disparate image.) She had unnerved me, unhinged me, taken me apart. And yet I was not angry. I felt I had deserved her lashing, that it was driving me somewhere, that a creative nerve had been scorched. Oh, I was not about to write a masterpiece. I had read too much fine literature to presume literary ambitions. No, she had not given birth to an artist. Her taunts had goaded my brain into an activity it could not yet understand, interpret, know how to pursue. But it would come. I would put together again what she had torn apart, and I would return in a blaze of glory.

I was reminded of one of my interviews before entering college. A weary old professor, who seemed eager to get it over and done with as soon as possible so that he could go for his beer or sherry or whatever it was had brought out tiny scarlet veins in his nose, imagined he had got rid of me with his first three questions.

'Have you read any Trollope?'

'No.'

'Have you read any Thackeray?'

'No, he's on my list, though.'

'Have you read Thomas Mann?'

'He's not an English writer.'

'I know he's not an English writer,' he thundered back, which sometimes paralyses sometimes stimulates me. I was feeling stimulated.

'I've concentrated on—' He didn't let me finish and explain that I had concentrated mainly on the moderns.

'I mean,' he thundered ahead, 'if you haven't read Trollope,

Thackeray and Mann what possible frame of reference can we have in common to begin your three years in this most hallowed of halls?'

'That we're both human, perhaps?' I ventured, and became bolder when his dull eyes suddenly lit up. 'That we've both lived, experienced much – you more than me, of course – that we share fears, hates, self-doubt, jealousy, bewilderment, sexual urges, and have opinions about the world that come at us from here, there and everywhere? Perhaps?'

We became good friends. His drink was whisky. He handed me down a taste for it.

There now. I've quietened. It will come. Whatever it is that's trying to be born in me will shape in its own time. Hurry nothing, Beatie Bryant. Be patient. All will be revealed.

10

I knew it would have to come out sooner or later

I knew it would have to come out sooner or later. Manfred was worried about me. I had worried him. I could see that. In his eyes, I could see it. He was watching me as though any moment I was going to leap off a balcony. It wouldn't be long before he would press me. I knew it. Manfred wouldn't be satisfied with any old dismissive explanation I might offer for my state of mind. He'd press, probe, again and again. I had worried him too much. And I understood why – I had worried myself! That dream had saturated me more expansively than I had thought possible. It was with me in my waking hours for months after, as though the panic had taken hold of me like terminal cancer. That's what panic is – a cancer, eating away sanity and serenity. Of course I was worried, and my worry communicated itself forcefully. I would have to betray Tina. I could see it coming.

'Of course you would have to betray me,' said Tina. 'Only I wouldn't call it "betrayal". You're so melodramatic. You're just getting something off your chest, as we all need to from time to time.' I thanked her.

'Pleasure,' she said.

'Now go away,' I said. She left obediently.

'*I will never see youth again*,' Manfred had said, talking about the young woman to whom he had spoken a few words in Shepherd Market. He was always meeting people, here, there and anywhere; and he had the facility to engage them in conversation, encourage their story. '*Everyone has a story*,' he'd say, and he got them to trust him with it, to reveal what perhaps they might later regret having revealed, but at the time of the encounter he could make himself their confidant, and out would tumble their lives, the stories of how they had made a mess of those lives, or of how *others* had made the mess. He was a good raconteur. I loved listening to his retelling of their tellings. But this time the telling was saddening. The young woman in Shepherd Market had made him feel old. It was my turn to console *him* and remind him of his stupendous achievements climbing mountains.

Of course Manfred didn't consider them as achievements, or not as *great* achievements. For him, he'd say, the mountain was a humbling place where he learnt to take the lesser role. '*The mountain dictated, I followed*,' he said. That I could understand – the mountain is a big bloke; you don't quarrel with big blokes. But I wasn't comfortable with everything Manfred said. Like: '*Mountains have mysterious ways.*'

'What "mysterious ways"?' I challenged. 'What's "mysterious" about a mountain? It's solid. It doesn't move. It's there. In the moonlight and in the mist I guess it must be beautiful and *appear* to be mysterious, but so would a river bank,' I pressed, 'or a house on a hill. Mist and moonlight do things to places – valleys as well as mountains. It's the nature of mist and moonlight to turn characterless places into mysterious places.' He tolerated what he called my pedantry with a superiority that I don't mind telling you irritated me. On the other hand perhaps I *was* being pedantic. If a man climbs a mountain you let him say whatever he wants to say. He's earned the right. So I let him see mystery and think humble. I knew he would dismiss my attempts to reassure him that he was as old as he felt and that he couldn't really be feeling old or he would fall down the mountains he was always climbing.

'Never mind all that,' he said in a way that reminded me he was the forceful one in our relationship.

Thornton Wilder in his novel *The Bridge of San Luis Rey* observed, or had one of his characters observe, that, of two people who love, one loves the less; and I think that in any relationship that lasts – whether between lovers or friends or colleagues – one is forceful and one is not. I'm not thinking of cruel force that renders the other a victim, simply of those who without question assume command of the moment; those who naturally take over the organisation of an event; those who make suggestions for an activity when a hiatus occurs. Just as, of two people who are intelligent, one is confidently intelligent, the other constantly doubts their intelligence. The confidently intelligent possess a sort of steamrolling energy that it's pointless to contradict. Unless their proposals are complete anathema, then of course we dig our heels in. Or I do, anyway. I don't mind going along with what Manfred suggests, mostly. Just occasionally what he suggests doesn't match my mood, and I cry halt! Does that make me a weak personality, I've often wondered? I don't think so, or I hope not so. My strengths reside in my work. I'm a good critic, knowledgeable and responsible; I don't care or need to enter battles of will over who takes charge.

But I digress. I frequently do – go off at tangents, feel things need more explanation than they do. Like now – I'm going off at a tangent to explain why I'm going off at a tangent.

So, 'Never mind all that,' Manfred said, 'I'm worried about you, your dream and the panic it has left behind. You know what I think it's all about?' I didn't need to answer him; he was going to tell me. 'It's delayed reaction to Tina's death. Two years is not a long time to absorb a loss like that. Consider,' he steamrollered on, 'in one death you lost a daily companion, a cook, a carer, a lover, an anchor . . .'

I blurted out my correction. 'Anchor, yes, lover – not.'

'What do you mean, 'lover not'?'

'What I say. Lover – not!'

'Now don't go to extremes,' said Tina.

'Quiet!' I ordered her. 'You can have your turn later.'

'Tina?' asked Manfred. I nodded.

'Look,' said a surprised Manfred, 'I don't want to get too personal. We're intimate friends but some things we need to keep to ourselves; on the other hand—'

I didn't let him finish. 'I don't need to "keep",' I snapped. 'What do I need to "keep" for? I've "kept" for twenty years. I'm tired of "keeping". That's why I'm having bad dreams because I've been "keeping, keeping".' I could hear myself becoming Jewish.

'Then stop "keeping",' Manfred urged. 'Explain!'

When it came to it I didn't think I could. I *was* tired of keeping in all that I felt and thought about my late wife, but she was A Person even if A Dead Person, and respect must be paid to persons dead as well as alive. Everyone adored her, besides. I had no right to blemish that memory. But, it had to be said, she bequeathed me panic in her will, a will she made out twenty years before she died, a will that many bequeath of a strong presence that hovers over our shoulders or inhabits our dreams long after they've gone. And now that panic which began mildly had, over the years, grown in intensity and was interfering with my work. *That's* why I didn't need to 'keep it in'. My book, my biography of Giovanni Marcantonio, had been coming together; the crochets and quavers of his life were beginning to harmonise with the crochets and quavers of his extraordinary music, and here was the old panic, induced by Tina all those years ago, surfacing again, terrorising me. The book was falling to pieces. I was losing control of it.

I was torn. To tell or not to tell. And what guarantee was there that telling would ease the terror?

'I'm having second thoughts,' I said. 'You're right. Some things are too personal even between old friends.'

'More than "old",' Manfred corrected me. 'Close. We're close friends.' I could see he had been startled by what I had foolishly let slip out, and I was really, really regretting the slip. Then just as I was regretting it, out it came, exploded, as though *I* had decided one thing and someone else within me had decided another. God knows who that someone else was, it didn't matter – he, she, whoever, had won! Out cascaded my hidden life.

'Tina stopped being a lover when she turned fifty. Even a little before, as though fifty on the horizon was a warning. At forty-five she transmogrified into one of those women who speak to their men like little boys, diminish them with indulgence, open their legs with a sigh saying, "Oh well, if you must." Loving becomes a favour they have paused wearily to bestow in the midst of more important things. It's not that desire dries up, rather it's that they have discovered power through not needing to love as desperately as their partner. Such women withhold the joy of physical contact until needed as a reward for good behaviour – sweeties to the child. "I don't know what I'm to do with you," she says as though a kiss were a request for money she couldn't really spare. And she discusses him with her female friends, reducing him to a burden she must bear, her cross in life. Tina wasn't quite like that. I don't think she would have been as vulgar as to discuss me that way with her friends. Neither do I think she was really interested in power games, but I did notice she held her head higher, that she walked, as it were, in triumph. She had administrative skills and she was sharp and witty but the interest she once had in my book on Marcantonio had waned, the intellectual exchanges ceased and overnight I felt in her shadow. She towered. And worse, she made me feel old. There's something about love withdrawn that makes the one who is bereft feel old. It has to do with being discarded – you discard old things, things that no longer function or no longer please.'

Manfred was astounded. We had fooled everybody, Tina and

me. And that's what Manfred was thinking – he'd been fooled.

'I know, I know! We'd projected the image of a tactile-loving couple who couldn't keep their hands off each other. I'm sorry. Forgive me. Forgive Tina. The reverse became true. She began withdrawing bit by bit by little bit. It was the most tortuous time in our marriage, and the worst part of it was that I couldn't understand why it was happening. Nor did she *talk* to me about what was happening. She just made it happen, or let it happen, or willed it to happen. Who knows! I understood nothing. And we kept it from you. Hid it. Forgive us.'

Poor Manfred. He, too, understood nothing because I was being neither clear nor specific, only vague and distraught, and I could see in his perplexed face and hunched shoulders that he was a man waiting for an explanation of the incomprehensible. I was uncertain whether to go on, the details were indeed very private. But what did I care? Perhaps if I revealed them, spoke them out loud, I'd begin myself to understand.

'We had a good sex life together,' I began. 'Only I don't like to call it a sex life. I hate that expression "having sex". It sounds like a course of hospital treatment. Too clinical! "I'm going to put you on a course called *sex*." No! Love making! I prefer "love making". We had a good love life together. More than good – adventurous! We tried everything, mostly at her suggestion; things I'd never dreamt of, or if I had dreamt of them I had never contemplated the possibility of exploring them.'

I could see Manfred waiting for me to go into detail. Maybe I would, maybe I wouldn't.

'It wasn't only the lovemaking that was glorious, it was the loving,' I continued. 'I loved being loved by her. When we drove places she'd take my hand and hold it while steering with the other. I let her drive, she enjoyed it.'

'I remember,' said Manfred. 'One or two friends were cruel about it. "Tina's in the driving seat," they used to say, maliciously.'

'I know what people used to say,' I replied. 'People! They need signs to let the world know they're in control. Me, I never needed such things. I was never in competition with anyone. Not even with myself. Some people compete with everything. They have to win – games, driving, life, to show who's boss, who's in control. Not me. So I let her drive and take my hand. We made long trips like that. In a car holding hands. It was so intimate, so very intimate. And sometimes, in the afternoon, as we got older, we'd feel tired and we'd lie on the chaise longue in my study, she on top of me, her head on my chest, and we'd fall asleep, and snore a little, or she'd dribble, just a little, and I loved that, it made me feel tender, as with a beloved newborn baby. Christ! What only we didn't do. It all floods back. We soaked in baths together, visited outlandish places in search of small concerts of obscure composers, and it seemed to me we made love everywhere – beneath hedges, in the back of the car, once in a public place against a huge tree on a stony path along which anyone could come at any moment. And we loved small things about each other. She loved my breath smelling of whisky; I loved the light hairs on her cheeks; she loved watching me sign my name on cheques or letters; I loved watching her walk – upright, her body slightly thrust forward, like a model. It gave her a strange pleasure to watch me draw a wallet from inside my jacket, or look at my watch. It gave me pleasure to have her hands come at me from behind while I shaved, long fingers with red nails spread over my chest, scarlet against the white. She loved me bringing her tea in bed – I'd have a cup myself and we'd sit propped up against the wall sipping and talking and oooing and ahhing. Small things. The pleasure of marriage is in the detail as well as the major events. And when they stopped I missed them, the details. Terribly. I missed them like crazy.'

I had to pause because I knew that if I didn't I would weep. Manfred could see that possibility, and sat back. Left me alone. No more urging. He could see I was not 'keeping in'.

'Sometimes we'd do wicked things like go to a movie in the afternoon, or she'd suddenly decide to strip and walk around naked doing some unnecessary housework, teasing me, playing with me, like a little girl. And she could carry it off. She was not lewd. Another woman might be tarty doing such things. Not Tina. She was mischievous and merry. I loved her mischievousness. We once took a visiting friend from Spain to see the flowers along the Regent's Park canal and I took photos. In one, as they were sitting side by side on a low wall, both staring at the camera, she opened her legs quickly and closed them again but not before I snapped. I have that photo still and I look at it every so often, not only to be reminded of the delights that lay behind that pair of white knickers but to gaze at that lovely, sunny face with eyes full of childlike naughtiness.'

I was weeping. I tried hard not to. I kept swallowing and blinking but out it heaved. I couldn't help it. I was too overwhelmed with a sense of loss. It was unbearable. We talk sagaciously of a sense of loss – old Freud counts it one of the great causes of unhappiness, but no one can understand it who hasn't actually suffered it. The heartache is tangible. You feel it. You really, really feel it. There, in the region of your heart, a weight. The heart must break, you feel. Surely it's going to break. And this profound sadness, this choking unhappiness, affects the way you perceive everything around you. Every object. A wineglass unwashed; a cup and saucer on the table; the sky outside whether sharply blue or grey with a hood of cloud; an article of clothing slung over a chair; a pen on a notebook on the desk; the paintings, drawings, photos on the wall – everything and anything that is touched by human hand, seen by human eyes, all seems sad, unbearably sad, and takes on the heartache. So I wept. Manfred moved to comfort me. I thrust out a hand. No. I would recover without help, thank you very much. What was I – an adolescent in need of consolation, of a parent's pity? No thank you. I could manage, I thought. I would carry on talking.

'Now here's a funny thing,' I said between clutches of heavy breathing. 'Well, not funny but curious. I can remember the first sign of her change. At least I think it was the first. Who can be certain? You look back to account for it all, to explain, to build a graph of the decline, and perhaps you imagine what wasn't there or your explanations take into account chimeras. Who knows? Anyway, it was this—

'You remember Tina, vividly I suppose. She was my height, even a little taller, half an inch or so; and in the early years of our marriage she only ever wore shoes that were flat. She imagined I was shamed by her appearing taller than me. Silly, isn't it? As if I cared! I didn't! Taller, shorter, less or more – what did it matter? But *she* cared on my behalf. So – flat shoes. Stylish but always flat. And then, a few years into her forties I noticed – her shoes had heels. Low to begin with but they grew. She never wore those really high ones, those thin things that always seem to me to be feet-cripplers, no – thick heels. Not middle-aged wedges but elegant. And she became taller! It didn't matter to me. She looked good in them. I enjoyed her looking good in them. But it was more than being taller, she was now also somehow less connected to me. The higher heels had taken her up and away. She was more belonging to herself – I can't explain it any other way – more, more independent. Fine! That was fine by me. In fact it didn't even strike me that way at the time. Only later, when she began withdrawing her favours, the high heels fell into place.'

I could see Manfred beginning to doubt me. Not doubting the facts, just my explanations of them. Or was it doubt in his eyes? Perhaps it was merely concentration. Doubt or concentration, I drove on.

'And you know what the second thing was? This will surprise you because it's something you never knew she did. Whenever I travelled abroad she used to pack my suitcase for me – which was lovely of her. I never asked, she just did it. I hated packing and I wasn't good at it so I appreciated it. But that wasn't all. Believe it or not she used to slip thin sheets of tissue paper between the folds of a shirt, a pair of trousers, layers of pants. And when I unpacked I'd usually find a little present – a bar of chocolate, or a photograph of the girls, or a note saying something like "don't forget me". And then she stopped. One day she was rushing around before she had to drive me to the airport and she apologised saying she was too pressed and would I mind doing it myself. I was no good at it but I did it. Packed the wrong things, folded shirts and jackets the wrong way, packed too much. And that was it. From then on I always did it myself. Nothing was said but a new ritual took over – me the packer!'

Manfred had turned pale.

'You've gone pale,' I told him. 'And you're holding your breath.'

'Pale?' he asked moving to look at himself in a Georgian mirror I'd not long ago bought, covered in Victorian painted flowers it had taken me all day to clean off. 'Pale? It's true. I'm pale. I can't think why. You're the one torturing yourself, why should the blood drain from me? I was holding my breath listening to you but that should make me turn red, surely?'

'Stop holding your breath,' I told him, 'and listen to this third change in her that I'm just remembering.'

'A third thing?'

'The saddest,' I said. 'Remember that Tina wore glasses?'

'I remember.'

'Well, it wasn't always so. Her eyes began to give out at the time contact lenses came in. She had a thing about glasses. She thought I thought they made her look unattractive. It was a misunderstanding. The first glasses she bought didn't suit her. Or at least I didn't think they suited her, and I said, "Those glasses don't suit you, Tina!" She thought I had said, "Glasses don't suit you", so she took to contact lenses in order to stay attractive to me. Foolish woman. Glasses, no glasses! What did it matter to me? I didn't care. I loved looking at her face and her eyes and her smiles whatever she wore. But then I noticed, round about the same time that she started wearing shoes with higher heels she also started wearing her glasses. Sometimes she wore contact lenses, but less and less. Breathe, Manfred, breathe!'

'High heels, packed cases and glasses,' he said, breathing out.

'And then the gradual withdrawal of lovemaking.'

'What only we don't know about each other.'

'The saga of that gradual withdrawal I'll save you, but I can tell you it was distressing. All our innocent explorations that we had mutually believed natural, now seemed unnatural, shabby, unclean. I don't think it was what she intended but that's how it felt. "Don't do that" she'd say about something she'd once thrilled to. "Stop that! No! Not that!" She'd push my hand away from an action I'd made a thousand times. *That's* what upset me most, the pushing away of the hand. That's the killer. "Not that! No! Stop! No more!" One by one, until that final utterance, I'll never forget it, it rings and rings in my ears: "I have," she told me, "nothing more to give to this relationship." Nothing more. Nothing! Gone! Chilling, no?

'I lived with that rejection for years and years and years. She brought it with her whenever she entered the room, whenever we went to our separate beds, whenever we went out together. It was there at my side. Rejection! She had found me sweet, and left me sordid. It was like a river drying up. Remember those trick shots in movies showing a fast-flowing river that slowly cross-fades into a dried-up riverbed? That's what our relationship became – a dried-up riverbed. We became strangers to one another. How could we become strangers? After such intensity – how? It's a terrible destruction the destruction of one's sexual gaiety. But it wasn't only the abandoned lovemaking. We had looked after one another. She had cared about my work, the Marcantonio biography, it was exciting for her; she was a help to me, we were soulmates. But she wasn't there. I needed her but she was no longer there. A stranger was there. Where did she come from, this stranger? I didn't know her. It was so painful and so bewildering. I was bereft. A good word – bereft! I was utterly, utterly bereft.'

'And you didn't separate, you kept her.' Rhetorical though the question, Barney answered.

'Of course! No longer desiring me was not a crime to be punished. She was the mother of my children, she had given me many happy years, I had reached heights with her. Such things have to be remembered, honoured, cherished, respected. It knocked me sideways, I didn't know where I was or who I was for years. My fires burnt out, and I lost my smile.'

I was silent for a long time after that. I could feel Manfred waiting for me to continue. There was little more to add.

'But,' I finished, 'I had a responsibility; and responsibility is responsibility.'

11

What my poor husband, Barney, now a poor widower, didn't realise was

What my poor husband, Barney, now a poor widower, didn't realise was that in some married women there is a celibate waiting to get out. They hanker to return to the state of virginity, to feel untrammelled, untouched, unviolated. The sexual act is a violation of innocence most women mourn having lost. He couldn't understand this. To slough off all links with a man was a need too alien for him to comprehend.

But there it was, this distaste that had slowly grown up in me. I couldn't help it. I didn't want his tongue in my mouth any more nor his shlong between my legs. I didn't want him in me in any way. I didn't want to be intruded upon any longer. He couldn't understand that, and I couldn't help him understand.

Nor was it only intrusion I didn't want. I didn't want to be needed, depended upon, expected from – it was all a weight, a burden. I didn't want any of it ever again. And that shocked me. When the girls were gone I thought I'd miss them but I didn't. *He* did, not me, and it made me feel ashamed. Shocked and ashamed. My daughters, my beloved daughters, the girls who filled the house with their friends, their screams at each other, their laughter – the thought of them going, the thought that one day they would no longer need me, and leave, was unbearable. But the reality, when they actually *did* go, was different. The pressure of not being needed, the weight, the burden, the expectations, the planning of meals – it all sloughed off. At last I could hear the air moving around the rooms. I could pause to smell smells. I could tend to my garden as it deserved, I could steal time to read. Ah! The relief! I became number one, the first at last. Me, me, me, the first at last.

And once I'd had the taste for it, once I'd sloughed off one expectation I wanted to slough off more. I stopped this happening, then that. I said no to this and then I said no to that. And I found I needed it so badly, this sloughing off, that I'm afraid Barney became *part* of the sloughing off. I stopped being a wife. Shocking and shaming. I know, I know! Wives are the ones they rely on to give them happiness. We give it, we take it away, we give it, we take it away. It's a terrible power we have and they resent it, our poor husbands. They resent it and it confuses them. Barney was confused. I sloughed off his happiness and he was hurt and confused and it all shocked and shamed me but I was powerless to do anything about it. I couldn't say anything because it would involve me in tortuous attempts to explain the inexplicable. All I wanted to do was send him silent messages of little endings leading up to the big ending. Over! I would look after him, the world would see a loving and caring couple, but I was done. Enough! *Basta!* What saddened me was that he interpreted it as riddance. It wasn't that. Or I suppose it was. But not for me. For me it was peeling. The skin of my existence had become hardened. I needed to peel it off and let fresh skin grow, if it could. Maybe it wouldn't but I had to try. I had been in a room full of smoke, and now needed to breathe.

That sounds awful, I know it, even from the grave. But what can we do, we women? The body becomes boring. All those same contours, groans and smells. I suppose it was the same for him with me but he never said so, he didn't seem to mind the boredom. Or maybe it wasn't boring for him. It couldn't have been, because he claimed every time was fresh, like the first time. Though I didn't believe him.

And I have to confess it got worse. I know how they used to think about me, talk about me. 'A powerhouse of action! A doer! A solver of problems! A bulldozing spirit!' That was me, for sure. I can't argue with it, but − I hated it and it tired me. I didn't slough off my girls; the inevitable rhythm of life sloughed *them* off. But I sloughed off Barney, and then I began to slough off my friends.

I didn't think it possible I could do such a thing. What, *me*? Tina the gregarious with 'an unending basket of appetites'? Tina whose arms opened wider than anybody's, who stayed up late cooking and preparing party after party, lunch dates, tea dates, brunch dates? Surely not. And then breakfasts began. The hard-working, ambitious, no-holds-barred Americans introduced breakfast meetings, and so Barney, who used to travel widely to review concerts and performers and who met everybody and invited them to come and see him, squeezed in breakfast dates. The girls loved it, naturally. Tamara especially. It helped her when she got to Oxford − she knew how to mix. They began calling *her* 'a doer', 'a solver of problems'.

Of course I didn't slough off *all* my friends. Friends are like the objects you collect and lay around in your house. One day you look at them one by one and think why ever did I bring those into my house? Who needs them around any more? They had a brief attraction but now, looking at them closely, you realise they no longer hold either interest or depth. Things of beauty may be a joy for ever, thank you, Mr Keats, but who has the eye to spot that beauty? A good first line, Mr Keats, but oh, those beautiful friends who are no longer beautiful. Painful, but I had to slough

them off and the emotion that accompanied them. Baggage.
Emotional baggage. I didn't want it. None of it. People, objects,
feelings – rid of them! I needed to travel light, I had this great
need to travel light.

12

Beatie used to be ambivalent about returning to her family

Beatie used to be ambivalent about returning to her family. The pull was always strong, the experience limited. Now her hankerings for the flat landscape were acute. She looked forward to driving her mother around old haunts, and found herself tolerant of her mother's endless repetition of stories that once hammered her into the ground.

And there was Stan Mann. Beatie was learning about Stan Mann for the first time. She had grown up with him as a drunken friend of her mother's, a man who'd once owned a fleet of cars for hire but who had slowly, over the years, sunk into decline from too many lagers and much else of excess. Now she was discovering another Stan Mann. Her unexpected education had brought him out. She had become someone he could talk to about ideas and his past. Stan had not only been a communist, he had fought in the Spanish Civil War as a member of the International Brigade, with responsibility for transport, one of the few departments of that chaotic conflict to have functioned smoothly under his control until he was wounded.

A lorry-load of armoury replacements had to be driven near Republican lines, and he knew how slim the chances were of getting there safe and intact. Stan had only Spanish boys available, none of whom knew how to weave a truck between bullets and shells as he did. As a commander he should have commanded. As Stan Mann the dry-humoured, cocky, Norfolkian who thought no man from the Fens could come to harm, and who couldn't bear the thought of spilt young blood, he volunteered himself to himself.

'Stan Mann,' he said to himself, amusing his young Spanish friends, 'I need you to volunteer.' 'Aye, aye!' he said to himself, and sped off with his vital baggage. He missed the shells but a bullet whistled through where a door should have been, and shattered his left leg. The young Stan who could run, jump, ride horses, swim and chase girls never overcame his disability. It defeated his spirits. He returned to Norfolk, found a nurse to marry, took to drink and burdened her with the rest of his life.

The need, however, to read, to talk, to animate a company never left him. And so – crippled though he was, drunkard though he was, bankrupt though he was – he was loved and indulged, and repaid those who loved and indulged him with lively conversation and stories. Beatie certainly loved this old man. Through him she felt in touch not only with an historic past but a past of solid, old-fashioned values of tenderness, tolerance, pity, awe and respect. He honoured and cherished the good and the great, and taught her the meaning of Schadenfreude. It was through Stan that she learnt to appreciate the sterling qualities of her family.

She enjoyed card games with her brother and his brood, and dinner plates piled high with not one or two vegetables – say potatoes and peas – but three or four – say carrots and beans, too. She enjoyed her nephews and nieces, whom she considered achievers against the odds. They were good people, her lumpy family, hardworking and generous, perhaps wanting only that spark of curiosity about the world abroad and a preparedness to accommodate the possibility of joy in the arts she had newly discovered and was eager to share with them but couldn't, only with Stan Mann; which meant that conversations soon wound down and Beatie became restless to return to the cultural energy that was London. But this trip home was to be different, for many reasons.

She stood looking down at the new shape of Liverpool Street Station that was emerging under reconstruction. She watched over the years the magnificent Victorian iron pillars and arches meld into the modern structures of steel and glass. The architects had designed the change with boldness and sensitivity. They had retained the best features of this famous 1874 railway station from which hundreds of London evacuees had been whisked away to avoid the threatened bombs of World War Two, to the alien villages of the Fens where there were cows and spiders and a way of life so utterly different from the slums of the metropolis that few remained unaffected.

As she watched, Beatie experienced a glow that she was coming to realise was part of her nature, a nature stroked and informed by Stan Mann. The glow came when confronting human genius. When she saw it honoured, when achievement against the odds was finally acknowledged, it brought a lump to her throat. Not that she had the opportunity to experience many such honourings in any than vicarious forms through literature or cinema – without which, she knew, she would be impoverished. Standing at street level looking down into the exhilarating changes of this railway station was one such opportunity. Somewhere someone in charge of money and planning had honoured these architects and designers by releasing their imagination and skills to transform this tired old station. Only one condition seems to have been imposed: don't destroy the past, weave it into the present, let human endeavour be seen to have continuity. And they were succeeding. The year was 1983, two years into watching the United States run by an actor. Part of Beatie's pleasure in visiting her

Norfolk family was to travel from Liverpool Street Station and
chart its transformation from the nineteenth to the twentieth century. It was scheduled to be finished in 1992.

She was early, with time to kill. Rather than sit around in a station pub, or eat Japanese sushi in one of the many new eating
places, or drink in Dirty Dicks, a cavern pub that once had walls
festooned with foreign money but now was cleaned and sanitised
and without personality, she decided to wonder through Stepney
back streets the other side of Bishopsgate. She didn't get far. One
tiny shop in Frying Pan Alley held her attention. It was a bookbinder's.

In the window was an old press with sheets of leather hanging
from it, and, scattered around at its base, an assortment of dusty,
newly bound leather books, some fully bound, some half-, some
quarter-bound, all cheerfully strewn as though to echo the hap-
hazard nature of the reality literature attempted to bring to order.
Beatie normally suspected indulgent readings of the outward
appearance of things, but looking into this window display, if display it could be called, she felt very strongly the display's message.
The bookbinder most definitely had a view of books, which con-
sciously or not he seemed to have demonstrated in the way he had
thrown his shop window together. She peered beyond the display
and saw that the bookbinder was not a 'he' but a 'she'. Beatie
made up her mind instantly; she would go into the shop – a
workshop, actually – and look around.

A feeble bell rattled as she opened the door reminding her of
the little greengrocer's in the village of her Norfolk childhood. A
voice called out:

'Mind the step.' It called just in time. Beatie hadn't seen it and
would have tumbled forward into pain and chaos.

'Good thing you warned me,' she said to the voice whose body
she still couldn't see.

'Had to!' snapped the voice. 'It's a reflex by now. The bell din-
glelingleings and I call out, "Mind the step." Had one or two nasty
accidents when I wasn't insured.'

'Doesn't surprise me,' Beatie said. She moved sideways between boxes that seemed both empty and to serve no purpose, and turned into a cluttered work space where a plump woman stood, poised over some leather she was gouging out, warmly dressed in an attempt to stave off the damp from what Beatie could now see was a semi-basement. 'Why don't you put a notice in the door warning of the step.'

'There is one,' grumbled the woman.

'I didn't see it.'

'No one does.'

'Perhaps you should make it in larger print,' suggested Beatie.

'I keep meaning to but you know how life is: full of "keep meaning to"s.'

'Don't I just,' replied Beatie in an attempt at camaraderie, but then reflected: I don't, just. Why did I say I do? I do more than just 'mean to'. I actually *do* it. I'm not a "keep-meaning-to" person. I'm an 'action' person. But she kept quiet about all that.

'You got something needs binding?' asked the woman.

'Will you throw me out if I say no?' Beatie offered her warmest of smiles.

'Not at all,' said the bookbinder, whose voice Beatie could now hear betrayed echoes of a North American accent.

'I just want to look around.'

'Look around,' the North American bookbinder invited, 'as long as you don't mind me working on.'

'Oh, please,' said Beatie. 'I'd be mortified if I stopped you working. But do *you* mind if I watch?'

'Watch away. Be my guest. Help yourself, and other such clichés.'

'To be honest,' said Beatie.

'Another cliché,' interposed the bookbinder.

'Although I don't have a book to bind just now, though who knows I might one day, like a battered old first edition to be rebound as a Christmas present or something – I *do* have another reason for looking in.'

'Tell me.'

'I didn't know you existed.'

'Story of my life.'

'I just stumbled upon you. Killing time waiting for a train but as soon as I saw your shop window . . .'

'Another "keep meaning to"?'

'Not quite. But I did think – fate! Fate or fortune has brought me here.'

'I don't understand.'

'I'll explain,' began Beatie, and she related the story of her distressing encounter with Lindsey Shackleton and how ashamed she had felt wanting to work with books not knowing what an 'endpaper' was. 'And so I thought if I watched a bookbinder at work I might learn a little more about books.'

'Books,' said the bookbinder, 'and by the way my name is Norma, Norma Shapiro, how do you do?' She offered her hand. Beatie took it.

'And my name is Beatie Bryant.'

'Books,' continued Norma Shapiro, 'are about what's inside them, not about how they're covered.'

'Yes, of course. But a good book jacket can help sell a book.'

'And leatherbound books are beautiful to look at, I know all that. But after years working in the trade – and I'm good at it, and enjoy it, and it provides me with my bread and butter and sometimes a little champagne without which bread and butter doesn't taste the same – after years working in the trade I've met people who are so obviously concerned only with outward show – the types that come in from the City, the financial sector which is round the corner as you probably know, and want, bound in full red calfskin, whole sets of Dickens which I can tell they're never going to read but they just want them on show on their shelves.'

Beatie was enjoying this woman and her relaxed, faintly sardonic tone. She seemed to have a handle on the world or at least that part of the world her profession occupied. She had taken up a slim metal tool but now slammed it down.

'I suppose you want me to give you a fifteen-minute Masterclass on how a book is put together, huh?'

'Oh, no!' cried Beatie. 'No, no, no!'

'What's the matter? Worried you'll lose your train?'

'Trains don't matter to me, there's plenty of them. Your time does. I wouldn't dream of wasting your time.'

'Don't sweat. I'm in control of my time. To be honest – that cliché again – I'm bored with my time. I'm efficient and so I'm ahead of myself; and the City types who spend a lot of time in a state of fury, and earn far too much money than is good for them or they know what to do with, spend it with me so I'm feeling flush, and I don't mind telling you I get lonely down here, and what's more I've never described a book to anyone before so it'll interest me, too, I might even get a taste for teaching, which I've always avoided because I'd have to take up the history of books and become a scholar and I'm not too certain I'm good at placing myself in that state of unknowing which is what makes a good teacher I always feel. Distraction! A bit of distraction telling you about the parts of a book might save my day. Want a drink?' She poured out two tots of whisky. 'Black Label acceptable?' Beatie raised her glass, clinked the bookbinder's glass and sat back to listen and watch a Masterclass on 'The Parts of a Book'.

She was amazed to discover so many parts to such an everyday object. Norma showed her a book she was working on, having to reconstruct it from scratch.

'Books are sewn in sections,' she began, showing her the sections she was sewing together.

'Do you mind if I write this down?' Beatie asked.

'Go right ahead,' said her teacher. Beatie reached for a small notebook and pen. 'Sections,' continued her teacher, 'your first part. Write it down. They're sewn in sections unless they're "perfect-bound". "Perfect-bound". Write that down, too, it means the book is glued together from single sheets, like most paperbacks and hardback novels, and of course has nothing to do with perfection as you probably know from all your paperbacks that have fallen to pieces. Now, each section has a number only it's not a number it's a letter of the alphabet: A, B, C etc, and these are called signatures. Don't ask me why. I don't know. It's one of those "I've been meaning to"'s. I've been meaning to find out but never gotten around to it. Some parts are self-evidently named. The front board is called the Front Board, and the back board is called the Back Board, but the front edge is called the Fore Edge, and the back, as you'd guess, is called the Spine. The top of a book is called the Head, surprise surprise. The bottom is called the Tail, more surprises. Not going too fast for you? I can tell you my life history in between your jottings if I am. No, on second thoughts you don't want to know. Shall I continue?' Beatie nodded. 'The right-hand pages of a book are usually the odd numbers and known as Rectos; the left-hand pages are usually the even numbers and they're known as Versos.'

'Rectos – Versos,' mumbled Beatie as she scribbled.

'Sounds faintly crude, doesn't it,' said the North American. 'Like a bum that can do all sorts of tricks. Forgive me. I'm being presumptuous. Now for me the really classy part of a book is the hidden painting you sometimes find on the Fore Edge. Here, let me show you.'

Miss – or was it Mrs (Beatie couldn't decide which) Shapiro reached for a small nineteenth-century book of verse by an obscure Victorian poet, Rev. R. Montgomery. A.M. Oxon Volume II devoted mainly to a long poem in three cantos called *Woman*, whose front and backboards had crumbled to dust. 'As had,' said the North American bookbinder, 'it is probably safe to say, the Rev. R. Montgomery. Look here.' The craftswoman flexed the book one way and revealed on the Fore Edge a 'painting' of red roses cushioned between a jungle of delicate green stems. 'Now,' she bent the book again, 'if I flex it the other way we reveal . . .' It was a 'painting' resembling a Stubbs painting of a lion about to pounce on a terrified white horse with its mane raised in terror.

'That's remarkable,' said Beatie.

'I'm glad you said it's "remarkable",' the sardonic lady observed, 'and not "amazing" or "brilliant" or "absolutely something or other" or worse still "brill". "Remarkable" is what it is, and clever, and skilfully executed but a little pointless, I feel. You paint on canvas, boards, ceramics, but books are for reading, and if you want to illustrate it you make prints for the pages, not the Fore Edge.'

'You're a purist,' observed Beatie.

'Nothing pure about me,' Norma Shapiro hastened to assert, 'soiled and sullied, me. I just think there's a rightness to life. Things belong only to certain things. You don't put salt in a fruit salad; you don't polish leather with Brasso; you don't light candles in the garden on a sunny day, and you don't paint paintings on the Fore Edge of a book. Or you shouldn't.'

'What about,' Beatie challenged her, 'all the great artists who broke the rules?'

'Ah! Rules you can break, laws you can't. Laws contain inherent truths about themselves.'

'What's the difference?' Beatie asked.

'Jean-Luc Goddard, the famous French film director, was once asked didn't he think a film should have a beginning, a middle and an end. To which he famously replied, "Yes, but not necessarily in that order." The law that can't be broken is the need for a beginning, a middle and an end. The rule, which *can* be broken, is that they don't necessarily have to be in that order.'

'I'm getting my money's worth in this Masterclass, aren't I,' said Beatie. 'And for no money, to boot,' she added with gratitude.

'There's more,' warned her teacher. 'You got time?'

'A little.'

'OK. I won't burden you with everything, just leather, and that's straight forward. There's cloth binding and leather binding. Cloth is the normal binding, naturally. I don't do cloth binding. Leather is usually calfskin or goatskin. "Basil" – a name for sheepskin – was a cheap nineteenth-century substitute for calfskin. Calfskin can be dyed many colours, and you can tool around with it more easily. You can pay a lot of money for a book fully bound in leather, or less for half-bound, and even less for quarter-bound.' With each she threw down a book showing which was which. Beatie handled them.

'Quarter-bound seems mean,' she said. 'Half-bound seems half-hearted. Seems to me there's no point having anything but the full-bloodied fully-bound.'

'If you can afford it,' cautioned her teacher.

'What are these called?' Beatie pointed to some raised ribs of leather on the spine of the fully bound book.

'Ah, yes. A part I forgot to name. See how I'd make a bad teacher? Do you know a poem called "Naming of Parts"?'

'You do jump around,' smiled Beatie, enjoying herself.

'Makes conversation interesting,' said Norma Shapiro. '"Naming of Parts" by Henry Reed. Not very well known these days, but one of the Second World War poets. He was naming the parts of a gun during a spring day. You have to ease the spring of a gun before you kill your enemy. Beginnings and endings. Very strong, very sad. Everything has a part that can be named, and these ribs are called Raised Bands. There are usually five on a spine. Between the first and second Raised Band is the Title, and even that part has a name. It's called the Tithing Piece.'

At this point Beatie had begun not to listen. Not because the bookbinder was becoming boring as she began to explain how the raised bands can be real – that is to say they can be moulded tight back into the leather, or falsely glued onto a flat spine before covering with leather; no! Beatie had excitedly been arrested by something the bookbinder had said: 'Everything has a part that can be named.' She didn't yet know why but that observation had instantly taken root in her imagination. What would sprout or blossom was not yet knowable, but something would. She made a mental note to look up the Henry Reed poem.

'You've wandered off,' said the observant bookbinder. 'Another reason why I could never be a teacher, I'd end up boring my students.'

Beatie reassured her. 'No, no. On the contrary. It was just that you said something so startling that my mind was instantly grabbed by it and I had to think about it but I didn't know *what* to think about it.'

'I said something startling?' asked Norma Shapiro in a tone that made Beatie understand why she was drawn to this woman. She didn't look like, but she *sounded* like, Barbra Streisand, her favourite singer. Beatie quite liked Streisand as an actress, too, but felt she had never stretched herself, and was capable of more. 'My, my! I said something startling,' said the Streisand soundalike. 'Care to tell me what it was? I might use it again. I often find myself at dinner parties looking for something startling to say.'

'"Everything has a part that can be named" is what you said.'

'What's startling about that? It's a simple fact.'

'When I know I'll come back and tell you. Now I must dash for my train.' Beatie expressed her gratitude and they shook hands. Norma Shapiro called after her:

'You go quiz that Shackelton lady about the parts of a book now, and have fun.'

The workbench seemed dreary after that brief encounter, and the leather to smell of dead cattle.

13

What made me confess all that to Manfred?

What made me confess all that to Manfred? How could I have betrayed you, Tina – even to such a close friend? And do I feel better for it? Go on, ask me, do I? Of course not. The loss, the pain, the ache is still there. Whoever said get it off your chest and you'll feel better, or a pain shared is a pain halved, spoke nonsense! People talk such nonsense. Yes, even you, Tina.

'I don't talk nonsense.'

'You do sometimes. Now go away. I'm talking to myself, you're not invited.'

I should have talked to Manfred about my book, with which I'm having problems, great problems. Manfred has a good mind – clear, strong, decisive. Well, decisive about everything excepting his personal life, anyone's personal life. He could have helped more with a book than with a dead wife. It upset him. All that about me and Tina – why did I upset a friend like that? He was off to Antarctica – cold enough there. Why should I have chilled him with tales of Tina chilling off me?

Or I should have talked more about my girls, my lovely twins who are no longer girls but young women whom I worry and complain about, but what father doesn't? Actually I don't worry about Tamara, she'll go places. With a cool head like she has she'll go to the top. The top of what, I don't know, but the top! Of course I know what top I'd *like* her to get to but dare I tell her? I dare not. Business, she's made for business. She got her degree in PPE – she should use it. A philosopher she's not. A politician only maybe. But economics and how the world of trade works and how to make a penny into a pound? *That* she knows. Right from the start, in school, a school we sent her to which, for some strange reason, was full of girls trading in something or other. Actually I don't think it was the school especially, I think it was that particular intake – the class of '75. They all, or it felt like 'all', came to school with something to sell. The playground was full of steamy adolescent entrepreneurs. This one brought in her old clothes, that one brought in her old dolls, another brought her mother's old clothes – scarves, shoes, last year's skirts; some of them could knit, others could embroider, and there were the artists – the wild girls with paint on their fingers who brought in huge canvases. At lunchtime the playground became a thriving, throbbing marketplace.

Only the poets suffered. They stood a long way apart from each other to recite their poetry and sell their sheets, but no one listened, or only a few. The lunch break was short and everyone was on the lookout for bargains. It was my Tamara who organised the poets. First she told them not to compete with one another but for only one of them to recite each day. Second, she advised them to put their poems together in one folder. The audience for poets reading in school playgrounds is small, she told them, don't dissipate your market. And you know what? The other girls *did* listen to the poems when there was only one of them reciting. They gathered round and they bought the folders with each poem signed by the poet. It was a bizarre phenomenon that hadn't taken place either before the class of '75 or after it. All phenomena come to an end. The market was finally broken up by the head-mistress after she received complaints from parents that some of their best shoes and jewellery were being stolen by their offspring in order to boast how much money they'd made by the end of the week.

Tamara could do nothing herself. Embroidery bored her; her fingers were not made for knitting; a painter she was not, nor a wordsmith of any kind either. But the marketplace was her habi-tat. From an early age she understood the game of Monopoly, instinctively knowing that you first bought up the slums – the Old Kent Road and Whitechapel, cheap to buy and cheap to build. Get rich before anyone else does, that way you can buy them out. And she won. Game after game. It embarrassed me to begin with, and then it reassured me, her future was secured. She wasn't unpleasant about it, she wasn't aggressive about it, and she didn't make you feel uncomfortable as some go-getters do, but a go-getter she was, and aggressive she was. She didn't have talents or skills of her own; she merely enabled those with talent and skill to exploit those skills and talents sensibly and to the full; she always had ideas how to make other people's ideas work. And that's my girl, an entrepreneur. The BBC is a prestigious item to have on your CV, but how high can a woman rise in such an organisation? Entrepreneur! That's her.

But I've gone off at a tangent again. In fact I'm all over the place emotionally, intellectually, professionally. I've gathered together this material about Marcantonio but it's sparse. There's not material enough for a book here, not a whole book, unless I pad it out which I don't want to do; there's just enough for a cameo. And who buys cameos or takes notice of them? I should content myself with organising concerts of his music. I know everyone there is to know, it should be possible. But I can't. I'm choking with the years. Manfred doesn't believe it's possible, but it is. The years like a tunnel. Like night falling. They talk about 'the twilight years' between evening and night, between the day dying and the night coming and it's true but people just think of it as poetry, as metaphor. Not me. For me it is all too real. For me night falling is life ending. I'm terrified of going to sleep. That dream of being in a tunnel, unable to move, the night tightening around me – it'll come back. I know it. Again and again. Time, like a noose. Panic. Round any corner. How can I write in such a state? How can I review in such a state? It's not fair on the musicians. Actually that's not true. I don't get into such a state when I'm listening to music. I become a pro when I'm listening to music. My critical faculties function when they're called upon to work. That's what I need, to be called upon. The night petrifies me, daylight calls upon me. As soon as there's light in the sky my humanity is beckoned. As soon as I hear traffic in the street, the sound of people passing on their way to work, the bustle of life – I'm fine. I'm drawn into living, into the purpose of things. But the night? Ugh! I hate the claustrophobia of night. I keep the radio going through the night. It doesn't keep me awake it just reassures me. Every so often I do wake, of course – a Shostakovitch crescendo or a folk singer from Algeria becoming excited that his love has said 'yes', or someone being interviewed laughs too loudly – but I soon fall asleep again. This way I have signs of the living even through the night. It's comforting. It mustn't stop. I can't bear the thought that living ceases. It must go on. I need to *hear* it going on.

14

The Worst Journey in the World

The Worst Journey in the World by Apsley Cherry-Garrard, the youngest member of the Scott Antarctic expedition, was published in 1922. He wrote of penguins that: 'They are extraordinarily like children, these little people of the Antarctic world, either like children, or like old men, full of their own importance and late for dinner, in their black tail-coats and white shirt fronts and rather portly withal.'

I, too, find them fascinating to observe. Survivors are utterly fearless. I keep my distance but watch them for two hours. They ignore me but I know they know I'm watching, and they seem to perform for me. They're kept constantly busy by their young, diving for food so that the chicks can quickly grow and take off on their own and leave their wearied parents in peace.

The old C-130 Hercules is noisy. Earplugs don't help. Through the tiny portholes the views seem endlessly the same – snow and ice. It has been a long journey. From London to Santiago, to Punta Arenas, the last civilised town of 125,000 inhabitants from where we fly to the uninhabited wastes of Antarctica, another six hours covering 3,200km. It is the coldest continent on earth, occupying ten per cent of the earth's landmass. Did those mad and wonderful people really walk those ice wastes for months on end to reach the South Pole? As we climb to 25,000 feet the cold intensifies. We're instructed to keep warm. I reach for gloves, hat, parka coat. Nothing seems enough. We are approaching Ellsworth Mountains, named after Lincoln Ellsworth, who made the first flight across Antarctica in 1935. Excitement is mounting. There are six of us – four paying adventurers and two guides. I'm hungry. Make myself a cheese sandwich. Need to pee. The curtain covering the toilet hides nothing. No one cares. Forty-five minutes to landing. Mount Vernon, the highest Antarctic mountain, is to our right. Soon we'll be landing on a natural blue-ice runway 1,000 metres above sea level. The noise of the plane is horrendous. We're warned to be careful not to slip on the ice when we get out of the plane. In my excitement on arriving I slip. I notice that no one notices. It seems to me that the first courtesy has been observed – you don't laugh at the mistakes of a novice.

The first stop is the Patriot Hills. This is base. From here we will fly to the South Pole when weather permits. There and back in a day. To be able to do this the weather must both be perfect and promise to remain perfect for twenty-four hours. A week passes before the pilot, a cautious, competent, laid-back Australian, deems the weather safe. I'm impatient to be there; and anxious in case the weather doesn't improve before I must leave. But I *must* be patient. I'm allotted my tent, unpack, explore facilities, spend the morning skiing with others and then finally have a great need to be alone.

There's no time to waste. I pack for my afternoon's outing, cover my face with sunscreen, my hands with two pairs of gloves, a heavy hat on my head, ski sticks in my hands and a small pot of New Zealand Manuka honey in my parka coat pocket. Soon there is a great distance between the camp and me. This is what being alone really means. No matter how remotely you may live in the Andes or the Fens or the Black Mountains of Wales you are still surrounded by nature: living, growth, movement – buds into leaves, dead bracken into live young ferns, the flutter of birds, the movement of mice, squirrels, insects. You are aware of busy company, of things furtively growing. Not here. Not in this desolate landscape of ice and snow. If anything is growing it's hidden from view. I wriggle a hole in the icy snow with my stick. A few inches down I'm touching snow that fell before I was born. Everything about this continent is unlike anything I have experienced before. Empty, raw and utterly without sound. At first I think I can *hear* silence. Is it an illusion? Is my memory of sound so strong that I *think* I hear it? There is also this about silence – you want to break it. Like someone's brilliance – it disturbs you, you feel you want to tumble them. No matter how modestly the brilliant mind conducts itself it is the nature of the brilliance that you want it to shatter. It intimidates. Like this silence, this utter silence. How dare it be so perfect?

I shout. Inane utterances. 'You can't fool me! You don't frighten me! You're only nature, I'm human! You can only remain where you are, I can move, I can invent aeroplanes to fly over you. I can shout! SHOUT! You hear me?' I stop. I would not have done that had I been climbing. Sound can shift snow and cause an avalanche, but here in the flat ice-covered wastes nothing can fall. But I stop shouting and am confronted again by the silence, and instantly feel foolish. Then angry. There is a huge immobility about the landscape that speaks of indifference. I am at once exhilarated by my surroundings and disturbed by them.

Why 'disturbed'? I'm occupied pondering this question as I walk further and further away from the Patriot Hill's base. Silence from people to whom one has written is called by sociologists 'passive aggression'. I wonder if that's what I see in this cold and bleak landscape – passive aggression. Perhaps what we see depends on our state of mind. One day magnificent, another day aggressive. Today, my first day, as I carefully crunch the snow and struggle to keep my balance on the icy patches, I am in awe. I may refuse to feel humbled by polar nature but I will humbly take my place as I climb the mountain ridge, breathe deeply and steadily from my lower abdomen and marvel at the rocks. I pick some to take home aware that I'm transporting in my pocket stones between 250,000 and 1,000,000 years old.

My bones ache. It's possible I've walked too far, overstretched myself. My body needs rejuvenating. I reach into my parka coat pocket for the Manuka honey. Of all honeys in the world, even more than the renowned honeys of the English Downs and the heather slopes of the Scottish Highlands, this honey from the Manuka trees in the remote, unpolluted forests of New Zealand claims health benefits and the power to revive like no other. A certain Dr Molan discovered a factor in this honey he called UMF (Unique Manuka Factor). Chemists had been able to identify the exact composition of honey but had failed to reproduce all it parts. There is a substance – no one knows its nature – that bees put into honey that chemists could not. Until Dr Peter Molan came along and identified this constituent, which he called UMF, as containing antibacterial properties so strong you can rub it into an open wound to assist healing. I take it three times a day and after I have engaged in extra-exertive activity.

On my way down I find myself thinking about Barney and his terror of the night. Would he feel less threatened here in Antarctica, where in the summer months there is hardly any night? He wants me to help him think through the problems he is having with his book on Giovanni Marcantonio. How can I? What do I know of music? I can only enthuse about what he has done so far, and I can do that because he himself is enthusiastic – about his material, not his achievement – and I enjoy other people's enthusiasms.

'Imagine!' he tells me. 'The birth of Western music took place in the arms of a paradox.' I ask what he means, which is what he wants me to ask. 'Greece, the cradle of democracy, tyrannically imprisoned music in the rhythms of words and the metres of a poem. Along comes tyrannical Christianity, and what happens? They free the music and reduce the words of a song to secondary importance. Gregorian chant is born.'

'Do you actually *like* Gregorian chant?' I ask him.

'As a matter of fact I don't. Too monotonous. But then? In those days? It represented freedom. No other art benefits from early Christianity – only music.'

I try to challenge him. 'And painting? Sculpture? The great cathedrals?'

'Later! Later!' he bursts out. 'All that comes later, in the Middle Ages. But to begin with who needs a cathedral to make contact with God? Who needs a representation in stone to pray to? All that comes later, but to begin with? Music! The early Christians recognised the relationship between divine revelation and the heart singing freely. Music! Everything aspires to music, as the philosophers say.' Which doesn't help him with his problems because *I'm* listening to *him* whereas he wanted to be listening to me.

A few days later the weather clears. Now I'm excited. Exhilarated. I feel like a child. I fear the others can see it. I want to burst out singing. The plane is a tiny Cessna 185. The distance to the Amundsen–Scott Base Station is 1,000km. We must stop once to refuel. Space in the small plane is taken up with – in addition to our own kit – many survival items: two/three person tent, food for eighteen days for each person, an ice saw and shovel, emergency locator beacon, several flares, portable radio, life vests, first-aid kits, mats and signal mirror. All in case the weather breaks its promise, turns treacherous and we have to make a forced landing in the desolate, barren wasteland between the Patriot Hills and the South Pole. I must confess to a degree of terror but it's the flight of a lifetime and I can't afford to waste time on fear.

At the refuelling stop – an area of empty whiteness except for about thirty barrels of petrol from which planes just help themselves – we're told to move fast. The cold is so bitter that it can affect the engine even though we've covered it with a tarpaulin sheet. The cap of the petrol drum is frozen fast, a hammer and chisel is needed to break it open. The refuelling operation takes thirty minutes. I have never been so cold, never stood for so long in such a frozen expanse.

Why am I travelling to the bottom of the earth? It's a question I keep asking myself – crossing deserts, climbing mountains, flying over icy wastes, what am I trying to prove? And to whom? Foolish questions. We keep asking foolish questions which complicate life and for which there are no real answers. I climb and accept hardship because that's what humans do – take on challenges, reach for adventure. I'm climbing mountains and crossing icy wastes because it pleases me. I'm trying to prove nothing. I hate the psychiatrist's dark catechism about motivation. Achievement is its own answer. I've always had this wish, this ambition to stand at the South Pole where stood the great explorers, Roald Amundsen on 14 December 1911 and Captain Robert Scott on 17 January 1912.

We land but cannot stay here for long. We eat, we're shown around, I buy cards and write them to family and friends who will enjoy the exotic ink postage stamps. There are many to choose from illustrating the variety of projects that have been carried out at the Amundsen–Scott South Pole Station in Antarctica. And finally here I am, in the vast white desert, the biggest in the world, standing where they stood, clutching the ball and stick that marks the South Pole. A childhood dream come true. Hampstead seems a long way away, and with it the nightmare that is blighting Barney's life.

But something else doesn't seem a long way away. The face of that young woman I met in Shepherd Market. I'm caught unawares by a longing to have her here with me. To share the experience. How strange to be haunted by a face so briefly glimpsed at. It is not the face alone, but those few words: '*Men always look. I'm beautiful.*' Why should everything else fade but not this young woman? I swear it's not an old man's sexual yearnings. Besides, I'm not that old. No, it's something to do with the whiteness of where I am. Here in these vast lands of snow and ice I'm overwhelmed by a sense of innocence. She belongs here. Her innocence and this southern continent are one and the same thing.

Nonsense! You're thinking nonsensically, Manfred. The majesty of the place has brought out pretensions. You are somewhere breathtaking, and the human instinct is to want to share such an experience, that's all. Yes, but why her? You've had many encounters in your time, known a pretty spectrum of female prettiness, why her – someone you know nothing about, neither name nor address, and so will never see again? Why her?

You're right, Manfred, idle fantasies.

15

The BBC was not Tamara's 'forever land'

The BBC was not Tamara's 'forever land'. She knew that for certain. She had glided up and down the long corridors for nine months now and could play a variation of her father's silly game. The BBC, she concluded, is divided between those whose eyes hold terror and those whose eyes hold contempt. The terrified ones look as though they're clinging to rafts in a turbulent, unpredictable sea; the contemptuous ones know that heavy waves are for surfing, and that they are strong surfers. Tamara was a strong surfer, and could be impatient with bureaucracy, over which, to the horror of her colleagues, she frequently rode roughshod. Her cool intelligence and effortless efficiency protected her, though she knew it would not protect her forever in an institution resistant to innovation.

The Beeb's central flaw would never be ridden over, not even by the cool and efficient, and once she had recognised this fact she knew the august establishment was not her forever-land, develop an affection for it though she had. My father is right, she admitted, I merit better. Well, not 'better' – the Beeb after all is an internationally renowned, respected and depended-upon institution – but 'other'. I merit 'other'.

The flaw she thought she had identified was the rigidity of its timed programmes. She believed that material – documentary, drama, series or whatever – should dictate the slot. A programme's material was more important than the need to fill a preordained slot of time. The powers that be, on the other had, considered their slots inviolable. There was the forty-five-minute or hour long documentary slot regardless of whether the material called for longer exposure. The afternoon play was thirty minutes long, no more no less. The material had to be squeezed or distorted to fit the slot. The public needed slots they could rely upon, argued the Beeb. Everyone needed a dependable routine. Well, if that was the way of the world, or the way of the BBC's world, so be it. Tamara could stay and accept it, or linger long enough for it to look good on her CV: St Hilda's, Oxford, a first in PPE; P.A. to various media chiefs; twelve months as a BBC researcher. A good start. But then? It would come. She would know soon enough.

Just now she was concentrating on collecting her lunch on a tray. She went, unashamedly, for the junk food – fish and chips and mushy peas – knowing that one day she would be eating only in the best restaurants. She shook vinegar liberally, sprinkled salt and prepared to enjoy it. A large woman approached. It was the badly dressed Matilda. Why, Tamara wondered, did overweight women wear clothes that clung to the lumps that emphasised their size? Matilda Hutchinson was a colleague, a researcher par excellence who by now, after working ten years for the BBC, knew all the right corners into which to peer for what she was called upon to unearth. She knew Colindale inside out for old newspapers; she knew the right departments in the right ministries and the people who headed them; she knew where to pursue which theme in the British Library; she had the phone numbers of all manner of celebrities or of those who knew someone who knew someone who could help her establish contact with a reclusive celebrity. She was flattered and sought after and offered vast sums for her files, and she dressed like a woman who ran a launderette.

'Mind if I join you?' she asked Tamara, approaching with a tray sparsely filled with salads and yoghurt.

'Of course not, Matilda. Come and shame me with your healthy eating.'

'It's all right for you, Tamara. You can eat stodge and it seems to burn away as it goes in. Got a little furnace inside you?'

'If only!'

They were joined by a third. A young man named Lee Danton who, Tamara noticed, had taken a shine to her and had been trying, as inconspicuously as possible, to be in her company or near her though he had not spoken a word to her. He was a trainee sound engineer and much younger than her, his looks and body language that of a puppy – floppy and eager and trusting. Occasionally she noticed that he seemed to take command when other trainees were around, as though he was the teacher. At such moments he was impressive. Now he seemed feeble, trying to pretend no other table had a spare chair.

'Sorry,' he said, 'it has to be here. Is that all right?' He hovered waiting for a response from the other sex whom he obviously thought the superior of the two.

'I've got nothing private to discuss with my friend here, young man,' said Matilda.

'Park yourself!' ordered Tamara feeling she ought to establish that their relationship was unmistakably that of the older woman to the younger man who, pretty though he was, did not seem to carry the intellectual weight she looked for in any companion – male or female: he seemed in possession of what she called 'a large-print mind'. Matilda was not an intellectual either but she carried history and secrets around with her; her company held electrifying possibilities.

An awkward silence hovered over the three of them. Tamara felt driven to break it.

'My father has a friend, one he's known for so long that I call
him Uncle, and they play a silly game each time they meet. They
divide the world into two sides, and they look for new divisions
to exchange with each other whenever they meet. They didn't
invent the game, it began in the early fifties in a play that ran for
years in the West End called *The World is Divided*.'

The young man with large-print eyes looked as though he
needed to have it explained in large print. Tamara obliged.

'I give you an example off the top of my head: there are two
kinds of people – those who *enjoy* what they see and experience,
and those who need to *explain* what they see and experience.' Lee
Danton looked admiringly at her, but lost. He understood not a
word. She drew him in. 'Come on, Lee. You have a go. The
world is divided between . . .' He blushed scarlet but caught on.

'Men and women,' he said.

'Excellent!' exclaimed Tamara. 'Now, go a little deeper, concentrate on women. The world is divided between women
who . . . and women who . . .' The women waited. The poor boy
blushed an even deeper scarlet. Matilda tried to help.

'You look ever so handsome when you blush,' she told him, to
which he replied with, Tamara thought, unexpected courtesy:

'Thank you.'

'Now he won't come up with anything,' Tamara said. Again,
unexpectedly, he did, albeit on the verge of tactlessness.

'The world is divided into women who are beautiful and
women who *wish* they were beautiful.'

'Do you think he's talking about us?' asked Matilda good-
naturedly. 'And after I'd paid him a compliment, too.'

'Come now, Matilda, let's not intimidate the boy with female
confidence. Let's hear how you divide the world.'

'Oh, easy,' she said, 'the world is divided between those who
fight with words and those who fight with fists.'

'I like that,' said Lee, who became a little more confident
because he had sensed these women were friendly and not hostile
as were many in this establishment. 'And I wasn't talking about

you when I talked about beautiful women and women who wished they were beautiful.'

'That's all right,' said Matilda, 'you could have been more brutal and said women were divided into the beautiful ones and the ugly ones. *That* would have hurt. But the truth is I *do* wish I was beautiful, and Tamara here has no need to wish. It was a valid division you made.'

'So was yours,' said the grateful trainee sound engineer. 'I think I might use my fists more than words, and I'm not proud of that.'

'But,' said the large lady, 'sometimes it's necessary to use your fists — either because there's not words that are adequate or because you know they won't be understood.'

'Not in the short run, maybe,' said Tamara, who would defend words to her grave, 'but the power of words is forever.'

'Oh, you don't have to tell *me* that,' said Matilda. 'I'll tell *you* about the power of words.' She embarked upon her story only after scooping up the last of her yoghurt as though she had to get rid of food before she could talk seriously.

'I'm thirty-five now, sober and mature and overweight, I know, but in control of myself. Very different when I was seventeen. At seventeen I was wild and cocky and rude and utterly indifferent to the feelings of other people. I shock myself when I think about it and perhaps I shouldn't have confessed it. Certain truths you should keep to yourself because, as Dr Johnson says, there's always someone around who'll store it away and throw it back at you. Anyway, it's out now. I'll trust you. And besides our lives are hardly likely to intertwine over the long years ahead. Right? So that was me — cocky and rude. And one day I was in the Underground with some friends and there was this old woman frightened to get on the escalator. We should have helped her but instead we watched to see what would happen. Finally she took the risk, and stumbled. And we laughed. I laughed loudest. Very raucous I was in those days. And behind us was an old man who said to me:

'"One day you'll be old like that."'

"'Yeah!'" I said, "but not for a long time.'"

"'Soon enough,'" he said. And I wish he'd have left it at that, but he didn't. He said more: "And I promise you that from here on, from this moment on, every time you step onto an escalator – in the Underground or in a mall, anywhere in the world – you'll think of this incident and how you didn't help an old lady onto some moving stairs, and you'll remember age. You'll be aware," he said, "every time you get on an escalator, how much you've aged. Every time. And you'll say to yourself, every time, 'One day I will be old. I'll age." And I did. Every time I got on an escalator, through the years, I found myself saying those words, 'One day I will be old. I'll age.' It was like a curse. He'd cursed me. He'd made me measure my ageing on an escalator and with words: 'One day I will be old. I'll age.' I can't get on a set of moving stairs without those words, that old lady and my raucous laughter coming into my head. And I bet it will be the same for you. From now on, now that I've told you the story you'll think about age and old women every time you get on an escalator. Words! That's the power of words, they live on in your head like a curse.'

A sombre moment settled. Tamara looked at the young man. He'd left them. The story had affected him. He was somewhere deep inside his own thoughts. She changed her mind about him. Here was not a large-print youth. Here was a sensitive youth – tall, broad-shouldered, short-cropped hair, sharp blue eyes, someone you could come to rely on. He could drive you safely on icy roads, change a tyre in minutes, take charge of a school group going on a foreign trip. He exuded a quiet confidence to match Tamara's. Her gaze lingered too long. He came out of his reverie and caught her looking at him. She returned hurriedly back to their conversation.

'It's not only words,' she said, 'anything can have that power. What about music? Music can bring back a landscape, a personality.'

'An action can do it, too.' Lee felt confident by now. He spread out his hands before them, palm down. 'Look! What do you see?'

'The back of your hands and dirty fingernails,' said Matilda, belatedly getting her own back. Women bide their time. Tamara had no revenges to take.

'I see beautiful cuticles,' she said.

'Exactly what I wanted you to see,' said young Lee whom, it was obvious to the women, was besotted by Tamara. Nor could she pretend to herself that she wasn't enjoying this adulation, albeit guiltily for he was surely under age. 'Now,' the young engineer continued, 'why are they like that?' He didn't expect either of them to know, and didn't wait for an answer. 'Because I have a cousin, ten years older than me, taught me many naughty things I must confess, but there was one thing she taught me that was not so naughty: how to keep my cuticles down. 'Every time you dry your hands,' she told me, 'push your cuticles down with your towel.' And I did. Still do. And I probably always will. And each time I do it I think of her.'

'And all the naughty things she taught you, no doubt,' said Matilda, who found that little item of information – much to her surprise, and later disgust – to be rather titillating. Young Lee had meant it to be, but not for her. Tamara knew for whom, though.

The lunch hour was soon over. They each disappeared their separate ways into rooms off long corridors on different floors. Or so Tamara assumed. She was surprised, then, when walking along one of the BBC lanes on the fourth floor she noticed a door open and a young man creep round with an extended hand. It was Lee Danton. He didn't grab her, he merely extended his hand leaving her free to walk past or take it. Everything she did from then on surprised and confused her. At first she imagined he had something he wanted to show her in the studio where he worked. But did he work there? Weren't the trainees on another floor? Why did she think that? Trainees were everywhere. They were assigned. Without coming to a conclusion she took his hand seeing it only as a friendly 'come here, look at this'.

Once her hand was in his he pulled her gently into the studio. It was both dimly lit and empty. He closed the door. She knew exactly what must now happen. From the moment she had agreed to take his hand she must agree to everything that followed. He eased her back against the door and brought his lips to hers. And she let him. He kissed her tenderly; nothing loutish about this boy. But she kept thinking, 'This is a boy, this is a below-age boy.' But was he? The truth was she didn't know. He looked fifteen but once his lips were upon hers she felt he was eighteen, perhaps even older. He pressed himself against her. She let him. She felt him go hard into her belly. She made no Mae West wisecrack, though when the famous line crossed her memory she smiled to herself in the dim light. He hazarded a tongue. She opened her mouth to him. He moved to raise her V-neck top. She stayed his hand.

'No fear,' he said. 'No one will come.' That confidence, there it was again. She withdrew her hand and let her arms hang limply by her side. The gesture told him: do what you want. He's a boy! He's a boy, she kept thinking. And the boy did, he did what he wanted. He raised her top. Her breasts were small, needing no support. There was no hook to struggle with though she guessed he would have handled that hurdle expertly. He circled her breasts with his fingers beautifully cuticled, taking his time to reach her nipples, which, to her mortification, hardened in anticipation. He scratched them lightly with long nails. She didn't look down to see that he had cleaned them, carefully, thoughtfully. She shivered. Moaned a little. He's a boy! He's a boy! His hands caressed the slight curve of a belly that she considered – though boasted to no one – was exquisite. He's a boy! He's a boy! He dropped to his knees pulling down her skirt, her tights, her knickers with one expert movement. A boy! A boy! There is a boy in my crotch who had a cousin taught him naughty things and taught him well. His mouth found her. She let him in, and writhed to his circling tongue. A boy! A boy! He's only a boy!

And he wanted nothing in return.

'The world,' he said to her between his farewell kisses, 'is divided between men who can give love and men who can only take love.' He opened the door for her to sidle out after he had checked the way was clear. 'Be careful of escalators,' he instructed, closing the door silently as though not to wake a sleeping child.

16

After so many train journeys in a short lifetime Beatie expected encounters

After so many train journeys in a short lifetime Beatie expected encounters. It was partly to do with the nature of train journeys, and partly to do with her attractiveness. Women sat opposite her feeling safe; men, hoping to flirt the time away. She was beginning to identify types, and made mental notes about the outcome of certain encounters, with either sex, testing herself to see if she was right. The most interesting encounters were with those she could not identify within a few minutes of conversation; they were the surprises, and as such the rewards of travel.

But this time, for this journey, she planned actively to discourage conversation, and listen instead to music on her beloved Walkman from which she drew endless pleasure on trains, in buses and on long walks. She couldn't wait to walk the familiar country lanes behind her mother's cottage listening to Elgar, Vaughan Williams, Mahler and the newly discovered beautiful *Nuits d'été* of Hector Berlioz. And with every note she blessed Ronnie for introducing her to classical music.

Beatie had left Norma Shapiro's bookbinding workshop in good time. She had a horror of being late for anything. There was a five-minute wait for the platform to be announced, another ten for departure. Time to find the carriage and seat she wanted; by now she knew the carriage nearest the Diss exit, and found a seat facing the engine, with a table for four so that she could spread her papers and Walkman and the half-dozen tapes she had selected to chose from. Soon Mahler's Resurrection Symphony was transforming the carriage into a concert hall. A middle-aged woman in her fifties sat next to her, and spoke, oblivious that she was addressing someone who wasn't there.

'I think I'll sit here as I'm getting out first stop. Save disturbing anybody.'

Beatie suspended one of the ears of her headphones by way of telling her neighbour that she was not in the running for conversation.

'Beg your pardon?' she asked. The woman ignored the hint, and repeated her words; an inocuous piece of information of a kind that told Beatie there was more to come if she didn't instantly return her earphones. The woman was not discouraged. 'Don't like disturbing people unnecessarily,' she said, working her way out of a dull-coloured but once fine-looking York coat, 'though sometimes you have to in this life, don't you? Not possible to go through this life without disturbing somebody.' Beatie simply nodded and turned away. To her consternation the woman ignored what was manifestly Beatie's wish, and continued speaking loudly. 'It's neighbours. I've just had to see a solicitor in London about my neighbour who's filled his front garden with a mountain of junk.' Beatie resignedly took off her earphones. At least the woman, having got her way and secured for herself a travelling companion, lowered her voice, though not much. '"Precious belongings"' he calls them. Precious? He's been going to auctions and car-boot sales for the last twenty years and there's a pyramid of old water tanks, building materials, bikes, rolls of carpets, and bags full of God know what. "They'll come in handy one day," he says. One day! I've been waiting twenty years for that "one day" and it hasn't ever come.'

'"One day's" never do,' offered Beatie sympathetically. 'So what did the solicitor say?'

'Health hazard! We'll get him on the health hazard of it all. The solicitor is going to write to the local council. They won't take notice of me but they will of a solicitor's letter.'

'*Is* it a health hazard?' asked Beatie as politely as she could.

'Health hazard, eyesore, bloody antisocial – it can't be right, can it? Twenty years' worth of junk. He'll have to shift it.'

'So who's the one being disturbed – him or you?'

'First me, now him. And not only me but the other neighbours, too, those the other side of him and those across the road from him. We've all clubbed together to pay for the best solicitor for the job. Came recommended. David Spiro and Partners. They say with his name alone everyone capitulates and doesn't bother to contest a case. I mean live and let live is all very well, and I agree with it most of the time, but who's letting who *not* live is the question that's got to be answered in this case. And his house is shabby, too. You should see the paintwork on his windows. I mean one day I might need to sell my house – who's going to buy it with a junk yard in next door's front garden? Live and let live is all very well but . . .'

It was when the middle-aged lady began talking about 'live and let live' that Beatie switched off and turned to look out of the window, captivated by a spectacular cloud formation. What was it called? She once knew the names of all the cloud formations but had forgotten them. Was it cumulus or cirrostratus? She knew they were very different but couldn't attach the right name to what she was looking at. And then she turned back so as not to appear too rude to her neighbour, just as the most breathtakingly handsome man, wearing an expensive Burberry raincoat and carrying a portable computer, appeared, looking for a seat, and obviously one with a table. The neighbour had been speaking so loudly that a number of passengers had walked past preferring not to have such a drone bending their ear. But the handsome man was more attracted to Beatie than he was repelled by the discontented neighbour who, when she saw him, lowered her voice even more as though royalty was approaching, and perhaps he knew she would, for he had that air about him of one who commanded attention in a crowd. Courtesy accompanied the looks, and a beautiful voice accompanied the courtesy. Women hate it when it happens but exceedingly handsome men do make them go weak at the knees. Some begin to speak gibberish, others, in self-protection, work hard to avoid becoming aggressively rude. He asked permission to join them.

The middle-aged woman said with excessive eagerness: 'Of course, of course.' Beatie simply nodded her head. He took off his Burberry, folded it neatly into the overhead rack and sat down to open his computer.

'Do you mind, ladies?' he asked. 'I know it's more polite to make conversation but I have reports to write that are long overdue.'

'We'll let you type if you tell us what the reports are about,' said the brazen middle-aged one, who was flirting more than being brazen. Beatie looked apologetically at the handsome man, though why she felt the need to apologise she didn't know. Who was she apologising for? The woman had nothing to do with her. Her sex? The young man then blundered, imagining he was being helpful.

'I also have a mother,' he said.

'She's *not* my mother,' Beatie protested too violently. The middle-aged woman looked hurt.

'I was only showing interest in the young,' explained the hurt middle-aged woman.

'Oh, dear,' said the courteous young man. 'How presumptuous of me. But I don't mind telling you what my reports are about. And I'm not, by the way, all that young. The truth is I've just landed this new job, which is also a newly created post so I'm rather excited by it even though I don't start for another three

months because I have to work out my current contract, and I'm
in that frame of mind where I'll talk to anybody about it. You
might even have ideas I could plunder.'

Mother and daughter they might not have been but now both
were as attentive as if they were; the older with a watery, mater-
nal look, the younger with lively curiosity. The handsome man
had the audience he was obviously used to commanding.

'I recently moved to Norwich from London, well St Albans
actually, thinking I'd find both a better job and a cheaper flat to
buy. I'm trained in marketing and soon found what I thought
was a job that couldn't be bettered – marketing the city of
Norwich to the world. The local council wanted to embark on
a drive to bring more tourists into the city. Easy, I thought to
myself. Here was a city that had ancient and modern side by
side, a flourishing university, a huge touring theatre for opera,
ballet and musicals, another smaller one being planned, an
annual music festival, a colourful open market in front of the
Town Hall – the lot. I hadn't been working there longer than
three months, in my stride, impressing everyone, enjoying my
days, lovely Viking women all over the place, when one day I
open my *Guardian* and see advertised a job for someone to plan
and draw up a report for making the London Underground a
more attractive experience. I couldn't rush into that one,
though. The London Underground is where only two things
happen – people linger and look, and people catch trains to
destinations. I knew nothing about the problems of transportation nor, as it turned out, was I expected to, but it was obviously
a major, if not *the* major, part of the experience of being in the
London Underground. Transportation would have to figure in
my plans somehow.'

The women were mesmerised. Not only by the details of the
work he was engaged in but by his manner of talking to them. He
appeared blessed with that special gift of making everyone to
whom he was speaking feel as though there was no one else in the
world, in the train, in the carriage, in the room, in his life; one of

those rare spirits animated by the experiences he was relating, and further animated by the people he was animating. It was an exciting prospect. Some people talk to you at arms' length, others hook you and draw you into their lives. Beatie worried about both. Yet she was hooked. Not that she minded for she knew that though she could contemplate making love with this stunning male she could never, ever enter his life. The older woman at her side was listening with her mouth open, accepting all, questioning nothing while she, Beatie, tried to identify what precisely it was that made her listen slightly askance. After a while she understood – he was not only animating his story and his listener, he was animating himself. There was an element of self-regard in his personality. But how profoundly did that disturb her? She was, she had to confess, excited by him. Nothing else – apart from this hint of self-regard – repelled her. He looked as though he could be tender, sensitive, thoughtful, sweet-smelling; and when he warmed admiringly to what she later contributed, she was ready to stay on the train with him to Norwich and not get off at Diss, the stop before, where her brother would be waiting. Exciting males who were also intelligent were hard to find. She would make it up to her brother.

Not so the middle-aged lady, who had to get off at the first stop, Colchester, and was thus deprived of the full story of the young man's new job with the London Underground.

'If I was younger and had no responsibilities like my young friend here, I'd stay on and miss my stop so as to hear how you were going to reorganise London.'

'Hardly London,' he told her charmingly as he stood to help her on with her dull York coat, which she now felt, for the first time, along with her entire life, was dull. 'But you never know, we might bump into each other again,' he said. 'I'm frequently on this train, or will be for the next three months until my six-month contract with Norwich Council is worked through.'

'Oh, don't you worry, I shall be looking out for you.' The middle-aged lady threw him a flirtatious look and imbued her

words with more hot-blooded sexuality than she thought herself
capable of. Which both surprised and pleased her.

'Well, she was a good audience,' he said to Beatie as the train
drew away from Colchester platform.

'Oh, come,' she played with him, 'you know you always have
good audiences.'

'I confess, I do enjoy talking about my work. My name's
Derek, by the way.' He offered his hand. Beatie took it.

'And I'm Beatie.' His handshake was firm but not too firm as it
is with some who wish to impress their strong-mindedness and let
you know they are not to be toyed with. She also noticed that
though she had made it plain that she was at ease and probably
attracted to him he did not take advantage of the fact to squeeze
her hand or let his linger sensuously. Everything about him paid
her respect. It seemed too good to be true. She delighted in it.

'You fed up hearing about my new job?' he asked, packing
away his computer. 'I don't think I'm going to be using this for
the rest of my journey, love my computer though I do. An interesting travelling companion always takes priority.'

'How do you know I'm interesting?' Beatie asked. 'You've
done most of the talking.'

'It's true,' he said. 'I'm sorry.'

'Don't be sorry. It's been fascinating. Certainly more so than
the story that woman was telling me.' Beatie retold what she had
heard about a feared London solicitor and an antisocial neighbour
who hoarded rubbish in his front garden.

'But that's intriguing,' Derek contradicted her. 'I love stories
about obsessives. I'm one myself.' She enjoyed him contradicting
her, and asked about his obsession. Curiously she found herself
anxious about his reply. She didn't want anything to spoil this
image of the perfect male before her. Was he about to admit to an
obsession that would reveal an absurd or infantile side to his character as a collector? Matchboxes, sugar wrappers, bar coasters; or
perhaps, and this, bewilderingly, she was the most anxious about,
he was going to confess that he collected art cards of nude women

as a way of introducing a touch of salaciousness into the conversation. None of them.

'I'm obsessive about interesting newspaper stories that I cut
out and file away labelled under the headings of "cruelty", "madness", "heroism", "eccentricity", "political moments", "bizarre
stories" – like the one about the neighbour who hoards rubbish
from car-boot sales. Don't ask me why. I imagine they'll be useful
some day. For what – God knows.'

'Not only God but you, too, surely?' Beatie chided him. 'That's
not an indifferent obsession, that's a very focused one. There must
be a reason, and you must know it.'

'I do,' he confessed, 'but I'm rather ashamed of my reason.'

'Trust me,' she tempted him.

'I'll trust you if you tell me what *your* obsession is,' he bargained.

'How do you know I've got one?'

'Hasn't everyone?'

'No, I don't think everyone has. You have to have an extreme
nature to be an obsessive. Most people are bland, I fear.'

'But you're not bland.' It was his first flirtatious comment.

'Obsessions require extreme natures,' she didn't allow even a
split second to hover over his compliment, 'but extreme natures
don't necessarily harbour obsessive natures.' She wanted to move
from the topic but wanted more to know what reason he could
possibly be ashamed of. She pressed. 'Now, why are you ashamed
of your reasons for collecting newspaper clippings?'

'I collect newspaper clippings,' he confessed, 'so that I can
glance at them before going to dinner parties and thus go armed
with topics to raise over dinner. Isn't that dreadful?' She wasn't
sure. Part of her thought yes, it was, it smacked of a social behaviour too calculated. On the other hand she was impressed by his
candour.

'Talk more about the new job you're preparing for. I'm
Norfolk-born so I love the London Underground. It's exotic for
me.'

'My job,' he didn't need much persuading, 'is mainly to pro-
pose new ways of using the space. There's space everywhere in
the London Underground. Walls on both sides of a platform;
walls in endless passageways, low ceilings, mini-piazzas at the
bottom of escalators, slim spaces above the seats inside the trains.
Everywhere! They've installed chocolate dispensers on platforms
but could there also be someone selling espresso coffees? No!
Because in rush hours you need all the space you can get for
waiting passengers. Should we legitimise and increase the number
of buskers there are, and have a selection committee to ensure
performers are of a high standard, like they do in Convent
Garden? The big problem is to bring the dead areas alive without
endangering life. And there *are* lots of dead areas, aren't there?
You feel as though you're descending into Hades when you stand
on those escalators going down; and if you have to change stations you find yourself walking endless walks as though in a
burial catacomb. They've started tiling some stations, rather
imaginatively, but I think they've run out of money to do every
station.'

'Perhaps,' Beatie was buzzing, 'walls could be painted. I bet
artists painting murals would be cheaper than tiles. Long murals
depicting the bustle of London life. You'd have the world coming
to see an exhibition like that!'

'Don't think I haven't thought of murals,' he said, 'but I fear the
really talented painters would charge the earth.'

'Then use the best students just out of art school. They'd love
the opportunity – to be able to claim that their first job was painting murals for the London Underground? They'd leap at it.'

It was now Derek's turn to be mesmerised by Beatie. He was
hearing her voice for the first time – low, mellow, infused with
controlled enthusiasm.

'Any other ideas?' he asked.

'Well,' she replied as though she'd been waiting to be asked, 'if
you're really interested, yes, I have. One that I've often thought
about as I've stood waiting for a train . . .'

'And waiting and waiting and waiting.' He smiled at her.

'... and that I'd like to see not only on the London Underground walls but on hoardings all over the country is "Quote of the Month" – the kind of quote to set people thinking, even talking among themselves. There! I've revealed my obsession.' He couldn't see how. Where was the obsession? She explained as she reached into her bag for a credit-card wallet from which she withdrew a small folded sheet of paper on which there was typing. 'I collect quotations and put them into an old leather-bound address book under their author. Here's a quote I think so important that I carry it around with me to bring out at the right moment.'

'Like now?'

'Like these days of IRA bombs going off, and hijackings, and Muslim kidnappings. It's from a lecture given by the philosopher Isaiah Berlin on the occasion of receiving the Jerusalem Prize in 1979.' She read it to him, bending close so as not to disturb other passengers, though she would like to have stood up on her seat and declare it out loud.

"The oldest and most obsessive vision or ideal is that of the perfect society on earth, wholly just, wholly happy, offering a final solution of all human problems within men's grasp, but for one – some *one* major obstacle such as class war, or the destructive aspects of materialism or of Western technology; or the evil consequences of institutions – state or church; or some other false doctrine or wicked practice – one great barrier but for which the ideal is realised.

"It follows that since all that is needed is the removal of this one great obstacle in the path of mankind, no sacrifice can be too great, if only by this means can the goal be attained.

"No conviction has caused more violence, oppression, suffering. The cry that the real present must be sacrificed to an attainable ideal future – this demand has been used to justify massive cruelties . . ."

When she had finished there appeared a new quality in his features. Before, he was animated by himself, and so Beatie detected
self-regard. Now the animation came from an outside force –
Beatie. It was different. She looked up from the little white sheet,
and saw it. He was excited. His eyes were bright with everything: the good fortune of a new job; the thoughts of Professor
Isaiah Berlin; the beauty of Beatie Bryant; the ideas of Beatie
Bryant, the possibilities that life offered. He felt himself on a high
cliff, the wind in his face, a vast world before him, youth on his
side. Beatie wondered if he was still with her, he seemed so ecstat-
ically gone. She brought him back to her.

'And if you look into yesterday's *Guardian*,' she told him, 'you'll
find an item for your folder marked "Cruelty", or perhaps you'd
file it away under "Madness".' He asked what it was about. 'It's a
story about an Iranian actress who is to be flogged for kissing a
man on his forehead in public.'

And now the dazzling Derek with the wind in his face and a
vast world before him and youth on his side fell from his high cliff
with just a few words.

'You can kiss my forehead anytime,' he said, as though unable
to help himself, 'and you won't be flogged.' He might have saved
himself at that moment had he not, after a theatrical pause, added:
'Unless you want to be.'

Beatie's disappointment was acute. He would misjudge many
more moments like that in his life, she knew. She smiled weakly,
and left at the next station, Manningtree, three stops before the
one she wanted. And there she stood on the platform looking at
the clouds and wishing fervently that she knew their names.
Naming parts created order.

She had fallen apart a little after her encounter with dazzling
Derek, and desperately felt the need to come together again.

17

'The great thing about business is that the customer pays for everything'

'The great thing about business is that the customer pays for everything.' Stan Mann was on his third lager, and in his stride. 'Raw materials, machinery, wages, packaging, marketing, transport, the interest on loans, profits, salaries, private schools for the boss's children, the boss's house, the boss's car, the demands and expectations of the boss's wife – everything! The customer pays! It's an important lesson to learn if you want to get on in life. What he has to do, the boss, is work out the logistics of putting the enterprise together, and he has to be possessed of a special brilliant ability to choose his staff carefully. Assessing character and skill, the right people to run the different departments – *that's* what justifies his large salary. And then he sits back or she sits back, works out the sums, decides which house to buy, which car, where to send the kids to school, where to go on holiday – and it's all paid for by the customer. Simple! So damned simple!'

Beatie asked him: 'How do you know these things?'

'How? Because I'm a good Marxist, that's how! Three of the richest men I ever met all used to be members of the Communist Party. Phil Piratin, one of only two communists who were ever Members of Parliament, became a banker. The first was Willie Gallagher, member for Lanarkshire. Willie became nothing, except beloved. Phil, MP for Stepney in London, was an uneducated Jewish street urchin who didn't have two pennies to rub together but he was a brilliant orator – the old Jewish prophets must have sounded like him – and he became filthy rich. Not from his oratory, you understand, but from knowing how the capitalist system worked. He knew – the customer pays for everything. So never mind about your publishing houses and looking for new writers,' he urged Beatie, 'business! Go into business!'

'But I don't have a business brain, Stan Mann.'

'You don't need a business brain, you just have to remember that the customer pays for everything.'

'You may not need a business brain,' said Beatie, 'but you need to *care* about business. I don't care about the logistics of putting a business together, I just have ideas. Ideas *for* business excite me because human ingenuity excites me. I'm an encourager.'

'What ideas have you got?' the old man asked. 'Tell me them, I'll tell you what to do to bring them alive.'

'I don't have any big ideas just yet, Stan Mann, only small ones. But I feel as though something is germinating, you know? Like you feel when a cold is coming on but you don't know if you're actually going to get it. You have to wait. There's this character in a play by John Osborne, *Epitaph for George Dillon*, about an aspiring playwright who—'

The old Mann interrupted her. 'I used to like the theatre. Don't get much theatre here. Sean O'Casey. Him. I used to like him. And Lorca. Real poets they were.'

'And this aspiring playwright,' Beatie continued, 'tells his girl-friend that he doesn't know if he really has a playwright's talent or

if he's just got the symptoms – "the pain, the ugly swellings". I'm
a bit like that just now. A little bit of pain. A slight swelling. I feel
I'm sickening for something. But what?'

Stan Mann reached for another lager. She asked him:

'Do you know the names of clouds?'

'That's a strange question,' he said, 'after what we've been talking about.'

Was it? She was fumbling.

'I was looking at a cloud formation the other day and I desperately needed to know its name.'

"Desperately'? You desperately needed to know the name of a
cloud formation? Whatever for?'

'I'd had a disappointing encounter on the train coming up a
couple of days ago. I'd misjudged someone and lost my balance
in life. And then I saw this cloud formation which, because I
couldn't name it, made me feel even more that I was losing
control.'

'Well, you've become an oddball, Beatie Bryant, that's for sure,'
said the old man.

'Oddball? Me, Stan Mann? Never! Normal as they come.'

'Only no one,' said the old revolutionary, 'ever comes normal.'
He wasn't going to leave her alone, and she had to tell him what
had happened. 'People disappoint,' he sympathised. 'Prepare yourself for it and they'll disappoint less. Just try not to disappoint
yourself.'

'Can't promise that, Stan.'

'Biggest cause of unhappiness,' Stan cautioned. 'We think we're
one kind of person, and one morning wake to discover we're
not. You look at people in the street next time you walk out in
London. Look at their faces. Ask yourself – are they happy with
themselves? Are their eyes dull, do their mouths droop at the
ends, do they carry leftover marks of discontent on the skin?'

'I'll do that, Stan Mann.'

She had an urge to leave the old man's company. Not that his
company didn't please, even delight her, but there are certain

personalities who can be experienced only in small doses; and more, she had a need to listen to music, to walk back to her mother's cottage with her Walkman wrapped round her head, and *The Dream of Gerontius* lifting her spirits.

18

The world is divided between . . .

The world is divided between those who know what they're doing and those who don't know what they're doing. I belong to those who don't know what they're doing. Well, sometimes I know what I'm doing but mostly not. Not these days, anyway. I've started to write the biography of a musician no one's heard of, whose music is complex, who lived in the sixteenth century about which I know next to nothing, and anyway how does one write biography?

Presumptuous of me. Audacious. Foolhardy. So little is recorded that I'm having to leave gaps, and leap across the years in the hope that what is known five years later will give clues to what happened five years earlier. I can identify the clues, build suggestions around them but I feel fraudulent; full merely of conjecture. It began fine. Excited myself. Even got Manfred excited. I mean I got him worked up about Christianity freeing melody from the tyranny of the word but I didn't have time to tell him how Christianity rejected harmony in line with its rejection of the flesh and all things earthy. Which is why Manfred and I find Gregorian chant boring and deathly – pleasure is denied, and delight. Gregorian chant may have freed melody but it blighted joy. There's ecstasy there but it's relentless, protests itself too much. Now?

The truth is I'm too old to have embarked upon such a project. Only one approach appeals to me – spelling out the history of music up to and beyond Giovanni's life. History excites me – one thing leading to another, connecting the parts that explain the whole; *that* I find satisfying and worth trumpeting to an interested public. Otherwise? He was born, lived, composed startling music, and died young. Where did he learn about music? From the Church or the troubadours? Not known. Neither could account for the outrageous Giovanni spirit. What did, then? We know he was imprisoned for murdering the man who raped his mother; but letters exist between him and his mother suggesting their love for one another was no ordinary love. Those same letters tell us she was a singer who incurred the wrath of the pious Church fathers for attempting to add descant to plainchant. After her battles with the fathers who were protecting the sacred, untouchable liturgy of the Church, she became a wild woman who perhaps put herself in the way of rape. The son inherited her fury which transmogrified into his exhilarating and sublime music with its breathtaking energy and heartbreaking lyricism of a tenor unheard of before, and was lost after death so that his genius was not permitted to shape the music that followed.

Domenico Gabrielli who, like Giovanni, lived only thirty-nine years, certainly didn't know Giovanni's music. Nor did Maurizio Cassati or Giuseppe Torrelli – all Baroque composers whose works could be shuffled and redistributed without anyone knowing the difference (though I'd never write such a thing for printing – I'd be decapitated, torn apart by colleagues). I don't know how but C. P. E. Bach, Johann's son, might have known of Giovanni's music if only because of the bold vivacity of the first and last movements of his glorious Magnificat, the exaltedness of which is as electrifying as the Concerti Grossi and Masses of my Giovanni Marcantonio. And there's Thomas Tallis with his powerful forty-part motet 'Spem In Alium'. How did the music of a little-known Italian come to the attention of the great sixteenth-century English composer for surely the power of that motet is touched by the power of Giovanni's compositions? Did it come through the Scottish composer, Robert Carver, whose Mass for ten voices must have been the inspiration for the more famous Tallis motet for forty voices?

And there's Vivaldi. Doesn't the *Gloria* possess the same kind of energy and lyricism? I have to admit. Though I've never heard a rendering of it that drives the energy to the degree I'm convinced Vivaldi intended, nor that found the true sweetness of its lyricism. And I've written about that lack on at least three occasions, but who listens to critics? We're ticket-sellers. That's all that's expected of us. Or not.

And then there's Handel. But there, I'm wandering off at a tangent again. The topic was 'what on earth does Barney Perl, music critic of the *Telegraph*, think he's doing with his life?' My darling daughters despair of me. They know I won't ever finish the biography of Giovanni Marcantonio, like that novel everyone knows is inside of them that one day, one day soon, one day not far off, they'll begin writing, but never do.

The world is divided between those who plan novels and those who execute them, those who tidy their desks and those who write on them, those who long for and those who act upon.

19

I didn't tell Stan the full story

I didn't tell Stan the full story of my stopover in Manningtree. Not sure why. Perhaps because I've not sorted it out in my own mind.

My normal response to those who say 'it's all a question of mind over matter' was dismissive. 'If you *think* you'll get over cancer,' they said, 'you will!' Balls! is what I said. If you get cancer your mind can do nothing about it – except be affected. Matter over mind is what really takes place, I said. But I've been wondering.

Recently I've noticed something about myself. A cold shiver goes through me if someone relates an accident, even a small one. 'Jack slipped on the ice today.' I shudder. 'Jill scalded herself with boiling water.' A cold sensation snakes down the back of my neck. 'He came off his bike with such a crash.' I feel it at the back of my legs. Sometimes I just think the thought myself, imagining something happening as one does going through nightmare scenarios in one's mind, and I can feel that cold shiver. It's most odd. My mind seems in such moments to be in control of matter.

More worryingly, however, is that I find myself thinking about violent encounters and my body tightens, tenses. I catch myself clenching my teeth and fists as though I am about to use them. At such moments I feel myself capable of anger and great violence. Anything can spark it off. I might be walking down a street and see a drunk approaching, and he may be harmless, just drunk, but I start to imagine what I would do if he accosted me, if he stopped me to ask for money and became aggressive when I refused – for refuse I would. Or if he walked past saying something like, 'Fucking stuck-up bitch.' Scenes take shape in my head, and I imagine exchanges of words. In the scenario where he becomes aggressive after I've refused to give him any money, he raises a fist, and I stop him with my tone of voice, which of course is fearless, full of authority and confidence. 'You as much as touch a hair on my head and I'll have you inside before you can remember your name.' Embarrassingly I find myself slowing down to deliver these words, and sometimes I even stop to place myself in the right physical stance. I've seen others walk past me with smiles on their faces as though they recognised what was happening, as though they'd been there themselves. Violence makes me feel violent.

But my mind taking over is not always to do with violence. One of the sweetest incidents in my short life was one day standing on the steps of the National Gallery deep in thought that was obviously shaping the frown on my face, when gradually I became aware of a well-dressed elderly man approaching directly towards me and shaping his face into the same frown that he could see was shaping mine. It was a lovely moment in which I caught myself reflected in another's sympathetic features. When finally I noticed him frowning my frown I smiled, and he smiled back with a look that said 'Nothing is ever that bad', and walked on past me to greet a very young woman whom I guessed must be his granddaughter. Lucky granddaughter.

All of which is a prelude to what happened on Manningtree Station, where I had to wait another hour for a train to Diss. I bought myself the *Guardian* but found I couldn't concentrate on the special prose that is journalism. Now, surely, was the time to listen to music on my Walkman. Manningtree is a dreary station.

I wanted to hear something lively, or demanding. Should the music be English or Russian, German or French? Choral or orchestral or chamber? I slid in the Prokofiev Classical Symphony. No, too jaunty. Tried the Elgar cello concerto. No, too familiar. Schubert? I had brought along the Trout Quintet specially because it had been a present, bought long ago by a friend, that I hadn't ever played. Now was the time to get to know it, sitting in a station where I shouldn't be, hadn't planned to be, and didn't want to be on this late spring morning in April.

Hovering near the station cafe on the platform across the track were three boys between the ages of fifteen and seventeen. The first word that came to me was 'louts'. Does one have the right to call such youngsters by such a name without knowing a thing about them? Except that one did. Instantly. From the way they slouched, dragged their sneaker-clad feet as though to lift them would be a sign of surrender to the better-off classes; from the loud decibels with which they communicated their banalities to one another; from the banalities themselves.

'Oo gives a fuckin' toss what 'e thinks?'

'I'm just saying he'll have to deduct money for not fuckin' bein' on the fuckin' job.'

'So fuckin' what! Let 'im!'

'It's only fuckin' money.'

'Right!'

'At the end of the day it's only fuckin' money.'

'Well, don't come fuckin' askin' me for loans for your fuckin' beer, that's all I'm sayin'.'

'Did I ever, cunt?'

'I'm just fuckin' saying, that's all.'

Did they really think that what they were saying was so interesting that everyone else on the station ought to hear and enjoy it? I covered my ears with my earphones. There I sat listening to Schubert, and watching three nothings storm at and circle round each other. Their words were blocked out but I could watch the gangling choreography of their testosterone-fuelled, belligerent restlessness. Which female of the species would ever want to make love to them? How could they ever be a partner, a soulmate, a father of children? With what language would they introduce themselves to bed? What wisdom did they possess to hand on to their children?

Then entered a fourth young man – black and taller than my three louts but carrying himself warily, like an everlasting foreigner. It was not that his blackness made him seem un-English – we are by now very multi-racially habituated – it was that a different atmosphere hung about his being. First of all he wore a suit and tie and shoes, which were in stark contrast to the shabby, boring clothes of my louts. And he seemed indifferent to them as though he understood precisely the kind of youths they were, and should keep his distance. Taller he may have been but he didn't possess their aggressivity.

I watched, and as I watched my imagination began forming a scenario. I saw those louts looking at the black boy, obviously sharing a banal joke about him, and I moved the action forward in my mind. They would shout obscenities at him, ask him which part of Africa he came from – I could see his was an Ethiopian face but for my louts all blacks came from Africa, which they thought was one country – and then they'd start circling him, taunting him with the myth of black sexual prowess.

'Yours a big 'un, then?'

'Spend your nights measuring it?'

'Prefer white girls to black ones, do yer?'

'Goin' somewhere nice all dressed up?'

''E's not sayin' nuffink.'

'Lost 'is tongue.'

'Finks 'e's better than us.'

'Takes our girls, takes our jobs.'

'Take every fuckin' thing if we let 'em.'

'But we're not goin' to let 'em, are we, lads?'

'Too fuckin' right we're not.'

All this was going on in my head. I was making up the

dialogue, like a playwright. And I hadn't heard a note of Schubert. I went further. They began pushing him, he was telling them he didn't want trouble, they were ignoring him; a fight was about to begin. And then the strangest of things – I leapt up from the green station bench where I'd been sitting, and was about to cry out 'Stop!' I suppose I was what is described as 'carried away'. My imagination had briefly taken over my body. My body had tensed, my fists were clenched, I was about to enter the fray. In fact – and this is what astonished me – I wanted to hurt my louts. I wanted them hurt. I wanted my Ethiopian to turn into James Bond and utterly decimate the three. I wanted them off the platform, off the streets, thrown into prison, thrown out of life. I could see no point to their existence. My feelings were violent, nothing had happened but I'd imagined a scenario so vivid that it had taken over my physical being. Confronted with hatred and violence, albeit imagined, I was filled with hatred and violence. It was disturbing, distressing, shaming. Was I not supposed to be a pacifist? Hadn't I marched against the death penalty all those years ago, holding Ronnie's hand and feeling I was making the world a better place?

I worried myself on that platform. My mind had taken control of the matter that was my body, and I was out of control, all over the stage. What was happening? I'd begun life post-Oxford with such confidence and calm. I didn't have answers, no sense of where I was going, no plan like some I knew who planned their lives ten years ahead, mapped out their futures. Not me. I was feeling my way, treading warily, thinking slowly, plotting carefully. But in control. I felt strong enough to be uncertain, confident enough to have doubts and failings, brave enough to take risks – but the two interviews, the disappointment over dazzling Derek, the discovery that I could feel such violence just by thinking angry thoughts – was making me fall apart. Meeting with Norma Shapiro, that was good; learning about the parts of a book, that was pleasing, reassuring, a contribution to my life. I have a fear of fragmentation. I needed things to fit as in joinery. I loved Ronnie's brother-in-law, Dave. He ran a joinery workshop and made everything from tables and chairs to bookcases and bank counters. His hands were never still – he sawed, chiselled and hammered home parts that it was deeply satisfying to watch come together into a whole that was both useful and aesthetically pleasing.

I want, I need to fit together like an elegant Windsor chair sitting solidly on the floor, inviting the weary to rest, confident that I won't collapse under their weight. I want to be solid and dependable for those who cross my life, and to be that I need to know the parts fit beautifully and peacefully and inevitably and gracefully together.

20

Off he'd gone through Shepherd Market

Off he'd gone through Shepherd Market with his shoulder bag, striding like a young man who could have been less than sixty, and Beatie knew nothing about him. He had been a strong presence that stayed with her as she went home but another strong presence had descended upon her that same day.

Beatie lingered over her coffee contemplating the attraction of older men. They would not have the sharp edge of urgency youth possesses; they would not be delightfully surprised as young men are who still have much to discover and experience; perhaps the older man's power to make love will have diminished and he might lack swift laughter, but his smile would be more knowing, and his knowing would offer comfort and security; urgency would be replaced by tried and tempered tenderness, slick wit replaced by wisdom, conversation would flow rather than be broken into five-minute bursts, and consideration would take over from selfishness; I would be taken seriously rather than casually, not taken for granted but pampered and spoilt and made to feel special rather than passing.

In the middle of which fantasy a surprised voice called out,

'Beatie?' She looked up from her reverie half forgetting who she was, and not in the least recognising the face that had uttered her name.

'Tamara. Tamara Perl. We were at St Hilda's together.'

'Good God! Tamara! What are you doing in Shepherd Market?'

'Looking for a flat.' They fell upon each other like sisters reunited and talked nonstop for the rest of their time together so that morning coffee crept over into early lunch, which they decided to stay and eat in the open as this spring day was warmer than those days English springs normally offer.

Beatie told her of the two jobs she was due to be interviewed for, and Tamara described what working for the Beeb was like.

'Do you plan to spend the rest of your life with the Beeb?' Beatie asked.

'No, no! Never! I plan to run a consultancy and become rich.'

'A consultancy? Consulting who about what?'

'I don't know. Like a husband for life I'll know it when I see it. You?'

'A bit the same. I'm hovering on the verge. I feel something approaching, or I'm approaching *it* but I've no idea what it is. This liver and onion is really tasty. What's yours like?'

'Caesar salad is Caesar salad.'

'Is that true?'

'Not really. I don't know why I said it. This one is good. The lettuce is crispy, the croutons don't taste as though they're yesterday's, just the right amount of anchovy, and the dressing is light and lemony and nicely peppery and not out of a bottle, and I think they've tossed it with raw egg which I've never had before. What made *you* come to Shepherd Market?'

'I wanted a touch of Paris. And because it's a touch of Paris I've just had an extraordinary encounter with an older man.'

'How old?'

'Not sure. He seemed very fit. Could be late fifties. Told me I was beautiful.'

'Why wasn't he a dirty old man?'

'You can tell. He was intelligent and shy and quickly left after a few words.'

'If he only uttered a few words how do you know he was intelligent?'

'Sharp as ever, Tamara. He looked at me with relish and then apologised.' Beatie described the encounter. 'And when he left he told me I was very kind to let him talk to me. Don't you find those words odd? "It was very kind of you to allow me to talk to you."'

'And then he left?'

'Not quite. He said something else that I found really, really interesting. "The world," he said, "is divided between people who are immediate and those who are hard work, and you," he said, "are immediate." Wasn't that lovely?'

'And a coincidence. My father has a friend with whom he's doing that all the time. They have competitions whenever they meet – who's found the sharpest division. Ever since that play called *The World is Divided* it's become a party craze among London's intelligentsia. I even play it myself sometimes.'

'Give me one,' asked Beatie.

'Just like that? OK, let me see now. I believe the world is divided between those who stand out and those who want to belong.'

'Oh, that's good.'

'You?'

'I've been trying to think of one ever since he left and I can't come up with anything really stunning. The best I could manage was one addressed to myself. The world is divided between those who know what they want to do with their life and those who don't!'

'And he left without asking for your name and address?'

'And I'll never see him again.'

'Would you want to?' The question made Beatie reflect.

'Yes. I think I would. I think I might like older men.'

'For love or company?' asked the sharp-as-ever Tamara.

'Not sure. Company, perhaps. Perhaps I'm looking for a father figure. I've got lots of ideas and I feel I need guidance.'

'I'm good at guidance. What ideas?'

'Oh, silly things just now.'

'Like what?' Tamara stopped eating to attend. Beatie laughed. 'How funny you look with your fork halfway to your mouth. Watch out, an anchovy is slipping down a piece of lettuce. Eat! Eat!'

Tamara obeyed, and repeated: 'Like what?'

'I'm not sure I should tell you, 'said Beatie. 'I remember you as such a high-powered individual, so quick to criticise and comment. Coming from Norfolk peasant stock, I found you a bit overwhelming.

'Gone! Changed! I'm reborn!' Tamara boomed out.

'You mean you've exchanged Jewishness for Christianness? And I know there's no such word.' Beatie became more softly spoken than usual as though to hint at the decibel level conversation should be maintained out in the open, narrow-way of Shepherd Market.

'Good Lor, no!' Tamara took the hint, and reduced her decibel level. 'Besides, I know some very loudmouthed Christians. They're called "louts".'

Was she angry, Beatie wondered? 'I'm sorry, I wasn't suggesting . . .'

'Don't apologise,' said a cheerful Tamara. 'That's Jewish family life. Jews argue! Everyone of them has opinions, and because every Jew has an opinion they have to shout loud in family circles to be heard. It's a Talmudic tradition.'

'What's "Talmudic"?' Beatie was ashamed to ask.

'The Talmud is a record covering hundreds of years of Jewish scholars arguing with each other over the meaning of the Bible. And each new generation of scholars argued about the interpretations of the previous generation. It's the argument that's enjoyed not the conclusions. There were no conclusions, or rather there *were* conclusions but the next generation questioned them.'

Beatie was curious. 'Give me an example of what they argued over,' she asked.

'Good God, don't ask me. I'm not a Talmudic scholar.'

'You must have picked up something along the way,' Beatie persisted.

Tamara thought a while. 'Here's something I remember my dad telling me. Three Rabbis – I can't remember their names but it was in a Palestinian academy of Jewish learning sometime BC where they were confronted with the question: Which is more important – study or practice? One rabbi says practice is more important than study. Another rabbi disagrees and says no, study is more important than practice. The third one brings the two together and concludes study is more important because study *leads* to practice. And this is argued about throughout the centuries. Study, thought, interpretation, debate – no right action is possible without them. Or is it?'

Beatie was enthralled. It was like being with Ronnie all over again. The feeling that his presence was around pleased and warmed her even though she knew in her heart there could be no coming together again. And she wondered would she ever find anyone to match him. Tamara continued.

'That's why Jews disturb other people – they question everything and everyone. No one is an ultimate authority for them, they have no respect for authority, only for those who do good deeds and achieve things. Achievers are the authority – the scientists, writers, philosophers – the thinkers. *They* were the authorities the Jews took notice of. Jesus belonged to this tradition, and gave rise to the most murderous argument of them all – was he the promised Messiah or was he just another false prophet? There were lots of them around, and many Jews thought he was one of them. Then along comes the very Jewish Paul, creates Christianity, and the slaughter begins. First the Romans slaughter the Christians, then the Christians slaughter the Jews and then each other – everyone has an opinion, it's in the genes of the Jews. Paul! It was all Paul's fault, I blame him. But I digress, like my

father, he digresses a lot, and now that he's a widower he argues
with himself.'

Beatie found all this familiar.

'I used to have a Jewish boyfriend,' she said. 'Couldn't stop
him talking, but I got to love his family, and they argued all the
time.'

'About politics, I bet,' said Tamara.

'Right!'

'And I bet they were communists.'

'How did you know?' asked an amazed Beatie.

'And your boyfriend argued with his parents because they persisted being believers against all the evidence of Stalinist tyranny.'

'Right.'

'And they all came from the East End of London.'

'Right, again.'

'And they were all kind and hospitable and opened their houses
to strangers and had special friends who were Gentiles.'

'Right, right! His mother had a circle of friends who were all
lonely and eccentric.'

'And at least one of them had to be a writer or a magazine
editor.'

'A writer. Golda. Golda Appelfeld. She published her own
novels because they were . . .'

'So obscure and so full of philosophical references that no one
else would publish them.'

'Exactly so! But how do you know all this?'

'My father's trying to write a book, a biography.'

'Of who?'

'An obscure sixteenth-century composer called Giovanni
Marcantonio who he thinks is the lost inspiration behind the
greatest of Italian composers, even Mozart who of course is not
Italian but my father thinks there's a link. Not even the Italians
have heard of him, this Giovanni. My dad wants to rescue him
from obscurity. Typically Jewish, wants to save people – not souls,
souls are your own affair. Saving souls is what the goyim do, but

the physical being, the material being, that's something else. The Jew feels it's a blessing to help the world be a better place. Heaven he can do nothing about. That's God's affair.'

Beatie was not going to let that generalisation go unchallenged. 'What about Christian Aid and all the good works of the nuns and priests in times of famine and disaster?'

'You're right,' said Tamara, 'but I'm not wrong!'

'Is your father still music critic of the *Telegraph*?' Beatie wanted to shift from generalities to the specific.

'He most certainly is, thank God. Music keeps him sane.'

'That's what my boyfriend was passionate about. Music!' Beatie surprised herself talking about him and enjoying it. 'I will always be grateful that he introduced me to music.'

'Yes, I'm remembering now. You talked a lot about him. Ronnie, wasn't it?'

'I'm impressed.'

'See! He didn't want to save your soul, he wanted to hand on something concrete – a love of music. I bet he played the piano, or the violin.'

'Nope!' said Beatie ashamed to feel a trifle pleased that the all-knowing Tamara had guessed wrongly for once.

'Then he wanted to be a writer!'

'Damn!' said Beatie. 'I was enjoying you getting something wrong.'

'Stick around,' said the confident Tamara, 'you'll see me get lots wrong.'

'That was terrible of me.' Beatie was contrite. 'I must watch out for this – this wish to see others fall. It's not really me, honestly.'

'Forget it!' Tamara reassured her. 'Schadenfreude – it's in us all to glow a little at the mighty fallen.'

'And it's a trait I despise.' Beatie was becoming upset. 'I really do. Despise it! College was full of girls who gloried in other people's failures and I could never understand it. But it seems some of it rubbed off on me.'

'If it rubbed *on*,' said Tamara eyeing her friend's distress and thinking I like this young woman, she's innocent, naive, fresh, 'then it can rub *off*.'

Beatie was mortified. Thoughts of the kind of person she might be that she didn't want to be always upset her – like Lindsey Shackelton's observation that she walked into a room with the air of imagining everyone in it is an idiot. She did indeed find many people idiotic but that is what she encountered not what she believed.

Beatie did not want to have to think about herself, preferring rather to return to the topic of Jewishness.

'Tell me,' she asked Tamara, 'what exactly is it to be Jewish? My ex-boyfriend and his family were not religious, they didn't celebrate the festivals, not even Passover. And though his parents could speak Yiddish Ronnie couldn't, and they were devoutly tolerant and believed in egalitarianism and that under the skin we're all the same – which I'm not sure I agree with, I must confess – and yet they felt fiercely Jewish, and I don't know what it means.'

Tamara warmed to her old college acquaintance more and more – even her questioning was innocent. She seemed like a modern-day Candide. Voltaire would have enjoyed her. It slipped out: 'Have you ever read Voltaire's *Candide*?' she asked Beatie.

'Yes,' Beatie replied. 'Why? Is that who you think I'm like because I asked about the nature of Jewishness? I just want to know. I left my boyfriend long ago and now that I've been through Oxford I realise how uncurious I was about a people and a milieu I loved.'

'I'm the wrong person to ask.' Tamara was being truthful. 'I know it's a question lots of people ask, especially Jews. They keep asking about themselves who they are. They should know but they don't. Or they know one day it's one thing and the next day it's something else. My dad and his friend I was telling you about, they constantly discuss the question between them. In fact my dad's getting fed up with it. "People are people!" he says. But not his friend, Manfred. I like Manfred. He climbs mountains for charity, and treks over icy wastes, and deserts, and he's a thinker. Not trained, not a philosopher, an accountant actually, but he loves rummaging around philosophical concepts and thoughts about the nature of this and that. And recently, because no one likes Jews much any more, he's taken to thinking about the nature of Jewishness. I'll introduce you to him one day. Now, tell me, like what?'

'Like what "what"?' asked Beatie, who was too absorbed with what Tamara had been saying to remember where the conversation had left off.

'You have ideas, you said. Like what?'

'Oh, ideas for this and that. Like advertising – and no, I don't want to be a copywriter. But I have this idea for an advert for Volvo cars.'

'Explain.'

'A family is coming out of their house and into the smallest Volvo on the market, and off they go. And they pass another Volvo, the next size up, and one of the children cries out: "Oh look, another Volvo." And you follow this Volvo with a family on their way somewhere and they stop for a picnic, and while they're eating along comes another Volvo the next size up, and someone cries out, "Oh look, another Volvo," and so on through the range – and it stays in your head: "Oh look, another Volvo."'

'Got any more like that?' Tamara was aglow.

'You've got a really expressive face,' Beatie told her. 'I can see thoughts passing through it as though your skin was thin, thin glass.'

'I know. Can't hide anything. More, more!'

'Well – shampoo. Have you noticed how shampoo adverts are all the same? Stick any brand name in the advert and it would fit. I'd like to see an advert that says simply 'Forget the hype – just try it!' Let's say the shampoo was called Gull shampoo – just imagine huge adverts with all that space uncluttered and only those eight words on it: GULL SHAMPOO. FORGET THE HYPE – JUST TRY IT! We'd all be saying it – "Forget the hype, just try it!"'

It was Tamara's turn to be enthralled, and Beatie was happy to have such an appreciative audience. 'But,' she said, 'I don't know why you're getting excited over ideas just for advertising copy. Lots of bright copywriters around.'

'Well,' said Tamara, 'you haven't shared any other kind of idea. Have you got any other kind of ideas?'

'Yes, but I've not thought them through, you wouldn't get excited by a half-baked idea, would you?'

'Try me.'

'Pennies! You know how everything costs something and ninety-nine pence, like £4.99 so you don't think it's £5, which of course it is but the retailers imagine we're stupid and that they've succeeded in making us think it's four pounds something instead of £5 less just one penny.'

'And they're right. Most people *are* stupid or gullible.'

'Or perhaps just resigned?' Beatie couldn't bear the notion of people as 'stupid'.

'What's your idea?' asked Tamara.

'Well, what if there were a row of government collecting boxes labelled "Education", "National Health", "Transport", "Art", "Environment", and customers were invited in every shop, all over the country, to put their penny change in whichever they thought was the most important problem needing assistance. I mean don't you feel silly holding out your hand for a penny change? And it must finally amount to a lot because governments are always talking about a penny increase in this tax or that tax.'

'Boxes wouldn't work,' said Tamara, already working on the idea. 'It would have to be in the till somehow. The assistants ask which one you want your penny allocated to and it's totted up at the end of the day. And there would have to be charities on the list, too – cancer, heart, wildlife, et cetera.'

'And think how many items a day one person buys,' contributed Beatie further. 'Say six, that's forty-two pence per week, that's – er – what?' She took out a little calculator from her bag. 'Forty-two times fifty-two that's £21.84 a year say £22 in round

figures and say only half the population participate, say half a population of fifty-eight million, that's twenty-two times
twenty-nine . . . that's six hundred and thirty-eight million to
distribute.'

'Lovely idea,' said Tamara in an efficient tone of voice.
'Romantic and generous – but I can see a dozen reasons immediately why it wouldn't work.'

'Like?'

'First of all there'd be protests that the government was obtain-
ing tax through the back door. And say there were twelve boxes
receiving equal nominations for the penny – it wouldn't be equal
of course but just to illustrate my argument . . . that's . . . divide six
hundred and thirty-eight million by twelve.' Beatie did so.

'Fifty-three million one hundred and sixty-six thousand six
hundred and sixty-six.'

'Fifty-three million! That's a lot of money. Cancer would be
grateful of it, and wildlife, and the Heart Foundation. But it's not
much for the biggies like transport or National Health. Still – it's
an idea with potential of some sort. I'll think about it.'

Of course they exchanged contact addresses. Tamara gave her
father's address and telephone number, and Beatie gave her
brother's address and phone number.

'I'm not looking for a flat just yet,' she said, 'but I soon will be.
I'm living over a Greek restaurant and the smell's driving me mad.
My brother will always know where I am.'

The spring day had become warm. Each went their separate
ways. Tamara to an appointment to view a flat that turned out to
be too expensive – which of course it would be, situated in
whoreland. Beatie returned to her food-smelly flat in north
London where she looked at herself in the mirror and thought
about the old man who had strode off like a young man with a
bag on his shoulder, and of whom she had asked nothing, and
would never see again.

She had two interviews for which to prepare.

21

I got me a toy boy

I got me a toy boy, or so it seemed. How old does a woman have to be for her boyfriend to be described as a toy boy? And how old does he have to be? I was approaching thirty and he was eighteen. It was many months later, after the BBC and I concluded we were too good for each other, and I answered an ad for a PA to the executive director of a business consultancy, I took him out to dinner. Lee, that is, Lee Danton. You can't easily forget a boy like that. He was still with the Beeb, of course – the technical side hung on to lads, the gals, being creative, became the producers and researchers. He was surprised that I wanted to date him.

'I thought you had dismissed me as being too young.'

'How can you be too young for a woman of thirty? What are you? Twenty-three, twenty-four?'

'Eighteen.' That's when I knew I had got me a toy boy. He continued: 'Then I thought you'd dismissed me as being too cocksure.'

'I like cocks that are sure,' I couldn't resist replying, instantly regretting my crudeness, and adding hastily, 'No, that's not why I've invited you out to dinner.'

We were downstairs in a restaurant, Trattoria Romana on Romilly Street, once the haunt of theatre folk along with Princess Margaret and Lord Snowdon. Now, fickle and itinerant as theatre folk are, after ten years of glamorising the Trat, they had found somewhere else, and a certain calm – dullness for some – descended upon the place. I used to enjoy it because the interior of glowing Italian tiles felt warmly familiar and reminiscent of the glorious days I spent in that rich and relaxed country. I fantasise about returning there when I'm rich and relaxed.

I had not eaten at the Trat in a long while. The management had changed and I wanted to see if the food had remained excellent despite the exodus of the glitzy ones, and if the waiters were still attentive without being obsequious. The food was good but the waiters were different, older it seemed to me, and the atmosphere seemed devoid of the gaiety it once had. It was to prove a mistaken choice.

'Why *did* you invite me to dinner?' he asked looking as boyish and handsome as ever with his short-cropped hair, blue eyes and broad shoulders so that I doubted my honesty.

'Let's order, first. What do you fancy?'

'Apart from you?'

'Stop that. My propositions are going to be serious.'

'You mean lovemaking isn't serious?' He was being mischievous. I enjoyed it but in my sternest of voices, which is not *very* stern, told him again to desist.

'I'll eat anything you offer,' he said in a tone suggesting he was *not* desisting.

'You want me to choose for you?'

'I like being chosen for. Saves having to make decisions, and it opens up new experiences.' Was he going to be like this all evening, I wondered? I'd have to rethink my propositions if so.

I ordered a *mozzarella in carotzza* each for starters, and for his main dish a *saltimbocca all'Alfredo*. For myself I indulged my love of veal escallops, and ordered *vitello tonnato* with its thick, rich tuna sauce. But it was the dessert of crêpes with a surprise filling that I really wanted him to taste.

'The world, by the way,' he said as he started on the dessert, 'is divided into those who are all of themselves and those who are only half of themselves.' He astonished me.

'That's good. That's very good. That's quite brilliant.' But I said it in the wrong tone of voice.

'Why,' he admonished, 'do you talk to me as though you're surprised I'm not an idiot?'

'Do I?' I was mortified. He had me on the run. 'Oh, my God, do I? I certainly don't mean to. Oh, forgive me, Lee. Really, believe me. It was just a stunning division that would have stunned me coming from anyone, a philosopher even. It's kind of abstract and poetic and so bloody true. Oh, Jesus, yes. So true. Did it just come to you, or have you been fashioning it and savouring it over weeks?'

'Came to me after our lunch with Matilda.'

'After the lunch or –' I wasn't sure how to describe it – 'or our incident together?'

'*Was* it an incident? You make it sound like a road accident or a fight outside a pub. What's wrong with "after our lovemaking"?'

'*We* didn't make love. *You* made love.'

'And what were you doing?'

'Standing there. Taking it. As most women do.'

'Now you make it sound like punishment you had to endure. Didn't you enjoy it?'

'I enjoyed it.' He really did have me on the run. If I wasn't careful I would not be able to have the serious conversation I had planned.

'Do you really think that's what most women do?' he asked. I had forgotten what I had said. He reminded me. 'You said "as most women do" – stand there, or be there, just taking it?' It was one of those careless, throwaway remarks but now that I had to think about I replied:

'Yes, I do, actually. Women mostly want to be made love to.'

'And men?'

'Their pleasure is incidental, it's a by-product of satisfying women.' Did I really believe that? I had not thought about it before, and to be honest I didn't want to have to think about it now. I had serious conversations to pursue.

We chatted through the first courses catching up with what the other was doing. Having been a whiz-kid and taken on before turning seventeen, and because his organisational skills and leadership qualities had been recognised – rare in one so young – he had risen speedily in the hierarchy of sound technicians. More, his innovatory talents had been discovered, surprising not only his superiors but himself as well.

'You know those cartoons,' he explained, 'where a goofy dog races through a room and knocks over a valuable vase and it smashes to pieces on the floor and then he says, this goofy dog, something like ". . . Er, gee, doh, doh, doh – let's do that again," and the sequence is played backwards with all the pieces of the vase flying together? Well, I'm a bit like that, I walk into a room or a situation and all the pieces of the vase fly together again. No matter how tidy or organised it is I can see at once the disorder, the pieces that don't make sense where they are, the people who aren't working together, who aren't saying the right things, who aren't *doing* the right things, and like that vase flying back into shape I can see how the room, the situation, the words and actions can fly into shape.'

I was mesmerised. I was also sceptical. If what he was saying was true then he was a goldmine for whoever employed him.

'You make your skills sound like the properties of an automaton from outer space,' I told him. 'Aren't you ever wrong? Don't you ever find you're fixing what doesn't need fixing?'

'Of course!' Even his admission of failure inspired confidence. 'It's a bit like – well, I was working on a TV programme last week, an interview with a painter. And we were filming him talking about what he was painting as he painted it. And there was one painting that he talked about saying that although he didn't know where the first stroke was going to be placed yet he knew pretty much where he wanted to go *after* he had painted the first few strokes. But with this painting that we were filming it wasn't coming out as he had wanted it to come out. He had an image in his head but he couldn't make his hand follow what he saw in his mind's eye. That's what happens to me sometimes. I see the shape of the vase as it should be but sometimes I don't always find the parts, or I put the right parts in the wrong place. I think, yeah, that part belongs there to make the shape I see in my head, but it doesn't. So, it goes wrong. Yeah, sometimes I get it very wrong.'

Where *did* this boy, this wunderkind, spring from? My instincts were right. He was just who I needed for my enterprise. I explained. He had his skill, I had mine. I was born to make other people's ideas work, and I needed someone at my side.

'The world,' I said, 'is divided into those who have ideas and those who don't.'

'Or those who make ideas work and those who can't,' he echoed, like a musical response for which I'm sure there's a musical term but I couldn't name it.

'Can't or don't,' I completed his thought. I explained my plans.

'I'm working for a business consultancy at the moment.'

'What's that?' he asked.

'Oh, businesses come to us and say they're having problems and we help solve them.'

'What sort of problems?'

'All sorts. Profits have been dropping – we identify where the leak is. Shareholders feel they're being screwed by their executives – they ask us to check it out.' Lee asked for examples. He wasn't content with generalities; he wanted specifics, concrete examples that he could visualise, like his vase. I gave him a current one.

'You know how everybody loves a certain kind of shop – a stationery shop, a tool shop, soap and perfume shops, a deli shop with lots of cheeses in the window? Deli-shop-lovers *have* to go inside and taste things. They need their tastebuds satisfied. They're also on the lookout for new tastes to take home and surprise their lovers or families with. Then there are those who can't stop buying tools because they have fantasies about all the shelves they're going to put up, or the furniture they're going to make. I used to have a passion for stationery shops. I once thought I'd be a writer and that all those white pages would inspire me. I loved the feel of pen and ink going over the soft sheets, sometimes white, sometimes coloured. And I'd buy each new gadget. You're too young to remember how the large heavy staplers began taking on smaller and smaller shapes; and then they devised that little gadget with four prongs that took out the staples from the documents we'd mistakenly stapled. I used to break my fingernails before that little device was invented.' I asked him did he have a favourite stationery gadget. He didn't.

'I'm into sound gadgets, remember?' he said.

He had been listening intently. I had watched him gazing at me, taking in everything, patiently waiting for me to come to the point. I didn't want to come to the point. I just wanted to come, to eat him there and then, to cease talking, to wrap him in an embrace. No man had ever affected me this way. Man? He was a boy, a mere boy.

I forced myself to continue.

'My favourite gadget was the "super clip", spelt of course S-U-P-A, a small metal clamp you shoot out of a dispenser with a spring inside. It clamps thick documents together. The normal paperclips twisted out of shape but this little device was simple and satisfyingly effective. Anyway, the compact stationer was more attractive than the large stationers like W. H. Smith but they couldn't compete with Smith who could cut down prices because of their ability to bulk-buy. Along come a couple of brilliant young business brains who could see the attraction of the small stationer – like the attraction of the corner grocery shop – and they established a nationwide network to which little stationers were invited to join as a member shareholder of a mutually owned chain run for the benefits of its members. Each shareholder could own only one share for which they had to pay £25. The chain was called "Paper Lovers", and the whole enterprise flourished. Five hundred Paper Lovers came into existence and provided pleasant incomes for the families who ran them.

'One day the shareholders, the owners of their beloved little shops, received a letter saying that their £25 share was now worth £2,500, and that they were going to receive that amount because the chain was being bought out for £7.5million by an Irish paper manufacturer who wanted to diversify. Wonderful! An unexpected £2,500. A windfall! But in order to receive it the chief executives were asking those five hundred shareholders to vote for the merger to go through. Few worked out the sums, but some did: 2,500 × 500 was £1.25 million. What was happening to the other £6.25 million? The suspicious shareholders came to us for advice. We found the other £6.25 million. It was being shared out by four greedy executives who had run the enterprise efficiently but were taking roughly £1.5 million each, which compared to the £2,500 offered to each shareholder was not a distribution in the spirit of mutuality. The idea of lots of small shopkeepers pulling together was lost, ignored, dispensed with. The greedy little pigs couldn't resist rich pickings. We leaked the news to the press who named names, and the four chief executives backed down and went home with their tails between their legs and only £300,000 apiece instead of £1.5 million – we're talking round figures here.'

'And the shop owners,' Lee calculated, 'had £12,600 each instead of £2,500.'

It was not simply that his blue eyes shone with intelligent attention, but that he had calculated the sum so quickly.

'How did you do that?' I asked.

'Do what?' he offered me an innocent, I-don't-know-what-you're-talking-about look.

'Work that sum out so quickly, what each shop owner had instead of the original £2500.

'I've got that sort of brain,' he replied. And I believed him. I didn't think to test him with other figures as Dustin Hoffman had been tested in that film *Rain Man* where he played the autistic brother alongside Tom Cruise, and could work out the answers to the addition, multiplication and division of fantastic figures. Had I tested him I could not have been surprised by what he later revealed. I was just too centred on what I had asked him to dinner for.

'Sounds like an exciting job,' he said, 'why cut adrift and sail alone?'

'I don't want to sail alone,' I replied, 'I want you to sail with me.'

'We're talking round figures here.' He smiled at me. 'One, two, even three, it's still "alone".' He saw and read the way I was looking at him. 'We'll make love later,' he said sipping his coffee and chewing a chocolate mint.

'Not sure I can wait,' I said.

'You'll have to. I want to know more.' A boy! A mere boy! 'Tell me why you're leaving such a job that's *got* to be financially rewarding . . .'

'It is, it is.'

'. . . and professionally gratifying . . .'

'It is, it is. Let's go now.'

'Behave!' He was only acting stern but even as playfulness it was a stern tone that commanded attention. I found myself thrilling to it. Me, who always had to be in control, in command, the one giving orders, the one wanting to get things done, no monkeying around.

'All right,' I said, 'another story. Shorter.'

'I hope so!' He smiled a smile that said everything: that he wasn't really being stern and that he, too, wanted soon to leave for bed and better times.

'One of our jobs is to help business executives who are in dispute with their companies. It's not something we encourage or pursue. We prefer to deal with, and help, the company not the individual. We made an exception in this case because the

executive concerned was also a shareholder. Not a major shareholder but a substantial one. The dispute doesn't matter. The
point of this story is other. The organisation was a large advertising one which has among its clients the makers of soaps,
shampoos, detergents, body sprays, bleach – you look in your
kitchen cupboard or along the bathroom shelves, or in the boot-
polish and Hoover cupboard under the stairs, and they're
responsible for most of what you see. A multibillion-pound
worldwide outfit, so we had to tread very carefully since his
group was one that we might one day want to do business with.
Unlikely, since they've been around for over a hundred years and
are not likely to get into any difficulty *we* could help them with.
As you can guess, this bloke was high-powered and responsible
for a lot of words on a lot of billboards and newspaper pages but
he'd been dismissed because sales had dropped. We talked about
the effectiveness and limitations of advertising, and I expressed
the view that the hype was counter-productive. "All advertising
for shampoo, whatever brand," I told him, "sounds the same.
Not one of them stands out. Leave out the brand name and they
could be referring to any one of themselves." He agreed. "That's
the problem. They dismissed me for not coming up with anything new." I told him I'd love to see an advert for shampoo that
simply said: "Forget the hype, just use it!" Nothing else. Brand
name shampoo followed by "Forget the hype, just use it!"
Repeated again and again on TV and on huge billboards – eight
words in an expanse of white space. Open your newspaper, your
woman's magazine – eight words: brand name shampoo –
"Forget the hype, just use it!" It could become a catchphrase, I
told him, people would say it to each other, give orders to each
other: "just use it". We advised him not to sue his organisation,
and put him in touch with another who promptly employed
him and – guess what?'

Either this boy loved looking at me or I told stories better than
ever I had ever imagined I could. Or, more likely, the way he
looked at me inspired my narrative skills. I've only ever lectured

on a few occasions – to girls just leaving college, advising them how to think about their future. I'm not normally that good at it but I soon discovered the important trick of finding an attentive and sympathetic face in my audience to whom I could address my words as though they were only for her. So it was with Lee. I loved telling him my stories. He made me feel like an oracle. It's the one way to a woman's heart – make her feel intelligent because most of the time most of us feel we're not.

'I can't guess,' said the enraptured boy.

'Can't guess what?' I'd forgotten what I'd asked him to guess.

'You put him in touch with another organisation, and guess what?'

I told him: 'Months later I saw adverts all over the place for a brand of shampoo that said: "Forget the hype, just use it!" The bastard had stolen the idea.'

'So you *do* have ideas,' he said.

'It wasn't mine,' I told him.

'Whose was it, then?' he asked.

'A friend's – or rather a college acquaintance – I'd bumped into. She was bursting with ideas and that was one of them and she'll think me a thief from hell when she sees it but that's how I came to understand that my role in life was to help other people put their ideas into practice and – it's no good, come!' I raised my hand for the bill.

'Why didn't you phone her?' My boy was meticulous. I had to lower it again.

'I lost her phone number.'

'She won't believe you.'

'She will. I'm an honourable woman and it shines through. Come, I can't wait any longer.' I called for the bill, and was about to pay it without checking, for what did it matter if they had got it wrong, I had got it right, here at my side, and soon between my legs, but he said:

'Whoa! Let's check. Always check the bill.'

'You check,' I suggested. I wanted to watch him check. I

wanted to watch him do everything. I just wanted to gaze and gaze at him. He checked.

'What's this item for?' he asked the waiter. The waiter looked.

'Your glass of water.'

'My *what*?'

'One of you had a glass of water.'

'From the tap. It was a jug of water from the tap. Not bottled.' The waiter was the impatient kind who had been a waiter too long and had seen too much.

'Speak to the manager.' Lee did just that. I was mesmerised. I was confrontational but not with waiters. Arguing restaurant bills hinted at tight-arsed natures protecting pennies. It embarrassed me. But not, curiously, with Lee. He was my protector, my knight. He stood tall and spoke with an authority that transformed the features of his young face so that he looked ten years older.

'I am not,' he adamantly told the manager, 'paying for a glass of tap water.' He looked and sounded awesome, but the manager was more experienced, and knew how to deflate my boy's confidence with a salacious upper cut.

'It doesn't seem to me that you were going to pay for anything.' He had caught me with my chequebook in hand, and was able to identify our relationship as what, it has to be admitted, it was: older woman younger man. I didn't care, and my 'toy boy' didn't flinch.

'I'm not going to let my girlfriend pay for a glass of tap water, either.' I thrilled to hear him describe me as his 'girlfriend', but the manager was not going to let go of this young man whose youth and handsomeness I could see from his narrow eyes he resented.

'Let me enlighten you about the way of the world, young man,' he began. 'I buy water from the Thames Water Authority. I buy the glasses that the water is served in. I buy the ice that goes in the water. I buy the labour to serve the water, and I provide the luxury surroundings for the water to be drunk in, and then again

I pay for the labour and washing materials to wash the glass after you have used it. And you think I should provide all of this for free?'

It was an impressive little speech. I could see the other customers had been listening and, like them, I was anxious about my boy's response. He thought for what seemed like minutes but was in fact seconds, maintaining a stern, controlled confidence throughout. I could see that even the manager was eagerly waiting for a response.

'Pay the bill,' Lee instructed me gently. As I wrote out the cheque he reached for his wallet and looked around counting the customers. There were twenty of them. He waved two pound notes and said loudly:

'Your tap water is on me, folks.' He lifted an ashtray off the counter, placed the notes on the surface and slammed down the ashtray. I took his hand, pulled him through the restaurant door to my car and drove to my flat as though I was an addict of some sort, and only home sweet home contained that which could assuage my need, satisfy my hunger, calm my fires and permit me to breathe freely for I was choking with desire as never before.

22

This is about two eighteen-year-old boys

This is about two eighteen-year-old boys who fragmented my life; intelligent, cultured, attractive personalities who committed something from which they may never recover. I have built up their characters and recreated their thoughts from talking with them. I must become their amanuensis in the hope that I can put the parts together again.

Castle College in Norwich is a sixth-form college to which the brightest from schools around, having secured their O levels, now needed two years to study for those A levels securing which would open up the gates of university and a purposeful life. There were three such colleges in and around the city. Castle College was the one most applied to, mainly because the principal had created an extra curricular programme of both sporting and artistic events. Students entering the building sensed that something interesting was about to happen at every or any moment of the day. Not only sports events like tennis tournaments and athletic competitions, or arts events such as concerts, recitals, plays and musicals, but also lectures given by students themselves on any topic or theme of their choice – to do with their studies or not.

He encouraged debates around current events: the recent death of Jean-Paul Sartre – was he right to reject the Nobel Prize? What did that say about the Colombian novelist Gabriel García Márquez, who accepted? And there were readings from those who were poets or considered themselves poets. The scientists and sportsmen were encouraged to sing in the choir and declaim Shakespeare on stage; the musicians, singers and actors were encouraged to run or play badminton. Future political leaders were hinted and glimpsed at; potential Oscar winners tested and proved their passions in the glare of spotlights. Unusual of all, perhaps uncharacteristically so for the English, was the generosity of spirit that abounded. Mockery and derision were frowned upon. The pupils all seemed to know the extent to which they needed one another, and were there with praise and encouragement, which in turn bred the qualities of courtesy and respect overspilling into other areas of behaviour. '*That one there's a Castle girl, I bet she'll help you carry your bags to the bus station.*' I wished such an A-level college had existed in my day. I might have been a more rounded personality instead of just 'round' – Rubenesque though it is described.

As can be imagined the brightest and most talented of Norfolk's youth inhabited the rooms and corridors of Castle College where the buzz of young humanity animated and announced the shape of things to come. Nor were the youngsters only from the rich or the middle classes. The principal – one of those inspired heads of institutions who make the best happen – scoured the towns and villages around talking and prying, hoping to discover genius among the sugar beet, and though he found no genius he did find talent and skills that he kept an eye on and guided in his direction. Lads and lasses from Castle College, recognisable at once for their bright eyes, fluent conversation and courtesy, were welcomed in all major universities.

The parents of Paul Zynowski and Solomon Beales were the proud, attentive and ambitious parents many young people envy their friends having. Father Zynowski, head of the best and most exotic bakery in Norwich, was the son of a Polish airman who hinted he descended from Polish aristocracy, and a gentle Norfolk mother who had died two years ago. Certainly the grandfather added to his grandson's sense of his place in the world, and complemented the virtues imbued by Castle College with an even deeper sense of honour.

Paul talked all the time, during our shared ordeal, of his sense of honour; not only of honour but of joy. His voice was deep. I imagined him singing church hymns in rich baritone tremors. It was a passionate voice, reckless; a voice that seduced. Women become vulnerable before such plumy cadences. The Poles, he claimed, knew how to enjoy life. His rundown of national characteristics was a little stereotypical. The Poles were joyous but the French were too narcissistic, while the Germans were humourless unless their laughter was prompted by the misfortune of others. The Americans were too in love with 'the bitch-goddess success' to know real joy, while the English were kind but bewildered to discover the rest of the world could get on without them. As for the Jews, with whom the Poles had a thousand years of history before allowing them to be slaughtered, they were too melancholy (surprise surprise). But the Poles had a capacity to generate joy, and despite that Paul's Polish blood was both once removed and mixed with the Viking blood of the Fens, he claimed those qualities of honour and joy.

Solomon Beales in complete contrast came from parents one of whom, mother Beales, was a brilliant intellect; the father, a painter. Both their qualities were marred by an eccentricity that resulted in a Bohemian home ambience bordering on squalor. There was nothing juicy about the way Solomon spoke. He, unlike Paul, didn't resist the Norfolk twang. Norfolk dialect is ungrammatical, Solomon loved the English language too much to structure his sentences ungrammatically but the dialect's musicality suited his dry, laconic sense of humour. It was probably Solomon and his sister, Sadie, who stemmed the waves of chaos their parents were constantly making. Like so many households the children rebelled against what they found at home. Had the Beales parents – whose ancestry went back into Fen country for centuries – been neat and orderly then no doubt Solomon and Sadie would have been untidy children. As it was they were thrown together in a battle to create order out of chaos, an order which did not prevent their emotional lives entering chaos. Solomon and Sadie were lovers, and had been since Sadie turned eleven and Solomon ten. Close from an early age as brother and sister, the physical relationship seemed to them a natural one beginning inevitably as curiosity, and moving gradually into fun, then pleasure, and with the passing of the years, into calm need.

It was of course initiated by Sadie. I don't know why, as a woman, I say 'of course'. It's to do with female determination. I recognise it. Women cannot understand why as soon as a need, emotional or practical, presents itself it shouldn't be explored, acted upon. Men are indecisive, as we often complain. If murder has to be committed then Lady Macbeth will ensure it happens; if lovemaking is in the air it is the woman who will let it be known her lips are ready, the man fears rejection; if a house has to be sold the wife, knowing men hate change, will find the new house to encourage the change; if a relationship must end it will be she who moves away. Life and literature are full of examples. And so it did not surprise me when Solomon described their first steps into incest. After our ordeal Solomon became unnerved, and chaos swam back into their sibling lives severing parts of themselves they were never able to fit together again.

Solomon and Paul were drawn to one another the instant they met in the college canteen. Both arrived in the queue for food at the same time, and both stepped back at the same time to usher the other ahead. After two or three '*No, you*', '*No, you, please*', '*No, you were here first*', '*No, it was a split-second difference*' Solomon stepped forward.

'Thanks.'

'Was that,' asked Paul, 'a battle of wills or a manifestation of politeness?'

'I was brought up chaotically,' replied Solomon, 'but politeness was a "must" in our household.'

'Honour and politeness was a must in ours, too.' He extended his hand. 'Paul Zynowski.'

'Any relation to Zynowski the baker?'

'My dad.'

'Best bread in Norwich.'

'I know. My dad will travel to the other side of the globe to pick up a recipe for bread.'

'Why can't he just read the recipe?' Solomon asked.

'He has to *see* how they do it. A perfectionist, my dad.'

'And your mother?'

'Dead.'

'I'm sorry.'

'Two years ago. Your mother?'

'Very un-dead,' replied Solomon.

'Wait,' said Paul, 'something's missing. I gave you my name but you didn't give me yours.'

'Solomon. Solomon Beales. Yes, I know, my Christian name doesn't match my surname. That tells you everything about my mother – she teaches philosophy. Or rather she tutors it. Privately. She's very bohemian, my mother, wouldn't fit into university life.'

'And she called you Solomon because she wanted you to be wise like Solomon.'

'You've got it!'

'And your dad?'

'A painter.'

'A good painter?'

'*I* think so, but the galleries don't.'

They bonded instantly. Of course I don't report this conversation as it actually took place. I've reconstructed it from what they told me. But I pride myself it's mostly accurate. I was very alert indeed when they were describing these things to me.

As they moved from sixteen into seventeen into eighteen they discovered other qualities in common, and they shared experiences giving them even more in common – especially when Paul passed his driving test and inherited his first car. They drove all over Norfolk occasionally straying into Suffolk visiting the stately homes in which the counties abounded. Framlingham Castle with its thirteen towers; Oxburgh Hall, a fifteenth-century moated manor house with its display of embroidery done by Mary Queen of Scots; Houghton Hall near King's Lynn was a favourite because of its model-soldier collection, though they confessed to me they quarrelled over it. Paul loved the exquisite details of costume and armour; Solomon considered Paul's pleasure in toy soldiers rather puerile but agreed to the three trips they made to the Hall because he was intrigued by the recreated battles. He was torn between disgust for the idiocy of men killing each other and admiration for the tactics of battles and the logistics involved organising them. They visited exhibitions in Kings Lynn, Ipswich, Great Yarmouth, and Norwich Cathedral, and particularly enjoyed the Georgian Assembly House in Norwich where they usually ended up eating after a Saturday's excursion, and talked over what they'd seen that day.

'What really gets me,' said Solomon after they'd seen the Queen of Scots tapestry, 'is the attention to detail and all the time spent in making artefacts. I mean you look at costumes through the ages, at all that cutting out and threading together, at the lace and the frills and the dye and the cloth itself and you think: someone's spent hours and days and weeks doing all that. And the armour; all that production of metal and the beating into shape; and they didn't only produce practical weapons, they decorated them as well! I find museums represent such a wealth of human ingenuity and endeavour – leaves me breathless.' Paul shared his admiration for human effort – as I have to confess I do. It's what contributed to making our shared ordeal more bearable – we discovered much in common.

'I first had thoughts like that,' he said, 'when my dad took me on my first aeroplane trip. To Italy. We flew over terraced vineyards and cultivated fields and villages on hilltops, and I thought – all that planning ahead, all that patience waiting for the grapes to ripen or the corn, or the olives and lemons, all that human effort. Mind-boggling!'

But they had their disagreements, too. Some of the stately homes they agreed were beautiful, others they were divided over. Solomon had a weakness for the ornate, Paul for the spare. Solomon considered the ornate – not to be confused with the ostentatious – an expression of delight in detail. Paul viewed the spare as an honest choice of essentials.

All this I learnt about them during our shared ordeal, and relate it because I hope one day to be able to reconcile what they did with who they were. At the moment I cannot do this.

As with all friends they developed rituals. Before the days of Paul's car they cycled everywhere. They would start at eight in the morning and stop two hours later for a full fry-up breakfast. This would obviate the need for a big lunch, a ploughman's usually, leaving them ready by four in the afternoon to look for a cafe offering 'a cream tea', for which they awarded marks one to five for the scones. The scones made or broke 'a cream tea' for them – lightness, taste, texture, did it crumble when the knife spread the cream? Was it the right size to enable you to take a bite of scone, cream and jam in one mouthful? Was the jam from a shop or homemade? They would write to the cafe telling them what marks they had awarded.

The ritual that couldn't be missed at any cost was the exchange over a meal in the Assembly Rooms of one news item that had, more than any other, grabbed their attention during the week of whatever nature. Solomon carried one such news cutting around with him. It touched on a topic about which he had developed a theory, and so he was focusing on news items that supported his theory: that all revolutions and coups, whether of the right or left, end by slaughtering their artists and intellectuals. This was from a *Sunday Times* report of 14 June 1981. He read it out during our hours together. I don't quote it all, just a relevant passage. It was about a military coup in Guatemala supported by the CIA.

> . . . More serious for the future of the country is the full-scale killing of the liberal, educated elite, considered by the right wing to be subversive . . . After the murder of 136 university teachers and professors at the National University of San Carlos in the capital in the past eighteen months the university is virtually paralysed. 'I consider the university to be the life breath of the guerrillas,' a highly placed colonel told a local academic. About 70 elementary teachers have been killed, 36 this year alone, and scores more are leaving rural areas in terror . . .

Solomon was now researching the Chinese so-called cultural revolution in which artists and academics had been sent into the fields to work and die as a lesson to those who 'thought themselves superior to the working class'.

'One day,' he said, 'I'm going to write a film script about the three black leaders of the Haitian Revolutions.' He explained how the eighteenth-century Haitian revolutions fell into three parts each headed by one of three men – Toussaint Louverture, Jean-Jacques Dessalines, and Henri Christophe. And he saw each phase as typical of all revolutions since. 'Revolutions,' said Solomon, 'begin with idealism, move into victory and a brief period of virtuous change, then they turn sour and end in tyranny.'

It all began when Solomon discovered that his father had once filed away newspaper clippings, sometimes whole sheets of news items. One was the complete page of the *Times* for Friday 31 December 1976 that listed a '*Diary of the Year*'. I later looked it up. It was indeed fascinating. I quote at random.

3 January: The worst gales and floods in thirty years caused millions of pounds of damage in Britain and at least fourteen deaths in Europe.
4 January: Five Roman Catholics were killed by gunmen in Ulster.
5 January: Ten Protestants were massacred in south Armagh; more

troops from England were sent to the area.

7 January: In Beirut, Palestinians successfully launched an offensive against the Christians; over 8,000 dead and nearly 18,000 wounded.

12 February: Thanks to a vigilant passenger, a 20lb bomb was defused at Oxford Circus station.

15 February: The Tate Gallery exhibited 120 bricks in a pile designed by Carl Andre.

1 March: Mr Alexander Solzhenitsyn, interviewed on Panorama, feared 'The sudden and imminent fall' of the West.

13 April: British Petroleum and Shell admitted that their Italian subsidiaries had made payments totalling 3.3 million pounds to Italian political parties.

9 May: Ulrike Meinhof, leader of German terrorists, hanged herself in prison in Stuttgart.

24 May: British and French Concorde made their first commercial London/Paris–Washington flights in just under four hours.

16 June: Mr F. Melay, American Ambassador in Lebanon, was murdered in Beirut.

20 July: The American space aircraft Viking landed on Mars and began transmitting photographs.

26 August: Following an enquiry into allegations of bribery by the Lockheed Aircraft Corporation, Prince Bernhard of the Netherlands resigned all his posts.

4 September: Headed by Mrs Betty Williams and Miss Mairead Corrigan 25,000 Protestants and Catholic peace-lovers marched in Londonderry.

3 October: In the German election, Dr Helmut Kohl was narrowly defeated by Herr Helmut Schmidt.

11 November: President Sadat of Egypt abolished the single-party system.

11 December: Señor Oriol, Spanish President of Council, was kidnapped.

20 December: A literary hoard, including Byron and Shelley manuscripts, was uncovered in Barclays Bank's vaults, London.

One day Paul arrived with a cutting about a fatal rape of the wife of a wealthy businessman by two electricians whom the couple had engaged to wire their house for floodlighting but to whom they had not paid the agreed bill in full. The businessman had told them he would pay the bill less the ten per cent he knew they had added because it was normal practice to add 10% knowing the customer would ask for that 10% to be taken off. That was the way all business was conducted. The two electricians told him they didn't conduct business that way, and demanded their bill to be paid in full. The businessman, used to having his own way, had told them they had learnt a lesson and would add ten per cent next time. The electricians learnt nothing of the sort. On the contrary they thought they would teach the businessman a lesson – you fuck with us we'll fuck with you, in the literal sense of the word. Only not with him but with his wife one weekend when they knew he would be away. His wife, though in her mid-fifties, was, as might be expected, an elegant and handsome woman whom they both agreed they had fancied though had no intention of pursuing even though they detected the beginnings of a lascivious smile on her face now and then while working round the house. The rape would be easy, therefore, they guessed. She would put up no resistance. Like so many men, the dazzling Derek for example, they had misjudged. They did not encounter a woman surrendering to dreams of rough trade but one who fought them violently. She suffered from a weak heart, and died after the indignity of two entries. They left traces of themselves all over the house as only those who knew the house intimately could have done. They were sentenced to five years each for rape with violence, and a further fifteen years each for manslaughter.

'Why have you cut out a news item about rape, for God's sake?' Solomon asked. 'It's a terrible story but it holds no significance about anything except male stupidity and bad luck.'

Paul disagreed. 'It holds a lot of significance. About crime and punishment, for starters. About how much blame lies with the husband, for seconds. If he had honoured his bill his wife would still be alive. And then there's the question of choice. They could have chosen to burgle the house rather than rape the wife. Why did they choose one rather than the other? Then there's the wife – did she or did she not cast flirtatious looks at the electricians? Had they been led on? And why did they choose to take revenge at all rather than leave it alone and learn a lesson for next time?'

They discussed and argued over the questions Paul had raised, until the perceptive Solomon said:

'I detect another reason for your interest in this story.'

Paul took a long time to respond, as though uncertain how this friend would react to what he was about to say. Finally he said: 'Rape intrigues me.'

'Intrigues you? *Intrigues*? That's a strange word to use,' his friend reacted. 'What's "intriguing" about rape? I hope you don't subscribe to the crude male fantasy that the fantasy of all women is to be raped.'

'Nothing as crude as that,' Paul retorted angrily. 'No, I don't believe women fantasise about being raped, or rather some may fantasise but wouldn't really want to experience it. Though,' he added, 'we all know about the pleasurable relief of having decisions taken away from us, which I suppose is part of that fantasy.'

'But even then,' said Solomon, 'the actual experience must be awful. Those brutal, insensitive hands all over you. And isn't language part of lovemaking? What words can a lumpen mentality utter – because of course the rapist would be lumpen.'

'But what,' asked Paul, 'if he wasn't?'

'Wasn't?'

'Wasn't lumpen. What if he possessed the power of language, what if his hands weren't brutal and insensitive, what if his main concern was to delight her, please her, be tender to her? What if he wanted to introduce her to a level of pleasure she'd never before experienced? What if she was a virgin and we gave her an experience that would set a standard for her? What if she were a bored wife with a disgusting husband and we introduced her to the possibility of an alternative so that she became determined to leave him and lead a new life with a new partner?'

Solomon was open-eyed and open-mouthed.

'Have you noticed what you're saying?' he demanded. 'Have you noticed how your words have changed from "what if he" to "what if *we*?"'

Paul ignored him as if driven by an inner demon. 'I don't believe women dream of rape but I'm intrigued to know how they would respond once they realised that no brutality was involved. How would they respond to a beautiful rape?'

'There's no such thing,' his friend protested, adding, 'and stop using the collective "we". I don't know what you're planning but leave me out of it.'

Paul said simply: 'Think about it. We'll stop talking now. But think about it. No violence, no brutality, but something sweet, a giving not a taking, her gratification not ours. Is it possible? Think about it. We'll talk again.'

They did. I am not yet ready to write about what happened.

23

Barney was seriously debating with himself

Barney was seriously debating with himself whether to continue with his biography of Giovanni Marcantonio when the telephone rang.

'Yes,' he said, never giving the number.

A plaintive voice asked: 'Can I come round, Dad?' It was the other daughter, Natasha.

'What are you asking for? Come! You all right? Come! I'm here. You hungry? Want me to take something out of the freezer?'

The twin to Tamara said: 'No, thank you. I'll be there in half an hour.'

'She thinks I'll listen to her?' Barney, like many who lived alone, talked out loudly to himself. Well, sometimes he did and sometimes he just thought he did when in fact he just thought. A fly on the wall would hear a disjointed train of thought, though to Barney it was continuous. He continued, sometimes talking, sometimes thinking. 'Children! Their first instinct is to say "no" to a parent. No matter what. "You hungry?" "No!" "You look tired." "I'm not." "You feeling ill?" "I'm fine." "How was school today?" "OK." What's "OK"? What does it mean, this "OK"?'

Barney looked through his freezer. Since Tina's death he had been forced to cook for himself. Nothing haute cuisine, just basics – meat sauces for pasta, chicken and rice dishes, and Jewish dependables like fish fried in egg and medium matzo meal, chopped liver and onion, chopped hard-boiled eggs, with crème fraiche and mustard cress, and barley soups. He enjoyed cooking. He couldn't invent but he was a faithful recipe-follower. Nor was he in the cooking mood every day, so he always cooked more than he needed to store away in his freezer for times such as these – a daughter coming unexpectedly. He searched. 'Soup. She can't say no to a plate of chicken soup. And *lockshen* – have I got *lockshen*?' He meant vermicelli. 'Lockshen', unlike other Yiddish words such as 'chutzpah' and 'shlep' and 'shmuck', hadn't yet entered the English language. He found a box of *lockshen*. He was a 'maybe' shopper as well as a 'maybe' cook. He bought for 'maybe' occasions.

'You never know who's coming, who may ring up from here or there. I wrote a glowing review of a Russian pianist and she rings up to say "thank you" – something she hasn't yet been advised not to do – and I say "You're welcome, come over for lunch." Or Manfred drops by. Or a fellow critic. Someone. You never know. So be prepared for "maybes", I think.'

Barney took out the plastic box labelled 'Chicken soup' – he always labelled and dated his 'maybe' stocks – and placed it in the microwave switched to 'defrost', but once he defrosted he didn't immediately put it on to heat. He knew his daughter. She was a bad timekeeper. She said half an hour but he knew she wouldn't be there for an hour at least, and how long does it take to heat up soup? He would put it on when he heard the doorbell ring or a few minutes before he sensed her arrival, which he was good at – sensing. Didn't he know his daughter? 'Don't I know my daughter? Whatever she says she'll be grateful to have a hot plate of soup waiting, ready, like a greeting.'

It was strange, this inability to keep time. It was a family trait. He had cousins who couldn't keep time, and he had a couple of friends, husband and wife, who split up because *she* couldn't keep time. She'd be the last one to arrive and the last one to leave. Finally the husband couldn't stand it any longer. He would arrive from his work to attend a dinner party and she would arrive an hour later leaving the hosts uncertain whether to wait or feed the rest of their guests. He would always advise to eat.

'I've never understood,' Barney mumbled to himself. 'Someone invites you at such and such a time, you have to make calculations. This long to shave and shower, that long to dress, to make up, to travel in a bus, an underground, the car. You've been alive a long time, you know these things, you should be able to calculate these things. But people! Funny creatures, people. They leave things to the last minute. I always try to teach them, my twins: be on time! You keep people waiting it's like an insult. "But who can foresee the unexpected hold-up?" my Natasha says. "So you allow for it!" I tell her. "That's life! You always allow for the unexpected. Like driving a car – you always calculate the other driver is a dangerous idiot." She didn't. Lovely girl, do anything for you – except be on time.

'And you've forgotten,' said Tina from her place of rest, 'she always lost her watch.'

'It's true,' Barney said, looking at the photograph of his wife that occupied a large part of the wall behind his desk.

'I've lost count of the number of times she asked for a watch as a present.'

'I remember,' said Barney. 'What did it mean? She lost time and she lost watches.'

'I have a theory,' Tina said. 'She didn't want to be dictated to. Time is a dictator – it's a framework within which certain things *must* be done or else. "Or else" – that's a threat.'

'You're right, sweetheart,' he said to the photograph, which seemed to change each time he looked at it. 'Natasha never wanted to succumb to threats.'

'Never!' Tina sounded proud as she spoke of her beloved daughter. 'She was a sixties kid – no one was going to dictate to her and tell her what to do.'

'Not even time, which waits for no man.'

'Or woman.'

'Or child.' They had become an harmonious team now that they were apart.

'Tamara on the other hand always listened.'

'You're right, sweetheart.'

'She always understood that time was a thief who could steal your life while you weren't looking.'

Barney wept a little. 'And you're so clever, Tina,' he told her.

'On the other hand,' warned Tina, 'pay attention to the quiet ones. I always say, the quiet ones, pay attention to them.'

'I miss you,' said Barney.

The father's estimate was correct. The daughter arrived an hour and ten minutes after her call. Hot soup was waiting.

'Mmm, lovely, just what I needed, Dad,' she said as though their earlier conversation had not taken place. Denial, he thought, children live in a constant state of denial, but he was a wise and considerate father who didn't confront his children with their inconsistencies.

'Eat,' he said, 'there's plenty more.' Tina left him alone for now. Was it because she knew what was coming?

'Tell me how the world's divided for you these days?' he asked his slurping daughter.

'The world's divided between men who are Gregs and men who are not Gregs.' Her reply filled him with dread. Her musician boyfriend had not been a source of pleasure for Barney.

'How *is* Greg?' he enquired.

'I don't know,' she replied, greedily slurping down the thin but tasty soup. 'This is good soup, Dad.'

'What do you mean, you don't know?'

'Well, he's not around, is he?'

'He's off on a gig somewhere, you mean?'

'Somewhere.'

'You don't know? He doesn't phone?'

'You know Greg.'

'I know Greg. Too well I know Greg. But he'll be back soon?'

'Not that soon.'

'What do you mean, "not that soon"? How far can he be gone in a country as small as the UK?'

'Who's talking about the UK? More, please? I'll help myself.'

'Take, take!' said her loving father, adding, 'It's like drawing blood out of a stone. Talk to me straight, Natasha, be a good daughter, it's lovely to see you but why have you come? You sounded distressed on the phone.'

Natasha sat down to a second helping of soup as large as the first.

'Greg's in Australia and I'm pregnant,' she announced.

'Go carefully,' said Tina. 'What you say next is very important.'

'What do you want me to say?' Barney asked his wife. His daughter responded.

'Well you could say "mazel tov".'

'I wasn't talking to you,' said her confused father. His daughter was regarding him quizzically. She could see he was deeply affected by her announcement, as she had expected.

'Then who *were* you talking to?'

'Sometimes,' he confessed, 'I hear your mother in my head.'

His daughter responded as though it was the most natural thing in the world, which of course it was: 'What's she saying?'

'She was telling me to go carefully because my immediate response to your news is very important.'

'She's right. What *is* your immediate response?'

'To say I love you.'

'That's all?'

'Ungrateful daughter! You could say "thank you" first.'

'Thank you. That's all?'

'Of course it's not all.' He rose, pulled her up from her chair and gave her a tight hug, kissing her lips, her cheeks, her forehead, and then another hug.

'Enough already.' She pushed him away and returned to her soup, which she was eating more slowly having realised she had taken too large a second portion. 'Now say something.'

'Didn't my embrace say enough?' God! How he loved her, the more so perhaps because he knew she was the less gifted, the less intellectually endowed of the twins, the less resourceful of the two. She had inherited, from who knows which side of the family, a fateful flaw: she assumed the habits and characteristics of those stronger personalities with whom she came in contact. She never sucked her thumb until she became friendly with a thumb-sucking infant in kindergarten. She abhorred smoking until she made friends with an older girl at comprehensive who smoked. Confronted with a boyfriend from Wales she developed a Welsh lilt in her conversation. When her sister, Tamara, brought home a black boyfriend she adopted the slang and cadences of West Indian speech. She was the dearest and kindest of souls who grew into one of those young women about whom the book was written: *Women Who Love Too Much*.

'You know I love your embraces. You and Mum made us very tactile human beings. Now I want your wisdom, not your kisses.' His daughter was serious in a way he had not seen since she was facing puberty.

'You haven't given me enough time to be wise,' he said wisely, 'I've got to get used to the idea of being a grandfather.'

'Who says you *are* going to be a grandfather?'

Her father was shocked. She had shocked her father and he couldn't hide it.

'Go carefully,' said Tina, 'carefully, carefully.' This time he didn't respond to her. Some part of him knew – that way lay madness.

'Natasha! What are you saying? Of course I'm going to be a grandfather. And your mother is going to be a grandmother.'

'Dad, stop that. It frightens me.' He crouched down beside her and took her hand in his.

'I'm sorry, darling, sorry sorry sorry. No upsets while you're

pregnant. I'll stop talking to your mother. I only do it for comfort's sake. I miss her – what can I do?'

'Any drink in the house?' she asked.

'Of course, what am I thinking of. A toast! Forgive me. I'll
open a bottle of champagne.'

'Dad!'

'Well, not champagne perhaps but a good sparkling white wine
from Spain.'

'Dad! I don't want a drink for a toast. I want a drink because I
need a drink.'

'All right! All right! I'll give you what you need, but you won't
mind if I raise my glass to the infant.'

'There's not going to be an infant, Dad. I'm going to have an
abortion. I've come here for your blessing and to ask if you'll lend
me some money till I fix myself up with a job. Greg's gone with
our savings, I need money for rent.'

Barney's heart broke that morning. He could only mend it by
giving his daughter all she needed, and more, but he did not want
her to abort his grandchild. Not that. How must he talk her out
of an act she would one day regret? Not by blackmail, not financial aid in return for birth, not emotional blackmail saying how
much, how desperately, he wanted a grandchild. No, somehow
reason, history, precedent must be employed. He had images he
dreaded. Like the one of his only spinster aunt who laughed a lot
until she found herself old and living alone with no children a
long way from anyone. He would tell Natasha about his aunt, her
great-aunt Freyda who died when she, Natasha, was six years old
so she wouldn't remember her.

'Darling,' he said, 'you will have my blessing whatever you do,
and I'll help you with money. Don't worry. And I won't make any
conditions, believe me. Just one. No, two. First, you'll let me say
something. Express an opinion. Talk to you. You'll let me talk to
you. Not orders, not demands, not big daddy talk, simply an old
man's wisdom. I don't have much, just a little, best I can offer,
collected over the years, made up of my own stupid mistakes.'

He moved to retrieve the bottle from the refrigerator in the kitchen. She called after him, defensively.

'You think I'm making a stupid mistake?' He hurried back with the bottle to rectify what damage he might have done with his careless talk.

'No, no!' he explained. 'Did I say that? "Stupid" – did I use this word to you? No, no! I used it about myself. Me! *I* was stupid.'

'And by implication, me.'

Barney tried evasion tactics. 'Here. Open this. My fingers seem to have lost their grip and besides I don't have as much experience opening champagne bottles as you.'

'Another mistake, Barney,' said Tina. 'Watch how she'll leap at you.'

'Why,' asked Natasha, 'do you find every opportunity to make a dig at me?'

'There! Didn't I tell you so?' said Tina. 'Right me or wrong me, that's young women. Watch how they'll pout, go dark, sink into themselves like young tigresses looking for something to leap at and dig their teeth into. They're angry. They don't know why but they're angry. It's a gnawing feeling inside them. Gives them heartburn. Makes them restless. They can't keep still. They have to pace and growl. And every generation is the same, they resemble each other. As one generation grows up, matures, along comes another generation with the same glares, the same discontent, the same angers, the same battles with life. They resent, they glower, they despise the old. Look at her, your daughter, she's simmering, waiting to erupt. She's made mistakes and she can't interpret them. What do they mean? How could she have made them? What do they tell her about herself? She doesn't know. She knows she's lovely and good and capable so it must be the world at fault, or him or her or them. Mystery! Unfathomable! But watch her, Barney. She's not as big a personality as her twin but watch her. Still waters run deep. She'll come to something.'

'Dig?' asked Barney. 'What "dig"? When did I make a "dig" at you?'

'Just now,' said Natasha. 'Saying I have more experience opening champagne bottles than you, thereby implying I drink too
much.'

'What funny daughters I have,' said the bewildered father.

'All parents since time began have funny daughters,' said Tina.

'And the second thing?' asked Natasha. Barney, eager to please,
to pacify, to be better, was confused and had forgotten.

'The second thing?'

'You said you'd help on two conditions. The first was that I
should listen to what you have to say, and the second was what?'

'I remember now,' said Barney. 'The second was that you
should think a little longer, reflect a little more. Look into the
future a bit, just a little way. Don't make hasty decisions. Think it
through.'

He said this last with weak effort, for Barney knew the one
thing this daughter had difficulty doing was thinking things
through. It was why his heart went out to her. She was a kind soul
who acted on impulse.

'Which is lovely,' said Tina, 'don't dismiss impulse and instinct
and spontaneity. I know about these things. But when I was alive
it didn't stop me worrying like crazy about the next thing Natasha
was going to do.'

'I have a story to tell you,' said Barney. 'Will you sit and listen
to my story?'

Natasha nodded. 'I'm listening.'

'I had an aunt, my father's sister, your great-aunt – Freyda. She
was the only other child to come over with my grandparents.
They came with my father and his wife, my mother, that is, and
with this aunt. Aunt Freyda. You'd have loved her. She laughed a
lot and was always doing things for other people. She loved being
needed. Someone like that should have been a doctor or a social
worker or a Member of Parliament. But there! You are what you
can be. She couldn't be any of those things and instead she became
an accountant working for a chain of clothiers. She studied, and
passed exams and rose high to become chief accountant.

'But her heart was never in it. She was a giver. She wanted to give. The only people she could give to were those at work, and it wasn't *real* giving, it was just favours. Babysitting for the young ones, shopping for the old ones. They began to think her a simpleton at work, and if she hadn't been such a whiz at figures, and honest and dependable as well, they'd have got rid of her because she was kind of embarrassing. She was too good to be true, and that's always embarrassing. But she couldn't find a partner, a soulmate, someone of her own to cherish and love, which she was so good at. No man seemed right to her – this one was too meek, this one was too arrogant, that one had dirty habits, this one was too cold-natured. Too silly, too solemn, too selfish, too something or other. No one fitted her shopping list. And it didn't seem to worry her. Outside of work she had a circle of friends who *knew* she wasn't a simpleton. And she rented a good apartment in an Edwardian mansion near Paddington that she filled with pot plants. Gradually she grew older, her energy waned, her friends died one by one and the time came for her to retire. Suddenly she was in her apartment alone. But she still had spirit and she still laughed a lot. And she had a special occupation that engaged her attention, passed the time away for her – she crocheted squares of coloured wool that she sewed together into bed-covers, and gave to people. Only by the end there were fewer and fewer people to give them too, and soon there were none. I used to visit her, and she used to visit us – you've forgotten her, you were too young.

'And then one day she stopped everything. She stopped washing herself, she stopped cleaning her apartment, she barely did any cooking and she paid a neighbour to shop for her. She sat in one armchair in front of her gas fire, and in the other armchair was an unfinished crotched bed-cover. She needed about fifteen more squares to complete it but she wouldn't do them. From one minute to the next she stopped, gave up, her spirit died in her. It happened. Just like that. There was no one in her life and her spirit died.'

'Why are you telling me this now about Aunty Freyda?' his daughter asked, suspiciously.

'Because I have this terrible fear, darling, this numbing dread that you'll end up like your great-aunt – no partner, no children.'

'Jesus Christ, Dad, that's so depressing. Is that how you see me? Someone who'll end up alone with a spirit gone dead?'

'I can't help it,' said Barney. 'You're my daughter. Your mother's dead but I have you and Tamara, and I want you to have your Natashas and Tamaras.'

'Do you have this fear for Tamara?'

'I told you to be very careful,' said Tina, coming back into the situation that Barney knew was becoming fraught and perhaps out of his control. 'And you haven't finished yet, have you? You're going to make it worse.' Barney slapped his head hard.

'What did you do that for?' asked Natasha.

'To get your mother out of my head.'

'What's she saying now?'

'She thinks I'm making a mess of things.'

'Don't worry, Dad, I'll think about what you said.'

'Haven't finished.' Her father looked straight at her to see how she'd take this.

'Then Mum might be right,' said his daughter. 'You might go *on* to make a mess of things.'

'Natasha, before your mum and me got married—'

'Your mum and I.'

'Before your mum and I got married she became pregnant and she had an abortion. It was mutually agreed, we couldn't afford to have a child so soon. Everything was uncertain. It was that period when I was realising I didn't have it in me to be a composer.'

'You agreed Mum should have an abortion but not me? Why? What crazy logic are you going to weave now?'

'No logic, my darling. My feelings are irrational but they're real.' He took a long pause thinking how to shape his next thought. It could misfire and come out maudlin. He opted for simplicity. 'I miss that child. I can't get it out of my head that there was a form in the shape of a boy that came out of your mother. A son. My son. I nearly had a son. As I've grown older I've thought about that son we didn't want, and it makes me weep. We had to do it, I make no moral judgement, it was the right decision for our age, our situation, our emotional state. But I miss that child. It was a life. It haunts me.'

'I'm going, Dad.' Natasha threw her arms around him. She had tears in her eyes.

'I didn't want to make you cry, darling.'

'But you did.' She reached the door.

'Wait,' her father called out, 'you wanted some money.'

'Oh, yeah. I forgot.' He gave her two twenty-pound notes, and next day transferred a thousand pounds into her account.

'You never ever told me how much reparations the Germans paid you, you know that?' said Tina. 'All our married life I never asked you and you never told me.'

'I was ashamed,' said Barney. 'I didn't want their blood money so I didn't want to talk about it.'

'Was it a lot?' asked Tina. 'I mean really a lot?'

'It was enough to take anxiety out of our lives and protect our children.'

Barney turned to his manuscript for which he had no appetite. He was exhausted. His past had exhausted him. Remembering his aunt reminded him that inside us all is a spirit waiting to give up. He realised – he had not been a composer and he was no writer, either. Giovanni Marcantonio would have to wait for a more capable champion. He closed the black plain-sheeted book that was really an artist's sketchbook, and decided he would never open it again.

'I'm sorry,' said Tina, 'I'm so sorry, Barney.'

'You fell out of love with me, who could help it? It happens.'

24

Stan Mann gathered his few friends together

Stan Mann gathered his few friends together. He hadn't gathered them for a long time, but with Beatie visiting he felt the urge to surround himself with folk he thought would enjoy meeting her. Beatie for her part was eager to meet them. Since marching through the gates of St Hilda's everything – people, places, experience – took on a different perspective. Literature had freshened up life for her as rain can cleanse and sharpen the contours of landscape. Those she knew from adolescence were like people she had never met before. She looked forward to Stan's gathering. His 'folk' were only eight people: three couples and two singles – both women, Mavis and Rosalind, intermittent girlfriends of Stan who over the last decades hadn't minded sharing him.

A certain relaxed atmosphere hung over this area of Norfolk. Heavy opinions were exchanged about such things as the condition of the roads, the functioning of the National Health Service, local rate increases, the demise of good neighbourliness; and there fluttered, like a butterfly, the usual amount of sour gossip about

him and her without which no community could operate happily.
Sexual morality, however, was left alone to find its own level like
water. No one minded who made love to whom. Love and let
love was the motto of this part of the Fens south of Norwich. Stan
had his girlfriends, and Stan's nurse visited men in need of her
ministrations. A warm, friendly and not overintense passion pervaded the area. You felt it in the pubs, the shops, in street banter.
'You will enjoy living here,' said the estate agents to house-buyers
from the cities. 'Flat landscapes and wide-open skies.' Anything
could happen beneath such openness.

Stan lived with his nurse, Hilda, in an early Victorian house
once handsome with architectural detail now chipped or heavily
painted out of sight. Neglected though it was, Stan loved and was
proud of where he lived. Beatie, too, had fond memories of her
childhood in the house with the odd name of 'Harry, 1825'. It
was not Stan's name for it, it was there engraved below the fan-
light, on an extra wide horizontal wooden bar of the door frame
known as the transom rail, the place where, over pub doors, were
painted in gold or racing green, words announcing licensing
details. Both the name and where it was engraved were unusual,
and it became a topic of discussion over the lamb stew alongside
which Hilda had piled, Norfolk fashion, boiled potatoes, beans,
peas and carrots, all from Stan's vegetable plot.

'It's the only exercise he gets,' complained his nurse.

'That and washing down my front door,' said Stan.

'Oh, yes. Forgot about his front door,' said Hilda. 'His pride
and joy. Ever heard of anyone whose pride and joy was his front
door?'

One of Stan's ex-girlfriends, Mavis, who worked for a solicitor,
said: 'What I've never understood is the name of the house.
"Harry"? What kind of family, or head of family, could name
their house by the common name of Harry?'

'Nothing common about "Harry",' Beatie corrected.
'Shakespeare had Henry the Fifth refer to himself as "Harry".' She
delivered the lines with a masculine bravura no one recognised:

'*The games afoot: follow your spirit; and upon this charge cry "God for Harry, England, and Saint George."*

The company applauded her. She blushed and protested.

'No, no! That's not me. That's Laurence Olivier, the way *he* delivered his lines in the film he made of *Henry the Fifth*.'

'I saw it,' said Stan. 'Bloody fine film, dubious text.'

'Oh, ho!' declared another of the guests, a jovial man stout from beer. 'Stan's questioning the Bard. Come on, Stan, let's hear you.' The stout man, Gaydon English, was proprietor of the Swan Hotel, a black-timbered Elizabethan building. He had married his cousin, Cynthia Howard, a gentle woman obsessed with her lineage, who had spent years cleverly researching and assembling a family tree. Every name was beautifully handwritten – she had made a study of calligraphy specially for this work of unearthing all the names and professions of ancestors, who included priests, butchers, criminals and aristocracy. Cynthia was a shy lady who needed no profession but who quietly brought up four splendid children. Her husband, the hearty Gaydon, who had just challenged Stan to justify calling the text of *Henry the Fifth* 'dubious', was the founder of the local amateur drama group known as the Swan Players – named after his hotel.

'Always worried me,' said Stan, 'that chauvinist speech before Agincourt, rousing his men to battle – for what? Colonialism, that's for what. To conquer the French. "*On, on you great Englishmen, teach baser men how to war . . .*" or something like that, I don't have Beatie's power of memory.'

Beatie reminded him: "*On, on you noblest Englishmen . . .*"

'That's it! "Noblest Englishmen", not "great Englishmen".'

"*Be copy now to men of grosser blood, and teach them how to war . . .*"

"Teach them how to war". I ask you!' spat out a contemptuous Stan. 'Teach them how to bloody war!'

"*And you, good yeomen,*" Beatie continued. "*whose limbs were made in England, show us here the mettle of your pasture; let us swear that you are worth your breeding . . .*"

"Worth your breeding".' Stan couldn't stop mocking. "Breeding". And didn't the French have "breeding"? Up the bloody English, everyone else is scum.'

'You're missing the point, Stan,' said Beatie.

'And isn't there a speech about how English soldiers will rape your daughters if you don't give in?'

'That wasn't Agincourt,' said Beatie, 'that was at the gates of Harfleur.'

'Remember those lines, can you?' Stan asked.

"*If not, why, in a moment look to see The blind and bloody soldier with foul hand . . .*"

Stan took over: "*Defile the locks of your shrill-shrieking daughters*". I remember that line,' said Stan, 'it came back to me. What a terrifying image: "*your shrill-shrieking daughters*". And there's one about babies, I think.'

"*Your naked infants spitted upon pikes.*"

'That's it! Terrifying! There he is, King bloody Harry, threatening the unimaginable. Where'd he get all that from if his bloody soldiers hadn't done it before? Murderous bastards, the lot of them. He wouldn't have written like that if he'd actually been in war, old Willy.'

'But isn't that what literature is about?' asked another of the guests in a well-spoken voice. She was Jenny Makepeace, a primary-school teacher from London married to a sullen farmer, Charlie Makepeace. An unhappy match. 'Isn't literature written by people who have the power to imagine what it's like to be someone else, to be some*where* else? You don't have to be a murderer to create a murderer in a novel.'

'No,' said her sullen husband. 'But I bet it helps.'

'I think Stan misses the point of that speech.' Beatie brought them back to Prince Hal before Harfleur. 'It's not that he and his men are a murderous bunch. On the contrary he wants the Governor of Harfleur to surrender because he knows what can happen, and he doesn't *want* it to happen. Once they do surrender he commands one of his noblemen, I can't remember which one, to be merciful to all of the inhabitants.'

'Yes, well, it's easy to be merciful when you know you've got the upper hand.' Stan may have become disenchanted by his experiences in the Spanish Civil War but the reflexes of a Marxist mentality persisted, tinged though it was with the cynicism that had encouraged Beatie to go into business remembering that 'the customer pays for everything'.

By this time the gathering had eaten and drunk and gone through the customary updating exchanges that take place between people who, though they know each other well, meet only occasionally. The third couple were the most eccentric, Kindred and Guinevere Lillywhite. With eccentric names like that, they felt, they might as well go the whole hog. They ran an antique shop selling everything from antique china and gnarled old walking sticks to period clothes in which they dressed up. Their speciality, however, was English silver. Entering their shop was always a surprise since they wore a different outfit each week. Of course the period clothes of, say, the Restoration, were nowhere to be found so they cheated, and attended auctions of period costumes from period films. Thus Guinevere could be Madame de Pompadour one week and Carmen the next.

'What I'm interested in,' said Kindred, 'is your door. I've never noticed it before though now it's come up I can remember always thinking how shiny it is, how polished. Tell us, what's special about it?'

'Look at the grain in it. I wash and polish it daily,' said Stan. 'Did you know that every part of a door is called "a member"?'

'And does each member have a name?' asked Beatie.

'The two uprights are called "stiles".'

'Wait,' said pleaded. 'I want to write them down.' She quickly found a biro and a used envelope.

'Stiles spelt with an "i",' said Stan.

'Go on.'

'And the bars across are called "rails". And the top rail is called a "transom". I have a suspicion,' he continued, 'that this transom, because it's so wide, was added in Victorian times, and I think they made it wide in order to have room for the name and date to be engraved.' He asked Beatie. 'Did you get down "transom"?' She had. 'And why do you want to write it down?'

'I don't know,' said Beatie, enigmatically. 'I've recently discovered an appetite for naming the parts of things.'

'Is that why you wanted to know the names of clouds?' her host asked. Hilda served up apple pie and custard as the sullen voice of Charlie rang out a singsong list.

'Cirrus, stratus, cirrostratus, altostratus, nimbus, cumulus, altocumulus, cirrocumulus, cumulonimbus, stratocumulus.' Everyone was amazed. His wife, Jenny, especially so.

'Charlie! How on earth . . .?'

'Don't ask me,' said Charlie, his sullenness ebbing away to be replaced by a blush of pride. 'I've always known the names of clouds. Like Beatie here remembers bits of Shakespeare I remember cirrus, stratus, cirrostratus, altostratus, nimbus, cumulus, altocumulus, cirrocumulus, cumulonimbus, stratocumulus.'

'But why? How? Since when?' His wife pressed with urgency, as though he had told her he'd had a mistress for most of their married life.

'Since forever. I once wanted to be a meteorologist, and I read up about it and read that to begin with you had to learn the names of clouds. I can't remember if that was during school or after it.' Nothing more came from him, and he lapsed back into sullenness as though the land of gloom was his natural habitat.

During the mmming and ahhing over the apple pie, the crust of which melted in their mouths, Beatie looked around the dining room with renewed interest.

'Do you know the names of the parts of anything else in the house?' she asked, 'That circular shape on the ceiling for instance, does that have a name?'

Kindred stepped in. 'That's called a ceiling medallion,' he said, and having started he continued, 'You see that up there between the top of the wall and the ceiling, that's called a cornice, and those mouldings in the four corners of the room are called crown mouldings, and you know what – I'm looking at this interior as though for the first time. You've made me open my eyes, Beatie, I can now see all sorts of original features I'd not noticed before. Look at the walls, they've got full wainscoting, and beneath it is the skirting board. The cornice was applied to hide the gap between the wall and the ceiling, and the skirting board was applied to hide the gap that developed between the lowere limit of the plaster and the floor.'

'Then what was the wainscot hiding?' asked Beatie busily writing down everything.

'Kindred is in his stride now,' said Guinevere who, by the way, was dressed in a black and red flamenco dress, 'you've set him off.'

'The wainscoting,' said Kindred, 'hides nothing. It serves a different purpose. Look at it, look at the top of it, there's a moulded rail protruding. That's to stop chairs banging against the wall.'

'What's the cornice moulding made of?' asked Beatie. 'Wood?'

'Too expensive,' said Kindred. 'Maybe in Queen Anne's time it was made of wood – walnut or lime tree, but later it became plaster. Fibrous plaster. And the best fibrous plasterers in England were Italian. Now here's a bit of useless information. Useless but fascinating: the Italian plasterers were so sought after and became so wealthy that they were the only craftsmen permitted to walk around with a sword. And that's my limit. All I can talk about from here on is English silver.'

'And he doesn't intend to do that, do you, dear?' warned his flamenco-clad wife, who knew how boring he could become on the subject.

Stan was an exuberant personality who commanded centre space in any gathering. His first dinner party in a long time was no exception, though to his credit 'command' did not spill over into 'dominate'. He conducted his gathering like a sensitive, albeit strong, conductor knowing who to encourage forth and who to calm down and when to bring in the right instrument to colour the whole.

They covered many topics, like the rise of the supermarket – it was before the days of the hyper-market though they were only a few years away – and the way in which high-street shops had lost the battle of competing with them once the Retail Price Maintenance had been abolished thus giving small shopkeepers no protection against undercutting. The economies of bulk-buying were overwhelming.

'Rosalind should know,' said Stan referring to the second of his ex-girlfriends, 'she ran a great little corner grocery shop in Norwich selling deli stuff you couldn't buy anywhere else, and then came Castle Mall, right, Rosalind?'

'It's a time I don't want to think about. It wasn't only me, it was lots of my friends. Little businesses closing all over the place – grocers, newsagents, butchers, ironmongers, cobblers . . .'

'And it wasn't only shops that went down,' said Mavis, 'it was a way of life. Thank God we still have a high street here.'

'How did it end finally?' asked Beatie. 'Did you own your shop? Could you sell it? Have a little capital at least?'

'Estate agents bought it,' Rosalind replied, 'and, difficult to believe this, they made me an offer that I thought was more than the property was worth.'

A sullen voice entered the exchange. 'That was because,' said Charlie, 'they knew what it *would* be worth in a couple of years time.'

Mavis, who worked for a solicitor, turned to Beatie and asked what she was doing in life. Stan attempted to answer for her.

'She wants to sell ideas.'

'Let the girl speak for herself,' ordered Hilda.

'Sell ideas?' asked Rosalind.

'Well, not quite that.' Beatie tried to explain but felt her explanation weak. 'I'm just amazed at all the people I meet who have ideas and do nothing about it. So I want to encourage them.'

'What kind of ideas?'

'*I've* got an idea,' Stan barged in again.

'Oh, do hush,' Hilda again ordered.

'Any kind of idea,' replied Beatie.

'I've got an idea, too,' came the sulky voice of Charlie wishing not to be left out.

'Let's hear it, Charlie boy,' said Kindred.

'How do you pull your legs out of Wellingtons without leaving your socks behind?'

'Oh my God, Charlie,' expostulated his wife, the schoolteacher, 'you are an embarrassment. That's not the level of idea Beatie is talking about.'

'I don't know anything about levels of ideas but you speak to anyone who has to wear a Wellington and socks, and ask them how often they lose their balance and fall over standing on one leg trying to keep the sock in place and then reaching into the Wellington to pull it back on.'

'Old men and young boys have that problem,' said his wife scathingly.

'So you say, so you say, but you've forgotten how often *you've* cursed after a morning gardening in the cold when you had to wear socks over your tights.'

'It's not important, Charlie,' insisted his wife, 'it's just not important.'

'So you say, so you keep saying.' He crawled back into silence with one last complaint. 'Nothing I do is important for you.'

Therein lay a relationship. One utterance can tell all. Beatie heard it and felt a tender wish to pull him back into the group.

'I'd like to know, Charlie,' she said.

'Don't encourage him,' said Jenny Makepeace.

Beatie overrode the spouse. 'How *do* you keep your socks on when you pull your Wellingtons off?'

Charlie almost whispered his reply, fearful that his wife might be right and he'd be an embarrassment. 'Tuck your trousers into them.'

'And what,' asked his wife, 'if a woman *isn't* wearing trousers?'

'Then she *should* be wearing them!' he hurled back at her.

'I think,' said Beatie, 'I'll always remember that – tuck your trousers into them. Thank you, Charlie.'

'My idea's better,' attempted a by-now hesitant Stan Mann.

'I bet it isn't,' said Hilda.

'Why is it,' asked Stan, 'that certain wives enjoy putting down their partners?'

'For the same reason certain men enjoy putting down their wives,' said Mavis. 'You should be the fly on the wall in my office when couples come in seeking a divorce. They don't only want to put them down they want them *put* down.'

'It's not only wives and husbands or husbands and wives,' said Rosalind, who now ran a stylish dress shop for outsize women, one of which she was herself never having lost the taste for exotic cheeses and creamy things, 'it's partners and partners.'

'Hey, hey, hey!' cautioned Beatie. 'We're not gathered together to quarrel. Ideas. I want to hear people's ideas.'

At which, up spake the quiet Cynthia who had learnt how to write beautifully in order to record and remember her ancestors.

'I have an idea,' she said with great shyness, overcoming which suggested strength of character. Her husband was an attentive soul, loving her dearly and wanting to support her in all she did, for she diligently supported him. She could claim no trained profession but rather made a profession of bringing up her children and caring for the home.

'What is it?' asked Beatie.

'It'll be something you didn't expect,' said Gaydon English.

'Don't say that,' said his wife. 'They'll all expect something sensational, and I ent got no sensational thoughts.' The company now hung on her words. 'I ent got no sensational anything,' she continued, which made them hang even more, expectant.

'Now look what you've gone and done,' she chided her loving husband, 'everyone's waiting for something special. You've paralysed me.'

'No he hasn't,' Beatie reassured her. 'None of us has sensational ideas . . .'

'I have,' intruded Stan.

'I'll hit him,' warned his chastising nurse, 'see if I don't.' Beatie had once again to separate belligerents.

But Hilda insisted, sensibly: 'If any of us had had a sensational idea we'd've been rich by now.'

'*My* idea will make you rich,' said Stan, like a disobedient child. His wife threw a nectarine at him hitting the side of his head. 'Ouch! That hurt.' He rubbed his head before peeling the soft fruit to eat.

'You're lucky it wasn't the candlestick,' said his Hilda, adding, 'Come on, Cynthia, we're listening.'

Cynthia began as though she was telling a story to a gathering of children, slowly and carefully.

'I have always thought: wouldn't it be a good idea if out of all the TV channels there was one, just one channel devoted to good news.' It was not an original idea but everyone fell silent contemplating what they thought of it and how they should respond. Cynthia, as though triumphant, helped them with a name: 'Good News Channel.' Mmmms and aahhhs trickled round the room.

Not surprisingly the first person to respond was Charlie in suitably sepulchral tones. 'Problem is – good news is no news.'

'Oh, I don't know about that,' said his wife, always on the lookout for an opportunity to contradict her husband. Charlie, because the evening was more electrified than most evenings of his life, bounced back.

'Well, you tell me – which newspaper would you reach for first: the one with the headline "I'll love him for ever" or "Two thousand feared dead in floods"?'

'Well, now you ask,' Jenny came back at him, 'I'd reach for "I'll love him forever".'

'Well, you'd be in the minority,' he snapped back trying to have the last word. She wouldn't give it to him.

'Who wants to read about disasters every day? You're just dismissing that idea because no one thought much of yours. Tuck your trouser leg into your sock – indeed.' Her contempt was well practised. He withered.

'Well, I thought it was a good idea.' Beatie came to his rescue.
'I think Cynthia's Good News Channel is also a good idea. A TV
channel you could turn to at any moment in a twenty-four-hour
day knowing that if you were gloomy, depressed, hating yourself,
feeling hopeless, unhappy, frustrated – you could switch it on and
there would be a good news item or a feel-good movie or a documentary about a person or a community overcoming life's
vicissitudes and winning through.'

'Put like that, I'd subscribe,' said Mavis, 'because I tell you by
the end of the day in a solicitor's office face to face with human
misery – well! No one comes into a solicitor's office in search of
joy, just one long, endless parade of people seeking justice for the
wrongs inflicted on them by cruel husbands, vengeful wives, or
other members of the family, or neighbours, or callous bureaucracy – you've no idea what people do to each other . . .'

'And what institutions do to people,' added Stan the Marxist.

'That, too,' said Mavis even though she wasn't a Marxist.

The company agreed that a 'Good News Channel' was a good
idea and would be a success if launched.

'But how do you get such an idea launched?' mused Rosalind.

'Probably have to do it ourselves,' said Gaydon English who, as
proprietor of an hotel and head of an amateur acting group, knew
how little you could depend on others warming to your suggestions. 'For every idea there are a dozen people with a dozen
reasons why it wouldn't work.'

'Especially in this country,' said Stan.

'Why do you say that, Stan?' asked Beatie. 'Have you been
trying out your idea, and banged your head against brick
walls?'

'Don't get him started,' Hilda pleaded as wives are wont to do.

'Does that mean,' asked Guinevere Lillywhite, 'that you know
what his idea is?'

'Oh, don't I know it just,' his wife's tone carried years of marriage in it, 'and I warn you, don't get him started. I won't have it
talked about at my table again. He did it once with a group of my

nurses I had round for tea and they all laughed at him. I didn't know where to put myself.'

'Not true,' Stan defended himself. 'Quite the opposite, Nurse Hilda. They laughed with approval, which, being nurses, they *would* do at such an idea. You got embarrassed because they participated a little too enthusiastically and you thought I was inviting them to be striptease dancers.'

'Oh my word,' said the shy Cynthia, 'what on earth kind of idea was he suggesting?'

'Sounds intriguing,' said Guinevere Lillywhite, clad in her flamenco dress.

'Come on, Hilda,' said the effervescent Kindred. 'Don't be a spoilsport. Let's hear Stan's idea.'

'No!' insisted his wife, 'Let him keep his ideas to himself. If he starts then I'm off to my bed.'

Beatie could see that the gathering was about to fall apart, and that Stan was looking dejected, even hurt to have been treated like a naughty boy. She embarked on reviving the evening's spirit.

'I had a very interesting encounter in London,' she began, 'sitting outside a cafe in a part of the city that looks as though it could be Paris, called Shepherd Market.'

'I was sitting having a coffee when I caught an elderly man staring at me who then apologised for doing so. I said I didn't mind, and we only exchanged a few words before he left. But something he said stayed with me. "The world," he said, "is divided between people who are immediate and those who are hard work," and just before we shook hands he said, "When I'm gone see if *you* can think of dividing the world that way." So I've been thinking and I've only come up with one that I like. The world is divided between those who have taste and those who have none, and those who *imagine* they have but haven't.'

'That's not,' said Stan, 'dividing the world into two kinds, that's dividing it into three.'

'I know,' said Beatie, 'I don't think I'm very good at it, which is why I'm interested to hear others do the dividing.'

'The world is divided,' volunteered the still snarling Hilda, 'into husbands you can take anywhere and—'

The husband you couldn't take anywhere didn't let her finish. 'And those you want to throw nectarines at.'

Rosalind, also anxious to keep acrimony out of the evening, rushed in: 'The world is divided between those who are players and those who are spectators.'

'That's right,' said Hilda, sulking, 'you encourage him.'

'I wasn't thinking of you two,' she lied, illustrating that the world is divided between those who have five minutes' worth of courage and those with a lifetime's. 'That's how life is for the majority – those who join in and those who stand on the sidelines.'

'Very good, Rosalind,' said Beatie, driving the evening ever onward. 'More! Come on, more from you all. One each at least.'

'The world is divided between those who live in the past,' said Cynthia, who knew about such things researching her ancestry, 'and those who live in the future.'

'Which never comes,' said Charlie, 'because as soon as it arrives it's the present, and a split second later it's the past.'

'Of course it never comes.' His battling wife, Jenny, got into a stride. 'That's the nature of the future, it stays ahead of you waiting to be transmogrified into something else.'

'Oh, you're too deep for me.' Charlie regretted even trying. '"Transmogrified?" Where did that word come from? I ent never heard you use that one before. Look it up in the dictionary before we come, did we? Armed ourselves with some new words to impress the company, did we? Ent I lucky to have such a clever wife?'

'I'm afraid I live in the past,' continued Cynthia, as though Charlie hadn't spoken. 'Not healthy, I know, but I have this great need to know where I come from.'

'I can't think of a thing,' said Mavis.

'That's because so many different types come into your solicitor's office,' suggested Stan.

'Correct! The world is divided for me into the strong and the weak, the winners and losers, the innocent and the diabolical, into cheats and loudmouths and thieves and the liars. Liars! Those are the ones I hate most.'

'You could say,' said Stan, 'that for you the world is divided into perpetrators of crime and victims of crime.'

'Could do,' agreed Mavis.

'I think,' said Jenny, 'the world is divided between those who build and those who destroy.' Not surprising from a schoolteacher who daily witnessed the creative instinct to put things together and the destructive instinct to tear them apart played out in her primary-school classroom.

'Well, I think,' said the man who ran a hotel, 'that the world is divided between those who know how to be good guests and those you want to murder.' Which made everyone laugh for they each carried within them the memory of such guests.

'Wonderful!' exclaimed Beatie. 'More! Kindred, Guinevere, Charlie, Stan. Come on!'

'I think,' said Guinevere, 'the world is divided between those who know how to divide the world and those who don't. I don't!'

'One of the best,' said her supportive husband, adding, 'I believe the world is divided between those with imagination and those with their feet in the mud.'

'Well, I can't compete with any of that,' complained Charlie.

'Of course you can,' urged Beatie.

'Something nice and morbid,' his wife encouraged.

'Don't miss a trick, do you!' he mumbled back. He rose, however, to her challenge and the occasion.

'I believe the world is divided between those who believe in an afterlife and those who believe that when you're dead you're bloody dead! Morbid enough for you?'

The company was surprised by Charlie's vehemence. Perhaps it was because as a farmer he had witnessed too much that had died on him – cattle, crops, the years . . . Autumns distressed him more than springs reaffirmed for him. His wife, being a schoolteacher, was devoted to nurturing growth and development. Farming should have made them complement each other. It didn't. Charlie resented his wife's cleverness too much. The sight of her reading a book drove him out of the house. It was a marriage that had begun well when they had been young and full of romance about the budding of nature and the gambolling of lambs. In those days a book in her hand had excited him. Now the sight of her sitting and reading drove him to the pub, its pints, and the commiseration of his thick, consoling neighbours.

'The world,' came the sad voice of Stan, 'is divided between those who hold on and those who let go.'

'Put that the other way round, Stan,' Beatie instructed. He did.

'The world is divided between those who let go and those who hold on.'

'Means something completely different put that way round,' she observed. 'Isn't that interesting? The first way round was gloomy, the second way round was inspirational.'

'That's words for you,' said Stan.

Stan's idea was simple but he was a performer. He needed to turn the evening into 'a happening' in order to demonstrate it. It was 'the happening' that drove an embarrassed Hilda to an early bed.

'Don't say I didn't warn you,' were her parting words. Stan prepared them as for a party game but they worried about her absence.

'It's not going to take place here,' he announced. 'I'm going to call you one by one into the bathroom.' The *where*? His guests jabbered, guffawed, and giggled at once. 'Now, who shall I take first?' He toyed with them. 'Think it must be a woman. Think I'll take the shyest first. You, Cynthia, come on.' He reached down his hand to pull her out of the company.

She rose to his pull but at once snatched her hand back. 'I'll come,' she said, 'but you promise me there ent narthin' sexual about your idea.'

'Promise.'

'Swear?'

'Swear.' She wasn't convinced. 'On my life.' She still wasn't convinced. 'On Beatie's life. There! I wouldn't commit my lovely Beatie to death, now would I? In fact I'll go one better – Beatie, you come in with me and watch it from the start. OK for you, Cynthia? Safety in numbers!' He reached out his hand to her again. She took it like a shy virgin. The young one, the middle-aged one and the old one left a bewildered company of people with uncertain smiles on their faces.

The bathroom doubled as a loo, and was spacious. It was also the most cared for room in the house, modernised with a fierce shower unit, glass shield and shiny brass fittings. The loo seat was polished pine rather than unpleasant black plastic; a spotlessly clean washbasin stood on an elegant pedestal, and the floor was tiled, covering underfloor heating.

'I've always admired this bathroom, Stan,' said a coy Cynthia still anxious about what was going to happen.

'Water, warmth and cleanliness – the only creature comforts I care about. Give me a strong shower and I'm revived no matter how much I've drunk the night before.'

'It's very changed from the days I came here as a girl,' said Beatie, remembering rainwater collected in oil drums.

'Is that what you've called us here for,' asked Cynthia, 'to praise showers?'

'No. Nothing to do with showers.' Stan adopted a new tone of voice as though to a child about to have its first inoculation. 'But before I explain why I've brought you here I want to point out that what I'm about to ask you to do may sound absurd, even vulgar, but believe me what's behind it is very serious.'

'Serious, Stan? In a bathroom with a loo in it?' Beatie was sceptical.

'Not without its humorous side but serious. Trust me.'

'I'm not sure we should,' said Cynthia. 'You're beginning to worry me.'

'Trust me.'

Stan waited and watched as Cynthia debated with herself.

'Oh, all right,' she said finally. 'I'm listening.' Just when she thought she had prepared herself to be game for anything there came Stan's question. It astonished her. Beatie, too.

'How do you defecate?'

Cynthia paused for a fraction of a second then announced: 'I'm going.'

'No! Cynthia, please, trust me. Have I ever been anything but a gentleman to you?'

'No gentleman would ask me a question like that.'

Stan could see the ice to be broken was polar thick. 'All I want you to do is mime the precise actions you go through when you . . .' He had become hesitant bordering on embarrassed.

Beatie suddenly understood why Stan had called her in, not merely to assuage Cynthia's fears and to support her but to support him, too.

'When – I?' Cynthia hung on.

'When you – you know, I've said it once.'

'I want to hear it again,' Cynthia pressed, 'because I'm not sure I heard it right first time round. When I—?'

'Oh, come on, Cynthia.' Stan rallied his confidence. 'There are billions of people in the world and they all do it, from the day they're born to the day they die.'

'Do what, Stan? What do they do?' Shy Cynthia possessed hidden reserves of protective scorn.

It was Beatie's moment to step in. 'Shit, Cynthia. The world shits. Daily. Kings, Queens, Presidents, movie stars, models – everyone shits.' Encouraged by Beatie's boldness, Stan's confidence returned.

'I'm not asking you to do it, I'm just asking you to mime the actions.'

Cynthia's protective scorn was not able to withstand two

people. All she wanted to do was leave as soon as possible.

'Mime it?' she asked plaintively.

'Mime it. That's all.' His kind, paternal tone reassured her.

She bent down to raise her long skirt.

'No, no, Cynthia,' he said tenderly. 'You don't need to actually pull up your skirt, just pretend. Look, like me unbuckling my belt.' He mimed the action of pulling his belt apart, then clenched his fists as though grabbing the top of his trousers, and mimed pushing them down after which he sat on the lavatory. 'See? Like that.'

It could not be said her heart was in it as off she went at breakneck speed like a child hating having to recite a poem in class. 'Pull up skirt, pull down knickers, sit, do it, pull up knickers, pull down skirt. Done! Can I go now?'

'Wait!' Stan was even more tender with his shy friend. 'That was fine, Cynthia, really. I'm sorry that you're so embarrassed but I promised you there was a serious point to all this. Now, the miming was excellent, really excellent, only it wasn't complete.'

'I'm not doin' narthin' else,' she snapped in her broad Norfolk accent.

Irritation had taken over scorn. Beatie said: 'Don't give up now, Cynthia, I'm intrigued to see where this is leading.'

Stan added his placations. 'No, you don't have to do anything else. I just want to fill in a couple of things.'

'What? What did I leave out?' An agitated Cynthia was now the irate actress who had been given a note she didn't think she deserved. Stan repeated her litany.

'Pull up skirt, pull down knickers, sit, do it, pull up knickers, pull down skirt.'

'Done!' Cynthia finished it for him.

'What about "wipe" and "wash hands"?' He waited for her response. She hadn't understood. He helped:

'Sit, do it, *wipe*, pull up knickers, pull down skirt, *wash hands*, then done?'

'All right,' said Cynthia sulking now. 'So I left something out.

I don't often get this request so it ent what you might call
rehearsed.' Which made them laugh which relaxed the tension.
Cynthia was not normally a woman of wit. She had surprised and
pleased herself, which rendered her more cooperative.

'Well go on, then. Beatie wants to know where this is leading.'

'Don't you?' asked Beatie.

'I'll wait till I know where it leads to before I know if I *wanted*
to know.'

'Right!' said Stan. 'Here comes the point of this little pan-
tomime. Why do you wash your hands?'

'Why *what*?'

Stan repeated the question.

'Why wash my hands?'

Stan nodded.

'I wash my hands, Stan Mann, in order to wash away impurities. Haven't you read those notices in the doctor's surgery about
bacteria here, there and everywhere?'

'You wash your hands in order to wash away bacteria?' Stan was
like a barrister about to play his trump card.

'Yes.'

'Why bother?' Stan's moment had not yet arrived; he was drag-
ging it out.

'Why bother?'

'Yes, why bother?' It was coming. 'Why bother to wash away
bacteria that isn't on your hands because you've already rubbed
them off on your knickers and your skirt and God knows what
other articles of clothing you've patted down as women do. And
let's not talk about putting your hand on a handle that's been
handled by someone else's unwashed hands.' Stan was now feed-
ing off Cynthia's widening eyes. 'And if it's a public toilet the
washbasin is outside the cubicle so with your hand full of someone else's bacteria you reach for your handbag, put it on your
shoulder and by the time you've reached the washbasin you're
crawling with a colony of alien bacteria who've met each other
for the first time and are dancing whoopee all over you while

you're pointlessly washing your hands that no longer have bacteria on them anyway.'

Beatie gasped a little laugh. The features on Cynthia's face rearranged themselves from irritation to thoughtfulness. Stan bent to reach for something inside an airing cupboard piled with neatly ironed towels, sheets and pillowcases. It was a clumsily nailed-together wooden dispenser in which lay 'wet ones' – a prototype of his idea. He took Cynthia gently by the arm and sat her down on the wooden-seated lavatory.

'Now,' he said, pressing the wooden box against the wall above the lavatory roll, 'supposing this was there, hanging?' She gazed at the dispenser of wet ones as though deciphering ancient hieroglyphics. A slow smile filled the features of her face with wicked pleasure. Stan incanted:

'Sit, do it, wipe, wet ones – *then* pull up knickers, *then* pull down skirt, *then* pat whatever you want into place. You can even wash your hands to be doubly certain.' Pause. 'Whad'yer say?'

'Gaydon,' she said, 'I want to hear what Gaydon will say. After all he runs a hotel. Gaydon next.'

And so one by one Stan's guests were invited to mime their toilet rituals and were presented with the idea of a dispenser of wet ones before touching their clothes. The idea was well received, but what startled Beatie was how everyone enacted a different, bizarre and idiosyncratic ritual around 'the act'.

Cynthia's husband's first actions were to open the window, summer or winter, and then sit to read the newspaper while waiting. Charlie Makepeace turned on all the taps to drown out the noise. Kindred and Guinevere Lillywhite each played a portable radio, very loudly. Jenny Makepeace was at first reluctant to participate.

'Two things you should never trust people with,' she declared. 'Your doubts, which always come back at you as truths; and your private actions, which are thrown back at you as your whole life.' Nevertheless she confessed to flushing before starting, and to wiping the loo seat under and over before flushing again and only then sitting. Plump Rosalind, who ran a dress shop, had no bizarre rituals other than spraying the air with scented freshener; while Stan's other ex-girlfriend, Mavis, revealed that she 'hovered'.

'My mother always warned,' explained Mavis, 'no matter whose lav – friends', relatives, even in home lavs you hover. In public lavs you most certainly hover! School was the first public lav in my life so school is where my hovering began. I first pull the roll, wipe the seat, flush, then I hover.' She hovered expertly, looking as though she were in the middle of a t'ai chi exercise.

'Wait a minute,' said Stan, 'even though you've meticulously cleaned the seat and flushed away its impurities you still hover?'

'My mum warned. Take no chances. You never know which bum was there before you.' It was her final action that astounded Beatie. 'I open the window and I wave the door.'

'You "what" the door?' Rosalind asked her. Mavis demonstrated. She cleaved a path to the bathroom door, opened it and flung it from one hand to another making of it a huge fan. When Stan revealed his dispenser of wet ones Mavis beamed.

'I use them myself!' Her legal mind flew into action. 'You must patent the idea at once. At once! I'll help you.'

'Problem is,' said Charlie, 'have a dispenser of wet ones in a public or a hotel toilet and the customers would empty them, like they take soaps and shampoos from hotel rooms. I should know – I've done it.'

'So what!' exclaimed Stan. 'It goes into the overall cost of a hotel room. The customer's bill will absorb the cost because the customer pays for everything!'

'And besides,' added Beatie, who, like Mavis, was focusing on commercial possibilities, 'even if no hotel in the world took up the idea there'd be all those millions of households around the world who would soon discover they couldn't live without one. I can see the TV campaign – people sitting on the loo looking high and low and later saying to their host in a disgusted tone of voice, 'How can you live without one?"

Beatie was the last to leave.

'Mavis was right,' she said to a host who had tired himself beyond his intentions, 'you must patent it. You could earn a small fortune.'

'Tell you what,' said Stan. 'I've no children, no family, Hilda will inherit the house and a little land when I go, and live off an insurance policy. You have it. I bequeath my idea to you, Beatie Bryant. You patent it, get it manufactured, make a fortune, and enjoy your life.' He patted her behind as she moved through the door. 'Off you go, and be careful. Don't put that bloody Walkman over your ears, you won't hear if someone's creeping up on you, or if a car is coming.'

She walked home to her mother's house through the dark night unafraid, feeling it was her village and that they were her country roads. She had grown up in them. No harm could come to her in the streets and byways of her childhood. Their familiarity was an integral part of her. She didn't place earphones over her head. It was not a night for music but for reflection. She was not sure it was within her but she was determined to enjoy life, to make all the parts fit, thank you very much, Stan Mann.

25

Go to hell, Miriam

Go to hell, Miriam.

Is it true that I'm trying to prove nothing? That I climb and accept hardship merely because that's what humans do – take on challenges, reach for adventure? Do I honestly climb mountains and cross icy wastes simply because it pleases me?

Where is Miriam in all this?

I know that's what I thought when I first began, as I ran up the hills of Hampstead and across the Heath – this is me I thought! This, I thought, is the inner me beginning to burst through the outer me even though notions of 'inner me' and 'outer me' are anathema to 'rational me'. I feel my heart pounding, I love that feeling, I said. I am gasping for breath, I enjoy my gasps, I said. And when the first exertion was over, when my training passed from its first phase to its second, there came to me an epiphany: the pounding heart and the gasps told me I was more than I thought I was, that everyone is more than they think they are. Better to gasp from effort than hold my breath in wonder. On the other hand I'm happy to do both.

There! 'On the other hand'. You're right, Miriam. I pause, I reflect, and your chiding has foundations. I have too many 'other hands'. I see too many sides. On the other hand – oops! – Barney sees me as a force. Neither is true. I'm decisive when decision is called for, and I'm of two minds when there's time enough for two minds. If there's no time – I'm not. Miriam! She has a battery of criticisms. My major fault is that I exist. Sorry, Miriam.

Dear Miriam, I am writing this letter in my head as we all write letters in our heads to our enemies, or have conversations in our heads with our enemies. And you are my enemy, aren't you? We must face that now, finally and irrevocably. Perhaps you were that from the start. I was your competition in life. Why on earth did you choose me, the one person who *could* be your competition? You are beautiful, one of the world's beautiful women, and you were so from babyhood into childhood into adolescence into young womanhood. A phenomenon. You knew how to be nothing else. People gasped at you, almost bowed before you. Your sense of yourself came from the way others perceived you – the most beautiful face they had ever seen.

And it was your curse. You don't see it that way, of course, but your beauty damned you, because when everyone looked at you that is all you ever saw – them regarding, considering, responding to you. You never learnt how to respond to them. People existed simply to look at and love you. It was not expected that you should have any regard for them. Homage was yours not theirs. And so you could relate to no one. To my shame that's why I chose you – your aloofness made me giddy, and your beauty reflected who I thought I was. With breathtaking beauty at my side I was obviously someone of substance who had earned, even deserved, the best.

Of course I *do* know why you chose me. I was the trusted accountant to a galaxy of stars. Stars of high finance and the arts. I had built up a firmament in which you knew instinctively you belonged. You didn't want to earn stardom, that was too vulgar. What nature had endowed you with was sufficient claim to fame, rightfully so, you thought. And because I knew how to handle stars you trusted me to handle you.

But I was not what you needed. I was also a star – clever and depended upon. People looked at you but they gathered around me. They couldn't hold back admiration for your beauty but they didn't want to be in your company. For advice and conversation they came to me. I was a good listener and told good stories, and I was wise and saw both sides of an argument. It distressed you; you couldn't understand how beauty was not enough. All your life you had been encouraged by your wealthy family to think that beauty was the highest virtue, the one sure passport to pleasure, and in return they were permitted to bask in the reflected glory of your perfectly formed features. Surely they were gods to have produced you. And now, to your chagrin, you were married to a man who siphoned off some of the attention you thought should be yours one hundred per cent; not a man who thrust himself forward, no, one who stepped back graciously at the right moments. But I was your equal. Equals are unbearable, they command half the light.

I don't know how I failed to see the hollow within your opal-black eyes, nor feel the chill from your skin. There must have been a sort of warmth in the beginning, words of endearment surely passed between us when we first made love. And was there not a tenderness of touch when you said yes to my proposal of marriage? I can't remember. It is so long ago. I just know I loved you once and in return you gave me pain, for you were not only endowed with beauty but cruelty, also. I had spontaneity once, you knew the way to cripple that through ridicule; I had easy relationships with clients, you knew how to poison them. Nothing shamed you. You could not see the discomfort and embarrassment you caused on public and social occasions. Every thing was justified if it seemed to sweep me away. It almost did. The sparkle went from me. I lost appetite for friends. Not all, some remained and drew closer to me and further from you. It gave me no satisfaction. Your scathing insults did not slide off me as they should have done. My skin was not a thick one. I am a good person, and sensitive. Your hurt got to me, and with each hurt you learnt how to hurt more, and more subtly.

We must divorce, Miriam. We have been living apart for so long you will not notice the separation. No acrimony, please. On the other hand if it will make you feel better – scream! I am selling the business and buying a house in Tuscany where I've always wanted to live and you always hated being. Your firmament will be gone but you will be well provided for.

Yours, Manfred.

Sincerely, Manfred.

Once upon a time, Manfred.

Hatefully, Manfred.

Damn you! Manfred.

God forgive you! Manfred.

Sadly, Manfred.

And now that letter has been posted I must concentrate on negotiation. I have been comfortably off, soon I will be wealthy, and then I will be useful. I will study philosophy, keep bees in Tuscany and climb mountains for charity.

Go to hell, Miriam. For wasted years in a once and only life go to hell.

26

I recognised the type at once

I recognised the type at once: the adored son of proud Jewish parents in whom all hopes – and much financial sacrifice – had been placed. Not spoilt, not bumptious, not arrogant but gentle, courteous, well mannered. I could hear the father telling his friends: 'We brought up a well-mannered boy, believe me. Taught him to be thoughtful and considerate of others. Taught him to be a mensch.'

It's an interesting word, this Yiddish word mensch. Although its literal translation is 'man' it is applied to both men and women. It means not only honourable and trustworthy, but carries within it a sense of grace, compassion, pity. A mensch is someone you can trust, someone who is neither mean nor petty. It is not always easy to live with a mensch. Their honourable nature can be a judgement of our own. Most, however, are sweet-natured and comfortable to be with. Putting us at our ease is part of what makes them a mensch. I have aspired to be a mensch, but I'm not sure my character was ever able to achieve that state of dignity and courage. I think I have just been a good man. Miriam wouldn't think so, but then it could never be said of Miriam that *she* was a mensch.

The young man sitting opposite me was not only a mensch, he was bright. He was not only bright, he was sharply bright. This was the third time we were meeting to discuss his purchase of my accountancy firm, and this time it was over a meal in Claridge's. I was dealing with no novice. He understood the relationship between capital structure, the composition of its assets and its potential for profit and risk. He had, during our first two meetings, asked his questions and inspected the books and the premises. His surveyors had found little wrong with structure but had advised renewal of the electrics, which I had alerted him to anyway so he had reason to trust me. I also advised installing a new heating system throughout the two floors, though he dismissed my advice on the advice of his surveyor. The money he planned to spend on rewiring, double-glazing, renewal of staircase, a luxurious reception area and repainting throughout was a colossal enough outlay in the first years. The heating system worked adequately if not economically. It could wait, his surveyor had said.

I liked him, this David of Davids. Why did I call him that? I knew so many Davids – David the Fantasist, David the Liar, David the Philanderer who grew old seedily, David the Power-Hungry, David the Punster, David the Know-All, David the Nebbish. Types, types! Jewish types! Most I didn't like but his type, David the Mensch, I liked.

Nebbish means pitiful. He who is a *nebbish* is a pitiful one. *Ach a nebbish* means 'what a pity'. The variation is *nebbech* (a harsh 'ch'), which means pity as opposed to pitiful. 'Ah, *nebbech*' – meaning 'ah, the pity of it all'. I wish I knew more Yiddish. I *do* know more, words here and there, but the language itself? Nothing! Or little. I can neither read nor speak it, and I regret it bitterly for it is a rich language that lends itself vividly to humour, insult, narrative, tears and pity. I am irreversibly an Anglicised Jew, which has its advantages and disadvantages.

What is it to be Jewish? I'm often asked. Good question. Jews constantly ask it of themselves, not realising that the very asking is

Jewish. Conferences are held, regularly, addressed by writers, rabbis, repudiating radicals all giving long, erudite lectures attempting to answer the simple question: what is it to be Jewish? And being Jewish they all disagree with one another, vehemently. There's nothing more endearing than two vehemently disagreeing Jews. They are also a type. Recognisable at once in that both argue as though God supported them and them alone, which, when I think about it, is true of most Jews. Not surprising since God commanded Moses to take charge of Ten Commandments, and Moses commanded his brethren to hand them down to *their* brethren who commanded *their* brethren to hand them down to their brethren who commanded their brethren to command their brethren to command their brethren who've been commanding one another ever since even though they've forgotten what it was they originally had to command one another to do.

It is a funny thing, this funny Jewish thing. Many Jews, not only artists and intellectuals but artisans and businessmen, claim a profound sense of Jewishness supported neither by knowledge of Jewish culture nor by religious faith. 'Impossible!' cry the orthodox ones. 'They have no right to such a claim. Adherence to the rituals and laws of Torah are what keeps the race alive and gives it identity. Only those,' warn the ritualists, 'who observe the rituals and of course descend from Jewish mothers can claim the mantle of Jewishness.' But they forget, those orthodox ones, they conveniently ignore the number of Jewish kings and princes who, the Bible informs us, married foreign, unkosher daughters for political expediency. Nor does Isaiah support them, those fervourists as I call them. From Chapter one, Verses eleven to eighteen:

> To what purpose is the multitude of your sacrifices unto me? sayeth the Lord. I am full of the burnt offerings of rams, and the fat of fed beasts; and I delight not in the blood of bullocks, or of lambs or he-goats . . . Your hands are full of blood. Wash you, make you clean; put away the evil of your doings from before mine eyes; cease to do evil; learn to do well; seek

judgement, relieve the oppressed, judge the fatherless, plead for
the widow. Come now, and let us reason together . . .

Now, *there* is one of the traits of Jewishness: *let us reason together.* A
foolish trait believing in the power of reason to combat hatred;
seductive but a liability since hatred is rooted in unreason. My
mother suffered from it: *come, sit down, have some tea, be calm, talk
to me, discuss, be reasonable* . . . How did it come to her, this self-
destructive Jewish trait? It is for sure she had never read Isaiah. I
keep looking for answers, Jewishness, what makes it?

Some of it is to do with a shared history of Jewish persecution
and Jewish achievement. That I know. But also there are certain
values and ways of perceiving the human situation, which per-
meate Jewish art: compassion, tolerance, a sense of justice, a sense
of humour and of the absurd. Values marked by an absence of
desire to revenge the persecution of centuries. And those values
drive a restless and questioning nature, inspire an international
perspective, a belief in the sacredness of life on this earth rather
than the speculative life hereafter. Values marked by an instinct to
build rather than destroy. All handed on from parent to child.

But is there more? I need to know. It matters to me. I was
looking at Genesis the other week:

So God created man in his own image, in the image of God
created he him; male and female created he them.

What does it mean? A strange concept: *in his own image.* I've been
thinking about it for days. Does it mean that God is more important for having created humankind or that humankind is more
important because it was created in God's image? Two conflicting
roots – between those who revere God more than people, and
those who revere people more than God. Take your pick.

Me – it seems to me that the bias of most Jews is towards the
rational rather than the mystical. Of course in some of us there is
the one and a touch of the other, but on balance it seems to me

that most Jewish writers and intellectuals are inheritors of the first: that reverence for, and greater preoccupation with, man and his ways rather than with God and the rituals glorifying his name. Judaism is an inheritance that judges action rather than religious opinions, good works on earth rather than orthodox observance for rewards in paradise; an inheritance of justice and tolerance, of prophecy as warning, of energy for action. How this energy was handed down, what paths it took even unto the agnostic son and daughter is something for which I can't account. It travelled through the ages, it touched me and many of us. We drew strength from it.

Look how I've wandered away from David who is going to pay me a lot of money over five years for the glittering list of my starry clients. He has politicians, professors and trade-union leaders on his books; he now wants to combine leadership with glamour, for I have film stars, best-selling authors, footballers, film producers and theatre and film directors on my books. I levelled with him about the emotional baggage my list carried – he would have calls in the middle of the night from angst-ridden novelists who had received bad reviews; he would have weeping starlets who were going through a period of neglect they thought would last forever; he would face hypocritical left-wingers seeking tax dodges, and film producers claiming expenses they could not really justify; and he would have to live through temperaments, insults followed by apologies and complaints that he was charging too much. But this David of Davids insisted he could handle them. He desperately wanted them. They matched his time in life.

He could have them. With my blessings.

27

He exhausted me

He exhausted me. Could I be that old? Thirty is not old. Forty is old, only ten years away from fifty, I'll worry then – but thirty? No, he exhausted me because making love is exhausting, especially with a young man under twenty who was an unselfish lovemaker, deriving the greater part of his pleasure from giving. I came eight times. That's not a boast but rather, to me, an amazing statistic. I don't discuss quantities of orgasms with every woman I meet, and for all I know there may be an entry in *The Guinness Book of Records* for twenty or thirty, and eight would be a paltry achievement so I would do better to keep quiet about it. (Of course the editors of the *The Guinness Book of Records* require verification . . . but let us not go there.)

That evening, after the dinner and water episode, it felt that surely death would accompany the ninth. He would not take his mouth away no matter how hard I pushed his head. He seemed glued there. Why was I complaining? Had I not always wanted a man who could breathe through his ears?

'At least don't move,' I begged. He listened to me, obedient but determined, withdrawing merely to ask: 'Is there another there?'

I was motionless, allowing energy to flow back till I could say: 'Yes, miraculously I think there is. Wait, just a minute, but yes, I think there's another one lurking there.' And the moment his tongue moved and circled in quest of it I felt as though I was embarking on my first journey of the night – a night that entered my annals as 'the night of nine first journeys'.

What did he smell of? Apples, I concluded, an attic floor full of apples waiting to become homemade cider. A warm smell – of late summer; the year's energy at a peak, full of sun and earth and all the goodness that both had produced. I had never before smelt an odour of such health, youth and endeavour spiced with musky, masculine sweat. I luxuriated in it as we moved in and out of sleep, his hand never letting go of a breast as though for comfort, or perhaps fearful that I would flee in the night. He would let go only when I removed it to crawl over and around him to lick his skin. The taste of him was intoxicating. I became drunk with sleepy abandon.

At around four in the morning we both, suddenly, were wide awake. He wanted a cup of tea, which I sprang out of bed instantly to make, as though I was to be this young majesty's slave for life. Of course I would not be. Being Jewish there is not a trace of the slave mentality within me, nor did I really imagine Lee had a desire to play royalty. But I did want to do things for him, buy him presents, visit cities with him, hold his hand to walk through the streets of the world and share all manner of experiences with him. I remember an aunt of mine once confiding that she knew a love affair was over when she no longer had the desire to buy her lover a present. But this boy, this one who came from God knows where, and who I must know more about, this one for whom I can see myself gazing into shop windows, wondering would he like this, and how well would that suit him, and isn't this just made for him, and that I must, absolutely *must*, buy for him. My life is going to revolve around Lee for sometime until he approaches thirty, and I'm past forty, and he will have had enough, and the windows will no longer compel me to hunt through them. But for now, the world had just been born, and paradise was around.

'I need to know more about you,' I said as we sat up in bed sipping our tea.

'Christ! This tea is hot,' he said.

'I know,' I told him. 'I can't bear tepid tea or coffee or tepid anything come to that so I heat the cup with boiling water before I pour it from the pot, which I also heat.'

'A person can burn their tongue,' he complained.

'I always warn people.'

'You didn't warn me.'

'I'm sorry. My head was full of other thoughts about you.'

'What do you want to know about me?' he asked, changing the subject not without an attractive hint of coyness.

'Your background first. Where were you born, grew up, what did your parents do?'

'It's good tea once it cools down enough to let you taste it.'

'You're not going to be evasive, are you?'

'I was born and grew up in a seaside town called Portslade, which is near Hove which is near Brighton. My father was an angry man who started little businesses that kept going bust, which was not surprising, my mum told me, because he insulted everyone, especially my mum who was cleverer than he was, which he couldn't bear so when I was five years old he upped and left and she carried on running the last shop he set up. I became her help, which is why I matured sooner than I should have done.'

'And you've not seen your father since?' I asked, thinking how succinctly he had etched in his early past.

'Nope!'

'No contact at all? No birthday cards, no phone calls checking on your health, no offers of a little financial help?'

'Nothing! Not a thing.' I asked him how that could be, how did he, Lee, account for it?

'I reckon he hated himself, low self-esteem, too ashamed to show himself.'

'Do you have a memory of him?'

'Not really, just of him shouting at my mother and slamming doors. I think I must have blocked out a lot.'

Now came the surprise moment. I asked what was the shop his father had abandoned that his mother had taken over and made a success of.

'It was a shop on the corner of Church Road and the Drive in Hove, a good spot. When I grew up and understood how it functioned and that it functioned well, I couldn't understand why he gave it up. If he'd've hung on a couple more years and seen how it turned round and thrived we would have grown into a happy family by now.' He said this in a tone that tried hard to mock the notion of a happy family but on the contrary betrayed longing behind the mockery; regret, a hurt, grief. It made me want to put down my cup of tea and take him into my arms but the gesture would have been too sentimental. I resisted. I love hugs and comfort but sometimes I think the world is too full of them, we're tempted to love the image of ourselves being comforting, so I avoid succumbing. Instead I asked:

'What did your mum's shop actually sell?'

'Well,' he said, 'now here's a thing,' he said, 'don't be angry when I tell you,' he said in a tone that alerted me to brace myself. 'She ran a shop called "Paper Lovers".'

'You!' I screamed, and nearly upturned tea on my sheets, which would really have angered me because I have a horror of stains like some have a horror of spiders. 'You bugger!' I slapped him. 'You let me tell that story without comment, without a hint, a sigh, nothing! And *that's* how you so instantly knew the figure of £12,600. You *don't* have "that kind of brain", you fraud you!'

'It's just that I thought it such an incredible coincidence,' he explained, 'that I thought I'd bide my time for the right moment to tell you and get the biggest and most amazed response possible. Which I've done.'

'You certainly have,' I said, 'but now, who intrigues me more is your mother. What kind of a person is she?'

'Very attractive, my mum. She's just past fifty but she looks after herself.'

'That,' I told him, 'is probably one of the reasons why she's made a success of the shop. Customers love bright, attractive personalities to service them. They come back again. It's a tonic.'

'That's what she is, my mum, a tonic. She says good morning to the morning. "Good morning, morning, and how are you this morning? What kind of a morning are we going to have today?" Honest! I love her but – I worry about her.' How odd to hear an eighteen-year-old talk about a parent as a parent might talk about an eighteen-year-old. I pressed him to explain. 'Well,' he continued, 'for a start she hasn't got a partner.'

'Women,' I pointed out to him, 'are quite good at living happily without partners.'

'I don't believe that,' he said, 'they may be good at it but I don't believe they're happily good at it. And why does she look after herself so carefully? It's confusing.' I didn't need to press for explanations; I could hear in his voice and could see in the way he was gazing into the middle distance that he was travelling a route he had travelled before. 'And she has pet hates.'

'We all have pet hates.' I was beginning to warm to her.

'But hers are neurotic.'

'Like?'

'Like, mayonnaise. And Oxfam shops. And car-boot sales. And launderettes. And high streets.'

'High streets?' That really interested me. 'What has she got against high streets?'

'They're full of ugly people badly dressed. She finds them depressing, yeach. I call her "the Yeach Woman".'

'But she dresses well?'

'Very well. She's an excellent housekeeper, and always has money left over for special clothes.'

'What kind of "special" clothes?' I asked.

'Designer special clothes,' he informed me. 'She doesn't eat much, either: salads, juices, muesli, grated vegetables, that kind of thing – so her skin is smooth, she keeps the wrinkles at bay, and she's slim, flat belly. But I think – what for? Why does she bother? No one's looking, no one's saying nice things to her.'

'That's absurd, Lee.' I had by now became his mother's champion. 'First of all *she* is looking. She's looking at herself in the mirror, and giving herself pleasure by what she sees. Self-satisfaction is an important element in a happy life. It keeps your spirits up and, by the way, attracts customers. You'd be upset if she was a slouch, if she let herself go, dressed badly, ate junk food and spread out like a couch potato, wouldn't you?'

'Yes, you're right. I know all that. In fact I would hate to see her rummaging around in car-boot sales, or waiting in the launderette. She's got style, my mum, I'm proud of her, but . . .' His anxiety lingered. 'But there's still something wrong. It's not only that she dresses well for no one, and stays slim for no one, keeps her skin smooth for no one – it's that she also spends her savings on reflexology and Thai massages and manicures and pedicures and facials and yoga lessons – it used to be t'ai chi – and she plays badminton, and walks endlessly on the sea front. It's . . .'

'She's looking after herself, for Christ's sake,' I exploded.

'She's pampering herself!' he returned.

'Yes! Pampering herself! So?'

'There's something desperate about it.'

'She's catching up on wasted years, perhaps.'

'It's more.' He seemed to be trying to understand there and then.

'Is it a crime to pamper yourself in order to keep your spirits up?' I was not going to let him get away with it, though what 'it' was I was not sure.

'No. But it worries me that she keeps her spirits up to share with no one.'

'Maybe she doesn't *want* to share her spirits with just anyone. It makes perfect sense to me.'

'Well, to me it's not healthy!'

'Maybe she hasn't found anyone worthy enough to share her spirits with.'

'She's not even looking.'

'Sounds like she's not the hunter type. Sounds like she's self-sufficient. Sounds like she's very admirable. You *are* funny, you blokes. Even at the tender age of eighteen you're funny blokes.'

'I'm not a funny bloke, I'm just a concerned son who wants to see his mother loved. Loving yourself has its limitations.'

'So has being loved,' I couldn't resist saying, and then regretted it. He looked hurt. 'Oh, not with you, honey, not with you. There, there – everything is perfect with you. It's just that most men can be tolerated for only small amounts of time. I read somewhere that no man is an endless book.'

'*No* one is an endless book,' he said tetchily.

'Are we having our first quarrel?' I asked with a smile I thought would win him. He ignored my flirtatious question.

'And here's something else that worries me – she refuses to take her yoga classes with other people. She'll only tolerate a one-to-one lesson. More expensive but she doesn't care. She cares more about avoiding the image of being part of a group of women in a hall together. She pampers herself but she can't bear the idea of being part of a group of women who also want to pamper themselves. Don't you think that's a bit snobby?'

'A bit,' I had to confess, adding, 'but there's a part of me responds to snobbery when it means wanting the best in life. The problem,' I ventured, 'is distinguishing between the snob mentality and the petit-bourgeois mentality.'

'What's that?' he asked. 'Petit – whatever.'

Why was I surprised that he didn't know what was a 'petit-bourgeois' mentality? I was beguiled by his maturity and expected him therefore to share all my cultural references, limited though they are. I wasn't sure how to define it without seeming to offend his mother. But what was I worried about? Was I not her champion? Didn't I have sympathy with her snobbery?

'The petite bourgeoisie,' I began my lesson, 'are people of small wealth and property, owners of little shops and single houses and perhaps a small plot of land. And because they had limited wealth they became regarded as people with limited horizons and narrow minds. And this view of them was supported by their own actions, because although they had limited horizons they aspired to greater ones that they weren't really up to. They weren't really equipped to fulfil those greater aspirations. So they were reduced to *pretending* their airs and their graces and their intellect. For example, they had shelves of leather-bound classics that they never read.'

'And they probably weren't real leather.' He caught on.

'And they lived at a level they couldn't really afford because that was the image of themselves they wanted to project upon society. They had a dread of seeming to be part of the great unwashed so they did everything they could to avoid being confused for them.'

'I don't think that's my mum,' said the loving son.

'No, it doesn't sound like her,' I confirmed.

'She just likes to look beautiful and be surrounded by beautiful things,' he said.

'Good on her!' I cried. But he was not convinced.

'She wants attention!' he cried out. 'What do you think all that pampering is about? Attention! The woman wants attention and she's paying for it. She's *paying* for attention, for Christ's sake. Paying to be touched and soothed and ironed out. *PAYING* for it! That's sad. Isn't that sad?'

I couldn't answer him. It was true. Many women, those who could afford it, were indeed paying for attention. We both sat up in bed contemplating the sadness of it.

He had not finished, however. 'What does the word "arid" mean?' he asked. I was sure he knew what it meant but just wanted me to spell it out for him.

'Dry, without water, nothing can grow in arid land. Deserts are arid. Ideas can be arid. Certain people are arid.'

'Can certain people be described as living arid lives?'

'Yes.' I was reluctant to go further. He was not, however.

'Can beautiful lives be arid?'

'I'm afraid they can, yes,' I replied.

'Well, that's it,' he declared with a eureka tone in his voice. 'My mum lives a beautiful life that's arid. She looks beautiful, she walks like a queen, she smells like spring, she's radiant and confident with fifty years of health and right decisions – a gorgeous flower burst into bloom, and there's no one around to enjoy her, she won't let anyone come near enough to share what she is. She nourishes nothing and no one, and no one nourishes her. It's as though she can't bear relationships because they make demands on her. She doesn't want to be disturbed by anything. She wants a minimalist life – with few possessions, few attachments, few demands. She just wants to be free to pamper herself and wear beautiful clothes and jewellery and be beholden to no one. Love should grow from what she is but nothing, nothing, just nothing grows out of her that gives pleasure. She's a wonderful mum to me and I know she's capable of being wonderful to someone else but there is no "someone else". She's warm to her son but cold to the world.'

'Not to her customers,' I reminded him.

'But that's not what life is for,' he persisted, 'to be kind to shoppers! Christ! There's more to life than smiling upon shopaholics, and I'm just worried she's going to miss out on it, and grow old and spinsterish and live out an arid life.'

'That doesn't sound possible,' I said, hoping I'd be blessed with such a son. 'From the way you're reading her she sounds to me as though she's poised, waiting, readying herself for the right man.'

'There's more!' It was as though he was a physician gradually revealing the symptoms of a terminal affliction. 'She talks too enthusiastically about the glory of being independent from men.'

'You can not,' I said with a bitterness I had not really earned, 'talk enthusiastically *enough* about the glory of being independent from men.' What on earth made me say such a thing? I didn't believe it. I fight hard not to be partisan in the gender debate but sometimes my responses are robotically female. I had responded too hastily. His counter reply was inevitable and shaming.

'Is that what those orgasms were – glorious independence?'

'Sorry,' I apologised. 'I was being too glib.'

'Seems like a female trait,' mused my serious young lover. 'My mum talks about the joy of returning to an empty house. Sometimes I believe her, sometimes I don't.'

'When don't you believe her?'

'When she says it again and again and again, whenever she can, to everyone, whoever is around. And when she is with other women who share her views then bells begin ringing, flags get waved and heavenly choirs take over. And I think – Mum, what about all those men who died in wars you insisted I know about? Women depended upon them, didn't they?'

'What did she say to that?'

"And who did those men depend upon at the battlefront?"

'And what did you say?'

'I said, 'Mum,' I said, 'we're not talking independence here, we're talking *inter*dependence.'

'What a remarkable young man you are,' I told him.

'Yes,' he replied, 'well, maybe, but I don't seem remarkable to myself. When I solve the problem of what to do with sound cables then I might be remarkable.'

'With *what*?'

'Sound cables. The biggest problem everywhere is cables, a nightmare, they're in the way of everything. I bet if I were to look behind your TV and hi-fi there'd be a tangle of cables, different cables for different pieces of equipment. Imagine what it's like in a recording studio. What needs to be invented is a wireless system.'

'Invent it!' I commanded.

'Easier said than done,' he retorted. 'In fact it *has* been invented. They've worked out how to send signals through the air directly into your equipment but there are particles in the air and they haven't made it better than using cables. There's no particles in cables like there is in the air. Optical cables are the best but they're too expensive.'

I had no idea what he was talking about, but I had to know how wedded he was to sound engineering as a profession.

'It's my life,' he was unequivocal. 'Too stupid to take on anything else now.'

I ignored his self-deprecation.

'Here's my proposition,' I began, 'I've taken a bit of my inheritance in advance, ten thousand pounds, and I think I can raise another twenty thousand from a government fund for new enterprises. The future is in the Internet. I want to set up a dotcom business called IDEAS.com.'

'Whose ideas?' he asked astutely.

'Theirs, of course. I want to help ideas into life.'

'Why not call it "yourideas.com", then? There's probably already an "ideas.com". Have you checked?'

I hadn't, and felt foolish not to have done. How could I be trusted to run an organisation when I hadn't done the most elementary groundwork? I could see my bright Lee eyeing me with bright-eyed scepticism.

'All right! All right!' I rushed to my defence. 'But I've done the most important groundwork. I've raised the capital . . .'

'Not yet!'

'As good as. And I've found office space.'

'Where?'

'A newly built block in Camden Town. Nice and central.'

'And expensive, I bet.'

'But worth it.'

'Everyone's moving out of the centre to the suburbs.'

'Camden Town *is* the suburbs.'

'Not any more it isn't!' Was he going to be as difficult over everything?

Perhaps I had made a mistake, perhaps I had chosen a young man still needing to assert his masculinity, a youth more driven by testosterone than the keen, sensitive youth I had imagined might be an intelligent partner? It seems I can't hide my features. His oh so handsome face broke into a smile.

'You're thinking you've made a mistake trying to haul me into your project.'

'Have I?'

'I thought,' he said with a smile of winning charm, 'that I had started working with you as soon as I'd begun asking pertinent questions about saving money.'

He was indeed a winner. Couldn't put a foot wrong. Not with me anyway. I asked him where else an office might be situated. He suggested that Finsbury Park or Crouch End were up and coming. Finsbury Park was on the Piccadilly Line. There was no Underground at Crouch End though, unfathomably, it was the more expensive area of the two.

'Best thing is to look around,' he said. 'We may end up with Camden Town but at least we'll have explored all possibilities.'

I wanted to say, 'Yes, sir,' and take him there and then in my mouth and not let him go until I had drunk all the juice I needed for the rest of my life, but lying in that bed for so long was setting dangerous precedents. Instead I informed him that I had also found a spectacular secretary – a thirty-five-year-old who had spent all her working years at the BBC and upon whom the accounts department relied helplessly but paid her insufficiently. I filched her with visions of a technological future and a larger salary. She was bored with the BBC, anyway. 'Margaret Bloom,' I told him.

'Margie from expenses?' he exclaimed. 'I used to fancy her rotten. Great choice!' My face betrayed me again. 'No,' he reassured me, 'she's not a threat, you haven't made a mistake this time, either.'

28

I think I have grown to love my mother

I think I have grown to love my mother. Not that I didn't love her before but I have grown to love her as if increase of appetite hath grown by what it feeds on, thank you, Will. Is that the pattern of all mother–daughter relationships, or most, or just some? And what is the precise nature of the change? After all she has always been a mother, the person who looked after me, ordered me, chided me. No longer. Perhaps that's what mothers do, perhaps up to a certain age a mother must be considered a parent; she only becomes a mother later. The parent *looks* after you, the mother *asks* after you: How's your health? Have you got a job yet? Are you eating well? Are you managing with money? Money! My poor mother never has any money for herself but she always buys me something at jumble sales. She has something to show me each time I visit her – a dress she thinks will suit me, or a blouse, or something for my flat. Mostly they don't fit or suit or please me despite that she has repaired, washed and ironed them.

'No matters,' she says, 'if you don't want them I'll soon find someone who does. I aren't short of people who know what to do with these.' On this trip she couldn't wait to show me some beautiful Sanderson curtains. She set them before me with a flourish and said: 'There! Guess what I paid for these? You won't believe it – only 50p. Course I knew where they come from so I knew they were good. They come from Mrs Goodall's that little lot do, her in the big house, and she don't have narthin that ent top quality. Feel 'em.' They were indeed handsome curtains. 'Now don't tell me you can't find a use for these in the flat you're going to rent you say.'

'I can and will,' I assured her.

'To be honest,' she told me, 'I felt a little guilty buying them for only 50p 'cos they're worth a lot more, but those poor ole gals they don't know what they're pricing.' She has a keen sense of class, my mother.

And I don't know how she does it but she remembers everyone's birthday including the grandchildren's, and she finds coins for their presents – Christmas, too. And to me these days, any excuse she can find, she slips a five- or ten-pound note in an envelope. How? Where from? I never understand. Careful household management, I suppose. Trained for it a lifetime – four children to feed on not much allowed her by my father. The only good fortune she had was in the early fifties when she won a thousand pounds on the football pools. And what did she spend it on? Clothes for her children and a trip to Ipswich for the day; and curtain material and paints and brush with which she painted our tied cottage from top to bottom. She also bought my father an armchair though she rued the day she did so, for it became his favourite sitting place in which he dozed and snored after his tea before my mother drove him in front of the fire into a tin bath that she filled with rainwater from a tank outside the kitchen door, and a coal-fired boiler that kept the kitchen constantly warm. He had that daily.

'He need it!' my mother would exclaim to the rest of the family rather than him. 'To get that smell of pig shit off 'im.'

I can't remember when running water with a real bath was installed. Not in Ronnie's time. Nor did it matter, because he loved that tin bath in front of the fire; it reminded him of tin baths he had when he was a child growing up in Fashion Street off Brick Lane in the East End of London. I retain one image he fondly recreated for me: the tin bath on the table, the towel getting warm on a brass-topped wire fender placed for safety in front of the fire, then getting out of the bath to be wrapped in the warm towel and hugged and rubbed down by his mother. My mother washed my father's back – something I love being done to me – but I have no memory of her hugging him with a warm towel. My mother is a generous-spirited woman; my dad was mean and tight. There was no love between them. I have recently discovered why – she was pregnant with her eldest when they married. Poppy Bryant was not the man she wanted to marry. It was a wasted life, which is why I feel so close to her now and come up to drive her around, give her days out, as often as I can, to compensate a little for what she never had. It's not much, a few rides out, some pleasant restaurant meals – modest crumbs off the table. But it's all relative, isn't it? Modest to me, glory days to her.

And she loves it, being driven around, getting out of the house to anywhere as long as it's out. I arrive and say: 'Where we going?'

'Anywhere! Just let's get on the road and drive anywhere.' And she tells me to turn left here, then go right there, you'll see crossroads soon with a telephone kiosk on the corner, then go right . . . She seems to know the landmarks for miles around. Even unmarked back roads. Knows them all, though sometimes we get lost because a smartarse has turned the signposts to face the wrong way. I never understand such pranks. Supposing a doctor is being called to a sick patient? My mother, who knows everywhere, gets confused, what chance a poor doctor? So – anywhere! On the road to anywhere. Well, not *anywhere*. She doesn't like the large cities. She doesn't want me to drive her into Norwich or Ipswich – Beccles, yes, and Bungay, Altringham, and Pulham Market with its thatched cottages and a good pub for lunch. The joy was not only the country lanes and pretty villages it was lunches and cream teas and stopping to buy things being sold along the roadside. And the sea. She loves the sea as I do, so it's Cromer and Lowestoft on many trips, and my favourite, Southwold. Her delight in all she sees is my pleasure – identifying crops: fields of wheat, barley and maize for the cattle. Sometimes she isn't certain and then I have to stop and let her out to get a closer look.

And she has stories about everywhere and everyone in everywhere. Here lived this one and there lived that one: 'Nor they wouldn't want to live anywhere else, no, that they wouldn't. Lovely house they have. That they wouldn't!' She drives me a little mad repeating her stories. To be honest I sometimes avoid certain routes because I don't want to hear the story again. But she's a game old bird, my mum, and sweet with it, and gracious. I had a happy young life – they didn't like one another, my parents, but there was no shouting, no quarrelling. She loved being a land girl, and she was bossy. Not unpleasantly bossy, a leader, an initiator, someone with all the ideas. Let's go dancing, let's go to the jumble sale, let's play cards. My dad wouldn't do any of those things. All he wanted was to sit in a chair. And then he had strokes and she had to look after him and that was the end of the happy life. The caring life took over, she looked after him, and when he died the lonely life took over. She had no one to care for, and that left her empty, which is why I take her out as often as I can into the country lanes she loves and probably knows all about from the days from when she was a land girl. A strong Norfolk woman she is. Cares about her looks. Keeps herself clean, tints her hair so that no one can see how grey she is. I have a feeling she was wild when she was young, and slept around. But she doesn't have a mean bone in her body.

Hardly a journey takes place without an incident. I love her dearly but one of her faults is her loud voice. I shrivel sometimes when she's being indiscreet. Yesterday we stopped in a pub for lunch and a woman walked in wearing a bright yellow dress loud with printed flowers.

'What do she think she look like?' my mother exclaimed in her loud voice booming with its impossible Norfolk dialect. People turned first to look at her then at the poor woman whose dress was the object of my mother's scorn. I winced, she blushed, the woman in the dress, and then looked daggers at my mother.

'She can look all the daggers she like at me, but that dress looks like she's brought her garden along for lunch too.'

'Mother,' I tell her, 'that's her choice, her taste, you can't go upsetting people with comments like that.'

'I was only telling *you*,' said my mother, honestly believing that to be the case.

'Me and the whole restaurant!' I whispered back, hoping she'd take the hint, and lower her voice. At which the man sitting at a table next to us said:

'I can't tell you what pleasure it gives me to hear a good, broad Norfolk accent. It's dying out, the dialect. You carry on, madam, sweet music to my ears.'

My mother should have been pleased and flattered but she didn't really understand what he was saying. There's a certain turn of phrase that to some is like a foreign language. 'It's dying out, the dialect.' Dying? How can a dialect die? People, animals, vegetation dies – a dialect is a sound, how can sounds die? They can get higher or lower, they can die away and even stop, but they come back again. Sound is not a thing that can 'die'. What was the man talking about? I could see the bewilderment on her face, and I knew, too, it would become one of her stories and that she would give the man a la-di-da voice because of course being educated he must be upper class. It turned out he was an actor – an amateur who performed regularly at the Maddermarket Theatre in Norwich, a company with a reputation as one of the best in the country. He told us all about it. Mother, so disliking the city, had never heard of the Maddermarket though she would from now on talk of it as though she were an authority on its history.

That was yesterday's incident.

Today was Beatie-being-foolish day. We drove to Southwold,

up to the sea front. Mother wasn't in the mood for getting out to
walk. She was content just to sit in the car and look out to the
North Sea, which was choppy this day. Not me, I have to brace
the wind that's chopping the waters, I have to feel my skin lashed
and pummelled. That's what I love – the fierce wind, the spray it
carries and the vastness of it all. I had to get out and walk and
stand by the water's edge. And as I stood gazing at the wonder of
it all and thinking of something daft a male friend from my
Oxford days had once said about hating the sea because it was flat
and endless and all the same, a man came and stood beside me and
observed after a few moments:

'It *is* rather mesmerising, isn't it?' I turned to look. He was
about forty, casually dressed, like a professional on holiday, in a
heavy black knitted sweater and windcheater, clean shaven, appar-
ently unassuming as though he would walk on after a few words.

'I love it,' I responded, hearing myself being too friendly too
soon. Is that what the Shepherd Market man meant by 'immediate'? 'And I was just thinking of what a friend once said about
preferring the mountains to the sea because the sea was samey
whereas the mountains held variety.'

'Your friend ought to be out at sea in a storm, he'd find all the
variety he wanted then.'

He sounded like an interesting man; his voice was considered,
thoughtful. I don't know why I thought it but he could have
been a judge. I didn't however want to become engaged in conversation. We had been out a long time and I wanted to take
Mother home.

'You live here?' His voice drew me into an exchange I was
reluctant to pursue.

'No, I'm visiting with my mother.' I turned and nodded
towards the car through the windscreen of which I could see her
peering with surprise and consternation. I found myself answering more questions and soon let him know that I wouldn't mind
renting a place for the holidays if I could find one. He said he had
a house, which he rented out and asked would I like to see it.

Why do I have no fear or suspicion at such moments? Most women would simply ask for the address and say they would come back with their husbands. Why do I foolishly believe everyone has honourable intentions? I agreed. The house was merely yards away, on the seafront, and wasn't my mother nearby?

It was indeed an attractive space for a holiday. He took me through the rooms finding every opportunity he could to brush close to me, and when it came to shake hands he held my hand too long. It was extraordinary listening to his voice changing timbre as we moved from room to room. He remained the judge into the passageway and the lounge – courteous and efficient. Then his voice sank into deep, heartfelt tones as he assured me he would give me a good price, and when we came to the large bay-windowed double bedroom the tone turned lascivious.

'I imagine this will be spacious enough for the two of you?' Why did he presume I was married? I wore no wedding ring. And why did I hasten to correct his image saying:

'One of us.' I realised instantly that could be misconstrued, and added, 'Though I might persuade my partner to take time off from his writing . . .'

'Your partner is a writer, then?'

'Hardly that yet,' I replied, not enjoying myself as a liar, and hanging on to a memory of Ronnie. 'Aspiring. He's been encouraged by an agent who's read the first three chapters.' This was me hoping it was the case with Ronnie, thus taking the edge off the lie. 'Now,' I said assuming the efficient tone he had abandoned for the lascivious one. 'Can you write down your contact address and number? I've kept my poor mum waiting long enough. She'll wonder what's happened to me.' He gave me a card.

'Well, she'll be delighted and relieved to know *nothing* has happened to you.' The judge had returned and laid emphasis on the word 'nothing' as though I had been in danger and he had protected me. Why are men so obvious? I withdraw that question. Men are various. I just happen to have had two recent unfortunate encounters. Though being various doesn't preclude them from being obvious. They are variously obvious.

'I watched you,' said my mother when I got back into the car, 'and I thought where in hell is that gal goin'? She's walkin' off with this man and they're goin' in a set direction, so they aren't just strollin' and I couldn't believe my eyes. Is she daft or something to be going off with a man she don't know? Whatever could have gotten into her? Blast! You give me a rough ten minutes, gal, I can tell you.' I apologised, and explained and she talked about it all the way home. 'You didn't know who he were. He could've been anybody never mind about having a voice like a judge. Anybody! I watched you and I couldn't believe my eyes. That gal's not right in her head I said to myself, and I started thinking all sorts of things.'

Our journey home was her chiding me and me apologising. She was right of course. I sometimes worry about myself.

29

It was now the 1990s

It was now the 1990s. Margaret Thatcher had reigned for eleven years from 1979 to 1990, pulled the structure of the country apart and put it together again as might a horrible child do with a clock, some parts fitting and other parts sticking out, not belonging at all. The trade unions with their huge boardrooms and luxurious holiday homes had become workers' institutions mirroring the power, bombast and smugness of the capitalist institutions they were set up to oppose. Thatcher clipped their wings, forcing them to concentrate on what they were founded to do – protect rights, wages and conditions in the workplace. So many working days had been lost by wildcat strikes that money for investment became scarce thus affecting industrial productivity and economic growth. Acts were passed by the triumphant Tories who, to the relief of a Labour leadership unable to confront the powerful unions on whom they depended for support, did away with the 'closed shop', banned secondary picketing and called for secret ballots before strike action. To her credit, Beatie conceded, she had attacked management as well as labour for their sloth and complacency, and she had rightly insisted that the individual must be freed from the tyranny of the state. The problem was she then exposed the individual to the tyranny of market forces.

Revolutionary was the Iron Lady's determination to help as many as possible own their own homes. Council rent-payers were given the opportunity to buy their houses or flats, which soon increased in value. The only problem was that the illogical Iron Lady then refused to allow local councils to build more houses with the money they received from the sale of the old ones. Alongside the increase of homeowners therefore was the increase of the homeless.

They were not happy years, those years of her reign. Thuggery inhabited the land. Courtesy disappeared off the roads. Car drivers drove threateningly near to cyclists whom they considered a species alien and impeding. Nor did they stop for pedestrians wanting to cross at zebra crossings, and they screamed abuse at each other as they competed for space on busy city roads. Competition that brought down prices in the marketplace raised the temperature of ugly argument in the street. Many felt free to swear insults at each other as they strolled through city centres looking for offence and a way to assert themselves. Beatie was astounded one evening, attending an RSC performance in the Pit at the Barbican Centre, to witness a loud-mouthed outburst from a young man who looked as though he had spent all day screaming purchases and sales in the stock exchange. The young man and his female partner had taken possession of four unnumbered seats – first come first served – and were waiting for their friends who were parking the car. Meanwhile the small auditorium was filling up, and other members of the audience were looking for seats, and protesting that he couldn't hold on to them forever as the lights were about to go down and they needed to be seated. At which he burst out in violent tones:

'I can hold on to these fucking seats as long as I fucking like. They're fucking paid for and they're fucking mine. Now you go fuck yourself and fucking look somewhere else.' She had never heard such belligerent vulgarity in a theatre, certainly not in one run by the Royal Shakespeare Company. Not happy years at all.

When asked by her brother, Frank, who was uncertain, whether she thought it a good idea to buy their council house, Beatie had no hesitation in siding with Pearl, his astute wife, who hadn't thought twice about it, staunch Labour supporter though she was. Property owners! Become one, urged Beatie, wishing that she too could become one, but couldn't because as yet she had secured no permanent job upon which she could depend to pay the mortgage. She had temped around for months in local council offices, the back rooms of banks, travel agents, estate agents, until one day she landed a job that she was tempted to hold on to for life, replacing the assistant to the secretary of a popular primary school run by a dynamic headmaster who set up such a buzz of enthusiasm among his staff and pupils, releasing skills and talents in both, that Beatie briefly contemplated changing course to train to become a teacher. She resisted, but her time temping in that north London school made a great impression on her even though it was not permanent enough to enable her to take out a mortgage on a flat.

Don Machin was a short, charismatic man driven by a passion for education, and blessed with gifts of organisation, judgement and an enthusiasm that was infectious rather than hearty. A man of infinite patience impatient with incompetence and negativity. Little was impossible to him, and what was impossible he had the common sense to recognise. The mixture of common sense and inspiration made his school sought after by the middle and upper classes, but he made sure that the classes were balanced. He possessed the knack of encouraging the uncertain children to recognise a potential they may have doubted, and exceptional children to exercise their skills to the full. His reassuring personality pervaded every aspect of his physical being from the swift and energetic way he moved to the reasonable, urging tone of his voice. He was everyone's big brother, reliable father and indulgent uncle. Beatie came under his spell immediately, and he, in turn, instantly recognised her intelligence and dependability. She would do nicely as a replacement for the school secretary's assistant, who was on six months leave of absence to give birth. He offered her the job on one condition.

'That you learn to type.'

'Type?'

'Won't take you long. You'll be grateful for the rest of your life. Trust me.'

'I will, I do,' said Beatie. 'I do, I do!'

'And the school will pay for it,' he set her mind at rest.

'Why would the school do this for someone who's going to be gone after six months?'

'Because,' he told her with a wicked look in his grey and handsome eyes, 'the school is going to squeeze a year's service out of you during those six months.' He made it sound like adventure rather than exploitation.

What attracted her most was his eccentricity, and that he surrounded himself with staff who were eccentric. Paradoxically he was a smartly dressed, dapper little man who dashed around wearing a clean shirt and different tie each day with jacket and trousers, and not infrequently a suit. For who he was and what he permitted to happen, such attire was eccentric. No high-necked pullovers, no strangely cut jackets, no long hair and ponytails – he considered all that to be external show hiding absence of skill and hollowness of purpose. Yet, a further paradox, he tolerated it in his staff. There was one red-haired mistress who, when her class was driving her to distraction, put feathers in her hair and danced a mock Red Indian war dance whooping and calling for silence. Of course she never achieved silence only great laughter. But the laughter broke the tension and the class loved her and gave her their all.

Beatie recognised the eccentricity of Don Machin himself very soon after commencing work assisting the school secretary. His room faced the playground; he always wanted to know what was going on with his children. The secretary's office was across a passageway, far from the noise that children made released from intensive work to playtime, or released from school at the end of day into the arms and cars of parents waiting reassuringly at the school gates. He wanted to make certain every child found a parent. Occasionally a parent was unavoidably late, and the Head would go out to comfort the child. Sometimes a parent was habitually late and he would speak sternly to them. Diminutive in stature though he was he commanded respect and attention and sometimes fear, for he spoke with the tone of one who knew he had right on his side, a tone informed perhaps by thirty years as a Methodist lay preacher. Not that he always did have right on his side, and when he didn't then a sober hesitancy informed his tone of voice, which again, in its own way, was reassuring. He was a man people believed, trusted. He was what the Jewish parents called a *mensch*.

One morning he beckoned Beatie into his office. He was standing by the window looking at something going on in the playground.

'Look at those two lads scrapping,' he said. 'Happens most days. They only have to look at each other and they start scrapping. And neither of them can scrap. Look at them. Flailing the wind and losing their balance. How many punches can you see landing?' Suddenly one of the boys, chubby and Jewish, received a blow that sent him reeling to the ground. He had been hurt, and began crying. Don Machin rapped on his window and waved the boys into his office. They entered sheepishly.

'I want this to stop. I wouldn't mind if either of you could box but you can't. You're bloody hopeless. You're like a couple of wet rags on legs flapping at each other hoping something will land. It landed this morning, I can see, but it was an accident. You!' He turned to the chubby Jewish boy. 'When you throw a left punch like the one you tried out there you leave yourself wide open for him to come in with *his* left, unless you've got your right up at the same time. You can't just jab. Like that.' He illustrated what he had seen happen in the playground jabbing into the air with his left arm while his right hung loosely at his side. 'No wonder you were surrounded by a group of laughing school-mates, they could see you fighting with just one hand. Stupid! Look at me.' He danced around jabbing with one arm, making them both laugh. 'Stupid! But I tell you what. You've given me an idea. I'm going to begin boxing lessons. I'll find someone to teach boxing after school hours. I hate bullies and I want everyone to be able to defend themselves against bullies.'

'Girls as well?' Beatie asked.

'Hadn't thought of that but yes, girls as well. Though some of the girls at this school don't need many lessons in self-defence, I can tell you.'

Within a week Beatie discovered most of what happened in that school. Don Machin was not an intellectual but he knew what was needed to stimulate intellect. He chose teachers who possessed not merely a passion for their subject but an imagination to invent ways to communicate it. A history teacher no longer with the school had instigated Radio Archway, named after the school. It did three things: played music, announced school events and listed the political and social events of the day touching on everything from the activities of Greenpeace to the setbacks in the health service and the development of 'in-vitro fertilisation'. That the population was growing healthier and living longer was also worthy of mention as was the Clean Air Act and the programme for immunisation against German measles. In 1980, many years before Beatie was temping there, a major announcement was made about the first heart transplant in Britain – little was con-sidered beyond the pupils' comprehension – all in simple language of course for these were five- to eleven-year olds who then talked about it with their teacher. Classes were forty plus with the bright ones sitting at the back and the less bright to the fore, so though they may not have excelled in subjects yet they felt cared about by their teachers.

The school hummed with activity both in sports and the arts. Pupils' paintings were all over the place, music floated through the corridors, and floors were thumped rhythmically by folk dancing. The boys made complicated models of famous liners like the QE2, and the girls sewed and embroidered. When a girl protested that she wanted to build balsa-wood models she was encouraged to do so. There were even boys who wanted to knit. No gender was forced to follow type but Machin observed how they just drifted into gender type, right from the first year. He had once conducted an experiment with his two- and three-year-old grandchildren – the younger one male, the older, female. He placed dolls and prams and toy trains and lead soldiers in his large lounge, and let the children in. Like birds with homing instincts the boy made straight for the trains and lead soldiers, the girl for the pram and dolls. The experiment did not, however, stop him from encouraging his pupils to consider preoccupations outside their gender.

Of all the astute teachers in Archway Primary, Dora Maitland, the geography teacher, stood out. She had put an idea to Don Machin who, as soon as she explained it, had no hesitation allowing her to go ahead. Using white, yellow and blue paint she painted a map of the world over the entire playground. The children thrilled to it. They made dates to meet each other in Moscow, Istanbul, Paris, Rio de Janeiro or New York, and made the effort to find out about climate and products and indigenous customs so that they could dress up, enact rainy or sweltering days, and have what to chat about. They planned world tours together working out the best routes and deciding which part should be travelled through by train, plane, ship or hired car. The playground map gave rise to all sorts of games devised by the pupils whose imaginations were stimulated by their newly discovered knowledge of where one part of the world was in relation to another. And of course the Greek, Cypriot, African and West Indian children developed a sense of pride and belonging to know that one part of the playground was theirs and theirs alone. An inevitable rivalry sprang up based on territorial rights – sometimes a completely different game having nothing to do with the map of the world would bring other children into the Mediterranean or parts of Africa, and there would be cries of 'Hey, get off my land.' But overall the map bonded pupils for they asked each other to show where they 'lived'. Those who had no exotic lineage and were merely Londoners sometimes adopted a territory that they claimed they had discovered, like Alaska or Antarctica or Japan. Not China because there were Chinese kids at school, children of Chinese-restaurant owners. And all of the children, those who belonged and those who adopted territory, would have to talk to their 'guests' about where they lived, what kind of animals were there, or what kind of food they ate. If you invited someone to your territory it was understood that you had to do a little research.

And so the school bustled with animated kids and their activity. Beatie loved the bustle and her entire six months in Archway Primary – an establishment those fortunate children would remember to their dying day. Don was right, he got a year's work out of her in six months because she never minded working into the evenings and sometimes on weekends. This dynamic eccentric infected her with his energy, and he was delighted to find himself matched.

It was during this six-month temp work that Beatie confronted what she thought was the betrayal of her life. One Friday morning waiting for her single-decker bus to take her to school and the last day's work of the week, her gaze drifted to a double-decker bus with a hoarding across the middle: GULL SHAMPOO – FORGET THE HYPE JUST TRY IT. She cried out loudly:

'Hey, that's my slogan.' The waiting passengers were startled, and she explained. 'Wait till I get my hands on her, that Tamara! She was supposed to have been my friend.'

One Sunday Don invited her home for one of his wife's traditional Sunday lunches of nicely underdone roast beef, vegetables and Yorkshires, and Beatie discovered that he had married a woman just as eccentric as himself. Of course. Why would he not! Griselda was taller than he was, and beautifully groomed. She hated sloppy clothes, and was well dressed even for cooking in the kitchen. She wore aprons and moved carefully in order not to splash her clothes with grease, but not even such slowing up induced her to be other than elegant.

When lunch was over Griselda played the piano for them, expertly and with feeling.

'She should have been a concert pianist,' Don said at a high point during the recital.

'I was not good enough.' His wife delivered the six syllables as though she had delivered them before. 'How many times must I tell you,' the syllables said. It was an exchange the couple had rehearsed over and over. Beatie could hear their married life in them.

'I can't bear wasted talent,' said Don.

'It's not wasted,' his wife retorted, patiently. 'It gives me pleasure, it gives you pleasure and look, it gives Beatie pleasure.'

'It gives me much pleasure,' said Beatie, 'but forgive me if I side with Don. I've listened to a lot of piano playing and I can tell – you play up there with the best.'

'Well, you can't have listened to enough,' she said sternly, authoritatively, ending a short piece of music with which Beatie was unfamiliar.

'It's from a piano sonata called 'From the Street' by Janáček. Heard of him?'

'Indeed I have,' said Beatie, pleased that she had. 'I love his operas.'

'Glorious operas,' Griselda echoed. 'That piece I played was called "Presentiment". Little known, his piano music.' Beatie asked to hear more.

Griselda was pleased. Everyone wants to be asked for an encore. Don retired to wash up.

'The second movement of "From the Street" is called "Death". I won't play you that one. Too morbid. Here's the first of the next sonata in the series called "In the Mists" – a short andante – a mixture of lyrical and dramatic.' And it was. Beatie had always been moved watching the faces of musicians as they played. The music seemed to feed back into the features of their faces. Each face was different. She noticed it from the first concert to which Ronnie had taken her. How, she had asked him, can a composer carry so many different faces in his head? Composers do not carry faces in their heads, he told her, they carry instruments, instruments that make different sounds in harmony with each other. She called him a pedant, a new word he had introduced her to and she was fond of using; he had missed the point.

When Griselda finished, Beatie clapped enthusiastically.

'I could listen to you all afternoon,' she said. At which moment her eyes discovered a photograph of a young man. 'Your son?' she asked.

'Hugo. Yes,' Grizelda informed her.

'Was your son eccentric in any way?' The question surprised her.

'Hugo? Eccentric?' Hugo's mother pondered and concluded, 'No, I don't think there was anything eccentric about Hugo.' Don returned. 'Don, anything eccentric about Hugo?'

Don paused in the middle of pouring more white wine, thought a moment, and decided: 'Yes. There was. I'll tell you what was eccentric about Hugo. He loved his cereals.'

'Nothing eccentric about that,' said Griselda. 'Quite normal for a child to love cereals.'

'But not all at once.'

'What do you mean?' asked Beatie. Don explained.

'He was a very decisive lad in most things but each morning he could never decide which cereal he wanted. It was an absolute agony for him to decide whether he wanted Corn Flakes or Shredded Wheat. Then one day they invented Shreddies, and that made it easier. He could have half a bowl of Corn Flakes and half a bowl of Shreddies. But that respite didn't last long because they brought out a new packet, and then he couldn't decide if he wanted Rice Krispies with his Corn Flakes or Shreddies. Or

Shreddies with Rice Krispies. And then they brought out more and more packets, and the mornings became a real agony, his angst grew, what to have with what.'

'Why,' asked Beatie, 'didn't he put a bit of everything in his bowl?'

'Good heavens,' exclaimed Griselda. 'That's *exactly* what he did. He ended up putting a couple of spoonfuls of everything in his bowl.'

'Everything,' muttered Beatie who went off in a daze. 'Everything,' she muttered again. 'That's it! A box of cereals called "Everything".' She emerged out of her daze. 'You often ask me what I plan to do with my life – this! Just this! Look out for ideas. And I've just found one.'

The Machins were perplexed. Beatie explained. She wanted to be a collector and inspirer of ideas.

'There are lots of people with untapped skills and intelligence bristling with ideas. I want to encourage them, help them put their ideas into practice. Problem is – I'm better at inspiring and collecting than putting into practice. I met someone from my old college who I thought I might work together with but she betrayed me before I've even got around to broaching cooperation with her.'

Beatie had to explain herself, and told them the story of meeting Tamara Perl in Shepherd Market, and how Beatie had told her of the slogan for selling a shampoo product and how she had seen it a few weeks ago on the side of a bus.

'You'll get a lot of that in life,' said Don. 'Prepare for it, harden yourself in preparation.' He spoke with pained authority.

'Shouldn't you contact her?' asked Grisdelda. 'Tell her off? Ask what the hell she thought she was doing?'

'I should have, I know and I've got a contact number for her, but here's my problem, I'm not confrontational. I hate scenes. I hate anger and loud voices. I should, I know, but there! That's me!'

'To your credit,' said Grisdelda.

'But no bloody use to her,' said Don. 'Might make her a nicer person but being nice won't get her on in life. I also hate being confrontational but I tell you what, no bugger's going to take advantage of me, do me down, let me down, betray me down. I'll confront them, sure as hell.'

'And what do you plan to do with Everything?' Grizelda asked.

'I don't know yet, I just feel that there's a market for a box that contains a mixture of cereals called Everything. *For those who can't make up their minds – buy Everything.*' Beatie was already making up sales slogans. '*For those who want it all – here's Everything. For those in a hurry – take Everything. Everything – for those with an appetite for life.* The slogans can be endless. Well, not endless, but lots of changes to be rung. Just have to fit the right idea with the right company.'

'And don't go around telling every Tom Dick and Harry your ideas,' Don cautioned.

'Got any more?' asked Griselda. Beatie told them about Stan Mann's idea for an addition to the toilet, describing the hilarity of that evening orchestrated around an aid to hygiene by an old survivor from the Spanish Civil War. The aid, she reported, was in the Patent Office awaiting a patent pending number.

'And then?' asked Don. 'When it comes through, what then?'

'Then,' said Beatie, 'I have to find out how to manufacture it, and how such things are distributed and marketed.'

'Shouldn't you be taking advice on how to proceed?' Don entered avuncular mode.

'What I've discovered about advice in my short life is,' countered Beatie, 'that two experts will offer advice that's conflicting.'

'True!' said Don. 'Which means you've got to develop the skill of assessing advice. We all have to do it, from Prime Ministers down to headmasters. We're surrounded by experts. I am anyway. All my teaching staff are experts in teaching methods, and they each differ and they each succeed. So who am I to listen to? It's a problem, I can tell you. There's no greater insult than to solicit someone's opinion and then reject it. I get it all the time.' He mimicked a hurt tone of voice: "Well, if you didn't want my opinion, why waste my time asking for it?"

'We're not talking about your bloody school,' rebuked Griselda, 'we're talking about Beatie's future. Christ Almighty! He brings every topic back to his problems at school. Drives me mad.'

'Right!' apologised Don. 'I'm an egocentric slob with limited skills who can only run a kiddies' school and wash up . . .'

'. . . and he's talking about himself again!' his wife interrupted him.

They were like a music hall act as some couples are who have lived relatively happy years together. Beatie had rarely felt so at home in other people's company.

Her journey from the gates of St Hilda's was becoming peopled nicely, nicely.

30

I had to return to Shepherd Market

I had to return to Shepherd Market. There's no need to ask why. It's obvious. I returned in the hope that he would be there. It was a stupid, romantic trip relying upon a million-to-one chance. Silly woman! Your problem, Beatie Bryant, is that you've seen too many films, and imagine your life could be like a film script with all the right lines written for you and all the right moments happening as you want them to happen. Life is more unpredictable. Why should he revisit these narrow lanes between Piccadilly and Curzon Street? It's not as though he had told you he takes his coffee there on a regular basis, or even not on a regular basis, just frequently. It's the kind of thing that kind of man would have said on parting: 'If you come here as frequently as I do, young woman, we might bump into each other again.' He said no such thing. On the contrary he seemed to flee as though he couldn't get away fast enough for having stared at me lasciviously. So why *did* I return? There were two other reasons: I was at a loose end having just finished six months working at Archway Primary School; and I enjoyed the ambience of Shepherd Market's streets. The real reason though, I feel foolish to confess, was this vague hope of meeting him again.

The bigger question is – why did I want to? Some people communicate and leave behind a powerful sense of themselves after even the briefest of encounters, and he had. What *was* that sense? He was an attractive man, for sure, youthful in that old man's skin. And the way he strode off betokened an appealing determination. He was resolved to go wherever he wanted to go and do whatever he chose to do. Am I responding to an elderly macho man? No, no, surely not. I don't like macho men. No, there was something else, a mixture of intelligence and experience. His voice sounded like the voice of someone who had solaced and guided many through dark and difficult times. I need such a voice, or rather the man to whom such a voice belonged. Such a man I would trust with my ideas and from him seek guidance and advice. Let me admit – I hanker after a father figure. That can be a trap – a father figure. It could lead me into all sorts of dire relationships if I'm not careful. Look! It has already led me into stupid actions like returning to Shepherd Market in the hope a briefly met stranger will also return. Why should he? I mean why should I think I lingered in his memory as he lingered in mine? However 'immediate' he thought me there is no reason why he should have given me a second thought the moment he walked out of my sight.

And yet I can't help feeling that he *did* remember me, that I did linger, that at certain moments – not every moment, just certain ones – I did re-enter his thoughts. I feel it strongly. It must be so because he looked at me and spoke to me in a special way. What special way? Be more precise, woman. 'Special' is a lazy word from romantic novels. Looked and spoke to you in *what* 'special' way? He thought he was looking at me lasciviously, and he was, a touch, a thrilling touch, but more he was looking at me with familiarity. His eyes said not only 'I desire you' but 'I know you'. That was his special look, a look that knew me, that knew me well enough to take my hand and say, 'Come, walk with me, we have much to talk about.' Of course he did no such thing, and even if that was what he was thinking he would not have carried it out because he knew it would frighten me. How unlike the 'judge' on Southwold seafront he was. And since meeting him, over a year ago by now, I would wager that I've entered his head half a dozen times. Sometimes, when his presence returns to me, I feel it's because he's thinking of me. I'm not of a mystical disposition, I don't believe in telepathy, I'm a solid, practical, down-to-earth type, but these moments, these sensations of his proximity, are strong when they hit me. I become filled with yearning. He looms as someone I'm reaching for, as though he is a part I'm missing in myself, one of many more parts I feel I'm searching for to make myself whole.

So, let me confess, I went back to Shepherd Market three times. At no time was he there. Those narrow streets gave me pleasure but the truth must be told, on the third occasion after I'd waited three hours going through a slow coffee, a glass of white wine, a languid lunch, and a large dessert I didn't really want and should have resisted for I felt a little nauseous, I knew for certain he would not come, not now or ever, and I doubted that I would ever return again. I felt so foolish, so lifeless, and with it, so vulnerable. I had exposed myself to myself. The yearning turned to loneliness. Irrationally I felt abandoned, though how could I feel abandoned by a presence that only briefly brushed my life? I seemed to melt out of existence. I could feel myself slipping away down the sides of the chair into the paving stones, running into the drains, when suddenly a voice screamed out:

'Thank God! I've found you at last. Do you know how many times I've been back here in the hope of finding you guzzling a large dessert? Beatie!'

She opened her arms and bent down to kiss me. Now I really wanted to be sick. It was Tamara. She who had betrayed me. Is that too strong a word? There was no other word I could find for the plagiarising of my advertising idea. She could feel my body stiffen at her embrace, and I think my look withered her.

'It wasn't me,' she cried in a plaintive voice that I instantly believed but resisted believing. 'I promise you, it wasn't me. I beg you, believe me. Can I sit down?'

'I'm just about to leave.' My voice was low and unfriendly.

'Have another coffee.'

'No, thank you.'

'A brandy, then. Have a brandy in your blood because I have a story.'

'No thank you.'

'Then I'll have one. Mind if I have one?' She sat, ordered her brandy, and began to tell me a story about her job helping dying enterprises come alive again, and how one man, a senior executive in an advertising firm, was in dispute with his partners and had come to her for advice and she had advised him not to sue, and how in conversation, just in passing, she'd let out the idea for the shampoo advert, and months later had seen it put into effect. *She* had been betrayed, it was not she who had betrayed me.

'I was stupid, perhaps,' she said, 'Fucking irresponsible, careless, unprofessional, but I would never, never, never, not in a million years usurp another person's idea. Especially not yours, Beatie Bryant. I promise you, swear to you, on whosoever life you want me to swear, my father's, my only remaining parent who I love, on his life. I swear.'

And then, most peculiar of all, she followed her swearing with a set of three unattached utterances.

'I know I am.' Pause. 'I know I am.' Pause. 'I know I am.' I looked at her as a person bewitched.

'You know you are – what?' I asked. She came as though out of a deep trance, and seemed not to know what I was talking about. 'You said three times "I know I am" and they weren't related to anything I had said.'

'You weren't supposed to hear those,' she said, and explained: 'My father and I have these conversations with my dead mother, who keeps popping in and out of our lives in moments of extreme feeling or tension, and talks to us.'

'And she was talking to you then?' I asked.

Tamara nodded. I asked what her mother had been saying. Tamara recited the exchange. '"You're an honourable woman, Tamara." "I know I am." "You're someone to rely on." "I know I am." "But you're a putz." "I know I am."'

'What's a "putz"?'

'Someone intelligent who doesn't always use her intelligence.'

It was fine from then on. We were back on course, and fell upon each other, greedily eating up each other's news and gossip. I told her about Stan Mann's lavatory idea stretching out with hilarity the evening spent by eight people in the lavatory. I described my six months with Don Machin's school, and how knowing him and his wife gave rise to my idea of a box of cereals called Everything; and told her that I could now touch-type. She thought the toilet attachment had possibilities but was uncertain about a box of Everything.

'But tell me,' she asked, 'are these the sort of ideas you really want to spend your life fishing around for?'

I confessed they weren't. 'No, there's something bigger out there, I'm not sure what but there's an idea just waiting for me to pluck it.'

'Do you think that's true for everyone?' she asked me.

'I'd like to think it is,' I replied, 'but in my dark and honest moments I know that it's not.'

Tamara told me about setting up – with help from her father's trust fund – her organisation for putting other people's ideas into practice, and how she'd gone into partnership with this wonderfully intelligent 'toy boy' who was an unbearably tender lover with a splendid business brain and an authority and maturity way beyond his years who had told a restaurant owner to stick a glass of water up his bum, and oh we were women together and she made me laugh and got me talking and made me realise what a lonely, loveless life I had been living.

'The world,' she said, 'is divided between those who make things happen and those to let things happen.'

'The leaders and the followers.'

'The doers and those who wait for it to be done.'

31

It began when he was young and vain

It began when he was young and vain. Manfred developed a taste for honey having read in a newspaper about certain villages in the Ukraine where men and women lived into their hundreds, and when asked their secret replied 'honey and yoghurt'. Manfred ate some every day until into his fifties when he lost the taste for yoghurt, but honey he ate with almost everything – tea, coffee, on cereals and in porridge, on matzos and Ryvitas, sometimes spoonfuls on their own. And he remained young. Young-looking that is, for: *Golden lads and girls all must/like chimneysweepers come to dust.* When people told him he looked young for his age he replied: 'You should see the painting in the attic,' until the Wildean conceit bored him; and he feared he would say it twice to the same person. But when they asked him what he did to *look* so young his reply was constant and repetitive – yoghurt and honey. Nothing boring in that, and he hoped others would take note for it was indeed a healthy combination.

The attraction of making his own honey was that others did the work for you – the bees! The beekeeper simply collected the results, golden sticky, full of identifiable nutrition except one which the scientists could *not* identify – a mystery element it was believed held the secret of longevity.

Manfred began with research. One book told him the word 'honey' derives from the Arabic for honey – 'han'. The Germans turned it into 'honig', which found its way into Old English to become 'hunig'. Another book revealed that a bee might have to travel up to 40,000 miles to fill a pound jar. One writer claimed without doubt that there was no honey in the world superior in taste and quality to that garnered on the Downs of England and the heathered slopes of the Scottish Highlands, and Manfred was amazed to read that there are more than 100,000 different flowers from which bees gather nectar.

Almost all aspects of bee life are known: that the bee is a structural engineer of astounding accuracy; that honey, like good wine, improves with time; it is also the only food that never deteriorates. The oldest known was nearly three and a half thousand years old, discovered by an American archaeologist who opened a royal tomb in Egypt where he found a jar of honey still in a partly liquid state. It had retained its full aroma and was as good to eat as when placed there.

Not much space was needed to house these busy, obedient creatures. The two acres of land Manfred owned was more than sufficient for his hives. Having sold the business for a vast sum, and the north London house for an even greater sum, he was able to buy a rambling old house among those promising English Downs. He enjoyed purchasing equipment and protective clothing just as he had enjoyed purchasing equipment for climbing and trekking. Purchasing held the promise of activity, and activity the promise of fulfillment. However, the equipment required for beekeeping was, curiously, more exotic: hives, frames, honey extractor, smoker, a hive tool, gloves, the bee suit, the veil, even the Wellington boots. He found a trustworthy local beekeeper, Jack Newsome, who sold him frames of bees, which Manfred had been advised was the safest way to start if he wanted to be certain of a healthy hive – an

unknown keeper might have sold him sick flyers with feeble hums
and a diseased honey sac.

Jack Newsome's strain of bees were Italian with three yellow
brown bands on their abdomen, and were much sought after
because they were docile, reluctant to swarm, seemed strongly
resistant to disease and were prolific breeders. The only disadvantage of the Italian bee, said his neighbourly beekeeper, is that its
brood flourished better in warm, Italian climates. But the bees he
was selling Manfred were third generation, and had become accli-
matised to English weather and, more to the point, were bees
reared in the area where Manfred would be operating. The keeper
advised him to buy spare frames and equipment in preparation for
an unannounced swarm. The thought that out of nowhere suddenly, uninvited, a swarm of alien bees might curve up to his
doorstep filled him, he had to admit, with a degree of terror. But
Manfred was of a cool, pragmatic disposition. His nature would
take the world's stings in its stride. After all had he not sold off his
motley chorus of artistic complainers and his castigating wife
upon whom he had settled far more than she deserved? The last
lap of his life's journey was clear, he could dictate the pace and
turn any corner inviting enough to turn. Manfred's new chorus
were not complainers. They were hummers who hummed a sin-
gular note and were good tempered. Jack assured him: 'You won't
find this lot either bothersome or prone to swarming.' Manfred
knew he would be relying on this man for the first few years. He
inspired trust and confidence.

Manfred's first question was: 'Is there one kind of hive that's
better than another?'

'Oh, yes, my Lord, yes.' The well-informed keeper of bees
listed them all. 'But if you want a hive that looks like everybody's
ides of what a hive looks like then you buy the WBC. Heavy, and
difficult to operate and move, but solid and lasts forever, especially
if they're made from red cedar rather than deal. Cost a bomb,
though.' Manfred knew that would be the one he would buy but
didn't say so in case it sounded as though he was flaunting wealth.

What fascinated him more than any other aspect of beekeeping, apart from the satisfaction of gathering the final result of his endeavours (the honey itself), were the rituals and hierarchical life within the colony. Manfred, like most laymen, knew that a colony was divided into three: the solitary queen bee, the worker bee and the drones. He also knew that the queen's main function was to breed and that the worker bee did all the work and the drones did nothing except fuck the queen – if they were lucky. Most never got the chance and those that did died quickly afterwards. When drones were no longer needed, usually around late autumn, they were starved of food and then banished from the hive to perish. He takes twenty-four days to be born; lives a short, pampered life entirely looked after and fed by the worker bee and when his hour comes dies swiftly whether he has fulfilled his function or not. The worker bee on the other hand makes up the majority of the hive's inhabitants, and though she does all the work she is also quietly in control, helped no doubt by having lost the ability to lay eggs, which leaves her free to do many other things. She's around throughout the year; cleans up the hive's detritus, feeds the young bees, attends to the needs of the queen, produces wax for the combs, which she also builds; collects and stores pollen and nectar and a strange resin from tree buds called propolis or bee-glue for cementing cracks in the hive, which she also stands guard over and collects water to spray and keep cool on hot summer days.

Manfred resisted making seductive comparisons between bee life and human life. Yes, in the hierarchy of ducks and bees each knew their place; but their lives were far less complicated than the lives of humans. People, it is true, found their intellectual, emotional or economic 'place' but there was always the possibility of change. Born into an intellectually limited family the child could always educate itself out of it; born into poverty the bright kid could learn how to manipulate the marketplace. But the queen reigns only to produce worker bees, drones and future queens. There is no breaking that pattern of behaviour. Worker eggs are laid in worker cells, drones in drone cells and queen eggs are laid

in a specially constructed queen cell where the royal grub is roy-
ally fed on vast quantities of royal jelly. The cycle, however
mesmerising, is repetitive and constant. It has its sad side as have
the cycles of human life, and its foibles, too. The virgin queen will
go through similar stages of growth as her worker bees, and when
she's grown and groomed she will fly off to mate with the dreary
drones on the wing well away from the hive because of course no
self-respecting queen, Manfred mused with a smile, would want
to be seen by her workers flitting and flirting with mere drones!
She can live for many years but it is the workers who will decide
when she has passed her prime and needs to be replaced. Poor, sad
queen. Only a drone for a partner, and the tiring privilege of pro-
ducing, at the height of the mating season, over two thousand
eggs a day, and then – dismissed. Purpose served. Was there any
sweetness in it for her, too? Manfred wondered.

Perhaps the most fascinating of the rituals was the dance of the
scout bee that flies off in search of nectar. When she returns she
has to inform the workers of two things: how far away the nectar
is, and in which direction. By a series of dances of different shapes
the scouts inform the others if the honey mine is near or far or
further away. The 'round' dance informs that the food is not too
far away; the 'sickle' dance indicates it's further away; the 'wagtail'
dance says further, further, further. What Manfred had difficulty
believing – he was reading the amazing studies of Karl von
Frisch – was, Frisch discovered, that if the bee danced up the
comb from bottom to top then her foraging recruits knew that
they needed to fly directly into the sun to find the nectar; if the
dance was reversed from top to bottom they had to fly away from
the sun. If the dance moved at an angle of say thirty degrees to the
right or left of the perpendicular from bottom to top then the for-
agers knew they had to fly thirty degrees to the left or right of the
sun. And they knew what kind of food they were looking for
because they could smell the pollen on the body of the dancers.
The length of time that the scouts danced also conveyed information about distance. And the bee seemed aware that the sun

was moving all the time, and so she made allowances for this in the way she danced. But clever though all this was, there was one last calculation that made Manfred hold his breath as he read it. If the informed forager encountered a wind that might blow her off course she would allow for that and fly a little to the left or right so that she would always be blown back on course.

What began as Manfred's vanity to hold onto youth ended as the passion of an ageing man. He loved the task of assembling his hive – he built only one to begin with – and inserting the frames full of bees. Jack Newsome stayed around to guide him through the first stages of establishing his nucleus of six frames. The bee-keeper had kindly agreed to deliver the frames one evening, 'Best time to move 'em' rather than make Manfred bring his hive to his territory, which is what normally would have happened.

'And don't forget – feed them a bucket of warm, thin syrup twenty-four hours from now and make sure every part of the hive is locked up securely. I know we've done it now but I also know you'll want to peek at them first thing in the morning. And don't be brave. Wear your veil and all the rest of the gear. You paid a lot for it, use it. A sting won't kill you but until your blood is used to them they're no fun either.' The Newsome man was friendly but stern. He had little time for dilettantes and half-hearted dabblers and, though he was an amateur himself, he was impatient with the amateur mentality. If a hobby, which at their age is what it was, was worth pursuing then it should be approached as though their livelihood depended upon it. Newsome had supplied and started off many such hobbyists and had, with contempt, watched their enthusiasm ebb after the first few stings or when realisation set in that there was more work and attention involved than they had bargained for. His last instruction to the newcomer was to remove the foam rubber from the elongated entrance at the bottom of the hive.

'You must never forget that, never!' he said. 'Imprisoned bees collect no honey, they just die.'

Manfred did indeed look at his colony next morning to make

sure they were still there and at home. And at home they were as if they had lived there busying themselves since the beginning of time.

He talked to them.

'Mind if I talk to you while you're at work?' he asked, feeling only a little foolish. 'I won't hang around long, just checking to see if there's anything I can do for you.' A fistful of guards flew onto his veil and made him go boss-eyed tracking their movements and attempting to gauge their intentions. 'They say,' he continued, 'that talking to plants helps them grow so I thought a few exchanges between me and my new friends might break the ice and reassure you that I'll be a good friend to my new friends. Besides, I'm a bit bored living alone in my head all the time. You know how it is — you talk to yourself and get stupid replies from yourself, or lies or distortions, and a man needs new angles on his thoughts, clever angles, and as you're clever little things I thought that maybe . . .' He paused, suddenly hearing himself. 'You thought what, Manfred? What did you think? What, what, what? Stop thinking, stop talking, look at the bees. The bees, the bees, look at the bees. Learn from the bees. Look and learn. Stop talking.'

He looked, it was all fascinating. But it was a lonely occupation being fascinated on your own with no one to share it. Barney! He must show off his hive and its clever occupants to Barney. He couldn't wait. It would mean buying another protective outfit but that couldn't be helped. In fact he would buy more than one extra outfit. After all, who else might I not want to show off my bees to, he thought. The moment he thought it he knew exactly to whom he wanted to show off his bees. Her. Her from Shepherd Market. She came into his thoughts again. Why? What *was* there about her that she lingered so? Would bees interest her? He would *make* them interesting for her, he said to himself. His mind was slipping into crazy meanderings. He had no idea who she was or how he was ever to meet her again. Crazy meanderings.

32

She had been ailing

She had been ailing. My brother Frank had been keeping me up to date about our mother with telephone calls every ten days to begin with, then weekly, then twice weekly, every other day, then daily.

It was not a named illness, not cancer or heart or liver. She just had high blood pressure and seemed to be in a constant state of panic. None of it was helped by her refusal to wear her hearing aid so that whenever I visited her there was a lot of shouting. Some weeks before the end I had come to attend the funeral of a distant relative whom I had not seen since I was an adolescent, and whose funeral I would normally not have attended. But with Mother beginning to ail I felt a need to drive up as often as I could.

After the funeral, people gathered in Mother's small room, one of three she had on this neat estate of sheltered housing, and everyone was shouting at the poor dear, and she was shouting back, full of her stories old and new. She was relentless. Ill she may have been but all her faculties functioned apart from her hearing, and her spirit remained indomitable. Frank's wife, Pearl, who to my shame was having to take the brunt of Mother's illness, rose to the occasion with sterling character. Curiously, she found she could converse more easily with her mother-in-law if she got on her knees, as though Mrs Bryant was more able to hear voices from the ground up than from heaven down.

On my last visit she had made me one of her huge meals of roast chicken, roast potatoes, peas, carrots and sprouts. And stuffing, of course.

'Get that down you,' she tell me. 'Vegetables! Good for you! And all fresh, look. I know where they come from. Jack Daniels, he give me them from his garden. Good ole bor he is. "I hear you ent too good," he say, "so I brought you these. Lots more where they come from," he say. Yes, good ole bor he is.'

The warden of the sheltered home installed an alarm cord by Mother's bed, and as the panic grew she pulled it more often. Frank would have to get up sometimes at four in the morning, and the warden, too. Soon it became too much and they had to put her into the Norfolk and Norwich. I went to see her. It was the last time. My poor ole mum, that energetic woman who made overflowing meals for everyone, painted her walls regularly, turned her own large allotment over and sent me home with bags of potatoes, peas, runner beans, onions and carrots to keep me for weeks, was flopped out in an armchair alongside her bed, exhausted. Life had finally exhausted her. She had given up. Her face was pale, the crevices in her skin deeper, her eyes dull and slow. She looked confused when I first appeared but then she recognised me and gave me a heroic thin smile before I faded out of her focus again.

Each time I came back into focus, I talked to her giving her tit-bits of information about what I was doing. She was pleased when I told her I was in partnership with a friend from college.

'You did well to go back to education, Beatie. Good on yer. Made me happy it did. Made me very happy it did. Good on yer.' And it made me happy to know I had given her pleasure. I wanted her to be proud of me. I don't think she took in much of what I said; for the most part she talked about the little bits and pieces in the house that she wanted me to have.

'Remember, there are lots of sheets in the cupboard. Make sure you get your share.' She spoke as though drugged, her voice slurred. My 'share'? What did I care? There were one or two mementos I had my eye on but in my heart I felt that Frankie and Pearl had earned what little there was. They had been the real carers. I told her I didn't want to hear talk like that. Neither did she, it seemed, for she said:

'I'll be glad to get out of this place, hell if I won't, back to my ole home.' But I could see that she would never again return to her old home, and I would never again take her on drives out to the countryside. Those glorious drives. It distressed me to gaze upon that once vibrant woman. You'll be ninety in three weeks' time, I thought, knowing she would never make it. Worse, I could see that she, too, could see she would never make it.

'I don't think I'll ever walk through Pulham again,' she said. Pulham? But she lives in Harleston. Then I remembered – I was born in Pulham. She faded, dozed away. I took advantage of her ebbing out, and found a staff nurse to talk to about her. She told me mother was up and down, and that they had done all they could for her. The problem was she was screaming at nights. The next stage would be a convalescent home. She could not have meant a convalescent home, what would she be convalescing from and towards? She probably meant a home for the terminally ill but was too delicate to call it bluntly by its name.

I returned to sit with her. She was awake when I came back and she looked at me as though I had just arrived for the first time.

'Hello, Beatie,' she said, 'I bin thinking about you.'

'I was only gone for a few minutes, Mother,' I said, and bitterly regretted it because I could see that it told her something about herself she didn't want to know. She drifted in and out of clarity. I watched her every movement and registered every sound. It made me so, so profoundly sad. That was my mother lying there, who had given me a loving, sweet childhood.

Suddenly she spun awake and said in her very loud voice: 'There's a woman in here got her body in tattoos.'

I looked around. The tattooed woman was sitting up in her bed across from us. When my gaze reached her she smiled and said: 'That's me, dear. I don't suppose there's many around like me. Your mother – is it your mother? – she's fascinated by my body. So am I truth be told. I look at it and say, "Daft old bugger, what on earth did you think you was doing?" And you know what? I've got no answer. I'll go to my grave not knowing why I covered perfectly good skin with coloured markings. Can't wait to get out of this dump. I had three husbands, they all died in this hospital and they were all fifty-two years old. Makes you not trust them!' I smiled but she laughed raucously. She had made herself laugh in a ward where there were five other old and exhausted women. Ward ten on the eighth floor.

I stayed a couple of hours all told. She kept dozing off. Sometimes she murmured incomprehensibly, sometimes she smiled. I sat as physically close as I could. I would like to have laid on the bed with her in my arms, though even had it been possible I have no doubt she would have rejected such intimate comforting. Or would she? We all have such unlikely perceptions of our parents. Who knows? All I could do was stroke her bare arms. I hated the thought of leaving her. There must have been something about my air that told I was leaving, that I was going to say goodbye. *She* wanted to comfort *me*.

'Now don't you worry,' she said. 'Don't you worry,' she repeated urgently. Three words, repeated. That did it. I fled from the ward into the corridor and wept. Inconsolable tears. I was near collapsing. A nurse hurried to hold me up and help me into a waiting room where she brought me a cup of tea.

A few days later I heard from Pearl that they had taken her to the home for the terminally ill. She had been waking in the middle of the night and screaming out everybody's name. The other patients had been disturbed. She had to be moved. It was not so easy for Frank and Pearl to visit her in the new hospital. I had made plans to visit. But she died before I could make it. She had carried on screaming our names in the night but the screams became weaker and weaker, and confusion grew. She never made ninety. None of us were there when she rattled her life away. I weep to think of her dying alone. We all have to die alone, I know, but it doesn't have to be alone alone.

It was a week before the funeral could take place. Mother had left some insurance to pay for her burial, and there was a little in her Post Office savings account. Frank and I had to top it up, and I contributed to the food that Pearl and some good neighbours put together for the gathering afterwards. I wanted to say something during the church service. It was not normal in our family circle. Rural reticence was rife among us. Eulogies were left to the parish priest whose knowledge of the deceased was scant, and usually garnered the day before from relatives. I was not going to allow my mother to pass on to the sound of a cobbled-together, indifferent speech full of overused words applied to hundreds of anys and others. My mum was not going off in silence. Here's what I said.

'I may have difficulty finishing this little speech, but I have to try. We can't let this remarkable woman go to her grave without a word about her life. She was a force, wasn't she? A vivid personality. You all here will remember that she was a force for getting things done, for offering to get things done, for saying it *could* be done when others said it couldn't be. And wasn't she a generous spirit? How she remembered all our birthdays I shall never know. She didn't keep a book of dates. They were in her head. Everyone had to be remembered. She was not a woman of intellect. She didn't think deeply, but she had a sense of simple rights and wrongs, and people were judged by that sense. Not only family and friends but famous personalities and politicians as they revealed themselves on telly. She could judge them. See through them. And she *felt* deeply. Not many people have seen her cry but I have. Not over things that happened to her, but to others. She was proud that I made it to university and that some of her grandchildren made it to university. And for each degree she shed a tear. And she was surprised, too. Not because she didn't think us capable but because she was acutely conscious of the changes in her life. She marvelled at machinery like washing machines. "None of that when I was a girl." And at the amount of cars in the roads where ordinary people lived. "None of that when I was a girl." And all the aeroplanes snailing across her vast Norfolk skies which she so loved. "None of that when I was a girl." And computers, and faxes, and televisions, and rockets to the moon. "None of that when I was a girl." And it's true. Her world and our world are almost like different countries, alien to one another. But some things never change. Some things go on and on being handed down from parent to child – both good and bad. She was proud of my university achievements and I was proud to have inherited her grit and determination and, I would like to think, her generosity of spirit. She didn't have the life she deserved. Perhaps none of us ever do. But I regret this: my mother loved company; she waited for that knock on the door and the chance to gossip and to share opinions about the state of the world. So I weep that she died alone, that none of us could make it to her bedside. I think I will regret that more than anything for the rest of my life – that no one was there to keep her company in those last moments. The world is divided between golden spirits and spirits of lead. You were gold, Mother, pure gold. Rest in peace. We shall all miss you like crazy.'

33

'Do you think we have double standards?'

'Do you think we have double standards?'

'Yes. But don't tell anyone I said so. And don't tell anyone we do.' Beatie and Tamara were sitting opposite each other either side of a huge green leather-topped desk in their office, a small space they and Lee occupied in Camden Town.

'Why that question all of a sudden?' asked Tamara.

Her unpredictable friend replied: 'I was playing chess with myself the other day, and I wondered – why was a woman, the queen, chosen to be aggressive, defensive and freewheeling while the king creeps handicapped across the board one step at a time?'

'Where's the double standard in that?'

'She's bound by no rules. She can do what she likes, one move one day a different move the next, and the same justification for each – to defend the king and strike down the enemy. She's amoral.'

'Can we talk about this some other time?' protested an impatient Lee. 'We have strategy to discuss.'

Their enterprise 'yourideas.com' was flickering but not flourishing. Stan Mann's toilet-dispenser idea was being contested by
the makers of 'wet ones'. It looked like being dragged out for
years by a firm of clever lawyers. Successful minor ideas were
allowing them to tick over but they were not storming the business world as they had dreamt, planned and fantasised six months
ago when they decided to pool their brains, energies and chutzpah, and launch their 'we-can-make-it-happen' promise on the
world, for what they had also pooled was their inexperience and
their innocence.

However, their innocence worked, finally and, unfortunately,
once only.

They had telephoned the Marketing Director of Volvo, a Mr
Malcolm Nugent, to say they were a new, young and dynamic
ideas group in possession of a wonderful film story for selling
even more Volvo cars than had already been sold and could they
please come and see him. It was Tamara who had spoken to him
in a voice she calculated to be a mixture of sexiness and hard efficiency that old-hand Nugent heard as a voice that tried too hard.
Out of curiosity he agreed to meet them and was amused albeit
nonplussed to be confronted by three confident, youthful enthusiasts who tripped over each other's sentences and informed him,
unaware they might be giving offence, that they had registered
their storyline with a firm of patent and trademark attorneys, and
that if he, Mr Malcolm Nugent, liked the idea they would go
away and make the film and then return to negotiate a fee.
Fortunately for them Malcolm Nugent was a middle-aged man
who happened to be involved in voluntary youth work and so
was of an indulgent nature predisposed to helping the young.
They had just started out; enterprise impressed and pleased him.
He wanted to help but their bubble and gabble had to be reined
in.

'Whoa, whoa! It's obvious you don't know the world of marketing.'

'What's there to know?' Tamara asked. 'You have a product,

you want people to buy it, you turn to us for ideas how to sell it.'

Nugent noticed Lee wince a little, and that Beatie turned to her partner with a hint of consternation.

'If only it were as simple as that,' the patient, paternal marketing man said. 'Tell me, is your idea a "marque ad", or a "range ad", or an ad for one type? Does it fit into a thirty or a sixty spot?' He knew they wouldn't know what he was talking about. Their blank faces confirmed this. 'See? Not simple. And do you imagine we don't have a long-established relationship with a major agency?'

'If,' Tamara blundered ahead, 'you have such a long-established relationship with a major agency why did you agree to see us?'

'Tamara!' Beatie cautioned, appalled, not believing her friend could have been so gratuitously confrontational.

'No, no,' said Nugent. 'She's right. Forthright and right. Why, indeed. The honest answer is that I agreed to see you, Miss Perl, because there is always the possibility something brilliant can come from left of field. And if your idea is brilliant and appeals we would want to buy it no matter where it came from. But I warn you, we might want to hand it over to be made by our agency of record.'

'You mean you wouldn't let us make it?' Lee asked, concerned.

'You'd have to do a lot of persuading.'

They were subdued. Tamara recognised the need to retrench.

'Forgive us. We're really novices.'

'You don't have to tell me,' Mr Nugent smiled. 'You've seen too many movies about successful go-getters, I fear.' His friendly tone took the edge off his sharp words but he thought it wise to add: 'And it doesn't inspire confidence.'

'But in the end,' said Lee, quietly, 'isn't it the idea that counts?'

'Ideas can be killed by bad presentation,' Mr Nugent responded. 'Now perhaps one of you should sketch it out to me. Whose idea is it?' He turned to Beatie who so far had said

nothing. His instinct told him the idea was hers. He smiled at her
and waited for an answer.

'We've written a script if you'd prefer to *read* it,' she said.

'And it's the script that you registered with your firm of "patent
and trademark attorneys"?' Mr Nugent teased, putting the firm's
name in faintly sarcastic inverted commas. Tamara tried to make
amends by drawing him into their innocence.

'Would you be kind and explain to us the difference between a
"marque ad" and a "range ad", please? If you can spare the time?'
She feared her voice was over contrite. It was. He forgave her.

'There are three basic ways you can sell a product like a car. You
can take one model and laud its virtues; that's called "the individual ad", more expensive because if the car manufacturer has three
other models then the manufacturer has got to consider making
three additional adverts. A "marque ad" deals with the overall
make of the car. Instead of "buy our Volvo model X1234" you say
"Volvos are best on the market because et cetera, et cetera". The
"range ad" says model X1234 does this, model X1235 does
that . . ." and goes on to cover the range of models. The range ad
is the most difficult to pull off. It's also the most expensive to make
but it's the most sought-after. What's yours?' Beatie's green eyes,
he could see, were sparkling with her answer. She was the one he
would prefer to be dealing with alone. Tamara was clever but too
calculating. The young man was obviously practical, the techni-
cian of the outfit but not worldly wise. This plump, green-eyed
young woman on the other hand seemed to be pulsating with
energy as though one day she would explode.

He asked: 'Will you leave the script with me?' When she hes-
itated he said, in the same teasing tone: 'It is after all registered
with your firm of "patent and trademark attorneys". I'm hardly
likely to steal it. Besides – don't I look honest to you?' It was a
head-on question designed to evince a smile and trust; instead it
made Beatie blush and splutter.

'Of course, of course! Of course we all trust you. Volvo is
much too important to want to play games. You must forgive us

if we've given any other impression. We're good sorts really, and hardworking, and I think you'll like our idea.' She would have handed him her wallet and contents at that moment.

They were together for no longer than fifteen minutes with Malcolm Nugent, whose office was in Mayfair, after which, in great need of a coffee and rich pastry, they at once grabbed a taxi to Patisserie Valerie in Old Compton Street where they conducted a post-mortem.

'Don't tell me,' said Tamara, 'I struck the wrong note. I know it and I kick myself for it and I'm going to put it down as a learning curve, and this Giotto pastry is going to help.'

'What's in it?' Lee asked. He had ordered a Fiorentina.

'Chocolate mousse with tiramisu cream on top. It's my weakness – tiramisu.'

'Not me?' asked Lee.

'Of course you,' Tamara paused to kiss his lips. 'You're my biggest weakness, my sweetest weakness, my helpless weakness, my weakness, my joy, my strength. Now, I've shown you mine you show me yours.'

'In my Fiorentina is a vanilla sponge, fresh cream with bananas and strawberries, pink marzipan – I think it's pink, and not a reflection of the strawberries – and nuts.'

'I've got a Selva,' said Beatie, 'that's that name I saw on the little flag anyway, and if it's what I think it is then it's a chocolate sponge with zabaglione. A bit gooey but delicious. Should have a crispy contrast like a biscuit curl, or a longue de chat, which is what they stick in a glass of zabaglione for dessert in expensive restaurants.'

'Are we avoiding saying it was a mistake to leave the film script with Mr Malcolm Nugent?' asked Lee.

'Not at all,' said Beatie. 'Couldn't you hear me?'

'Could we not?' said Tamara. 'Effusive, that's what you were. But I've gotta admit, I'm worried.'

'Not me,' said Beatie. 'I liked his face.'

'Only because he liked yours,' said Tamara.

'Good reason for liking anybody if they like you.'

'Groucho Marx doesn't think so,' Tamara challenged.

'Well, Groucho Marx got it wrong, didn't he! I would want to be the member of a club *only* if it wanted me as a member. If Nugent trusted me I'd have to view that as good judgement, and if he has good judgement I've got to trust him. QED.'

'Not sure about that,' Tamara mused. 'I would trust someone more if I'd *done* something to earn their trust. But just to look at me? To listen to my voice? Gaze into my eyes? Not sure I'd trust a judgement based on those things. As the rabbis say: "A man will be judged by the way he lives his life not by what he says he believes."'

'You made that up,' said Lee.

'The words, yes, not the sentiment. Christ! You're dangerously perceptive as well as gorgeous.'

'What goes into the making of zabaglione?' asked Beatie suddenly.

'Why you changing the subject?' asked Lee.

'Sorry, just wondered. The structure of things. What holds anything together?'

'What's that got to do with our idea for selling Volvo cars?' Lee wanted to keep them focused. 'Anyway, what's the big deal? You look up a recipe book and it'll tell you what goes into the making of a zabaglione.'

'You're right,' Beatie conceded. 'Back to our problem. The film script. Should we have left it with Nugent or not? I say it was OK to have done so.'

'I'm uncertain,' said Tamara.

'I don't think it matters now,' said the young and practical Lee. 'It's done. What we have to consider are the possible outcomes and our attitudes towards them.'

'Lay them out, lover,' commanded Tamara.

'There are two outcomes, as I see it. He likes it or he doesn't like it. If he likes it there are two further outcomes. He asks us to make the film or he asks their regular agency to make it. If he asks us to make the film there are two questions to consider: do we take the risk remembering we have no experience, or do we confess our lack, and pass it back to him in return for a fee, and if we do that, what sum do we ask? Then, going back to the beginning, what if he doesn't like it? Do we just walk away, abandon the idea, offer it to someone else? Or do we say, "He'll like it when he sees it," and risk investing our limited capital on a project that has a forty-sixty chance of succeeding? Maybe less!"

'When his brain goes into action like that,' sighed Tamara, 'all I want to do is take him home to bed.'

'Tamara! Will you be serious, for Christ's sake?' her lover chastised. 'It's mostly your father's money that's in this, remember.'

'I remember, I remember. You don't have to remind me. I'm just trying to reconcile desire with high finance.'

'Looking after our double standards, are we?' taunted Beatie. The taunt struck home.

'Lee,' Tamara sobered up, 'you're the technical one. Do *you* think we can make the film? We have half the team: the writer, Beatie, with a little help from her friend; and the lighting and soundman, my beloved here. All we need is a cameraman, and I bet between Lee and myself and our BBC contacts we could find one of those.'

'And the director?' Lee challenged.

'Me!' said Tamara. 'Nothing to it. I've seen directors fuck up documentaries they should never have been allowed to see, let alone make.'

'And you've also seen brilliant directors at the Beeb. Come on, Tamara.'

'I know, I know. All I'm saying is I think I can direct this little number.'

'And the actors?' asked Lee. 'Thought about them?'

'Ah! The actors. No. Forgot them.'

'Volvo has four models in the domestic car range,' Lee began.

'What other range is there?' asked Tamara. Beatie informed her.

'Trucks, Tamara, trucks, lorries, buses. But we're not handling those.'

'So,' continued Lee, 'four saloon models, that's four families. Twelve actors at least. They don't come cheap and they have to be found.'

They each felt the need for another coffee and pastry. Tamara went for the Black Forest gateau heavy with chocolate; Lee chose the alcoholic Cortina – chocolate sponge, fresh cream and rum; Beatie's choice was more sober – a traditional eclair with its crispy choux paste, crème patissiere in the middle and coffee covering. It was their main meal for that day.

Three days later Mr Nugent phoned to say he and his team liked their idea. He would be putting a proposition in the post, and looked forward to their reply. Tamara had taken the call and had graciously thanked him but could not resist adding that she hoped they were going to be allowed to make the sixty-second advert. There was silence at the other end of the phone.

'He's thinking about it,' she whispered to the two eager faces hovering before her. It didn't *seem* a long time before he spoke again, it *was* a long time.

'We advise against it,' he said. 'For two reasons. One, we know our agency very well, a good rapport exists. Two, if you get it wrong you could end up losing a lot of money.'

'Mr Nugent,' said Tamara ignoring Lee's whispers of 'Let's talk about it', 'I don't mean this to sound rude but would you let us worry about what we can lose or not lose. You see, we're looking all the time for as much experience as possible.' There was no response from the other end. As an inspired after thought she added: 'How else can novices learn?'

'Forgive me,' said an avuncular voice at the other end, 'I don't mean to interfere in your affairs, but aren't you supposed to be an ideas group? Didn't you tell me that you seek to put people's ideas together with those who can make ideas happen?'

Tamara, who indeed was the mistress of double standards, argued her point. 'Precisely so. Beatie had an idea, we contacted you, you will help us make it happen.' He realised the nature of his opponent – she would have the last word. He retreated.

'Thank you, Mr Nugent. We look forward to receiving your proposals. We're all very excited here.' She put down the receiver. 'We must buy one of those gadgets that enables us all to hear a telephone conversation at the same time.'

She reported what Nugent had said. Was he right, they wondered? Were they shifting their goalposts?

'I don't see what's wrong in shifting goalposts,' Tamara argued.

'Double standards,' sang Beatie, 'double standards!'

'Not double standards.' Tamara was not letting go. 'It's called being flexible. What's right on Monday may not be right on Tuesday.'

'Double standards, double standards,' sang Beatie again.

'The challenge in life is to survive,' Tamara persisted.

'That,' said Beatie, 'is why the queen moves up and down, left and right, one step, five steps, the whole board – whatever it takes to protect her man.'

'And the family!'

'Do you think,' mused Beatie, 'that's why men hang on to women? Women can argue different positions on different days. We're amoral. That's what we are, amoral. They depend upon us.'

'And thank God for it!' was Tamara's Amen.

They talked back and forth, sometimes defiantly confident, sometimes terrified confronting their paucity of experience and the prospect of losing a lot of money. The day passed between bouts of verbal exchange and stretches of long, contemplative silence. Each one of them felt challenged. Beatie, whose idea it was, wanted to see it happen as she had envisaged it; Lee had never put a technical team together and was excited to do so; Tamara had harboured a secret ambition to become a film director, and now saw an opportunity to test her talent. But they were not in a bargaining position. They could only threaten to offer their film to another car manufacturer. They didn't want to, the advert belonged to Volvo. 'Oh, look, another Volvo,' sounded right. 'Oh, look, another Mercedes,' didn't ring as resonantly. Nor 'Ford', nor 'Vauxhall', nor 'Volkswagen'. 'Oh, look, another Audi,' might work, but Volvo was better. The ad and the car name were made for each other, Beatie felt. They all felt.

Everything hinged on how eagerly Mr Nugent wanted their idea. After all, if they failed they could always hand it over to Volvo's agency to remake it. No skin off Volvo's nose. What they had to consider was the cost of laying down what should be viewed as the seeds of a possible future. Only one of the trio didn't see it quite like that – Beatie. She had no secret ambition to write film scripts. Something else was in store for her. She was not certain what it was, but that nagging feeling had persisted – something was there waiting for her to pluck it. The Volvo ad was an isolated venture. All that interested her was to see if something she had conceived matched its realisation.

The team – which was to be short-lived – came to an agreement: the commercial was theirs, for them to make it, no one else. They asked to meet with Mr Nugent one more time. Over strong coffee, and with him watching them very closely, they persuaded him. He was not certain he was right but he found their confidence and enthusiasm irresistible. They shot their commercial. Somehow. Somehow such risk-taking works. Mr Nugent, having allowed himself to be persuaded against his judgement honed over twenty years, got behind them with advice and encouragement. *Oh, look! Another Volvo* was to become a catchphrase among both adults driving Volvos, and kids walking to school on the lookout. It cost them £25,000 to make, and Nugent paid them £50,000 for the UK copyright. There was more to come, he rang one day to tell them. It was one of those rare commercials that travelled across frontiers. Other Volvo marketing directors were asking for it. There would be more usage fees over the next twelve months. He congratulated them and said they could come to him any time for advice. It had been, he told them, a happy meeting of personalities.

'You might have got a marketing sod of all sods.' They could all hear him at the same time. 'I was the right man to meet. I find it gratifying to give young people a chance, especially those who surprise me and prove me wrong.'

They liked Mr Nugent, and ordered Berry Brothers to deliver him a bottle of vintage champagne with a card saying how grateful they were that such as he lived in the world.

34

We agreed to see someone

We agreed to see someone who had written to us about an idea he was convinced would make him and us a fortune. Understandably he didn't outline his idea on paper but I should have guessed all would not turn out well after five minutes talking with him on the phone. In my defence it was the kind of exchange one only understands in retrospect. At the time I could not have understood that the calm and considered tone was too considered, too calm; that the reassurance was too warmly reassuring; that the reasonable refusal to give even a hint of the field in which his idea would function was weirdness dressed up as reasonable. This man had been touting his 'idea' around for twenty-five years and had become canny in the way he approached his victims, practised in his responses to their doubts, devious in the way he manipulated their attention. I could not know all this from our brief five-minute telephone conversation. And besides, I'd come through the gates of St Hilda to meet the world.

He arrived on time, carefully dressed in grey trousers and a grey houndstooth check jacket that looked expensive but on closer

inspection was recognisably a Marks & Spencer garment that
would soon lose its shape. His shirt was white with a frayed collar,
and his tie was black and white – an outfit harmonised like a
cheap melody. He entered our small space with a military-style
raincoat over his arm that he carefully set down on the back of his
chair saying, 'Tidy house, tidy mind,' and placing his briefcase
between his legs as though to protect it from theft. 'A habit,' he
said apologetically, aware that his action might be offensive. 'Better
safe than sorry.' They were the first of his fund of clichés. We
shook hands, all three of us, and were immediately put at ease by
the friendliness of his manner.

'I didn't imagine,' he said, 'that I would be greeted by such a
youthful committee. How pleasant. I love young people. Our
hope for the future – if,' he added, and we should have been
alerted by what he added, 'if there is a future to be had.'

We attributed the remark to melancholy wit rather than
gloomy nature. I told him: 'My colleagues stayed behind to meet
you but in fact they have to leave, and it will be just you and me.
I hope that's all right?'

'All right? Why should it not be? Each of us must conduct our
lives and affairs as we must. "To thine own self be true".' He
quoted Polonius as though no one in the room could ever have
seen or read *Hamlet*; and in so doing reduced poetry to a cliché.
Later, when he had no poetry at hand to clichify, he used, and
why not, a cliché itself. 'I would not presume to tell you who
should be here and who not, and when. Time and motion.
Tempus fugit and waits for no man. Or woman.' Every word
delivered was dramatically delivered, ponderously, as though he
was imparting wisdom. He could have replied simply 'perfectly all
right', instead he chose verbosity.

What was there about his accent? It was familiar yet illusive.
The courtesy seemed 'county', a courtesy anxious to anchor itself
in an old-fashioned world. A bygone courtesy. Not that I think
courtesy is old fashioned, not at all. I enjoy courtesy and having
compliments paid and car doors opened for me. But our Mr

Allerton's courtesy was too studied, as though it were not his nature but part of a contrived personality. 'I'm impressed and flattered that you stayed behind to greet me. I shall remember that, and deem it an honour and kindness.' Having shaken the hands of Lee and Tamara on arrival he now, a few minutes later, had to shake them goodbye. And he stood up to do so. Everything about his reverential courtesy confirmed contrivance rather than innate feeling. My friends gave me pitying looks of guilt as they kissed me goodbye.

The door hadn't closed before Mr Allerton called them back.

'Excuse me, but would you mind if I took a photograph of you all? It might become an historic photo one day.' He took control and arranged us behind the green leather-topped desk where in different poses he snapped and snapped and snapped away. Suddenly recognition dawned. The man's accent. It was American. American trying to be more English than the English. Here was an Anglophile. Harmless. Pedantic perhaps but harmless. When the others finally left I turned back to him.

'Nice people,' he said.

'What part of the States are you from?' I asked.

'Ah! You could tell, could you? No fooling you, eh? I'm from Boston. And you? That's not a London accent.' I told him I was from Norfolk, and we engaged in the sounding-out chatter of the newly acquainted. He was from Plymouth Brethren stock. He had, he said, traced his ancestry back to the Allertons, who crossed the Atlantic in the *Mayflower* in 1620.

'I'm not entirely proud of my ancestry. Unlike the Howlands who spawned such as Franklin D. Roosevelt and Humphrey Bogart. Isaac Allerton was a tailor from London who rose to become assistant to Governor Bradford and then, through various unauthorised deals on his trips back to England, landed the colony in debt. He had to flee. To New Haven, where he set up again, successfully trading with the Dutch. Unfortunately I inherited none of his business sense though his offspring did, and a small fortune was amassed of which a tiny portion came my way, which is how I live, I'm ashamed to say. Not ill-gotten gains but bequeathed ones. I've earned not one penny of it. Dreadful, isn't it?'

I kept trying to get him to lay out his 'idea' but he seemed more interested to expound on what I soon realised was the nonsense of an obsessive who derives his greatest pleasure from notions of doom and stories of gloom. Try though I did I could not ground him. I gave up and listened, only now and then punctuating his flow with a question. He spoke slowly and deliberately, dramatising his anecdotes with a body language that was mesmerising. He had little packages held together with elastic bands: a wallet bound to his passport, tickets and itinerary, and what looked like a wadge of calling cards. It seemed imperative to check every ten or fifteen minutes that everything was still there, that his world was still intact, that his possessions were still about him. His briefcase was full of such packages. There hovered over him, the atmosphere of a bag lady.

'Of course I believe in synchronicity rather than coincidence. Nothing that happens in this life is coincidental. Everything that happens was meant to be.'

'Even the slaughter of six million Jews?' I couldn't help asking.

'I'm afraid so,' he repeated apologetically, as though it was he who had been the slaughterer. I hate such notions. I become angry when I hear them. "Convenience notions", I call them; they conveniently require neither explanation nor outrage. Easy accountability. Ah, well, that's that; nothing to be done; walk away from carnage, betrayal, rail crash, usurpation of sovereignty, violence and murder. It was all meant to be!

Don't ask me why I didn't throw him out immediately, I don't know; morbid fascination, partly, and to begin with, I have to confess, he was beguiling.

'I'd really like to be a writer,' he said. 'I have this idea for a novel about Christopher Marlowe and William Shakespeare, because you know,' he whispered to me, 'it was Kit Marlowe really wrote all those plays.' He was sharing a secret he had discovered.

'Why,' I asked, 'would Kit Marlowe want to hide behind the name of William Shakespeare?'

'Because,' said the descendant of the *Mayflower* Allertons, 'Marlowe was homosexual and Catholic, and they were accusing him of being a spy, which was treason and punishable by death.'

I became wicked. 'And so one day, hearing that he might soon be arrested for spying he sat down and wrote thirty-two plays to protect himself? *Hamlet, King Lear, Richard the Third, Romeo and Juliet, The Tempest* – rather like Scheherazade who had to keep telling stories to the Sultan to stay alive, so Marlowe had to write play after play after play in the name of Shakespeare to stay alive? Is that it?'

'I think,' he said, reaching for his camera, 'that you're making fun of me.' Click! 'But I tell you,' click, click! 'there are lines in Shakespeare that are word for word lines from Kit Marlowe.' Click, click, click! 'Tell me, would any but the playwright pinch lines from his own play?' Click!

It was the logic of madness. I wanted to scream. Instead I said, cowardly: 'Of course!'

'Did you know,' he said apropos of nothing he had said so far, 'that the Mayan prophecies of five thousand years ago forecast that we are living in the last of what they called "the fifteen-year windows" and that on December 21st, 2012 there will take place the end of civilisation as we know it?' This announcement of the end of the world caused his brow to furrow deeply and his eyes to stare. His delivery became more deliberate. 'Two thousand and twelve. And what really happened to the Atlanteans was that they destroyed their own civilisation. That lost city was a city of technological geniuses who long ago invented the equivalent of our technological age. They had cures for all illnesses, and they could fly. They flew on long beams of crystal, and they had submarines to go underwater. They came after the lost continent of Mu whose inhabitants knew nothing. The people of Atlantis knew everything.' He didn't simply *relate* his doom-laden tales, he *performed* them, swinging on words for emphasis.

'Are you aware,' I asked, 'that you act out all that you're telling me?'

'I wanted to be an actor,' he explained with disarming geniality. 'I've always had this histrionic streak. What can I do? Forgive me!'

'But,' I persisted, 'with all this heavy acting you're sending me a message that your substance is so thin that you have to emphasise words that can't carry such emphasis. You're taking away from your credibility. You're not letting the story speak for itself. It's as though you don't think there's enough substance to allow it to speak for itself.'

'I know, I know,' he said with a confessional air that craved forgiveness. I might have forgiven him his absurd stories had they not been so full of boring detail and if I wasn't so frustrated unable to pin him down to explain his idea. The worrying thought flashed through my mind that he had no idea for 'yourideas.com', and that instead his life consisted of wanderings round the world in search of listeners to his tales of doom and his theories of conspiracy. Once such a thought came to me I felt pity. My goal changed. I would listen and humour him and not attempt to prise out a non-existent idea. If an idea finally did emerge it would be a bonus.

'How do we know all this about the civilisations of Mu and Atlantis?' I asked.

'James Churchward,' he replied. 'Heard of him?' I apologised and confessed I had not. God knows why I was being apologetic to this man whose tone of unarguable, indisputable fact was draining me. He claimed possession of the truth with such certitude that I felt dismissed, like a child for whose education he had Jesuitical responsibility. I knew I had to begin protecting myself, or at least steeling myself. 'James Churchward,' he continued, 'discovered sacred caves full of the Atlanteans' records. The Tibetan monks allowed him to take them away and study them, and they gave him the key to the codes of the books. That's how we know all this, through James Churchward and the Tibetan monks.'

Tibetan monks? Where did they come from? Was he confusing James Churchward with John Chadwick who, together with Michael Ventris, had deciphered the writing used by the Mycenaean civilisation of Bronze Age Greece? I think part of my fascination hinged on his logorrhoea and how it enabled him to leap seamlessly from one unrelated topic to another. 'And the souls of the drowned Atlanteans have been waiting for this technological age so that they can be reincarnated as the new technological whizz-kids. Which has happened. They *are* the new technological whiz kids; or technological whizz-kids like Bill Gates are the reincarnated Atlanteans and they're going to lead us to destruction with their television sets and computers just as the earlier Atlanteans destroyed *their* civilisation.'

'Why is it,' I asked him with reckless temerity, 'that all these forces are forces of evil or doom, never forces of good and triumph? And why is that we always get to know about them only in lost or heavily coded books? Do you believe evil will triumph in the end?' Why was I taking this man seriously enough to pose a rational question? Mr Allerton was a sad, damaged soul. His life was draining away through the cracks of his life's mistakes. He had fallen in love with an image of himself that never came into existence. His search for it left his personality sprawled all over the place.

'No, God not evil will win out in the end,' he replied.

'But you only offer evidence of destruction,' I foolishly reasoned, 'none for the triumph of God.'

'There is none,' he replied limply, his certitude ebbing briefly away. But not for long. He reached out for the security of a cliché. 'Greater the rewards in the life hereafter than in this one.'

'You don't agree with the Jews, then, that life this side of heaven is more important?'

'Well, the Jews *would* think that, wouldn't they? That's what drives them to control the world, isn't it?' My temerity burst its banks.

'You mean the President of the United States is Jewish? And

the President of Russia? And the Pope? And the Royal Bank of
Scotland is really the Royal Jewish Bank of Scotland? And the
rulers of China and India – Jews? And all those oil-rich Arabs –
more Jews pretending to be Arabs? I never knew!'

Sarcasm slid off his thick skin oiled by years of rejection and he
had a capacity to ignore all counter-arguments as though they had
not been uttered. I came to recognise when he knew he was
without words to reply – he would dip into his briefcase and
bring out another little package held together with a wide elastic
band. This time he brought out two packages – one was a small
wallet, again with an elastic band though the band seemed to
serve no other purpose than to keep the wallet together; and a
small bottle of Volvic spring water with a little schnapps size plastic cup banded to it with the ubiquitous elastic band. He had
brought his own water with him.

'Do you mind?' he asked. 'It's not alcoholic, but ever since I
nearly died from polluted tap water I drink nothing but the bottled stuff.' I waved him to go ahead, declined his offer of a
tumblerful, and took advantage of this lull in what was a much
longer diatribe than I have dared relate to arrange things on my
desk hoping he would take the hint that I had work to do. His
insensitivity was profound. There was no other world to live in
but his, and he drew one into it ineluctably. He carefully replaced
his bottle and plastic cup into his briefcase and then turned to his
other package, the wallet, from which he drew a small passport
photograph of a black man with a halo of curly hair and a sickly
smile of beatitude. His right hand was raised in salute.

'Sai. Sathay Sai Baba,' he announced. 'A living god with a following all over the world who can perform miracles because of
course . . .' (always 'of course', that adjunct to indisputability)
'. . . because of course he is the reincarnation of Jesus who was
himself the reincarnation of Abraham.'

'Why Abraham and not Moses?' My temerity knew no
bounds.

'Because Abraham was the reincarnation of Moses.' It seemed

heretical to point out that Abraham come before Moses, nor did I believe it would matter to him. 'Sathay Sai Baba,' Mr Allerton continued, 'born November 23rd 1974. The kind of miracles this man performs is to walk through dry land and make mango trees spring up so that weary travellers can satiate their thirst. One day the authorities told him he was earning income and therefore he had to pay taxes. Baba agreed with them, telling them that he was not running a business but . . .' This man, who by now had been with me so long that the drone of his voice was beginning to drone over me, sending my mind adrift so that I lost parts of his stories. For the sake of coherence I'm stitching together the parts I heard as though every part belonged to its previous part. For instance I don't know which authorities told Baba he must pay tax. I don't know even know if he was in the United States or an African country. As I was wondering how I was going to get rid of him I re-entered John Allerton's world where he was relating that: 'Baba took the tax men to a small shed that was unlocked and invited them to look inside. They did, and found shelves and shelves of gold bullion. "Help yourselves to all the tax you want," he told them. They went away and returned with the chief inspector who looked at the gold bullion and went off to get a truck big enough to take it away. And,' his voice grew darker, 'and when they came back the shed had disappeared.' Those last words came out of his mouth low and slow and very carefully articulated. 'The – shed – had – dis – app – eared.'

There! What do you think of that? How's that for a miracle? How's that for a moral tale of good and evil? 'Dis-app-eared!'

I said to him: 'Do you realise, Mr Allerton, that everything you have told me has come out of books, something read, or heard from others? You've not told me anything that is rooted in your own experience of human nature. You reach out to a fantasy here, a miracle there, but you reach into nothing of yourself.' His response was so sad that I regretted my probing.

'Why should I reach into myself? There's nothing there. I'm boring. I'm a bore and a loser. I know that. So I reach out for the fantastic, do my little bit of good in life, write my trifles, that's the best I can do.' He had laid a trap and I slipped effortlessly into it.

'You write?' I said. He reached into his briefcase for another package, this time a much larger one wrapped in brown paper held together by the broad bands of elastic.

'And here I come to why I asked to meet with you.' He was in control of the moment. I felt he had perceived that he had over-stayed his time but he was one of those people who didn't want to be asked to leave, he wanted to announce that he had to be going. I suspected he was the same on the telephone, that it was he who had to end the conversation and say goodbye first, perhaps even before the conversation had come to its natural end. And now, rather than have me press him to describe his idea, he wanted to deliver before I asked. He unwrapped the brown-paper package and laid a thick manuscript on the desk.

'You say you're looking for ideas to help people exploit? Well, here's an idea that will stir up the world and earn us both a great deal of money. Remember that novel about Kit Marlowe and Shakespeare that I told you I wanted to write? Well, it's written! I was kidding when I said I *wanted* to write it, the truth is – I've written it! There it is. A lifetime's work, fifteen years spent researching it, another fifteen spent writing it.'

'A labour of love,' I said, not knowing what else to say. Not true. I *did* know what else to say. 'But, Mr Allerton, we're not a literary agency. We don't read manuscripts.'

'You're called "yourideas.com" are you not?'

'Yes. "Yourideas.com" not "yournovels.com" or "literarya-gency.com". There are experts in that field. We are not they.'

'Nor is this a novel.'

'But you just said . . .'

'Don't tell me what I just said. I know what I just said.'

Was he becoming belligerent the nearer he drew to the all-familiar rejection he had sustained all his life?

'I called it a novel because that's the description the world understands. To call it what it really is would call down the wrath of the international theatre and literary world. This is not a novel, this manuscript is a revelation, contact with which will alter human beings' perception of the world.'

'But, Mr Allerton . . .'

'Let me finish! Please!' I could see the man was struggling with a deep fury. The laconic eyes, which on first encounter were courteous with certitude, were now ablaze for having been challenged. I was frightened for the first time. Had we let in a dangerous madman? Something told me not. Behind the glare of fury I could see fear and distress. 'I'm a bore and a loser,' he had said. Out of such knowledge comes violence, I know. Not from this man, though. His voice was violent and that was unpleasant enough but something about him told me – nothing physical would take place. In fact I resisted an impulse to take him in my arms and pat his back. But pity did well in me. I knew if I shouted 'boo' he would deflate. 'Please let me finish,' he repeated. 'It is not fully understood, not fully appreciated the extent to which the world and its perceptions of the human condition are shaped by the works of this man they call William Shakespeare. And if, suddenly, that face, that famous image of the bearded, semi-bald-headed man was replaced by another face, another image, if suddenly everything that the civilised, literate world knew or imagined it knew about William Shakespeare was wiped away, do you not think – can you not imagine the devastation that would follow? Every book, every essay, every manner of production of and about the plays of the man would have to be rethought, revised, rewritten. A revelation to cause a revolution!'

'But, Mr Allerton,' I began in the softest most placating voice I could muster, 'a rose by any other name would smell as sweet.'

I smiled my sweetest smile and made a gesture I thought would speak of gracious endings. What happened next was swift and instant. The man growled with anger from the pit of his stomach starting low and rising to a peak, which ended abruptly once he stood up. He spoke with his old hollow charm as though nothing had happened.

'I will leave it with you,' he said. 'Read it and let me know. Here's my card. Thank you for your time. Goodbye.' We shook hands, and he left without turning back. *He* had decided to leave. It was his decision. No one was going to tell him the meeting was over and that he must go. He was a profoundly sad man whose demeanour was that of one who knew he had lost the battle but didn't know how to walk away.

I looked at his card. It said all. It was in the style of a roll of ancient parchment. Nips had been cut away on all four sides of the oblong shape. The edges were faded brown with mock antiquity. In the top left-hand corner were the traditional masks of comedy and tragedy. The typeface was Olde English. Everything about it was pretentious. My pity faded. I read the first few pages of the manuscript. The prose was portentous. Here was a man writing as though commanded by God. I skipped to the middle and then to the end. God never left his side.

35

Tamara thought it was about time Beatie met her father

Tamara thought it was about time Beatie met her father. It was, after all, his money that was funding their enterprise.

'You'll like him,' she said, 'he's a bit intense, a bit humourless but his passion for music is infectious. He could have been a bore about it,' she said, 'but he's not, thank God.' She rang him and he at once invited them for dinner. 'He's a good cook,' Tamara promised, and checked with Beatie that there was nothing she disliked or couldn't eat. Beatie told her she could eat anything and, as she wasn't cooking it herself, would.

Beatie reflected, as they approached Barney's house with its quaint architectural features, how she loved London and its different areas. She had to acknowledge that she didn't know south London but the north had variety enough for a lifetime – from the bustle of markets: Ridley Road, Columbia Row, Petticoat Lane and Camden, to its *quartiers*, Hampstead, Muswell Hill, Golders Green, the City, the West End, black Harlesden, Asian Stepney. From its churches to its theatres, from its parks to its pubs, from its state and royal buildings to its galleries and concert halls; and from its highest views of the city as from St Paul's and the Monument to its low vistas as from Kenwood or Primrose Hill, or, spectacularly, from its bridges – Waterloo, Westminster, London and Tower Bridge. It was a glorious city, a loved and cared-for city, a city whose humanity accommodated most. And if one looked closely at the architecture one could see the centuries – Queen Anne, Georgian, Regency, Edwardian, Victorian, with splashes of invention belonging to no time but the builder's idiosyncrasies, and here and there art deco, mainly in the shape of cinema frontage. Ronnie had taught her to look up.

'Look up, look up, look at architectural details, the different styles of buildings next to each other. Look up at the variety within a street. Look up! Look up!'

Which is what she did when Tamara led her to the Edwardian house in which her father had his cluttered world. They had taken the Picadilly Line to Finsbury Park and from there a W7 bus to Heathville Road in Crouch End. Tamara had her own key to her father's flat. Beatie was surprised. Didn't she allow him his privacy?

'He always knows when I'm coming,' Tamara reassured her. 'I would never surprise him.'

'Does he have a key to *your* flat?'

'Of course!'

'Is that normal among Jews?'

'I would have thought it was just normal.'

'Not in Norfolk,' Beatie explained. 'Children nearly always have the keys to where their parents live because that's "home", but parents are rarely permitted to have keys to the houses of their children.'

'How strange.' Tamara looked perplexed.

As they approached the door they could hear loud male voices engaged in what sounded like a quarrel. Tamara waited before turning the key.

'Listen to them,' she said with a smile. 'Dad's got his oldest friend with him, Manfred Snowman, very rich, very civilised, very eccentric, very Jewish. Looks like there's going to be four of us for dinner. They're always quarrelling over something. I wonder what it is this time. Ssssh!' She turned the key gently, and they crept into the hallway. She wanted Beatie to listen before they announced themselves.

'You should always know what you're walking into,' she said. Beatie was not sure why her friend was making such an 'event' of their entry, especially as there was something familiar about the tones and cadences seeping through the thin plasterboard wall.

Two Jewish men were debating a current topic of the day. It was familiar to her. She had listened to such heated exchanges in the Clapton council flat of Ronnie's parents where tenacious Bolsheviks furiously argued with disillusioned Bolsheviks, of which Ronnie had been one. But there was something else filtering through the voices she was hearing. She couldn't discern what it was but found herself listening intently, as though, to mix metaphors, she had been given a dish to eat and asked to identify the surprise ingredient. What was it? She knew it and didn't know it, like seeing a familiar face in strange surroundings. The features had a place but not the place she was looking at. Could it belong to one of that circle of lonely and eccentric friends of Ronnie's mother? She knew the voice but it was not coming from where she had heard it before. All she knew was that the surprise 'ingredient' excited her.

And what were the voices arguing over? The Rushdie affair. On 26 September 1988 Viking Penguin published Salmon Rushdie's novel *The Satanic Verses*. The following month it was banned in India, and a month later, in November, it won the Whitbread Prize for 'best novel'. Bannings followed in Bangladesh, Pakistan, Sudan, Sri Lanka and South Africa. On 14 January 1989 Muslims in Bradford burned a copy of *The Satanic Verses*, and the news hit world headlines. But not as much as the Fatwa, a word unknown outside Islam but now common parlance.

On 14 February that same year Ayatollah Ruhollah Khomeini of Iran pronounced on Tehran radio: '*I inform the proud Muslim people of the world that the author of* The Satanic Verses *book which is against Islam, the Prophet and the Koran, and all involved in its publication who were aware of its content, are sentenced to death*'. Anyone, he went on to say, who dies in the cause of ridding the world of Rushdie '*will be regarded as a martyr and go directly to heaven.*' He had not, of course, read the book.

The exchange upon which Tamara and Beatie were eaves-dropping was taking place against this background.

'I don't think it helps to talk about what "causes" it. What "releases" it makes more sense.' Beatie knew that voice but in gentler mode, more relaxed, less strained to convince. The other voice was more anxious, familiar anxious, familiar Jewish anxious.

'You and your distinctions!'

'Distinctions matter, they clarify confused thinking.' Not only was the voice familiar but so, too, was the sentence structure, the reasoning and the rhythm.

'My thinking is not confused,' protested the anxious Jewish voice. 'It doesn't need clarification. The facts are simple and clear. Salman Rushdie recanted and asserted his faith in Islam and the existence of one God with Mohammed as his prophet, and the Ayatollah Ali Khomeini said it doesn't matter how much he recants, the death sentence remains. Look, I'm not making it up, here, in the *Guardian*, they report the Ayatollah's words "*The Imam's edict and the Muslim's commitment to implement it are bearing their first fruits on the scene of confrontation between Islam and world infidelity. Western arrogance, which had attacked the sanctities of a billion Muslims as a prelude to degrading Muslims and the Islamic renaissance in the world, has been forced to retreat in disgrace . . .*" etc. etc. *What* "Western arrogance"? *Which* "Muslim sanctities" have been attacked? The unsurpassed wealth of Muslim nations rests on the application of Western technology. What is the crazy man talking about? Tell me he's not suffering from an inferiority complex. Tell me the whole of Islam is not suffering from an inferiority complex. And tell me what difference whether we ask what "caused" it or what "released" it.'

'I'll tell you what difference.' The 'familiar' voice again. 'If you believe that the riots in Kashmir protesting about the book are "caused" then you look for who or what is to blame, and you imagine that once identified then the riots will cease. If on the other hand it's understood that rioting is "released" then you have to ask the question: what needs to be *contained* so that the rioting is *not* released? "Caused" assumes the evil can be cured; "released" accepts that the evil is ever present, and can only be minimised by containing it. The surface of gentle humanity has flaws, like the earth's crust, through which eruptions burst. There was a religious eruption called the Inquisition; there was a nationalist eruption called Nazism; there was an ideological eruption called communism; there was a racist eruption called apartheid. Something, some madness, some murderous intolerance is always there, lurking, waiting to erupt. Nothing *causes* it – like anti-Semitism and stupidity it's there in the bloodstream of humanity waiting to erupt through flaws in the skin. The question is: what can be done to minimise the flaws, to stem them? Politics, like health, should be concerned with prevention perhaps more than with healing.'

'I think,' whispered Tamara to Beatie, 'that's a good point to enter.'

She knocked on the door in the hallway and burst in upon her father and his friend. Beatie entered the room and froze. Manfred froze, too. Barney and his daughter didn't freeze but entered a kind of slow motion, as though they had to move through the next minutes very carefully or they would fail to understand them. Understand what?

'What is it?' Barney asked as though he had made a terrible mistake but didn't fully understand the nature of the mistake.

'This is unbelievable,' Manfred said.

'Unbelievable,' Beatie echoed.

'Is it really you?' Manfred asked.

'I hope so,' Beatie replied.

'*What* is happening here?' Tamara asked in a scolding tone, irrationally feeling left out of a momentous event. Manfred and Beatie spoke in unison:

'Shepherd Market!'

'You mean,' said Tamara, 'it's *him*?'

'It's him.'

'You mean,' said Barney, 'it's *her*?'

'It's her.' Manfred and Beatie from here on behaved as though the other two were not in the room.

'I shouldn't tell you this,' said Beatie, 'but I went back a few times to see if I'd bump into you again.'

'You *should* tell me this,' Manfred confirmed, 'because I did the same. In fact, it's absurd, or no, it's not absurd, but it's something strange that in those few minutes you made such an impact on me that I've thought about you constantly. No, not constantly, but disproportionately, unreasonable, illogically.'

'How's your back?' Beatie asked, stemming his declaration of love before it burst into flood.

'My back?'

'You stood up – I see it very plainly and I remember every word – you stood up, put the backpack on your shoulder instead of your back, offered your hand and said "it was very kind of you to allow me to talk to you."

As Beatie uttered that sentence she realised why the other sentence, the one she had heard through the plasterboard wall, had sounded familiar. People *did* have recognisable ways of structuring their thoughts and sentences. 'Distinctions matter, they clarify confused thinking.' 'It was kind of you to allow me to talk to you.' The same number of syllables. Thirteen. Beatie continued. 'I thought what a strange thing to say. *Allow* you? I wasn't *allowing* anything. And then you said, "The world is divided between people who are immediate and those who are hard work. You, my dear young woman," you said, "are immediate." And as you walked away I thought to myself – if he continues carrying a backpack on his shoulder he will strain his spine. Did you strain your spine?'

'No.'

'So you didn't end up on your back?'

'No, I flew to Antarctica and walked the frozen wastes and thought how much more of an experience it would be if *she* was with me. I didn't know your name. I could only think of "she" and "her". I still don't know your name.'

'Beatie,' she said. 'Beatie Bryant.'

'Manfred Snowman,' he responded.

'How do you do?' said Beatie. 'I'm very pleased to meet you.'

'And I'm very pleased to meet you, too.' They should have shaken hands at this point but neither moved. Or rather they did but imperceptibly, a tiny shudder forward as though both were on a narrow path and were uncertain how to let the other pass. Finally Beatie uttered a cry of three words that belonged to the end of a heated, internal, exchange, one that could only be guessed at by the nature of the three words themselves.

'I DON'T CARE!' she hurled at her interior opponent, and leapt into two arms that knew she was coming. They kissed on the lips and hugged with the passion of long-parted lovers. Tamara was thrilled to witness it, her father was appalled.

'Stop this, Manfred, stop this. Have you lost your mind? You're embracing a minor!'

Beatie laughed. 'Thank you for the compliment but I'm nearly thirty.'

'That may be, but Manfred is one hundred and thirty.'

'Don't exaggerate, Father,' said his daughter, 'and don't jump to conclusions. They're not lovers in the throes of a passionate reunion, they're strangers in the night in the throes of amazement. And you've got to admit – it *is* pretty amazing that your friend and my friend should meet briefly in Shepherd Market, never expect to meet again, and then do so eighteen months later in your apartment. Come, old man, what are the chances of that happening? A million to one? Stop looking so judgemental and meet my college friend or I'll think you're jealous. Beatie, this is my dad, our benefactor, but don't leap into his arms because I don't think he'll be there for you.'

'Yes, he will,' said Beatie, and although it was nowhere near the quality of the leap she had made towards Manfred it was a warm, friendly and fond embrace acknowledging her debt to a man whose blood money had paid her wages these last twelve months, and in whose space there now pervaded an atmosphere of gaiety releasing the spontaneous part of them each.

'You're right, Manfred,' said Barney completely won over. 'She *is* very immediate.' Manfred and Beatie – whose incredulity lingered like a fire refusing to die out – could not stop looking at one another and smiling throughout the evening. But it was an evening during which their emotions calmed, and they were given time to reflect. Their reflections entered parallel lines.

Both very much wanted to be alone with the other, and both knew they had to work hard not to make their friends feel uncomfortable by showing it. It was not easy, for though they participated in conversations and even initiated some they did so with too much of an eagerness to please that the astute Perls could discern. But neither of them could hide their lapses into reflections. This is an attractive man, thought Beatie. Intelligent, original, assured and obviously dependable. But he's more than twice my age. What on earth am I contemplating? Lee looks acceptable alongside Tamara because although she's obviously an older woman she is not an old woman. This man, for all his vigour and health, not only looks as though he could be my father but will inevitably behave like one. How could it be else? We could walk arm in arm along the street but never hand in hand. On the other hand – why not? Would I care what we looked like together? He doesn't have that many wrinkles – a few on his forehead. But around the eyes? They come from laughter. He's a man who smiles a great deal. As she thought about what they would look like walking hand in hand she was overcome with a great urge to run her fingers around his eyes, to feel the wrinkles, kiss them. Were her first impressions of him being sustained as the evening progressed? She remembered thinking how youthful he was in that old man's skin; now she could see he was not that youthful but neither was his skin the skin of an old man. It was his mischievous eyes that had given him an aura of youthfulness. There was still a kind of mischief in his eyes but it was of the contemptuous kind; his eyes laughed with contempt at the idiocy of the world.

The Rushdie affair was picked up again.

'I feel very strongly about the Rushdie affair,' said Beatie. 'The man has been made a prisoner in his own country by a foreign power. There's madness for you. He's a prisoner of Iran in the UK!'

'And for what?' exclaimed an outraged Barney. 'For writing a book! We thought that went out with the Nazis. No more burning of books. Who could believe it?'

'But not just any book,' Tamara thought it necessary to remind her father. 'A blasphemous book.'

'It's his right to blaspheme,' insisted Barney, who was rummaging among his books for a copy of the Koran. 'We all have a right to blaspheme. It's actually impossible *not* to blaspheme, an inescapable hazard of living, and it's a sign of intellectual and emotional maturity to accept this. Listen, the Koran, the chapter called "The Proof". *Nor did the people of the book* – that's us – *disagree among themselves until proof was given them . . . The unbelievers among the people of the book shall burn forever in the fire of hell. They are the vilest of all creatures.* And this from a chapter called "The Believers". *We have revealed to them the truth but they are liars all. Never has Allah begotten a son, nor is there any God besides him . . . Exalted be Allah above their falsehoods.* Now, should Jews and Christians find that offensive, blasphemous? *Never has Allah begotten a son.* What, no Jesus? And *they* want to burn books? Perhaps the Ayatollah is right. Perhaps the world *is* divided between Islam and the West.'

'The world,' countered Manfred, 'is not divided between Islam and the West as the crazed Ayatollah would have us believe, it's divided as it has always been divided between the rational and the irrational, the tolerant and the intolerant, the mindless and the thoughtful – divisions which can be found every century in every country.

'Excluding, of course, the land of Israel,' said Tamara provocatively.

'Don't rise to my daughter's taunts,' warned Barney.

'*In*cluding Israel,' said Manfred, not rising to them. Beatie dared enter the fray.

'You mean as Jews you're not supportive of Israel?'

'My country right or wrong?' posed Manfred. 'No! But we're all aware how that poor beleaguered state has had three wars declared upon it, and it's not even as old as I am.'

'It's the old problem for Jews,' said Barney, 'to whom do we owe allegiance?'

'It may be a problem for you,' said Manfred. 'Not for me. And come now, Barney, I don't really think it is for you.' Beatie heard a depth of feeling in that friend's voice addressing his friend. 'We none of us round this table, the three Jews that is, I can't speak for our lovely Gentile here, we none of us claim allegiance to either a religion or a nation but to a long line of freethinkers who've stood out against human injustice, cruelty and pathological fanaticism of any kind since the beginning of time. And such men and women have come from different religions, different cultures and different nation states.'

'And they are the glory of the human race,' said Tamara.

'Amen!' said Barney.

That 'amen' should have brought the Rushdie topic to a halt, but did not. It was an issue being discussed and argued about worldwide. It was a difficult issue to alight on and then fly from, galvanising attention as few others did. People had died in riots over it, the Japanese translator of the book had been murdered, its Norwegian publisher had been shot and wounded and intellectuals quarrelled over it as they had quarrelled over little else. Rushdie himself could move nowhere without police protection, and had to be kept moving around the country with his bodyguards scouting out the land before he arrived anywhere. And in the boots of their cars was a Hollywood array of arms to cover all possible eventualities. Clear thinking was at a premium, and all manner of sophistries and intellectual contortions were printed in the press. A history of those days has yet to be written.

Out of the silence and hiatus following 'amen' came the question posed round many a dinner-party table.

'Has anyone here actually read *Satanic Verses*?' It was Tamara who asked, adding: 'Because I must admit I haven't. Slim Hemingways and McEwans are all I can manage these days.'

'I've read it,' said Manfred.

'So have I,' said Beatie.

'I tried, and gave up halfway,' confessed Barney.

'Did either of you two enjoy it?' pressed Tamara. Both said they did.

'Though with a mixture of absorption and ennui,' said Manfred.

'I have a theory about Rushdie and his book,' began Beatie. Suddenly she was the centre of attention. 'We're talking about a highly intelligent and very literate writer here, one who has read not only the giants of the past – your Lawrences, your Balzacs, your Tolstoys – but also contemporary giants – your Kunderas, your Roths, your Bellows, your García Márquezes. And he's seen how writers of all religions have felt free both to evaluate their different religions – Catholicism, Judaism, Protestantism – and to play with them, some harshly, and some, horror of horrors, irreverently. I think of Voltaire, Rabelais, Swift, and leaping forward, the novels of the American and European writers like Heller, Mailer, Kazantzakis, Joyce . . . Rushdie must have fed on such works with their enlightened free spirits, and challenged himself to add to this body of literary irreverence from his own culture. But he forgot one thing – Judaeo-Christian evolution had produced a tradition of doubt and questioning. Writers had adapted to their times. Rabbis had questioned rabbis. Priests had questioned priests. And today many of them question the literalness of the Old and New Testaments. It didn't happen in Islam. The mullahs preferred power to enlightenment, and kept their believers in a state of unquestioning ignorance. The once glorious leaders of learning stood still for a thousand years. Scholarship stultified. No art, no literature, no humour, no reassessment. Rushdie hit a humourless blank wall. The Jews talk to God on familiar terms, but Moslems can't talk to Allah like that. He thought his readers would only be Jewish! Big mistake. People with fragile egos and inferiority complexes are looking for a fight.'

She paused. They waited. Tamara was amazed at this from her college friend. They thought she would continue. She was stirring them up, they wanted her to continue. Beatie, however, was preoccupied by other stirrings. While talking with mounting excitement, realising how articulate and lucid she had become, something was happening to her body; that is to one very special part of her body – her nipples. They were becoming erect. It was not Manfred and sexual arousal stiffening them, it was intellectual arousal. It had happened once before at university. She had stood up nervously during a student debate about the rights and wrongs of the Falklands War, and had argued an unpopular position – she had seen it as a war against tyrannical generals who had usurped the sovereignty of their people. She had not been emotional; on the contrary she had been controlled and reasonable and had marshalled her argument with great clarity. But while arguing her case she was acutely aware that her nipples were protruding through a thin blouse and brassiere and she had difficulty bringing her argument to an end as she noticed a male student nudge his friend and both stare at this unaccountable occurrence. Now, presenting her explanation of how Salman Rushdie had misjudged the possible reaction of the Muslim world to his novel, Beatie was aware, once again, of the rising of the tips of her breasts. Was adrenaline always going to affect her nipples thus, she wondered?

'I sound clever, don't I?' Beatie coyly returned her attention to the company. 'I'm not really. It's just that ever since your daughter,

my friend here, explained something that I should have known
about, to whit, the Talmudic tradition; and especially ever since
the publication of *Satanic Verses* I've been boning up on comparative religions, and that's my theory, folks. Rushdie read too much
Jewish literature and developed his writing skills in the wake of the
dangerous Jewish tradition of irreverence. At worst he must have
thought he would go through what Philip Roth went through
after writing *Portnoy's Complaint* – Jewish Roth faced Jewish
wrath, but it was verbal wrath confronting verbal Roth – no
sticks, no stones, no bullets, no death-demanding fatwas. The
Jews argued, they used words, which is what you'd expect from
the people of the book.'

Manfred interposed: "Come now and let us reason together',
says Isaiah.'

'Precisely!' continued Beatie. 'So Roth got away with it, and
Rushdie thought he would, too. Big mistake, big, big mistake.
Don't be surprised if his book ends up as the spark that inflamed
the Third World War. Thank you and out, Mr Rushdie.'

'Are you sure you're not Jewish?' Tamara asked.

'Positive. Very un-Jewish in fact. Very Viking un-Jewish. I get
strange sensations in the presence of Viking boats rather than the
Sabbath candles. Though I love the Sabbath ritual – a taste
acquired through my Jewish boyfriend, Ronnie Kahn.'

They covered many topics during Barney's four-course meal.
He was a limited cook, or more accurately a good cook with limited repertoire. But the handful of dishes he offered on the rare
occasions he had guests were carefully cooked and exquisitely
presented. They covered Rushdie before and during the chopped
liver; the progress of 'yourideas.com' during and after the beef
stroganoff; Barney's abandoned biography of Giovanni
Marcantonio during and after the dessert of bananas with
Cointeau; and Manfred's beekeeping ambitions during the selection of cheeses and grapes followed by coffee and brandy. Manfred
brought the red wine, a Gigondas and Chianti Red Ruffino,
which by chance fitted with the stroganoff; Beatie brought a

newly discovered white wine from the vineyards of Chile, which were beginning to make their impact on the British market. A 'revelation' they all agreed.

Manfred wanted to know what kind of ideas were being handled by 'yourideas.com'. Tamara and Beatie listed them: the Volvo advert, the toilet wet ones, the Everything cereal, the penny for ministries and charities idea.

'Downing Street,' recounted Tamara, 'found the idea of pennies towards our favourite cause – the arts, education, health and so on – "fascinating, absolutely fascinating", but backed away explaining how they would become an easy target for Tory mockery if they invited taxpayers to spend spare pennies on more tax.'

'And they were right, of course,' said Beatie. 'But one charity, for installing computers in underprivileged primary schools, took up the idea. We commissioned an advertising firm to design an illustrated cardboard container for the penny-box and it caught on. The schools sent their pupils off to local shops with the boxes, which pick up two hundred and fifty pennies a week. Ten shops can produce one hundred pounds a month. That can buy a computer in a year. Some raised enough to buy three. The problem is,' she continued, 'that people don't come with ideas, they come with ambitions.' She related the story of the American and his ambition to publish his novel proving Christopher Marlowe wrote Shakespeare's plays. She related it well and vividly, recreating the personality of the man as well as remembering his utterances and clichés; and as she was doing it she realised she had inherited her mother's skill of storytelling, warming to and intoxicated by the laughter and wrapt attention of her audience. 'And there was the young writer who came in with a film treatment for what seemed to us a perfectly good film involving the English passion for gardens. But we had to point out that we weren't film agents, though perhaps we should be that as well, intermediaries for the arts – films, plays, concerts, exhibitions – as well as intermediaries for shampoo and car adverts. What do you say, Tamara?'

'Don't!' intervened Manfred deep from his experience of being an accountant to artists. 'The arts are a minefield, full of third-rate middle-men and women who are first-rate opportunists. Individual artists may be a beacon of light unto the world but the arts market is a temple of slaughter, back-stabbing, bloodletting and betrayal. I know the practitioners intimately. Don't! Stay away! Sell adverts and ideas for cleaner toilets. Less fraught.'

'What about,' asked Tamara, 'ideas like the one that came in last week? A father – a parent father, that is, not a Church father – came in with a drawing, a rough drawing he'd made of our universe. There was the sun, and the planets revolving around the sun at different distances, and the moon going round the earth, and he asked us, "Do you know which way the earth spins? From left to right or right to left? And do you know how many times a year it tilts on its axis?" He didn't give us a chance to answer. "Nor do many children," he said. "Now," he said, "what I want is to be able to buy a kit where you can assemble the universe wired to a power box which you plug into the mains, flick a switch, and the whole caboodle starts moving so that my kids can see what's going on out there. I can buy them a globe of the world that revolves and glows but I can't buy them the universe. Now" he said, "is this an idea that could be put into practice or not, and are you lot up to it?"'

'What did you tell him?' asked Manfred.

'We told him it surely was a good idea,' replied Tamara, 'and that we were up to it, and I have to inform you that as we speak it is being looked into.' But very little else was working, they had to admit. 'Yourideas.com' was not as good an idea as they had anticipated. The most they now hoped for was to earn sufficient royalties from the Volvo advert and pay back Barney his initial investment with some 'redundancy' cash left for themselves. Barney protested that he didn't want his money back, he was content for Tamara to hold on to it until her future to be or not to be a film director became clear.

It was Beatie who turned the conversation away from themselves and expressed dismay that Barney had given up on the biography of the unknown Italian composer.

'It's very important,' Barney responded, 'to know one's limitations. Neither to overestimate one's talents and skills nor to underestimate them. I have intelligent things to say about the composition of new music and the performance of the classics. I don't always get it right, who does? But I mostly do. Reconstructing a life, on the other hand, is beyond me. The quality of imaginative transferral of who one is into the being that one is not requires leaps of imagination and perception I do not, believe me, possess.' Beatie attempted to protest. 'Dear soul,' Barney addressed the assembly, 'she wants to think everyone capable of realising their ambitions. She has not yet identified that human predilection for *articulating* aspirations in place of *fulfilling* them. She hasn't yet learnt that though people are born with equal basic human rights yet they are not, lamentably, born equal. But Beatie, *meine leiber*, the heart must face the unhappy fact of unequal endowment. Everyone has a story to tell, it's true, but not everyone's story is one they, personally, are capable of telling.'

'I may come to accept this one day,' combated Beatie, 'but confronted with someone as intelligent and articulate as you, Barney, I here and now find it difficult.'

'I'm won over!' cried a flattered Barney. 'Your friend, Tamara, is a darlink, a darlink. Nevertheless, Beatie, you must believe me. Here, let me tell you a story. There was once a music critic, the name's not important, who woke up one morning and tried to remember the opening of Shostakovitch's Eighth Quartet, the one with the rhythmic Yiddish melody, which he'd heard the night before, and had to review. He worked that way. Some critics wake up to read a novel they're reviewing; writers wake up remembering where they left off the day before, wondering about how they're going to continue. This critic woke up going over the music he heard the night before. But on this morning he couldn't recall the notes, and he thought – well, maybe it's too complicated for 7.30 a.m. So he tried to recall the opening of the Mahler First Symphony, and he couldn't recall that either. Never mind, he said to himself, Mahler is not early morning music anyway. But he was beginning to be worried so he went for a pop classic, Beethoven's Pastoral Symphony. Nothing! He couldn't recall any part of it, nor the Grieg Piano Concerto, nor the Bruch Violin Concerto. He managed the opening of the Beethoven Fifth because schoolboys made jokes about how those first notes came about. And he managed the driving insistent opening of the Rachmaninov Second Piano Concerto, presumably because the opening drives insistently. But little else. And he panicked. Snatches of music floated through his memory like detritus in a cyclone but he couldn't remember what the names were and he couldn't fit together the parts. He had to give up, after which his life began to fall to pieces. He couldn't make sense of anything. Neither life nor music. For years he lived off his savings and a small pension until one day he read a profile of the playwright Arthur Miller, and discovered that Miller's great hobby was carpentry. Miller made furniture. My colleague was amazed. A great writer like that and he enjoyed putting pieces of wood together. This appealed to him, my colleague – chipping and sawing and making holes to fit things into. His life had fallen apart because music had fallen apart for him, perhaps putting together parts of furniture would help him put together parts of his life. He sold up his London house, moved to near Aldburgh, which he'd come to love from his music-critic days, and set up a little workshop where he taught himself rudimentary carpentry. He makes furniture. I don't think he's a great craftsman but he's an adequate one. He hasn't made a fortune but he lives, he makes a living. His memory for music came back, not as before, never as before, but sufficient to give him occasional solace. The point is that music came to an end for him. Silence took over in his head, and he had to face that fact.' Barney's story came to an end but had to be rounded off. 'And I have to face the fact – I'm not a writer. I can't write about another person's life. Believe me. I'm not normally modest. Believe me.'

'What a story!' exclaimed Beatie. 'And you didn't make it up?'

'Such a story you can't make up,' said Barney.

'It's haunting. Music falling apart. Parts not fitting. Furniture made up of parts. One doesn't think of a piece of furniture as being made up of parts. A chair is something you sit on, you don't think you're sitting on parts. Haunting. I'll be haunted for life by that story.'

'As I'll be haunted by the story of the old woman who was afraid to go on the escalator in the Underground, said Tamara.'

'We're all haunted by something in our lives,' said Tina.

'No one's asking you,' said Barney, 'so go away.' Everybody knew Tina had entered their evening, but no one wanted her to stay so she left. Not without whispering first in her daughter's ear: 'Ask him about Natasha.'

'Go, Mother, go!' said Tamara. And she did. 'How's Natasha, Dad?' she asked her father.

'She told you to ask about Natasha?'

'She told me.'

'Don't you,' asked Beatie of Manfred, 'find their conversation with the dead a little creepy?'

'To begin with,' said Manfred. 'But when you get used to it it's rather touching.'

When Barney had announced to her sister that Natasha was pregnant, Tamara's response was that she hoped her sister was not going to keep the baby. Barney became angry, and they had quarrelled.

Tamara's reasoning was: 'She doesn't want it, she's not ready for it, there's no father to father it and she's not capable of being a single parent.'

'You have a bad habit,' he told her, 'of making decisions for other people.'

'Those aren't decisions, they're facts and opinions. She doesn't want it – fact! She's not ready for it – opinion! There's no father for it – fact! She's not capable of being a single parent – opinion! *He* made a decision for *her* – him, the guitar player who's gone off to Australia as though being the other side of the world means it's not happening. Bloody George, Jack, Sidney – whatever his name is, was.'

Barney had persisted: 'After all, remember, she has me for the grandfather and you for the aunt. What more does she need? And you know what, darlink, it could be the making of her. We unsettled her – me involved in music, you going through university – unsettled, confused her. What we were she wasn't, and she found nothing to fill the void. Maybe motherhood is what she was made for, and I don't care what the feminists say it's one of the most noble and honourable professions in the world.'

'I don't think,' had replied his daughter, 'that the most intelligent feminists—'

'Among whom you place yourself.'

'Among whom I do indeed place myself, would disagree. The problem is that mothers too frequently have to pay an unacceptable price to perform that most noble and honourable profession in the world – domestic drudgery, long hours, loss of freedom, loss of independence, relegation to the fourth division of existence, no cake, no cream, no topping, no thanks.'

What had finally persuaded Tamara was the story that had finally persuaded Natasha – about the brother they nearly had. Tamara had wept and Barney had comforted her and mused how young our children always seem.

Natasha had since given birth to a seven-and-a-half-pound son, and both grandfather and aunt had been thrilled with their new roles, which they fulfilled with much fussing and loving and purchasing of everything a baby needs – clothes cradle, carrycot, pram, mobiles that tinkled and spun and of course stuff that would not be needed for another eighteen months like a playpen, a high chair and toys that had to be wound up, and played music unwinding. Tamara had been amazed to find herself going daft over dinky shoes and socks and colourful hats. Barney of course had opened an account for his grandson's university education, and all three had quarrelled round her bedside over the different lists each had made from which he was to be named. They quickly dismissed the Russian names like Fydor, Vladimir and Sergei; then the rosy-cheeked English names like Tom, John and Peter; followed by the biblical names like Adam, Aaharon, Samuel, Saul and Luke; till finally they were left with a list of six that seemed to belong to no category – Max, Terence, Maurice, Kevin, Ralph and Boris. Boris had difficulty being on the list because it sounded Russian but gradually everyone not only accepted it but chose it. It seemed European. The name was at home in more than one country.

'So,' asked Tamara of her father, 'what do you have to tell me about Natasha? It can't be anything I don't know because I spoke with her two days ago.'

'Why do you think your mother asked you to ask me? You must have detected something in Natasha's tone of voice.' There was silence all round as Tamara tried to remember if there had or had not been something in her sister's tone of voice that had let her mother in. Beatie was beginning to understand – Tina entered their lives when something was worrying them. How peculiar. She had not come across such an occurrence before. What a strong personality Tina must have been.

'Yes, I had noticed something,' said Tamara at last.

'I was going to wait till this evening had come and gone,' said Barney, 'but your mother – well, it's out now. Greg has come knocking at Natasha's door to be let back in.'

'Greg the guitarist?'

'Him!'

'Greg the fucking slinking-off, thieving, third-rate guitarist from Australia?'

'Yesterday. No announcement, just a knock at the door and "Can I come in."'

'And she let him in?'

'Of course she did.'

'Of course she fucking did, my soft-hearted sister.'

'"He's the father," she said.'

'The fucking *what*?'

'Tamara, darlink, be a good girl, don't swear so much.'

Manfred stood up. 'I think,' he announced, 'it's time to leave this family alone. Beatie, can I drop you off anywhere?'

She accepted eagerly. When she hugged Tamara goodbye she whispered in her ear: 'You will make sure your sister throws him out won't you?'

'Of course,' her friend whispered back. 'And you will tell me what happens tonight with you and him, won't you?' Beatie made no verbal reply, simply uttered a sound that revealed uncertainty. A 'hurrumph' that could mean either 'Don't be silly, nothing will happen', or 'You must be crazy to imagine I'll share such a thing with you'.

In the car both the young woman and the older man became shy and embarrassed. The passion of their first meeting a mere four hours ago seemed an eternity away, as though those two shocked and excited beings who had leapt into each other's arms were now utter strangers to one another. They felt like two people who had met for the first time and were now searching for car-journey conversation. Manfred wanted to say, 'Would you like to come to my place for a drink?' but it had sounded corny even as the question formulated in his mind. He felt ridiculous. She's only thirty for God's sake and you're sixty-one. Beatie for her part toyed with asking him in for a coffee but couldn't bring herself to utter such an invitation, filled as it was with obvious, ulterior expectation. Both were in turmoil, having a great deal they wanted to say and ask of the other; and physically tense with the effort of reining in what they wanted to do with their hands. Each slid away from the other fearing they might be hinting at an intimacy the other did not want. Each was uncertain whether the other was feeling what the other was feeling, and each dreaded making a fool of themselves, feared rejection. Their shyness with one another was remarkable to them both. And when Beatie said: 'Here will do,' and the car stopped and they turned to face one another for goodbyes each deliberately letting the other know the farewell kiss was to be on the cheek. Manfred made a wide

semicircular movement forward and round to his left that said 'I'm
going for your left cheek and certainly not for your lips', while
Beatie pointedly pulled back and offered her left cheek.

'Goodbye,' said Manfred, 'I'm sure we'll meet again now we
have the Perls in common.'

'I'm sure we will.' She should have got out at that point but it
seemed like a blunt point, a pointless point. She hovered, shifted
awkwardly as though she didn't know how to wriggle out of a car.
Manfred attempted to help.

'Perhaps you'd like to see my beehives sometime,' he suggested,
and felt crass. 'It used to be etchings.' Beatie in her confusion had
no idea what he was talking about.

'Etchings?'

'It used to be 'Would you like to come up and see my etchings?''

'Oh, I see.'

'Now it's bees.' His sense of crassness deepened.

'I see.'

Manfred tried humour. 'Either way you might get stung.'
Beatie's confusion had blunted his wit.

'That would be nice.'

Now it was Manfred's turn to become confused. 'Nice? To be
stung?'

'No. To see your bees. To see your bees, that would be nice.' At
which she fled, blushing to have used the word 'nice'. Who was
it said 'mittens are nice'? It was a word she normally tried to
avoid, like 'interesting' and 'basically' and 'actually' and
'absolutely'.

36

She asked if he knew the parts of a bee

She asked if he knew the parts of a bee.

'Not off by heart,' he had replied, 'I try to avoid overloading my head with facts that can be referred to in a book.' They were standing beside one of his beehives dressed like astronauts in protective clothing. He was pulling out frames of busy, clinging bees that seemed startled to be exposed to air for which they were not yet ready. Many had just arrived with nectar for honey, and were not in the mood to cope with more air.

'Looking at this seething lot,' said Beatie, 'the expression "a hive of activity" takes on its real meaning.'

'I can name you parts of a hive without reference to a book,' he said. And he broke down the structure of a hive for her. There were seven parts. 'So, not many parts to remember – the floor, the entrance block, the brood box, the queen excluder, the super box, the crown board and the roof. Seven parts to produce the sweetness of life. Satisfying, no?'

Of course there was much more to explain of the process of beekeeping and honey-collecting, and Manfred explained it well, lively with metaphor and imagery. Did she know that grass plants are pollinated by the wind, and flower plants are pollinated by bees? Did she know that the human eye can distinguish about sixty different colours but the bee sees only four: yellow, bluey-green, blue and ultraviolet, which is invisible to humans? Did she know that butterflies taste with the tips of their legs?

'What really fascinates me,' he told her, 'are their parallels to human behaviour. As in life, there are only a few bees who dare take on the pioneering role of "scout". The majority prefer to wait to be told where food is.' Which led him to describe how the scout bees dance their information to the rest of the brood. 'But one of the most poetic aspects of bees is that because there is a close relationship between the bee's sense of smell and sense of touch so, in a way, the bee can smell form. Isn't that poetic – to be able to smell form?' Beatie agreed it was, and kept asking for more, more information about bees. Manfred was happy to share all he had learnt from books.

It was their first meeting after dinner at Barney's. When Beatie had fled using the word 'nice' she feared that her last image for Manfred was of a blushing, foolish young woman who had talked too much about that of which she knew little – a couple of books on comparative religion and she had held forth as though an authority. She despised this trait in others, those who read a little, learn a little and then know everything; overnight instant author-ities. Her dread had made her sweat. She needed a hot bath.

The bathroom had become one of her favourite rooms in this Belsize Park flat she had moved to from the one over the Greek restaurant in Crouch End. She luxuriated in it as she luxuriated in the area. Everything was nearby – Hampstead shops, the Heath, Kenwood House with its walks and summer open-air concerts, the Everyman cinema, Hampstead Theatre, Camden Market and Belsize Park underground to everywhere.

She soaked and wondered – *had* she made a fool of herself? She enjoyed spontaneity but had she presumed too much before those old men? Old? Barney was old but Manfred seemed not to be. Why was that? Was it because Barney was a defeated man who

gave the impression he had no right to be in the world whereas
Manfred seemed comfortable in the world as though he owned it?
There are such souls, they have a stillness about them. She had
watched him throughout the evening as constantly as she dared,
perhaps too brazenly so. Had she hidden how lustfully she had
wanted to kiss his lips, his full-blown, unashamedly sensuous lips
again and again? He moved them, played with them, licking them,
chewing them, protruding them. Did he know he was doing it?
Did he know she was watching him? She thought – men can't play
the game of subtle revelation as a woman can. They had no cleavage with which to tantalise, no thigh to show when they crossed
their legs. Many men sprawled but their open legs revealed no
secrets as alluring a woman's. When the wind blew they wore no
dress through which their shape formed, as did the curved shapes
of women in the wind. If men stood with the sun behind them no
suggestive outline was revealed. The most to be enjoyed of a man,
Beatie thought, was a hairy chest through an open shirt – though
not if a chain hung round the man's neck; and firm buttocks
encased in tight trousers; and 'the bulge'. But she personally did
not find any of these things alluring. Perhaps all that was left with
which a man could allure were the features of his face, the thoughts
in his eyes and the gentle play of his lips. True or not Beatie had
more than anything that evening just wanted to kiss those lips and
bite the lower one that seemed pleading to be bitten.

Nor was that all she remembered wanting to do; and now, as
she soaked and softened in her perfumed, oily water, she was
overcome by a certain desire of which she was slightly ashamed.
Manfred's age was an element in her desire; she felt his sexuality
had long been dormant; a sleepy, tired sexuality, perhaps one that
had forgotten itself, lost faith in itself, was perhaps even fearful that
it might no longer exist. It excited her to contemplate reviving it,
making his sexuality aware of itself, being the instrument of his
renewed energy, the conduit through which his desire might flow
again. She wanted to run her nails along the furrows of his
forehead and nibble the lobes of his ears. She noticed hairs in his

nostrils and longed to cut them with her small nail scissors. Soon she found herself speculating about his size and whether it was true, as they said, that old men have difficulty rising to the times. Her musings mortified her. Surely these were the ruminations of idle adolescents, the topics of blowsy, disappointed wives, the tittle-tattle over the washing line, surely these were the kind of thoughts which fed superior giggles in smoky pub corners where men were diminished, put in their place by women angered by encroaching wrinkles. But nothing could stem the flood of her speculation and imagery. What did he smell like? What did he taste like? What would he feel like in her hands, between her teeth, in her mouth? What was his weight? How heavy would he feel? She wanted the length of his body on her, the weight of him, the bulk of him, and then, as they exchanged smiles, she thought: he can see me thinking these things. He knows what's going on in my imagination, he can see through me. Oh Christ! He knows, he knows! And she understood it was he who could bring her alive. *She* would submit to *him*. It was she who had most to learn. Like a camera her point of view had changed. From fantasising about taking him in her arms she now thought only of folding into his. Instead of images of what she would do to him she switched to images of what he might do to her. She would lie and wait and submit. But she realised, having soaked and aroused herself, that whichever fantasy proved correct, his age remained a potent factor in her desire. A month passed before he called.

When Beatie had fled blushing – Manfred glimpsed the blush in flight – his first thought was he should have been bolder. His second thought was how wise that he had *not* been. Throughout the evening he had exchanged smiles and eye-contact full of queries and hesitant sexuality, but felt ashamed to be so doing with one so young. Old men longing for younger women, he thought, can only appear pathetic. He was a helpless romantic but dreaded appearing absurd. How could he ever contemplate embraces and fond partings in public, holding her hand in the street, kissing those full lips? Surely everything he longed to do would invite her scoffs; she would not squander her passion on a lifeless old man, surely she would flinch from the coarse skin of his fingers upon her; surely she would calculate that when he was seventy she would be only forty, and oh the prospect of having to look after an old man when life would be still ahead of her? Surely, surely all these things and much more?

On the other hand did he not climb mountains, trek across deserts and icy wastes? His back was not bent, he did not puff when he walked, no aspect of him was feeble, nor was the skin on his fingertips coarse, and he never allowed any roughneck to get away with insult, abuse or violence on the street. His voice commanded an authority his physique supported, and no woman would ever have to care for him for he possessed the means to pay for caring. Nevertheless age was age and youth was youth, and no matter what level of independence he could count upon, no matter how strong his body, the years were etched upon him as they were not yet upon her.

So throughout the evening he had veered from glances of longing to feigned looks of disinterest, though he could not be certain which she believed. All he knew was that by the end of the evening he had exhausted his power to take control, and the afeared side of his nature won. He could not bring himself to sweep her up in his arms and take for himself the prize for which he had longed all evening, longed since their first encounter in Shepherd Market if the truth be told. To risk making a fool of himself, of appearing ridiculous, he dared not. Her cheek was all he would hazard kissing, and an invitation to see his beehives all he would offer. And even that had taken him a month to dare.

'How serious are you about wanting to know the parts of a bee?' he asked as they stood outside the shed that housed the protective clothing they were now unhooking and unzipping.

'Serious about wanting to know,' Beatie replied, 'but not sure why.'

'Be more explicit,' he commanded, reaching for a book on a shelf in the shed, which she noticed was immaculately ordered with pegs from which implements and clothing hung, and with shelves upon which lay not only books about beekeeping but empty jars and gloves and boxes of gardening aids – to root, to kill, to help grow, to frighten off. The air of tidiness both satisfied and worried her. She recognised a need within her for objects to be in their place but worried that tidiness left no room for spontaneity – a quality she valued while fearing the chaos that might follow. On balance, though, it was upon impulse that she normally acted, knowing her impulse would be an informed one; she possessed an internal calculator that went into action, and computed the pleasure, the pain, the rewards and the consequences that would inform her this impulse would work or that one not.

She attempted to respond to his invitation to be explicit.

'I seem to be intrigued by the parts that go to make a whole. Why I'm intrigued I don't know. I've started to keep a box index file. So far I've got three "C"s, one "B", one "F", and one "T".'

'What are your three "C"s?' he asked.

'Cathedral, clouds, car.'

'Car? You've broken down a whole car into its component parts?'

'Most of them.'

'And a cathedral?'

'The cathedral was easy – spire, steeple, porch, nave, chancel, quatrefoil and lots more I can't remember but all lovely, ancient-sounding names. Now I'll have another two "B"s to add – beehive and bee. Seven parts to a beehive you said, but,' she looked at the page in the book he'd given her and counted the bee's anatomical parts as described, 'but according to this book it seems there are ten parts to a bee's anatomy.' She showed him the page. 'That can't be right. This diagram only shows the internal organs. I don't see antennae named, or the legs on which they do the dancing you described.' He apologised.

'I'll see if I can find you a more detailed book of bees. Now, are you ready for a drink?' Inside the house, as he poured a full-bodied white Sancerre, he asked what the other letters were.

"B" for parts of the body, with subdivisions for parts of the parts – like an arm is part of the body and an elbow is part of an arm.'

'That's a mammoth task,' Manfred interrupted. 'You'll have to break down the limbs, the ear, the parts of the eye – it's endless.'

'Don't tell me. I know.'

'But why?'

'Don't ask me. I've told you, I don't know. Yet. All I know is it intrigues me to list the parts that make a whole.'

'And the "F" and the "T"?' Manfred asked clinking his glass to his young guest's.

"F' is for flower – stem, petal, stamen, et cetera, and "T" is for tree – bark, branch, leaf, et cetera.'

'What will you do,' asked Manfred, 'when you come to carpentry?'

'Why? What problem will I have under carpentry? I'll have a subdivision named "joints" – like tongue and groove, and dovetail; and another one for tools – like plane, saw, spokeshave and so on.'

'Yes, and you'll have to break down the plane into its own parts, but . . .'

'But?'

'But what happens when you have a card named "Tools"? Will you duplicate your list and have a section called "Tools – carpentry" and "Tools – engineering" and "Tools – gardening"?'

'I don't know,' said Beatie. 'Give me a chance. I'm just playing for the moment. I'll cope with each problem as it comes up. If I continue with my – my what? What do I call it? Hobby? Pastime? Obsession?'

'I don't know,' said Manfred. 'All I know is I'm interested to be kept in touch as to where it leads.' It was not so much the request he regretted making as the formulation. He heard himself sounding like a professor to a student, an employer to an employee, and – yes, damn it – a father to a daughter. How could he possibly kiss her the way he wanted to kiss her having spoken such words in such a manner?

Manfred spent the rest of their evening together trying to find the right tone of voice. He did not want to flirt nor did he want to be solemn; he longed for Beatie but did not want to be caught needy; and he certainly wanted to be longed for. As he stepped from topic to topic he became subdued by a sense that he had lost who he was. In trying to find the 'right' tone of voice he had lost his *natural* tone of voice. This is foolish he told himself, you're stuttering around like an inexperienced adolescent with his first girlfriend. Finally he said:

'Have you noticed I'm having difficulty talking to you?'

'I had indeed,' she replied. Nor had she helped because she had observed his awkwardness and had been *trying* to help. Between them they had discombobulated each other and finished off the bottle of wine too swiftly. He stood to go to the loo and tripped over the magazine trolley that was at the end of a low, long coffee table either side of which they had been sitting.

'And have you also noticed,' he articulated his words too carefully, 'I've become a little unsteady on my legs?'

'Not until just now,' she replied reasonably and too carefully. 'Until just now you had been sitting. Steadily enough, I thought.'

'What a logical young woman she is,' Manfred said to the door through which he was about to enter. 'I think,' he said returning later through the same door, 'that it's time to eat and sober up. What do you fancy?'

'What's your favourite food?' Beatie asked.

'Honestly? You want to know honestly what my favourite food is?'

'I hope you're not going to say baked beans on toast.'

'Why do you hope that?' It seemed to him an odd thing to hope.

'Because I don't like people who flirt with working-class foods thinking it makes them interesting. In fact I don't like anybody who flirts with anything thinking it makes them interesting. I met them at university – flirting with left-wing politics, or alien religions, talking Cockney talk, or swearing in Geordie or Scottish dialects that were not theirs. I have a horror – a bête noire, you might call it – of people who attach things to themselves that don't belong either to who they are or where they come from.'

'No,' said Manfred, 'I was not going to say baked beans on toast, though I confess I loved it as a child and have been known on occasions to revert to childish things.'

'I understand that,' said Beatie. 'Just don't let it develop into an affectation or I won't like you any more.'

'Yes, ma'am. Of course, ma'am. I won't, ma'am.'

'So tell me, what is your favourite food?'

'Fresh, newly baked bread, preferably a Jewish *chola*, with slightly salted butter thickly spread. I could live on it.'

'No you couldn't, but I know what you mean.'

He took her to an Italian restaurant where he was known and effusively greeted by the short, stocky Italian owner who immediately sent his staff in all directions to bring fresh *bricatta*, butter, spiced olive oil, dishes of green and black olives, a jug of water, the wine list and the hors d'oeuvres menu. The main dishes were chalked on a blackboard above a fireplace that heated two rooms either side of a dividing wall. Those seated too far away had to rise to read what was on the board, but it brought them before the flames, which was cosy. Manfred, it was known, did not want to leave his table, and so was always seated near the board.

'The reassuring thing about a chalked menu,' he explained to Beatie who had pleasurably taken to the venue, 'is that it suggests the meals can vary greatly from week to week, even day to day.'

From the printed hors d'oeuvres list Beatie chose *carapaccio*, and from the blackboard Venetian-style red mullet.

'I'm a fish man, too,' said Manfred, 'but tonight I fancy veal – *scaloppini alla Parmigiana*, with Parma ham and melon for starters. And let's have a gentle rosé even though it's wrong for the food we're eating.'

'Do you care about such things?' Beatie asked, surprised.

'I do, but I've never taken the trouble to make myself an expert on what goes with what.'

'But you enjoy being known here?'

'I confess I do. Is that awful of me? Vain? To enjoy someone saying, "Good evening, Mr Snowman, how are you, Mr Snowman, welcome, we have a good menu today, Mr Snowman." Is that a despicable thing to enjoy? And why *do* I enjoy it? Power – am I enjoying power?'

'Don't be silly, Manfred. Of course not.' Beatie betrayed a little impatience, which Manfred found himself enjoying. 'To command recognition in a restaurant is minuscule power. Harmless. If it brought you attention ahead of customers who came before you, that would be reprehensible. But that's not you, is it? And you're not that rich. Really! Where do such guilts come from?'

'You're right. It's not me. But I am – well off. I'm a long way from being among the top five hundred in the country but I don't have to worry for the rest of my life. Not financially, anyway.'

'Does your money arouse envy in other people?' Beatie asked, thinking it was a daring question.

'It does, and I don't enjoy it. It's not a pretty sight watching people fawn before mediocre businessmen who are good at nothing else but making money, nor do I respect the sense of superiority it engenders, or the special privileges it earns—'

'Except,' interrupted Beatie, 'being addressed personally in restaurants.'

'And even that embarrasses me a little. But I have a good friend who is *really* rich. I mean super-rich, from newspapers and publishing. And I confess that I like him. My good friend – who shall remain nameless but we'll call him Sam – was one of my first clients and I had been his accountant from the day he began building his empire. He travelled widely, and he frequently took me along on his trips.'

'And you enjoyed it.' Beatie was ahead of him.

'And I enjoyed it! Yes, I did. I'll be honest. When Sam arranged that we went straight through customs and passport control, and ensured that we got the best attention at the airport, and were greeted by beautiful women in Hong Kong I felt a buzz. I couldn't do it for myself, wouldn't want to, but Sam revelled without qualms, without ambivalence, and everyone revelled with him. He'd ring the Mayor of New York to tell him he was coming on a business trip, and the Mayor would ask him if he wanted a police escort from Kennedy, and Sam would decline knowing the Mayor would press until the right moment when he'd say, "Oh, well, if you think so." Such things matter to Sam but not to me. He *has* to phone an airline manager to make sure it's known that he's aboard that Concorde so that an air hostess is there to say, "Welcome aboard, Mr Sam, we've reserved your seat for you," and to tell him that they've chilled his favourite bottle of champagne. And he turns to make sure his companions notice it all, and we smile admiringly, and he's happy like a kid.'

'He sounds most unpleasant,' commented Beatie who, it was obvious to Manfred, was nevertheless fascinated.

'And if you think he's unpleasant you're very, very mistaken. He's a charming, warm-hearted, generous man. He loves making a buck, it's true, who doesn't? But it's hard work being a tycoon. I couldn't ever bring myself to work so hard. I won't go out of my way for that extra hundred thousand pounds. Sam does. What does it matter if he spends five thousand pounds flying Concorde to New York with wife and friends for a long weekend, staying at five-star hotels and being driven from apartment to apartment in a stretch limo if in the end he can say, "I've just made a hundred and twenty-five thousand pounds"? His real passion, though, is setting up concerts for under-privileged children. He takes over entire theatres so that fifteen hundred children from all over the country can attend performances of, for example, the New York Harlem Ballet Company. I couldn't afford that. I have to climb mountains before anyone will give me money for *my* charities. Everyone used to think me dynamic at work but my secretary would often come in and catch me asleep. There was always five minutes in the day when I knew people were watching me so I'd start reaching for phones and looking at balance sheets and that's when I'd get all my work done. The rest of the time I was bone lazy, plotting treks across the Gobi Desert or studying maps looking for mountains to climb. Not Sam. I'd go with him to Hong Kong but he'd never climb a mountain with me.'

'It's an alien world,' said Beatie. 'Foreign and strange. I wouldn't know how to conduct myself in it.'

'You'd be surprised how quickly you would learn,' said Manfred refilling her glass with the 1983 Anjou Rosé.

'Are you trying to corrupt me?' Beatie asked. It was a flippant question but the moment she asked it she knew that a lot depended upon her companion's reply.

In the seconds he took to refill both their glasses there flashed through her mind many possible answers. 'Of course' – flirtatious. 'I wouldn't know how' – falsely modest. 'Isn't that what you'd like?' – caddish. 'Why, are you incorruptible?' – cynical. 'Only if you'd like to be corrupted' – sinister and supercilious. The reply he actually gave was what she had hoped for.

'If I thought you seriously thought I was trying to corrupt you I think I'd tell you to pay for your own meal.'

'No, you wouldn't,' she said, relieved. 'You're too much of a mensch.' She was delighted to have found an opportunity to use the word, and he was impressed. 'And I'm sorry to have asked such a crass question. Even as a pleasantry. I do disappoint myself sometimes, I really do. And it depresses the hell out of me.'

'Tell you what,' said Manfred more and more enjoying this young woman who was a mixture of honest and unworldly, 'let's continue with the "best" exchange. Like "what food do you like best" – we've done that one. Let's exchange others.'

'You mean "what is your favourite" something?'

'Yes, exactly that.'

'I hate those games. "What is your favourite piece of music", "What is your favourite book". I don't have a favourite piece of music. I need different music for different moods. I don't have a favourite book, there's too much literary talent in the world to prefer *Bleak House* above *The Idiot*, or *Rouge et Noir* above *Tender Is The Night.*'

'My, my,' said an abashed Manfred. 'You *are* a stern young lady.'

'I'm not, I'm not,' Beatie protested. 'I just love the variousness of everything. My Jewish boyfriend's family and friends used to quarrel constantly about the great strengths of this writer over that, as though the writers were boxers and they were their managers.' She mimicked what took place. '"Sholem Asch!" one of the old men would say, a friend of my boyfriend's father, "Now *there's* a writer." And then another with a name like Slansky, or Poliakoff, or Aronovitch, or Bronowski, they all had names like that, I loved the sound of their names, another one would say, "Asch? Pah! A provincial! I'll give you all the novels of Sholem Asch for just one of the novels of Kafka." And Ronnie's father would pipe up: "Pah! Give me one Dostoevsky for all of Kafka!" And someone else would cry out "What do any of you know about literature?" and they'd all quarrel, those impoverished old Jews with leather patches on their elbows, pulling the masterpieces to master pieces, reading loudly to one another from this novel and that novel, great diamonds of prose and revelation, and the little council room would throb and glow and I had never heard of any of those writers, and the next day I'd be with Ronnie and *his* friends and they'd do the same thing – argue the merits of D. H. Lawrence beside Henry James, A. J. Cronin beside Howard Spring, more writers I had never heard of. And that was my introduction to the world of literature – a battleground in which the fate of the world seemed to be at stake. I loved it. I understood little of what was being discussed but I loved it all. I'd never met people who cared so passionately about things outside their own life although they made it seem as though literature *was* their life. And from them I learnt to have no favourites. *They* had favourites but because they each loved a different writer or group of writers they passed on their loves and I benefited by loving them all.'

There is a vivid word in Yiddish to describe the feeling of pride a parent has for its clever, beloved child: *kvell* – to swell with pride, to sigh with satisfaction, to purr with pleasure. She was not his daughter, nor even his beloved, but listening to Beatie, Manfred *kvelled*. His instinct on first meeting her for so brief a moment had been vindicated. Here was a special young woman, a unique being. He must handle her very carefully. She must not be hurt or damaged.

'All right,' he said, 'I loved all that and we won't play "What is your favourite", but because it sometimes helps to get to know one another we can play a variation of it. Not "What is your favourite?" but "What do you like?" or "What impressed you?" For example – can you recall not your happiest moment but just one happy moment? Or not "What is the most weird, bizarre story you know?" but "What is the weird story that stays with you?" Not "What is your saddest memory?" but "What is just one sad moment you remember?"'

'And meanwhile,' said Beatie, 'we're not paying attention to our food. This *carpaccio* is delicious. I've only eaten it once before and I've been hoping for another opportunity ever since.' So there was silence between them for a while as they ate, except for a word or two because in truth total silence was difficult for them both. Each was bursting to tell and ask.

'I won't ask you what your Parma ham and melon are like,' Beatie broke the brief silence.

'You mean,' responded Manfred, 'because melon and Parma ham are simple and unchanging?'

'Preciously so.'

'Well, you'd be wrong. The melon could be over-ripe, the Parma ham could come out of a packet and be too leathery, or it could be sliced fresh off the bone too thickly, lots of things could be wrong.' Beatie didn't know how to respond to that. He was right but it seemed silly to apologise. The truth is she felt foolish for saying something else crass, and Manfred regretted correcting her. Having a few moments ago observed to himself that Beatie was someone not to be hurt or damaged here he was diminishing her in her own eyes. The silence stretched as both silently castigated themselves, till Manfred asked:

'Do you think that what makes people laugh tells you about them, reveals the kind of person they are?'

'Doesn't everything?' Beatie replied in a tone that, to her mortification, sounded like a sulk. Manfred had hurt her and knew he had. He regretted it. On the other hand if she was unable to absorb contradiction had his instant assessment of her in Shepherd Market been incorrect? Beatie, for her part, hoped that he had not heard the petulance in her response, or if he had that he would understand it stemmed from her self-contempt and not from any irritation with him.

It is in the nature of amorous relationships that much is unsaid that could ease them along. Why is it that two people so attracted to one another remain silent about their anxieties? Do they fear rendering themselves vulnerable? Are the explanations of feeling and counter-feeling too complex to embark upon?

'Are you about to tell me a joke?' asked Beatie.

'Not if you're one of those who don't like jokes,' Manfred responded cautiously and as gently as he could. Just as Manfred had heard the sulk Beatie heard the gentleness.

'I love jokes,' she exploded, grateful for the opportunity to make amends and come close to him again. Her words came out in a rush. 'I have a Tommy Cooper one. Can I tell it? I bet you've heard it. Tell me if you have. Don't let me go to the end so that you have to give me a polite smile. Do you like Tommy Cooper?'

'I'm not an expert on him, but . . .'

'Nor am I, but I heard this one on the radio, a programme about humour, about what makes people laugh. Do you think there is a basic language of comedy that can work the world over? Like the same things can make people weep the world over is there also a world-over joke?'

'I'm listening.' Manfred offered her the listening look. Beatie composed herself like a performer. She had to get this right.

'Tommy Cooper is sitting in his lounge and his wife enters the room and asks:

"'Do you notice anything different about me?"

"'You're wearing a new dress."

"'No."

"'You've got a new hairstyle."

"'No."

"'Then you'll have to tell me."

"'Have one more guess."

"'You've got new shoes."

"'No."

"'Well I don't know. You tell me what's different."

"'I'm wearing a gas mask.'"

Manfred laughed so suddenly and loudly that everyone in the restaurant turned and looked at him. It was a deep, rich laugh. Infectious. It made her laugh, too. And it went on. They would stop to eat and then it would catch them again – real merriment. Beatie loved his laughter, it sprang from joy rather than cheap ridicule, which is what the English seemed to enjoy most – a chance to diminish, belittle, laugh at the discomfort of others.

'Stop it,' she whispered to him. 'Everyone's looking.' But she didn't really care.

It was turning out right. Her sense of crassness evaporated, she had told the right joke the right way, she was with a man who knew how to laugh, her tension eased, and the laughter helped. 'Stop it, stop it. You're making me laugh at my own joke, which a joke-teller is not supposed to do. Tell me yours.'

'Oh, I've got lots,' Manfred gasped. 'It's difficult to know which one to choose.'

'Well choose two and I'll tell you one more and that'll be enough for one evening.'

'Agreed. I hate those joke-tellers who can't stop telling them. Have you noticed? It's a kind of affliction. They get such appreciation for the first one that they become hooked on appreciation, and go on and on in search of more. And as each joke receives less and less laughter they tell another and another and another hoping to recapture that first laugh. Like the compulsive gambler who wins once and doesn't know how to walk away with his good fortune.'

'Stop procrastinating,' said Beatie. 'Your joke. Tell it.' Manfred obeyed.

'A Tsarist officer gets into a carriage and sees a Jew there. He grabs him by the collar and demands:

'"Why are you Jews so clever?"

'"It's because we eat herrings," the little Jew answers.

'"Hrumph!" says the Russian officer and lets him go. A little while later the Jew takes out some herrings and begins to eat them. The Russian officer asks if he can buy them from him. The Jew says he can, for twenty roubles. The officer pays and begins to eat the herrings. After a while it dawns on him.

'"Hey! I could have bought these in the market for two roubles."

'"You see,"' said the Jew, '"it's beginning to work already!"'

Beatie didn't laugh. She just smiled.

'You didn't find it funny?' asked Manfred.

'I found it very funny, but not to laugh at.'

'Perhaps we used up our day's ration of laughter on your joke.'

'Perhaps.' Pause. 'No, Jewish jokes are melancholic.'

'But that was not a story about a melancholy Jew. He was a clever Jew, a witty Jew.'

'I was more distressed by the officer grabbing the old Jew by the collar than amused by the old Jew's wit,' Beatie explained.

'But he had survived,' argued Manfred. 'He had outwitted the Tsarist officer.'

'By cunning. It's a joke perpetuating the myth of Jewish cunning.'

'It's no myth,' said the Jewish Manfred to the Gentile Beatie. 'Survival is a deeply rooted instinct in all living species but when you've been hated and persecuted for as long as Jews have the instinct goes deeper. You know what they say – Jews are like everyone else, only more so! Anyway, who's the Jew here?'

'I have this thing about Jews,' said Beatie. 'I feel more at home with them than with Gentiles. Ronnie had all these Ashkenazi aunts around him – I loved them. Tender, warm, energetic, embracing and funny funny funny. They made me feel like their treasured daughter. So I get anxious about Jewish jokes. I get protective.'

'I don't think we should go for joke number two,' Manfred said as their second course arrived, brought by the owner himself.

As he laid down the food he said: 'You were laughing. Such laughter.'

'I'm sorry,' said Manfred. 'Were we too loud?'

'No, no, no, no! I like it in my restaurant. Makes the other customers feel good. Adds joy to the atmosphere.'

They ate for a long time in silence, merely commenting on how good the food was, and tasting a little of each other's dishes. Until –

'One of my clients,' began Manfred, 'was a very brilliant historian with a mind so animated by his intellect and scholarship that his body couldn't keep up with him. It jumped about all over the place like a firecracker seconds after its explosion. He seemed always to be looking for himself. His mind was never where his body was. He'd expound brilliantly, stop, then his body moved to accompany what he'd just said. His body seemed to arrive after his mind had left. It was as though he was never there when he came through the door, as though he came through the door looking for himself. Really disconcerting.'

'What made you tell me about him?' asked Beatie.

'Don't know,' replied Manfred. 'He just came into my mind. I thought you'd enjoy the image of a man entering a room as though he was looking for himself.'

'I do. It's vivid. You must have met so many interesting personalities as a high-powered accountant.'

Why was the evening going flat? Beatie wondered.

Why is the evening going flat?
I wondered

Why is the evening going flat? I wondered. Do we have too many heavy expectations of one another? Have our anxieties got in the way? We aren't walking in step. He makes a leap, I make a leap. There's no rhythm. We're gawky and awkward – a music-hall act. Gawky and Awkward, entertainers, the couple who when they're not tripping over themselves trip over each other. I'm Gawky he's Awkward.

No, I'm just too young for this man, that's what it is. I look at him and feel I'm being taken out for a treat by my uncle. Chance encounters, no matter how electrifying, are unreliable guides to compatibility. The chemistry of that meeting in Shepherd Market was a freak coming together of elements that might never come together again. And yet – here's the inexplicable paradox – I'm enjoying myself. I am enjoying being in his company. Of course we're awkward with one another, this is our first date. Date? Good God, I'm on a date with an older man. Young women aren't supposed to have 'dates' with older men. Dates are with guys. With older men it's called 'an evening out'. But I don't feel I am sitting across the table from an older man. It's a lively intelligence sitting across the table from me, a vibrant one. His body is not hunched, the back is straight, his head sits firmly on his shoulders, his eyes are not dull, they're animated, they transfix me, always on the verge of a thought, a comment. And his voice sounds young as though it hasn't caught up with its years, as though it refuses to relinquish the energy of youth.

He's talking. He's telling me something. No, he's asking me something. Is my red mullet all right? Yes, it is, thank you. A little dry but fine with lemon squeezed over it. What is his veal like? Just as he likes it, he tells me. I ask him:

'Do you always choose the right dish?' He answers my question with a question.

'What is the "right" dish?'

'A dish that is actually one you want rather than what you *think* you want. Don't you sometimes order a dish,' I continue, 'and then when it comes realise it's not want you want?'

'No, never,' he tells me, confident in his skin.

'You're fortunate.'

He says: 'You're very concerned with things fitting, aren't you? The music must fit your mood, I notice the colour of your sweater is a shade that fits the colour of your skirt, you're upset when you've chosen a meal that doesn't fit the taste you want, you've got a box file full of parts that fit together to make a whole.' He is pausing. He looks as though he's about to ask a question he's not certain he should ask. He freezes in midair. I know what he wants to ask. I can read him – his features, his eyes, the tension in his body. Here it comes.

'Are you also worried about whether *we* fit together?'

'Yes.'

'I thought so.'

'You did?'

'I did.'
'Well?' Why am I being so monosyllabic?
'Well, what?'
'What do *you* think?'

38

What indeed do I think?

What indeed do I think?

'I think,' I say, 'that fitting or not fitting is a question we should not trouble ourselves with yet.' As I say it I'm not sure it is the right thing to say.

'Why not?' she asks, pressing forward. 'When this meal is over you're going to wonder if you should invite me back to your house. And I'm going to wonder if that will lead to an invitation to your bed, and if it does I'm going to wonder what I should reply, and you're going to wonder how you'll feel if I refuse, and then . . .'

'Whoa! Whoa!' I say, putting my hand on her arm. 'Neither of us can know how to behave with the other until we've met a few more times. We'll know the right thing to do and the right moment to do it, believe me. We'll either please one another or disappoint one another but we won't know which it is until we've shared more experiences. We'll either slide together or slide apart. Fit or not.'

'I'm sorry,' she says. 'I've been crass again.'

Her consternation becomes clear. She is seeing me as the wise old man alongside whom she can only make mistakes. My heart goes out to her.

'There is no way you can ever be crass. You are intelligent, well read, bursting with ideas and opinions, and you are both beautiful and sweet-natured. And I think it's time for that second joke.'

She says: 'No jokes, but I'll tell you something funny. My mother, who died recently, had a dry old sense of humour. All Norfolk humour is dry, no laughter accompanying it.'

'Did you get on with your mother?' I interrupt her.

'I loved her very much.' Beatie's tone is so tender I want to kiss her now. Here and now. She continues. 'And my mother was a keen gardener. She grew her own vegetables and she cultivated flowers that grew all round the three sides of her house – it was a semi-detached tied cottage that the farmer let us live in after my father died. My father looked after the pigs. And in this garden were fruit trees that kept us going in tarts and jams throughout the year ever since I can remember. But there was one fruit tree that never produced its fruits, and it was the one I was given the task of pruning and looking after from the age of seven. But no matter what I did it never produced its fruit. Until one year I went outside to scoop up a bucket of rainwater from the rainwater tank by the back door and I screamed because I saw blossom on my tree, and I rushed into the house crying, "Mother! Mother! Looks like my plum tree is gonna produce fruit this year, won't that be something?" And when I drag her outside she look and she say "Yeap! That really will be something if that produces plums this year – cos thaa's an apple tree!"'

I laugh loudly and again the other customers stare, and again Beatie is trying to 'shush' me. 'It's not *that* funny,' she says.

I tell her: 'Everything is that funny when you're happy.'

'Have I made you happy?' she asks.

'You've made me unbelievably happy,' I tell her. 'And to reward you I won't tell you another Jewish joke but I'll tell you a strange true and happy Jewish story.' We have finished our meal, and the plates have been cleared. Beatie is taking my hands in hers. It's a gesture of joy rather than a sexual opening. I see she is happy to have made me happy.

'You know, of course,' I begin, 'that the majority of Jews killed by the Nazis were Polish Jews?' She nods. I continue: 'But not all the Jews were handed over by the Poles. Some were saved by them. One young Polish woman hid a Jewish neighbour throughout the length of the war and when it was over he emigrated to the States. What was there to hold him in Poland? All his family had been slaughtered and there was nothing amorous between him and the Polish lady even though she had been widowed when her communist husband was killed in the Warsaw Uprising. And in the States this man worked hard, thrived and became a very rich banker. As soon as his wealth was guaranteed he began sending money to the Polish woman who had saved him. Modest to begin with, but when the collapse of communism occurred the sums increased. She turned out to be a very efficient administrator, and saved the money in an American high-interest bank account. The town where she lived depended mostly on the fortunes of a steel mill that was on the verge of closing down because it lacked modern equipment. Jobs were threatened, small shops were flagging. She wanted to save the mill and the livelihoods of the little town's inhabitants, and wrote telling her banker friend about her plans. He not only sent her more money – and I'm talking big money here – but persuaded his banking friends also to send money. She accumulated thirty million dollars, and was able to save the steel mill and three hundred jobs and a dozen dependent small businesses. And the money keeps coming in. Her next project is to get the local hospital out of debt and re-equipped.' Beatie has enjoyed my story.

She says: 'And the moral is – be kind to Jews and you'll prosper!'

'Amen to that,' I say.

'You know,' she says, still clutching my hands across the table, 'I think I measure the humanity of people by the way they treat Jews.' I say again:

'Amen to that, too.'

We sit in the car outside her flat. I realise that no matter what either of us has said there still hovers over us both an uncertainty about how to behave, what to do next, what next to say.

'Do you have many stories like the plum tree one?' I ask.

'Not many,' she says. 'I'm not really a good raconteur. But you are, I can tell.' She is not making a move. I can feel she is waiting for me to shape the ending of the evening.

'We'll meet again?' I ask. She laughs at me.

'Of course we will.'

'Why are you laughing?' I ask her.

'You're not really a shy man,' she says, 'but you've gone all coy.'

'You understand why, though, don't you?'

'Of course I do. I'm frightened of appearing crass because I'm younger but you're frightened of making a fool of yourself because you're older.'

'I don't enjoy not knowing how to conduct myself,' I tell her.

'I know you don't. Men of power are only comfortable know-ing exactly what they're doing, who they are, where they are and what's expected of them.'

'Come,' I tell her, 'let's not exaggerate the "power" thing. I'm a retired accountant who dealt with people of achievement and influence. My power and my glory were reflected rather than actual.'

She doesn't want to leave, I can see. She wants the evening to continue. I am not going to encourage her. In fact I think that's also what *she* wants, not to be encouraged. She wants to make love, I can smell her ardour. I also know she wants to resist it for now, and she wants me to help her resist it. Which I'm prepared to do. But she doesn't know how to let go of the evening. She procrastinates.

'How different are you now from when you were younger?'

I answer her: 'When I was young I delighted. That doesn't sound like a finished sentence, does it? But it is. Like "When I was young I laughed" or "When I was young I dissembled" or "When I was young I soliloquised". It is a state of being. I could have said, "When I was young there was much that delighted me" but somehow that seems clumsy. I delighted. I lit up. I thrilled. The window displays in the Jaeger dress shop on Regent Street delighted me, and the longing curve of the Hammersmith Flyover delighted me. The Regency sweep of Park Crescent delighted me. The way women dressed, made up, strode streets delighted me. I delighted in the first coffee shop in Northumberland Avenue where, for the first time, half-bottles of wine could be bought. But, I hate to admit it, being older, I find I delight less. How about you?'

'Oh, me. It's easy. When I was young I was ignorant, knew nothing. These days I may know all that I don't know but I do know *some*thing. So I have much that delights me. Human ingenuity and enterprise – that delights me, and people's imagination, their spirit, their courage to dare the unexpected, their generous wish to please. Oh, lots of things. But you know what – I don't want to talk any more. I'm going.' At which she turns to me, heaves herself towards my face, and kisses my lips. It is not so much a kiss as a laying of her lips upon mine, lingering, without pressure, just enough to allow me to feel their texture. Her mouth barely opens, no tongue is searching, we simply seem to be breathing each other's breath.

At first I think this is a daughter's kiss, a light, brushing goodnight. But the longer she lingers without pressure the more sensual it becomes. I know I must not alter the pressure nor raise my arms to embrace her, but I can't simply hover like this in midair. I must make a sign that I am content with what is happening or else she will think I am just waiting for it to end, for her to withdraw. I raise a right hand to touch her face but this action brings me to brush her breast. I make a small sound that I hope sounds like 'sorry', and drop my hand to where it was. She reaches to retrieve it and lay it on her breast. I don't squeeze her breast, I cup it. I love the ways women have of telling you what they permit, what they desire. Beatie lets me know she does not want a passionate goodnight that will suggest she is ready to be made love to now. No, she is telling me that I attract her and that intimacy may one day be a possibility. I must now wait for her to withdraw. She is the pacesetter. For the first time in my life I feel helpless, and I enjoy it.

39

When I heard Stan Mann was ill

When I heard Stan Mann was ill I rang my brother to reserve my bed and took the first possible train to Diss. In Diss I hired a car. My mother was no longer there to be driven around but I thought perhaps Stan might like a drive out. When I saw him I realised this ole bor was not for sightseeing ever again. Looking at that gaunt face with its dark, hollow cheeks and eyes sunk deep into their sockets I wanted to cry.

'Don't tell me I'm looking good and don't ask me how I am cos you can see I'm not looking good and you can tell how I am.'

'Oh, Stan!' I said, taking his hands and kissing them.

'Well, this is it, gal, ent it? The end. Gotta end sometime. The one thing that's certain about this life. Can't be sure of anything else, just that – it ends.'

'It's difficult to believe, Stan Mann, your voice sounds so strong.'

'That's cos I always knew how to talk. Always enjoyed holding forth. You never heard me give a speech, Beatie, did you? In my young days I was a political firebrand.'

'I wish I had, Stan, really. I wish I had.'

'A political hothead — foolish and full of daft dreams. Don't regret a moment of it, though, not a moment.'

'Nor should you.'

'Don't regret it but I miss it. That's my problem — I'm ill, I know I'm ill but I'm not tired. I'm weak but I'm not tired. I always wanted to be tired so's I wouldn't mind it all ending. People used to ask, "Are you afraid of dying?" and I used to reply, "I won't mind dying if I'm tired, if I feel I've had enough. Let me be tired and I'll be ready to go." But I'm not tired, Beatie. Not as tired as I wanted to be.'

But he was. He was exhausted. It was just that he had a mind that didn't stop turning, deluding him that he wasn't tired. But he most certainly was. Washed up, used up, nothing left. Everything about the way he lay there, with Hilda fussing around him, spoke of last days. I just hoped he couldn't see it in my eyes.

'How's "yourideas.com"? Made a fortune yet? Sold my idea to anyone yet?' I brought him up to date.

'It's not really working, Stan. Your idea is a sound one but news is coming through that wet tissues are being superseded by an alcoholic gel. They're in hospitals in the States. You just push a button and the gel comes into your hand and you rub and hey presto — you're antiseptic. No water, no towels, no hot-air blowers. We can't patent that, it's already patented. All we could do is become the UK representative and sell them to homes and hotels. But that's not our job. We're not salesmen. Besides, they say the germs are adjusting to the gel!'

'And no other ideas come in?'

'Yes, lots of them, but they're mostly done ones or dud ones — ideas someone else has already thought of. Many are just complaints. Complaints about bottles and jars that can't be opened; about bottles of shampoo and shower gel that can't be read in the showers by people who need glasses to read; complaints about noisy neighbours, and about buses and trains that don't run on time, you know — all those things that make up life's little irritations and spoil the day. Accompanied, of course, by impossible remedies like hosing water through the windows of your noisy neighbours.'

Stan's eyes had closed. I had sent him to sleep. I rose to leave him in peace. He heard me shift.

'Don't go,' he said.

'I'll let you rest,' I told him. 'I'll just go to the kitchen and talk with Hilda. I've come here to be with you so I'm not going anywhere.'

'I know I must be dying,' he said. 'Hilda's stopped scolding me.' I bent down to kiss his forehead. 'Wish you'd've been my daughter,' he said.

'I am, Stan, I am.' With his eyes still closed he smiled.

In the kitchen Hilda was rolling pastry.

'I don't know what I'm doing this for,' she said, 'apple and plum pie, his favourite, but he can't eat it. He can't eat anything except a thin soup.'

'Chicken soup is best,' I told her.

'I know,' she replied, wearily, 'and I put a few strands of vermicelli in it, the only solids he can keep down.'

'Anything I can do to help?' I asked.

'Not really. Unless you like ironing.' She pointed to a pile of washed laundry on the sofa. I set up the ironing board, plugged in and slowly ironed shirts, pants, teacloths, towels, pyjamas, dressing gown and a lot of handkerchiefs.

'He refuses to use Kleenex,' she said. 'It has to be a real handkerchief.' I asked what the prognosis was.

'If you mean how long has he got,' she said, 'well, I don't know is the answer. Neither do they. But all my experience in nursing suggests it's weeks rather than months. It's the liver, see. Diseased. He needs painkillers every three hours. It could even be tomorrow.' I focused on the ironing until I found the silence oppressive.

'What'll you do, Hilda?' I asked, and as soon as I asked I knew I should not have done because it was an acknowledgement that one day soon he would not be around. But she had given me permission for such a question by saying 'It could be tomorrow'.

'I don't know.'

'Of course you don't. Silly question.'

'No, not silly,' she reassured me, 'cos it's one I ask myself constantly. It's just that I'm taking it a day at a time.'

I carried on ironing in silence. Hilda made her man his pie that he would never eat, and stuck it in the oven.

'I'll make some custard for that,' she said. 'Perhaps he'll keep that down.' She disappeared into the larder on the pretext of looking for the tin of custard powder but I could hear her sobs and her struggles to hold them back. Soon she was controlled enough to return.

'I know I'm not supposed to,' I said, 'but I enjoy ironing. Something very satisfying about smoothing out crumples and creases.'

'He led me a dog's life to begin with, you know.' I made no response. I could hear she wanted to talk. 'But I bore it because he was a good man. And an interesting man. He was full of opinions and ideas and bits and pieces of knowledge. That's what upset him most – that he only had bits and pieces of knowledge. It didn't seem like that to me. Seemed to me like he was rich in knowledge cos he read so much. But for him each book he read told him more about what he didn't know. So he was in a constant fever of frustration and the only way he could reassure himself was to go off and find another woman. I minded at first. I minded very much at first. But then I could see that he was going to look after me. And he always told me about them. The women. Not flaunt them, I don't mean that, but he always answered my questions about where he'd been or where he was going. He never excluded me. He had these women but I always felt part of his life. In a way I didn't blame him. I didn't look after myself, see. He liked style and I had no style. See all the ugly furniture here? That's mine. The beautiful antiques are his, and the paintings and prints on the walls.

His. I've got no eye. No taste. No style. Didn't care about makeup or clothes or hair do's, and I let my skin go rough. I was one of those stupid women who declared "love me for who I am not what I look like". But what I looked like was part of who I am, and I didn't really understand that till it was too late. He had to look at me day after day, plain and rough and with hairs on my chin, and it didn't for an instant occur to me that it might give him pain.' She paused to think and regret. I was not going to interfere with her thoughts, I was there to listen. 'I'm not a reader, either,' she continued, 'I was not his intellectual equal. He needed someone he could talk with. I couldn't, and it brought him down. If you only have a brick wall like me to talk with you lose heart. Poor man. No heart to lose now. But he tried. He tried to talk to me about what he read, he tried to share it with me. And so I didn't mind when he neglected the business, and the fleet of cars got fewer and fewer. There was always money around, not loads, but enough. I think secretly he squirreled some away and we lived off the interest. Cos you know they weren't just any old cars, no, they were vintage Daimlers and Rolls-Royces for posh weddings and civic occasions in Norwich. So when he sold them he must have got a fair ole price for them. I never knew. I asked about his women but never about his money. There! Go and make sense of that.' I waited to see if she wanted to tell me anything else. I think she did but thought better of it.

'This house must be worth quite a bit,' I said.

'Oh, I'll be all right when he's gone,' she said. 'And I won't stay here long. Too big for two let alone one.' This time she could not control her tears. I took her in my arms and we wept together.

'Well, this won't do.' She disentangled herself. 'Will you stay here the night? Shall I make you up a bed?' I could see that Hilda, normally a strong and independent woman, needed company. I said I'd like that and offered to help but she would hear none of it. 'I'll make your bed and prepare us something to eat,' she said, glad to be needed and useful. I rang my brother, told him of the change of plans, then took my Walkman and sat beside Stan's bed listening to the Beethoven string quartets, gazing at that face I had known from my childhood. He was breathing heavily and with difficulty. Once he opened his eyes, smiled at me as though thanking me for being there and closed them again. I was grateful for the opportunity to be with him and return the comfort he used to bestow upon me when I fell or lost a quarrel with my siblings or friends, or complained about my mother because she wouldn't let me have my way. I remembered something he frequently said: 'Nothing stands still, Beatie. Everything changes. Not necessarily for the best, but it changes. When you grow up,' he promised, 'your brother and sisters will be your friends instead of your enemies, and you'll discover all sorts of hidden qualities in your mother.'

The combination of my old friend dying and the Beethoven quartets on the Walkman was overwhelming. I had to leave. I moved as quietly as I could but not quietly enough.

'Don't go, Beatie,' he whispered gaspingly.

'I'll be back, I'll be back,' I assured him. 'Must pee.'

'When a gal's gotta pee a gal's gotta pee.' I heard him snort a sort of laugh as I went to pull myself together in the lavatory where I did indeed sit down, but not to pee. Rather to reflect instead on how a person can find humour at a time like this.

'Oh, Stan,' I mumbled to myself, 'I'm so sorry, so sorry. I wish you wouldn't go. I need you in the world.' What on earth was I doing talking sentimental nonsense to myself. This was no state to be in for the comforting of a dying man. When I returned he asked me:

'What are you listening to on that contraption?'

'The Beethoven string quartets.'

'Which one?'

'I don't know, Stan, they're all on this tape and I just start at the beginning and go through to the end.'

'You got the Razumovskys in that lot there?'

'I wish I could name everything I listen to,' I said forlornly. 'But the awful truth is I'm never too sure when listening to a Brahms symphony which one it is. Same with a Mahler symphony or any of the great piano or violin concertos. I know them, I love them, I can sing along with them, but am I listening to the Beethoven or the Mozart? The Max Bruch or the Mendelssohn? The Shostakovitch or the Prokofiev. Shocking, isn't it? I'm ashamed of myself not knowing which is which.'

'Do you like Richard Strauss?' he asked. I hadn't been aware he was *so* into classical music.

'Yes, I do,' I told him.

'The Last Four Songs,' he said, 'swap them for all your Wagner any day.' He was making a desperate effort to talk clearly, as though he had important thoughts to catch up with before fading away. 'Can't stand Wagner. He's sinister. Frightens me. Not Strauss, he moves me, and Sibelius. Sibelius is noble, Wagner is triumphalist. Beethoven is inspiring, Wagner is rabble-rousing. Mozart makes me wants to embrace the world, Wagner urges me to conquer it.'

'Stirring stuff, though,' I interrupted his flow. Stan would give no quarter.

'Stirring, but unhealthily so. Not to be trusted. Driven by an ugly spirit. He didn't like Jews, what can you expect?' I was uncertain whether more such conversation would overexcite him, but he seemed hungry for exchange. I continued:

'I once met a German academic, female and nicely acerbic, who hated Wagner. When I suggested he had given us one or two good melodies she said: 'Yes, for hunting!''

Stan had been stifling his smoker's cough during his Wagner diatribe, heaving and gasping between words. Now he let it out and collapsed into a fit of coughing. I moved to raise him up. He sank back into my arms. I held him tight till his coughing fit subsided and then positioned myself to become his pillow.

'Where I've always wanted to be,' he said, randy to the end.

'Shut you up, Stan Mann,' I chastised, 'I'm supposed to be your daughter.'

'Oh, I forgot,' he said snuggling comfortably, if lasciviously, into my breasts. Normally I would have pushed him away. Now, it seemed mean-spirited towards a dying man. It added to my amazement that lust as well as humour lingered. Perhaps the old bugger wasn't dying after all. Perhaps he was just seeking sympathy in these, his last years.

'You still walk at nights with that contraption of yours?'

'I can still hear the world outside, Stan,' I reassured him.

'If it's string quartets, maybe. But if it's a loud passage in a Beethoven symphony, or some choral work, you'll hear nothing.'

'You stop worrying about me, Stan Mann, you've got enough to think about.'

'Got nothing to think about, me. Not no more. That's my problem. It's all taken care of. From here on God takes over. I've done my bit.' I could say nothing to that. He had the measure of things now. All we had to do was wait and be attentive.

'Know what Woody Allen said about Wagner?' I did not. "Whenever I hear Wagner," he said, 'I feel I should be invading Poland." I laughed, which made my breasts bounce up and down. 'Nice!' he said.

I told him at length about Manfred. 'Lucky man, lucky man,' he kept saying as I described how we met and parted and met again, and how we hadn't yet succeeded in getting past the awkward stage but enjoyed each other's company. 'If he's rich I hope he's spoiling you,' Stan whispered, his voice weaker.

'He tries but I won't let him.'

'Let him, let him,' Stan urged. 'Lucky man, let him.'

I talked on and on about Manfred but knew Stan didn't hear me all the way because his breathing changed and his throat rattled a little. Not wanting to disturb his sleep I lay there still, without moving, though by now I was a little uncomfortable. And I, too, dozed off, until I was woken by Hilda who had come to tell me supper was ready, and was now stood in the doorway looking sadly down upon the two of us. At first I thought she was gazing upon a sweet scene, then I saw her sadness was resignation, and I felt that Stan's weight on me was heavier, leaden. He had died in my arms.

40

There is only one way to do this

There is only one way to do this, I said to myself. Just go there, knock on the door and tell him to get out of my sister's life. Would my sister let me through the front door? Do I have the right to interfere? It's a fraught question, this, of the extent to which we should step in and take over someone else's situation that's out of control. Especially when that 'someone else' is your twin.

Every situation is different. It's a question of authority, moral rights and responsibility. She's my sister – that makes me respon-sible. I've shown her love and dependability – that gives me moral rights. I'm an organiser, I can help physically, I'm supportive – that gives me authority. But—

'Don't give yourself "buts",' said Tina, my mother. My late mother, that is. 'You're doing fine so far.' But, I insisted, she's also an individual, my beloved sister, with free will. She must be allowed to make her own choices.

'Be simple,' said my mother. 'The man is a prick.' Really, Mother! 'An irresponsible prick to boot. He brings trouble with him. Trouble is his companion in life. There are people like that;

wherever they go they leave a trail of destruction behind them. They're not even bad people – just disaster areas. Greg, the father of your nephew, of my grandson, is a disaster area. Is that what you want for your nephew? A life of disasters?' She's right, my mother. Why do I complicate matters by involving morality?

'Good girl.' I just knock on the door, go in, and say this has got to end.

'Good girl.' If he's left once he'll leave again.

'Right! And he's a thief. He took all her money.'

'He did! He did!'

What am I wavering for? What am I hesitating for? Why am I procrastinating? I'm off!

'Good girl, good girl.'

Thus I psyched myself up and knocked on the door of my sister's flat in Kentish Town. Greg the guitarist opened up and stood there with the baby in his arms. Not a good start. He looked caring and protective. Fortunately his absence of grace and warmth glared back. No greeting, no sense of welcome, just his sullen, uncommunicative, hostile old self.

'Go for him,' hissed my mother.

'What do you want?' asked Greg, knowing it could not be anything of benefit to him.

'Hello, and how are you, too?' I said, hoping to shame the unshamable.

'Go for him,' hissed my mother again.

'I've come to see my nephew,' I said, plucking Boris from him, and plucking up my courage too, 'and to suggest to you that my sister will be happier and feel more secure if you got out of her life.' The moment I said it I felt pity for him. He looked crest-fallen. Helpless. Stunned. And miserably hurt. He had met dislike and displeasure in his life, he was used to being disregarded but no one had ever been so brutally upfront with him. He looked knocked out in the first round.

'Don't pity him,' warned my mother, 'he knows how to use pity. He's a very experienced pity user, I've watched him closely.'

'Why don't you like me?' asked the guitar strummer, disarmingly.

'Careful,' said my mother.

'I don't dislike you, Greg,' I replied, weakening, 'but some people just obviously don't belong together.' It was not easy. I was holding this gorgeous, cooing baby who I wanted to smother with kisses and attention while confronted with the unpleasant task of sacking somebody. I had to put Boris down in his cot, the two tasks were incompatible. As soon as he went down he began whimpering.

'Pick him up,' commanded my mother. 'He needs your warmth and the vibration of your voice going through him.'

'I can't go for Greg and comfort Boris at the same time,' I said.

'Who are you talking to?' Greg asked, as though fearful I was assembling an army against him.

I ignored his question and picked up the baby again. 'You left her when she was pregnant, you took all the money, you didn't phone or write or show any interest in your partner's condition, and one day you turn up on the doorstep as if nothing had happened. Why should you be in anyone's life, let alone the life of my sister who I care about more than anyone else in the world? Answer me that.' I loved holding Boris and he loved being held.

'You should have one yourself,' said my mother.

'Before or after marriage?' I asked out loud.

'What?' Greg was becoming confused, I could see.

'Answer me that!' I told him. 'Why should you be in my sister's life?'

'Because I'm the father of our son. And I'm a good father.'

'But are you a good provider?'

'I'm a good cook.' Oh, he knew how to disarm opposition.

'So is Natasha,' I countered.

'And I don't mind changing nappies.'

'Bravo!'

'And I shop economically.' I suspected all these things were true but the overriding fact was that Greg the strummer was a bore and a wimp with no conversation in him, no curiosity about the world, about other people's lives, not even about his own life. He was flotsam, driftwood, the currents and eddies took him here and there at their will, and good cook though he might be there was no predicting where the fickle winds would wash him up next. I couldn't tell him these things.

'And by the way, where *is* Natasha?'

'I don't know.'

'You don't know?'

'She didn't tell me where she was going.'

'You didn't ask?'

'Why should I ask? If she wanted me to know where she was going she would have told me.'

'And what about emergencies?'

'What emergencies?' I gave up.

'Greg,' I said, 'I'll give you a thousand pounds in cash to go and not come back.'

This was his test. Was it a fair one? He could answer in a number of ways. I was curious to see which he would choose. Reluctance? Offence? Pride? Indignation? Anger? Violent refusal? Violence?

'Did you know I compose music?' he asked.

'Well, that surprises even me,' my mother says. It certainly surprised me.

'Music?' I asked. 'I mean – real music for lots of instruments?'

'No. Nothing as complicated as that, but melodies, just melodies for words, for singers to sing, and such.'

'And you sing them?' I asked, regretting that I might be sucked into one of his fantasies, fearful of being distracted from my original intention to throw him out of our lives.'

'Yeah. I sing them.'

'Where?'

'Oh, here and there – the Underground, markets, Covent Garden, street corners.'

'So you earn money?'

'Yeah. A bob or two.'

'I give money to people like you. Don't give them to beggars with placards round their neck but buskers, people who add to the gaiety of street life – I like that. Why didn't Natasha tell me you contribute to the family?'

'Because it's not much,' said Natasha who had returned in time to hear the last part of the exchange, 'and it's none of your business.' She had been shopping. She dumped plastic carriers on the table and took Boris from me as though at last she had arrived home for her badly needed fix. Boris needed his fix, too, as he gobbled at her breast looking up at her to make sure she was going to stay around long enough for him to have his fill. I bent down to kiss her.

'Of course it's my business,' I said, 'just as I'm *your* business.'

'If he went out more often, secured more sites for himself, it could be a sizeable income. In the right place for a couple of hours, he could pick up thirty pounds. More. He's got a good voice, and his melodies aren't bad, either. I know he's going places.'

'Yes – Canada next time,' said my mother.

'You didn't warn me about talent, Mother,' I muttered.

'Go away, Mother,' Natasha cried out. 'We're grown-ups now, we can manage.'

'So you think! A singer of songs! Pah!'

'What's she saying?' asked my sister, who was rocking her baby too contentedly to be really angry. I told her.

'Greg,' she nodded at his guitar. 'Sing them a song.'

'"Them"? "*Them*"? You're weird, you lot. A weird Jewish family.' He reached for his guitar, tuned up, and sang.

An extraordinary change came over him, over Greg the strummer. This sluggish, shuffling personality who seemed happiest when no one around was talking and making demands upon his intellect, when he was left alone to exist seemingly with no purpose in mind, now came alive as though electric wires had been placed in vital parts of his body. His eyes, his dull eyes, took command over his features. They shone with meaning and understanding, and told his audience that this is what he and his body were made for: to stand before an audience and sing. Any place in the spotlight was his home. Here was no Mick Jagger strutting, no Tom Jones gyrating. Nor did he look as though he was about to smash his instrument, rather he held on to it as though it dovetailed into his body, belonged to his arms. I looked at him and thought, yes, the parts fit. Beatie would enjoy seeing this. I wondered if she had begun breaking down the parts of musical instruments.

The song Greg sang was a love song. A ballad. It was not identifiably English, there was something European about it. French, Italian, Spanish European rather than German. It wasn't Jacques Brel or Piaf or Serge Reggianni or Ewa Demarcyk but all of those brewed in the best of American song writing from Cole Porter through to Burt Bacharach. I was impressed and surprised, and asked for another one, which pleased them both. He glowed even more the second time round knowing he was appreciated.

'Did you write the lyrics as well?' I asked. We all – Barney, me, my dead undying mother, would have to step carefully now, reassess, perhaps make a volte face.

'No. Can't string words together to save my life.'

'Whose are they, then?' I asked. His old, vague, slothful self returned. It was extraordinary to witness the difference when his guitar was in his arms and when he was without it. Two distinct personalities. Or rather, armed with his guitar there was personality, without it there was none. He mumbled a story about a scruff who had stood watching and listening to him in the underground, had thrown some coins in his case and had then engaged him in a brief conversation. The scruff had wanted to know if he wrote songs as well as sung them. And when Greg told him he had never tried to write music the scruff had thrust some folded sheets in his hands and told him that if ever he thought about composing melodies here were some lyrics to work on. There had been three of them.

'I liked them. They set off something in my head. I didn't think I had melody in me but those words set off something. I wrote two and lost the other sheet.'

'Did he ever come back?' I was by now intrigued.

'No.'

'Was there a name, address, a phone number on the sheets?'

'No. Or rather I think there was but it was on the sheet I lost. I think he was pissed, or high. And I thought – he's gone round to lots of us and given us all his sheets of lyrics, and then he's forgotten who he gave what to, and he's tried to find us and forgotten where we were, or just missed us.'

'Have you got the two sheets?' I asked. To my surprise he was able to reach for them instantly. Poetry they were not as is often claimed for pop lyrics. But they had an atmosphere about them of pained adolescence. I was curious to know what the third one would have been like. Greg said it was much shorter and that he regretted losing the paper. Of the two that remained it was the shorter one I liked best.

You surely know it's me
It's me you love
You surely know
Your pain will tell you
Please don't go
Remain with me
My love
You surely know.
What do you see when you look in the mirror
Look at your eyes
What do you see when you look
Just sad goodbyes
What do you see
Your eyes are dead
Your happiness has fled
Because

You surely know its me
It's me you love
You surely know
Your pain will tell you
Please don't go
Remain with me
My love
You surely know.

'How old was the scruff?' I asked.

'God knows,' Greg replied. 'That's the thing about scruffs – all you see is their scruffiness. Could have been thirty, could have been forty.'

'He wasn't a kid, then, a teenager?'

'Nah! Too grey to be young.'

I tried to create the character of the scruff in my head. A would-be poet who didn't possess the talent, and then one day heard that all you have to do is write a successful lyric, just one, and you're made for life, and so he set to and wrote reams and reams of lyrics hoping one of them would break through. But he couldn't get them either to singers or to composers so he thought of the idea of buskers. He first tried the serious student buskers from the musical colleges but they were all performers not creators. Then he just went looking for good voices among the pop street-musicians. But why Greg? What made the scruff choose Greg?

'I think,' said Greg, 'he could hear how I played. I don't simply accompany myself with chords and a little strum. You heard, I improvise a lot. He must have heard something in me that I didn't know I possess.'

'Gonna leave us alone now, sis?' my twin asked, not without a hint of triumph in her voice. I still didn't think they were meant for each other but the ground was taken from under my feet. He was a provider. He had a certain talent. He loved his son. And although Natasha didn't seem deliriously in love she did radiate contentment, albeit, I guessed, a contentment stemming more from her glorious babe than its sullen father.

I must stop calling him 'sullen'. That shift from forlorn nonentity to startling performer was a transformation difficult to forget. I understood now why actors confess to being dull company off stage. I had thought they were being modest during their radio and TV interviews, but no, for many life began and ended on stage, they came alive inside other people. I left the trio with love and apologies, and ordered a large bunch of flowers sent round to complete my grovelling.

'Mother,' I said as I walked away from the flower shop, 'you're supposed to know these things from the other side of the grave.'

'I beg your pardon?' said a stern stout black mamma passing me.

41

A pattern entered my life

A pattern entered my life. The pattern pleased but left me unsettled because it was not the pattern for which I was looking. *Was* I looking? *Actively* searching? Not really, I was waiting for my life to dovetail, fit into place. There! That need again for the parts to fit. I felt sure they would as long as I kept the workbench clear, the saw and chisel sharpened, the word primed and ready, and providing I committed no major error of judgement. Work in the office of 'yourideas.com' turned over slowly. We were living mostly off the Volvo money and some technical innovations Lee had managed to sell to the IT industry. Negotiations with the cereal makers to market Everything – the idea I picked up in the house of Don Machin, headmaster of Archway Primary School – had come to nothing. They were insultingly dismissive. It demoralised us, especially as we had tried the idea on many people who confirmed that indeed they did mix as much as they could in their bowl. One woman had bought a large glass jar in which she shook up her favourites. The idea had a market. We had even scripted the advert. But we were outsiders, intruders. What could *we* know!

Unfortunately most of the ideas that filtered through to us were more 'tips' than ideas. It gave Tamara the idea to create 'yourideasmagazine.com' into which we poured those tips. They were not revolutionary tips but, argued Tamara, they were too useful to dismiss. We paid five pounds a tip, printed it in our on-line magazine for which punters subscribed one fee for life if any of our headings interested them: *The Kitchen*, *The Bathroom*, *The Workshop*, *Table Laying*, *DIY Carpentry*, *DIY Plumbing* and so on. Tips came from all over the world covering a wide spectrum of professions. One academic sent in a tip for twisting a half-empty packet at the point where the bulk began, and folding the top part down over the bulk thus ensuring the contents were airtight. The ground coffee remained fresh, the frozen peas no longer fell out in the freezer, the corn flakes stayed crispy. Tips such as our mothers handed down like washing in cold water the fork or the whisk that had whipped the eggs because hot water coagulated the remnant yolk and albumen. New generations emerge that don't know such things and have to learn them again as most things in life have to be learned again and again. History! Repeated mistakes! Recurrent types! Not that our on-line magazine of tips had a section headed 'Philosophic tips'. Perhaps it should.

And in between attending to our dotcom business I have been researching, to no purpose, the parts of things. I have about one hundred and fifty objects broken down into their component parts typed on card files. Why I'm doing this I don't know. I suppose I've become a collector. Not of coffee cups, nor postage stamps, nor thimbles, silver spoons, first editions or autographed letters, but of nouns. Not all nouns. 'Love' may be a noun but into what *parts* can love be broken down? 'False love' or 'puppy love' or 'oppressive love'are not 'parts' of love, they are subjective *views* of love. They are not component facts as hydrogen and oxygen are factual parts of the noun 'water'. 11.188% hydrogen and 88.812% oxygen, as I discovered the other day. That went down on an index card. 'Love' on the other hand is part of the noun 'feeling', of which hatred, fear and exaltation are some of the other parts. The pleasure I derive from this little hobby of mine comes from discovering facts such as the percentage difference between hydrogen and oxygen present in water; and having to distinguish between natures such as love and feelings.

And then there is Manfred. Such a complex relationship, I don't know how to begin describing it. We have not made love. It is obvious to us both that we *want* to but we are unable to begin. We seem not to know how to arrange our bodies in order that making love appears natural to us, inevitable. I understand *his* problem – he thinks that at his age any advance he makes will be construed as taking advantage of vulnerable youth. There is no logic to this but it explains his hesitancy. I know he wants me to take the initiative so that he doesn't run the risk of rejection, but I can't, I don't. Why not? I don't think it is his age that inhibits me – I *know* it is not his age. What is it, then? His wealth, probably. Not 'probably', most certainly. He fears the image of cradle-snatcher, I fear the image of fortune-hunter. And I do not, absolutely do not want to be thought of, not for a second, not for a split second, as a fortune hunter. He must know this by now because I have turned down all his invitations: an afternoon flight to Paris for dinner at Café Lipp, a known haunt for politicians and actors; a ten-day trip down the Nile; a weekend in St Petersburg to visit the Hermitage, to New York to visit the Frick and Guggenheim; to Philadelphia to visit the Barnes collection. I declined them all though I was very tempted by Philadelphia and the Barnes about which I have heard so much. I agree to theatre and dinners in London, and treat him as often as I can and he permits; and sometimes I drive us to places around England that neither of us has seen like the Lakes, the Yorkshire Moors, and the cathedrals of York Minster, Durham and Wells. It is important to build up a body of shared experience. I want us to have a background, to establish, if we can, an easy rhythm of movement and conversation; to test our inclinations and tastes, to sound out what might be anathema. I suppose I want to see if his presence becomes a need without which I could not live. I want us to become addicted to one another. From such a secure relationship might come a moment when our bodies will drift together, slip into place.

I fear I'm being romantic. I fear I'm being heavy. I fear I'm being formulaic – this should happen, then that, then maybe this will follow. I fear I'm not relaxed. I fear.

Why do I fear?

I should learn from Tamara. We talked about it some weeks ago. She told me she's taking life and Lee in her stride. She knows it will end, must end, but until it does they're in ecstasies of passion. She has no complaints, no regrets. He works hard, is bright, thoughtful and considerate, never bores her, frequently surprises her.

'He's too good to be true,' she says. 'I expect him to kiss me one day and say goodbye, just like that. "Goodbye" and walk away. Am I prepared for it? Ask me, am I?' I ask her. 'No, I'm not. I think about it, I picture it, I hear him say it but after that the screen goes blank. I faint.' I ask her where she wakes up. 'I don't,' she says.

'But we all do,' I tell her.

'Yes. I know it. But will I want to? Look! I'm full of heartache just thinking about it. Let's drop it. My life is sweet just now. A bit pointless but deliriously sweet.' She wants to know about Manfred and me. I explain. With difficulty. Even our kisses are chaste, I confess. She can understand none of it.

She tells me about her sister and Greg the guitarist. I am particularly intrigued by the 'scruff' who thrust the three lyrics into Greg's hands. She promises to take me to visit them and hear the songs.

'He's got a really good voice. And the melodies are surprisingly affecting. I was wrong about him. And about my sister, too, if I must be honest. I hate being wrong about such things. Makes me wonder about my judgements and opinions in the rest of my life.' I remind her that she is human.

'I don't want to be human,' she cries. 'I want to be superhuman!'

'The world,' I tell her, 'is most certainly *not* divided between those who are human and those who are superhuman.'

'I know. More's the pity.'

'Come, Tamara, you wouldn't seriously want to be superhuman.'

'Give me three good reasons why not.'

'I'm not even going to try,' I tell her. It is at that moment, over a glass of wine after work, that she says:

'We're going to have to wind up this outfit. You know that, don't you?'

'I know it,' I sigh.

'We have about three months' grace.'

'Missed it, haven't we?' I say. 'That one idea that seems to have made others millions – we just didn't have it. Do you have any idea what you're going to do?'

'I know what I *want* to do.'

'Which is?'

'Produce films.'

'You'll be very good at it,' I assure her. 'I, on the other hand, have no idea whatsoever what I want to do.'

That conversation took place a month ago. Nothing momentous has happened since. I have taken up swimming. That's momentous enough I suppose since I have been terrified of water all my life – a fear handed down to me through my mother who had it handed down to her by her mother, my grandmother, who lost two brothers at sea in World War One, and my mother lost one of *her* brothers at sea in World War Two, so water was not spoken of kindly in my childhood, and I was not encouraged to swim. It is not easy for me at this late age to splash around in the pool, to leave hold of the bar and wander away from safety, to dip my head under water. It is such an untrustworthy element, water. My instructor is trying to get me to float on my back. The day I float, he says, is the day I will have learned to trust water. Most things come to the surface, he assures me. Yes, I say, but they drown first! Sometimes I manage it when he holds me under my legs and back and when he lets go I float for a second or two. But then my bum slowly sinks and I panic, and struggle to make my feet touch bottom and desperately stretch out for the bar.

'Thrust your pelvis up,' he orders. I do but somehow that pushes my head back and under. I can't bear the water over my face. It lets in terror and dead uncles. But I'm getting better each time. It helps when Manfred accompanies me now and then. He can put his hands under my bum and the back of my neck. The poor instructor wanted to but dared not. Manfred has got me to lie on the surface for sometimes as long as thirty seconds. I am trying to make forty-five seconds, and am even beginning to enjoy the sensation. Best is that I can bounce up and down and feel the buoyancy, and submerge my head. Manfred is taking me through that in stages, too. I'm up to five seconds with my head in water and the terror ebbs away second by second.

When I told Manfred about Greg and the Scruff he said:

'I envy him. Greg, not the Scruff. If you asked me what I would have liked to be in this world I would have said – a composer. Music! How I would love to have been able to compose, to make music. Everything, says Barney quoting the philosophers, aspires to music.'

'Why don't you take it up now?' I asked him. 'Drop bees and honey and learn composition. Sweeter!'

'There is not,' he said, 'a single melody in my entire body.' He sounded the saddest I had ever heard him be.

'How can you know?' I pressed.

'Because I once bought myself one of those computerised electronic keyboards, you know, where you string notes together and the machine records them so that you can play them back and make changes and add backing for them – all I could possibly need to help me compose. And nothing came out. I punched up notes and created nothing. Nothing! Not a single melody took shape. If I stop and try to empty my head to let in melody nothing enters but other people's melodies. I hear John Lennon singing, or Barbra Streisand, or Johnny Mathis, or Pete Seeger. It's a terrible lack, this inability to create music. Pains me.' I could offer no consolation.

It's beginning to worry me that Manfred and I haven't made love. I'm not really sure why it is. I reason explanations to myself but they're not satisfactory. We have hit it off at every level except bed. We talk with ease, travel with ease, we share driving, respect each other's privacy, accept each other's tastes – though mostly they coincide – and it's obvious that we care for one another. When he's not around I miss him, and he claims to miss me. We have become a strong and needy presence for each other. I can't imagine my life without him, which is curious considering how central is the physical part of a relationship. The most curious aspect of this omission, however, is that we don't talk about it. All we do is kiss and hug endlessly, and if someone sees us doing this on greeting or parting they would at once assume we were lovers. And here's an even curiouser fact – our kisses are innocent. No tongue passes a lip. Whether he has an aversion to exploring my mouth – or any woman's mouth – I can't tell. I know only that men and women have aversions that are as strange as their predilections. Some women can't engage in fellatio but weaken to cunnilingus. Some men can't abide the vaginal smell and refuse to pleasure their wives that way. There are women who can't bear their nipples being touched, and men who will hit out if their anus is approached. I have, to my knowledge, no sexual hang-ups but I have not been invited to discover if Manfred has. So far it is not unsatisfactory; I don't have a regret that I'm missing any-thing. But I will. The day will come when I will. I know it. But today I have a great need to spend time in Norfolk, to gaze at those flat landscapes and vast skies and play cards with my brother and his family. Now *they* can become addictive – family and skies.

42

She had gone for a walk

She had gone for a walk from her brother's house, along the roads and lanes of her childhood. It was a warm autumnal evening. She had walked for longer than planned. By eight or thereabouts the dark evening had drawn in. A pink glow lingered from sunset. The last thing she remembered was wondering, as the Mahler Resurrection Symphony was climaxing to its reaffirming end, whether it was possible she would ever tire of this man's music. There had been a time, once, during the Ronnie Kahn period when, after he had introduced her to Sibelius, she had played the second symphony again and again until it disintergrated. It had splintered off into all its movements and parts of movements and parts of parts. She had no longer been able to hear the whole, only the bits. The links ceased to link. Symphony No. 2 fell apart for her and took years to reassemble.

Stan Mann had warned her – if the music was too loud she would not hear anything.

There was the Mahler ending, and then – something over her mouth, after which – nothing. Nothing until she came to, and even then she understood nothing of her predicament. All she felt was nauseous. Three things prevented her vomitting. One, she was strung up with her arms and legs apart, so she couldn't move. Two, she was blindfolded and didn't know where she was – she couldn't permit herself to vomit, it might be on someone's carpet. Three, she heard voices, which distracted her from her nausea.

As she came, over minutes, to comprehend her situation, or rather the limitations of her situation, one terrifying fact struck her immediately. She had been divested of her tights and knickers. She could feel dank warmth gliding up from the ground around her legs and inner thighs. Socks had been drawn over her feet, as though to keep them warm, but it prevented her from gauging where she might be standing. She pushed away the first fear that came to her and explained the absence of undergarments as a thoughtful gesture: she had wet herself, and her abductors had not wanted her to wake up in an embarrassed state. Why was she attributing the best motives for her plight? What inane mode of reasoning was taking over her fear? She did not yet want to face the worst explanation for her situation. Instead she must try to understand her plight, and make decisions. She must first fathom where she was. Her instinct was to call out to the voices for help. But whose voices were they? Her abductors? Or voices outside belonging to others who were not aware that a body was somewhere near and in need of help? The voices were not muffled, which meant they were not coming from the other side of a wall. They were with her, in the same space, but a distance away. It was a big space she was in – a school hall, perhaps? They must be the voices of her abductors. Two of them. They seemed unaware that she was stirring into consciousness.

The voices were youthful, not the gruff and coarse voices she associated with brutal acts. That was reassuring. More, not only were they youthful they were also – it was confusing, Beatie could think of no more apposite description – civilised. But as consciousness sharpened, reassurance ebbed. Panic and fear were taking over and she was searching for any reassuring sign that nothing horrendous was going to happen to her. It was not simply that the tone of the voices was reassuringly civilised, it was also that the substance of the debate was to do with literature.

She could hear names mentioned. A Paul was talking to a Solomon. Her abductors were no longer anonymous, they were humanised by names. Now she could go on to speculate why she had been abducted. It couldn't be for her purse. A cosh on the head, a snatch would have sufficed for a mugging. Nor would she be strung up for her Walkman. Why, she chastised herself, are you playing with all these pointless speculations? You're being evasive, she told herself; you're evading the obvious truth, she told herself; you've been rendered helpless and you're exposed down there, she reminded herself. Face it, you're here to be sexually assaulted.

The phrase, once shaped, made her want to cry out. She stifled the cry. She needed to find out more before she drew the attention of her captors. Where was she? Was she somewhere where she could scream for attention the moment she was touched – assuming it would be hands that touched her and not knives. Somehow, from the voices and what they were talking about, she didn't think knives would be used on her.

She was becoming aware of smells. What were they? If she could identify smells then perhaps, when it was all over, she could help the police discover where she had been. Hay. Musty old hay. A barn. That's why warmth was rising into her. But derelict or one in use? Horse dung. Was that horse dung she could smell? Was it fresh? She couldn't be sure. Wood. Wood shavings. She was in a barn that was also a carpenter's workshop. Oil. Was that oil she could smell among the other smells? If it was oil then maybe there was a tractor around. Someone would soon turn up, perhaps? She couldn't be sure. Perhaps it was light oil, to be smeared over an oil-stone in preparation for sharpening tools. She had seen her father use one for sharpening his knife, which he always kept razor keen. 'Always need a knife sooner or later,' he told his daughter, 'for cutting, carving, sharpening a stave, cutting off a dick!' 'Oh, Poppy!' she used to exclaim in mock horror. Now she couldn't be sure what she was smelling. Damn it! Why wasn't her nose accustomed to such things? Coming from her background it should have been. She would concentrate on smells from now on, that's for sure.

There was something else. This one she knew but couldn't place. What, what, what was it? She focused hard, and remembered. Twine! She had bought a ball for tying up packages when she moved from Crouch End to Belsize Park. Was she somewhere where twine was required for baling straw or hay? And what time of day was it? She couldn't hear birds so it must still be night. And how long had she been unconscious? And why was she so very warm if it was still night-time? It was at this point that she realised she had a scarf around her neck. She hadn't been wearing one when she left her brother's house for her walk. Had her captors put it round her neck against the night chill? Socks and scarf – that was thoughtful of them. If they were that thoughtful then they wouldn't hurt her – unless the scarf was there in preparation to be pulled. The thought brought on claustrophobia. Sweat gathered and dripped down the back of her neck. She felt a desperate need to wrench off the scarf, and because she couldn't she felt even more trapped, more helpless. Now she must call upon her captors to release her, to at least take off the blindfold and unwrap the scarf or she would pass out.

But who were her captors? Youths, she was certain, but which kind? She must concentrate on the voices; try to discern what they were saying. To deal with people, you need some idea with whom you're dealing – class, location, level of intelligence.

She heard this:

'I can't remember which paper it was, an old *Guardian* I think. Should have cut it out, but there were these six photographs of Auden from the age of twenty-two to sixty-six, the year he died, and it showed his face getting craggier and craggier. Amazing transformation. Real evidence of time passing.'

'Time ravaging too. I don't go great guns on Auden.'

'How can you not like Auden? One of the greats of the twentieth century?'

'Can you quote any of his work?'
"Lay your sleeping head, my love,
human on my faithless arm . . ."
'No, no! Everyone quotes that.'
The Auden-lover began again:
"Hausman was perfectly right.
Our world rapidly worsens:
Nothing now is so horrid
or silly, it can't occur.
Still, I'm stumped by what happened
to upper-middle-class me,
born in '07 when Strauss
was beginning Elektra,
gun-shy myopic grandchild
of Anglican clergyman,
suspicious of all passion,
including passionate love."
I stopped there but I plan to learn the rest by heart.

They were literate. Poetry was part of their lives. Beatie grabbed that fact as a lifeline. The Auden-lover, who was Solomon, spoke with Norfolk cadences, in which Beatie found further comfort. The other voice, Paul's, was less reassuring. Its deeper tones seemed capable of both menace and culture. She remembered how cultured the Nazis were supposed to have been. Fear re-entered her heart.

'Right!' said Paul. 'Now – we haven't exchanged news items this week, what have you got for me?' It was a ritual, obviously, thought Beatie. Would the news item each chose, helpfully reveal something more about their characters?

'Mine's depressing,' said Solomon.

'So is mine,' said Paul.

'Should we be depressing each other in view of what we've ahead of us?'

'Mine's about human stupidity, we'll need a sweet antidote for it.'

'Mine's about human brutality,' said Solomon. 'Nothing is an antidote to that.' In fact both were about human brutality stemming from different kinds of stupid fanaticism.

Paul began: '"Jairo Astudillo, one of the great defenders in Colombia's national football team, was last night murdered outside the restaurant where he was dining with friends. Astudillo, who scored a brilliant goal against England at Wembley last year, had, the previous Saturday, in a match against the Americans, leapt to defend a shot from an American player but instead helped the shot into his own goal. As he was walking to his car three men got out of a jeep and began to push and shove him and insult him about his poor performance in the World Cup. One man, with uncontrollable rage, took out a gun and shouted, 'Thanks for the own goal,' and shot him in the face and chest. With each shot the frenzied men cried, 'Goal! Goal! Goal!' Astudillo was known as 'un caballero', a gentleman, who usually dressed in a jacket and tie in contrast to the flashy silk shirt and gold chain beloved by most other players. He was the pin-up of teenage girls and a hero to Columbian children. Tens of thousands turned out to pay their final respects."'

'He was probably murdered,' said Solomon, 'not for scoring an own goal but for wearing a jacket and tie, for not being flashy like the others, for not being one of the lads.'

'Yours?' asked Paul.

'Mine comes from the *Daily Telegraph*. A short item. "A Pakistani woman, Nasem Bibi, aged forty-five, has been beaten to death by fellow prisoners while in jail on blasphemy charges after allegedly burning a copy of the Koran. Her lawyer, Pervez Aslam, claimed that his client was falsely accused by a neighbour whose advances she had rejected."'

The stories added to Beatie's distress. She couldn't suppress a whimper. Paul and Solomon leapt towards her. She felt an onslaught was about to take place.

'Please, please,' she cried out, 'don't hurt me, please don't hurt me.' The two figures stood in front of her.

Paul said: 'We're not interested in pain, only pleasure.' His voice was determinedly firm, perhaps too much so.

'Are you all right?' asked Solomon anxiously. Instantly Beatie gauged her abductors as young men not too sure of themselves. A divided army. It gave her courage to be angry rather than frightened. She could go on the offensive.

'Of course I'm not fucking all right, how do you expect me to be all right strung up like this with a blindfold? Take off the fucking blindfold.'

'We can't do that,' said Paul. 'You'll identify us.'

'Do you know me?' Beatie asked. 'Have I been selected because you've been checking on the kind of person I am?'

'No,' said Paul, 'you were a random choice.'

'Pity, because if you knew me you'd know you could trust me. Untie me!'

'It's your eyes,' said Paul. 'Your watching would inhibit us.'

'From what, for Christ's sake? What do you plan to do? Untie me!'

'We were driving around,' said Solomon, 'and we drove past you and thought . . .'

'Thought what? That two hefty males could handle a solitary little female like me? Brave of you! Now fucking untie me!'

'Please,' urged the gentle Solomon, 'don't upset yourself, nothing bad is going to happen to you.'

'If nothing bad is going to happen to me then why am I strung up like this?' Silence was their answer, and silence was unnerving. 'Please take this scarf off my neck or I'll faint.' The scarf was unwound very slowly by a hand anxious not to frighten her. When it was off she thanked them. 'Now untie me? Please?' Her tone was as warm and friendly as it could be in the situation. Again silence. The only response was a hand stroking her right cheek, twice. He's left-handed, she guessed. 'Was that Paul or Solomon?'

'How do you know our names?'

'I've been listening to you for quite some time.'

Paul. Paul was left-handed. She must remember that.

'Are you hungry? Thirsty?' That was Solomon asking.

'I'm nauseous.' No response. 'I'm not hungry but I would like something to drink, please.'

'We have wine,' said Solomon, 'some miniature spirits, Diet Coke, a flask of tea, a flask of coffee and plain water.'

'You didn't imagine your captive would drink wine with you, did you? I'll have tea. Very sweet.'

'Honey or sugar?'

'Honey? In tea? What strange people you are. I have to call you "people" because I don't know who you are or what or your ages – nothing! Take the blindfold off?'

'Let's take the blindfold off,' said Solomon. 'We're not really going to go through with this, are we?' Quarrel, said Beatie to herself. Quarrel! Quarrel! Disagree! Argue! Split up! Fight!

'We'll maybe take the blindfold off afterwards.' Paul was the leader.

'After what? What, for Christ's sake?' Beatie was trying to go on the offensive again.

Sweet tea was brought to her lips. She was grateful. The thought crossed her mind to spit it back at whoever had offered it. Even to bite the hand. Something held her back. What it was she refused to acknowledge. It was only later, after the ordeal, that she would know it was curiosity had held her back. Her fear had been assuaged by their strangely gallant treatment of her. She now believed she would be able, slowly, to take over control of the situation. She was wrong. Hubris, hubris, she was wrong.

One of the boys – she could think of them only as boys – stood in front of her. She sensed his face drawing close to hers, his breath – smelling of peppermint – heaving with what she guessed was unsteady excitement. His lips wanted to kiss her. She swivelled her head away. His lips chased her. She swivelled back and forth. She would not. 'No!' She would not. 'No!' She would not be kissed. 'No! No! No! More tea, please.' The intruder backed away. She was certain it was Paul. The other 'boy' stepped forward with more of the hot, sweet tea.

'Thank you, Solomon,' she said with a gentle gratitude she hoped acknowledged kindness, and would encourage more.

'She knows who we are.'

'Not *who* we are,' corrected Paul, 'but which one of us is which.'

'You mean she's identified our different personalities?'

'Clever lady. We've chanced upon a clever lady.'

Solomon responded to her tone. 'Nice with honey?'

'Yes.' Adrenaline fed her instincts. She must keep things as normal and as human as possible. Engage them in conversation, at least Solomon. Develop a relationship. 'I have a partner who keeps bees.' No response. 'They produce an excellent honey.' No response. She heard one of them crunch his way behind her. There was warm breath on her neck. 'Did you know that when the most daring bees return from scouting out the best areas for food they do a special dance that informs the others how to get there? No! No! Take your hands away.'

One pair of hands with aromatic cream was slowly sliding up and down from her ankle to her calf, the fingertips massaging her tired muscle. Another pair of hands was unbuttoning her cardigan, and beneath that a blue denim shirt. It was Solomon, she knew. When his fingers with their long nails scratched awkwardly round her waist and belly she shuddered. I must not, she commanded herself, shudder. Stiffen! Wriggle! Show distaste. Make everything difficult for them. Her binding was slack, allowing her to move violently and interrupt what they were doing, or at least make what they were doing seem clumsy and absurd. She also thought it was time to scream. At first, words: 'Help me, help me, please help me!' Then just screams as of one being slaughtered. The hands withdrew.

'Scream all you like,' said Paul, 'but you don't imagine we'd bring you somewhere near habitation? There is not a house for miles around. Your screams are absorbed by the night, and you'll damage your throat if you go on.'

'But it might disturb your pleasure. I bet you won't enjoy what you're doing if each time you touch me I scream.'

'Try it,' said Paul who resumed massaging her legs. She was right. Screams and violent movement were not conducive to love-making. Paul was also right – her throat began to hurt. Her screams subsided into tears.

Curiously they had not anticipated tears. Everything had been planned carefully to ensure it would be a beautiful, comfortable rape, except the reaction of the victim. Yes, a little resistance, protestation, anger, even a sob or two, but surely all would melt away at the touch of two gentle gentlemen who, it would soon be apparent, were concerned to give pleasure and not pain. But Beattie was sobbing helplessly. The boys were distressed. And ceased.

'We will be patient,' said Paul. Solomon wiped away her tears, and whispered close in her ear.

'We are conducting an experiment. Let it happen. It will be over soon.'

'No, it won't,' said Beattie. 'If you want to bring me to orgasm it won't happen. I feel humiliated. How can you expect a woman to function sexually if you humiliate her?'

'We're not humiliating you,' said Paul, 'we're paying you homage.'

'Bunkum! Bullshit! Stop this nonsense. Untie me and take this blindfold off and let me go home and I'll forget all about it. The alternative is jail and the end of whatever future you're planning. And from the way you both talk you sound as though you might have bright futures. Now untie me!' She heard herself sounding like a school mistress.

'We'll see,' said Paul.

'You'll be caught, you know. Forensic science has made great strides. There's not much can be hidden these days.'

'We'll see,' said Paul again. She could hear determination in his voice, but also the merest hint of uncertainty.

'I know what's happening,' she said, now in control of her voice and her thoughts. 'You've got some theory in your head

about rape, I don't know what it is, rape without violence, trying
to prove that women have fantasies about rape – God knows!
And this theory, this daft, perverted theory has grabbed hold of
you and won't let go. You were reciting poetry a minute ago,
Solomon. Words! Don't you know the power of words? You must
surely know the power words have. Formulate a decision with
words and you can't break that decision. You've got to go through
with it. Not to go through with it tells you that you're a coward,
that you have no strength of will, no willpower, no resolve. That's
what words do to you – they form notions that imprison you.
Unless . . .' She was talking rapidly, nonstop, talking talking talking her way through their defences, hoping she was talking talking
talking her way through to their reason. '. . . unless you're strong-
minded, unless you're really strong-willed enough to question
your notion, your theory, your resolve, unless . . .'

'That's a woman talking,' said Paul.

'Of course it's a woman talking. I'm a fucking woman. Now
untie me.'

'You change resolves daily.'

'Yes, yes! It's called 'flexibility'.'

'It's called unreliability.'

'It's called survival, for Christ's sake. Women are pragmatists –
now un-fucking-tie me.'

There was no further response from either of the two young
men. Soon she felt their hands upon her again. The argument
ended. There was no roughness in their handling of her, they were
simply continuing their argument in their treatment of her. She
struggled and gyrated some more but her will to fight had left her.
Resignation set in. She understood that she was not going to be
hurt. She decided – let what may, happen. When it was all over
she knew that had been the wrong decision. There is hurt and
there is hurt.

Paul's hands were firm, and his meandering subtle. Solomon
had found the back clip of her brassiere. Her breasts were accessi-
ble to his lips and caresses. Nothing frightening was taking place

but her anger was deepening. She could, if only by a fraction, obliterate what they were doing to her by focusing on what she would do to them when it was over. She would hound them. She would remember every detail – their voices, their mentalities, the setting, the odour of each of them, which was different and distinct. Paul's sweat was heavy and masculine. Solomon's was faint and fruity. And she would not let the police rest until they had traced these two young men who must surely be identifiable friends in a good Norwich college.

So engrossed was she in contemplating retribution, so concentrated on what she was determined to remember, that she had ceased feeling what was being done to her. What brought her back was a tongue on her clitoris. Suddenly she was awake to a myriad of sensations. Her nipples were being sucked, her juices lapped, her buttocks caressed. Four hands and two mouths were all over her. Body and mind were separating – mind observing, body functioning out of her control. Wriggling for avoidance had become writhing to sensation. Small moans escaped tight lips. Her body was moving, despite herself, towards orgasm. Somewhere she had read that the rape victim must not struggle nor be ashamed if orgasm was experienced.

She tried not to be ashamed as her body responded to the young men's stimulation. For a second she contemplated that if all they wanted was to hear her ecstasy she should fake it. But she had never faked an orgasm. Now it was too late. She came, moaned, then wept. They left her alone for a long while to recover. Then hands soothingly dressed her; guilty hands eager to make amends. Her brassiere was rehooked. Her legs were released from their bondage one by one as her underwear was drawn back into place. Every care was taken to ensure she would feel robed as she had done when abducted, which was absurd, for though they had thought of much they had not thought of everything. Only the blindfold was left and the rope binding her hands behind her back. They explained what was to happen. They would drive her back to where they had found her, she would be taken out of the car with her blindfold still on, the rope would be loosened so that she could, in a minute or so, be able to free herself and remove the blindfold. By which time they would be gone.

They sat her down on a rickety wooden chair and offered her more sweet tea.

'Please untie my hands and take off this blindfold.' They didn't respond. She correctly guessed a silent exchange was taking place between them and knew it would be Solomon nodding his head, and Paul showing doubts.

'I promise, I swear, it will go no further. You've conducted your experiment. Whatever it was to prove you've got your proof. Now untie me. Please.'

'Will you stay a while and talk?' That was Solomon.

'Is that what Paul wants, too?'

'Yes,' said Paul. 'It's what Paul wants, too.' She thought about this. She was drained, shattered and shamed but perhaps, who knows, talking and looking at their faces and into their eyes, might ease some of the shame. It was at this point that she recognised, and had to face, the existence of curiosity. The truth was she desperately wanted to know who they were. They had violated her privacy but not violently. Their voices were not offensive, their words were not coarse, there was even a confusing courtesy about them. And, having brought her to orgasm against her will, they had taught her what unrelated lives were lived by body and mind. She wanted to know them. And something else was nagging her, as will be seen.

They first untied her hands doing which drew her attention to another facet of their characters: they had not allowed rope to be in contact with her flesh, neither at her wrists nor at her ankles, instead they had placed wedges of soft cloth-encased foam between the rope and her skin. They had wanted to make her as comfortable as possible and not leave the raw bruise of a tight rope. As soon as her hands were untied she leapt at them with her fists.

'I didn't say I wouldn't beat you, though, you stupid impertinent, impudent intruders, you! I'll fucking murder you!' All they did was shield themselves as best they could without retaliating. Her blows landed painfully as she pummelled their heads, faces and ribs, kicking their shins, muttering her expletives with each kick and blow. She was not a street scrapper, and following her tiring ordeal she was soon exhausted, falling in a heap on the straw floor.

Two things struck her – she was in an abandoned old barn, and the boys were handsome and contrite young men. They fed her more hot tea and opened a packet of Duchy biscuits, and watched her with the curiosity of anthropological observers as she wolfed down the crisp, tasty things. After the third biscuit she glared at them, putting as much hatred in her eyes as she could muster. But she couldn't muster much, they looked so contrite and childlike.

'Satisfied?' she snapped at them.

'Aren't you?' said Paul who regretted but couldn't resist the quip, and paid for it dearly. Beatie found a little more energy to jump up, throw the remains of her lukewarm tea in his face and hit him on the head with the mug.

'Ow!' he cried. 'That bloody hurt.'

'Good!'

'I'll get a bump from that.'

'Good!'

'It's bleeding.'

'Good! I hope you bleed to death, you smug brat.'

'And that hurt, too.'

'What?' Beatie asked.

'Calling me a brat.'

'Well that's what you are, a brat! Didn't I "feel satisfied" indeed! No, brat! I did not feel fucking satisfied. I came, that's all, it had nothing to do with me, brat. Brat, brat, brat! It had nothing to do with me because you took away my freedom of choice. *My* choice, my fucking choice you fucking stupid little brats, both of you. And you've taken away a part of me that I can never get back. Don't you understand that? It had nothing to do with me, it had to do with my freedom. You usurped my fucking freedom.

Rape is denial of freedom. All crime is a denial of fucking freedom. You think police are guardians of law and order? They're
not, they're fucking freedom fighters. I want to walk my fucking
streets in freedom, you fucking brainless, cowardly, idiots you.
Now take me home!'

But she didn't really want to go home. She didn't want to
move, she didn't want to have to talk to her brother and sister-in-
law. Neither did Paul or Solomon want to move. They felt a need
to explain themselves. Not explain why they had done what they
had done but to talk about themselves, present other sides of
themselves. Their goal had been a woman's pleasure. The woman's
loss of freedom had not occurred to them. They imagined they
had talked it all through, accounted for every eventuality, every
response. Now they were ashamed, even more so because they
had chanced upon a woman whom they had come to respect and
like. They were eager to be questioned, grateful for the opportunity to present an honourable, intelligent and amiable part of
themselves. They had as great a need to talk about themselves as
Beatie had to find out about them.

She listened but not in a relaxed state. She didn't know it but
she was still in shock, uncertain how she should behave.
Conversation was what she was good at, mainly as a listener, and
this is what she allowed to happen veering between controlled
attention and jerky contributions delivered in a voice she hardly
recognised as her own. Every so often she would remember where
she was, what had happened and who these young men before her
were, animatedly relating their backgrounds, social lives and aspirations. They described how they met, the college they attended,
their rides out to the great houses. Thus she learned about Paul's
Polish lineage, and that his father was the baker of her favourite
bread. She scoffed as he talked of his family's sense of honour but
she warmed to their description of the rituals developed over the
years – the cream teas, the way they allotted points, the exchange
of newspaper items to which she had been privy; they extracted
pieces of newspaper from their pockets and read other items to

her, anxious to show her what caught their attention. When Solomon spoke of the film he was one day going to direct about the three black leaders of the Haitian revolution she felt like a careers advisory officer conducting a workshop with young students about their futures. She was amused at the portrait Solomon drew of his eccentric parents and the bohemian squalor in which the family lived, and was touched by the son's loyalty to his father's paintings. She listened without comment or judgement as Solomon spoke of his love for his sister, Sadie. And finally they told her about the two electricians who had been denied their full payment and of the revenge they took and how it had led them to conceive of this night's 'experiment'.

Now was the time to leave. They did not need to bind or blindfold her. They knew she would keep to herself what had happened. They drove her to her front door where her brother and sister-in-law rushed to greet her with great consternation. It was one thirty in the morning.

'Another hour and we were going to report you missing,' said Pearl.

'Well, where have you been all this time?' her brother, Frank, asked. She had never seen him so close to tears. She turned to wave as Paul and Solomon drove away.

'You won't believe this,' she lied to them, 'but I was so absorbed in my music that I lost my way and ended up dozing in a barn. When I woke I got back to the road and hitched a lift with those two young men.

'Christ!' said her sister-in-law. 'You were taking a risk weren't you?'

'I had no alternative,' said Beatie knowing more what those four words meant than ever her relieved relatives could.

She slept deeply that night, overcome with exhaustion. In Diss she caught an early train back to London, where shock set in.

43

She wept for a week

She wept for a week, and pleaded a severe cold to Tamara and Manfred. Between bouts of weeping she attended her swimming lessons. A great need to swim, to be immersed in water, overcame her fear of it. When she was not taking a lesson she was forcing herself to swim width after width. To begin with, just once across without resting her feet on the bottom, then back and forth without resting at all so that by the end of the week she could swim a length from the shallow to the deep end where, unafraid, she finally dared to tread water. That was her great achievement – to stand where nothing solid was beneath her. Having conquered that fear she could not stop facing it. Had Manfred been there she would have cried out like a child, 'Look at me! Look at me! I'm standing on nothing!'

Nor was that all. She walked daily up hill from Belsize Park to Hampstead Village turning right to the Heath where she jogged. She had this need to exert herself, to feel the element of wind as well as water about her. More: her 'hobby' in search of 'parts' grew dangerously close to an obsession. Everything she looked at she saw as a whole made up of parts, and she felt driven to seek

out and name the parts. Birds, bodies, parts of the parts of bodies,
trees, dogs, clothes, bicycles, religions, alphabets, geometrical
shapes, parts of geometrical shapes, parts of grammar, motorbikes,
earth, tobacco, fire, fruit, vegetables . . . her list grew. Each new
item broke down into parts that led to other items. Birds led to a
heading 'Extinct birds' like the archaeopteryx bird from the
Jurassic Period, which led to a heading 'Extinct reptiles', which
led to a heading 'Geological strata', which led to a heading
'Minerals'. The element 'water' led to 'ships'. Different centuries
in different countries produced different ships, so the heading
'Ships' had the subdivisions 'Countries' and 'Centuries'.
'Instruments' was broken down into the four parts, wind, brass,
strings, and percussion; and each of those had different instruments that had parts. Sometimes it began with a part. A leaf on
the ground had prompted her to think of 'trees'; an orange pip on
her breakfast table had prompted her to think of 'fruit'. It was
strange this wanting the bits and pieces of life to make a whole.
Strange and obsessive. Most people seemed able to live with fragmentation. She feared it. The parts had to be named, she needed
reassurance that a whole would always be whole because of its
constituent parts.

Of course she did not research all those items in a week, she
simply listed the lists that loomed for future research. One item
she was determined to learn by heart – clouds. On her first day as
she sat in the rhododendron garden to the west of Kenwood
House recovering from a long jog, she watched a spectacular,
dramatic cloud formation, constantly reshaping, frustrated not
being unable to name it. Next day she found a sheet on the
Internet, printed the names and shapes and took it with her the
second day she jogged the Heath. The rhododendron garden
became her 'cloud' studio from which she gazed and named and
learned by heart the seven shapes. To make them easier to learn,
Beatie arranged them by endings: stratus, cumulus, nimbus; and
the alto before cirro:

Cirrus, stratus, altostratus, cirrostratus

Cumulus, altocumulus, cirrocumulus, stratocumulus
Nimbus, cumulonimbus.

She recognised the dramatic clouds of her first day as cumulonimbus. It should have rained but the winds must have reformed them into bright cumulus clouds. The skies mesmerised her, and each day she learned more. Clouds led her to atmospheres:

Exosphere, ionosphere, stratosphere, troposphere.

Atmospheres led her to vegetation:

Tundra, coniferous forest, broad-leaved forest, tropical rainforest, monsoon forest, Mediterranean scrub, grasslands, savannah, semi-desert, desert, subtropical forest, dry tropical scrub.

The week became two weeks, then three, then a month, two months, three. Manfred expressed concern, lamented that he missed her and couldn't understand why she didn't want to linger on the phone and talk as she normally did. When she didn't respond he said:

'OK, something has happened, you'll tell me about it when you're ready. Meanwhile I'm happy to know it's not physical. You're in one piece. That's all that matters.' And he patiently waited and sent her flowers and chocolates twice a week. She was falling apart but she was being wooed. One morning she didn't get out of bed, and lay listlessly for most of the day neither washing nor dressing. She could smell herself but didn't open windows. It was the nearest she could get to hurting herself – by becoming sluttish. But she could not sustain it. After a restless night tossing and turning in her sweat-soaked bed she spent two hours the following morning in the shower. Or rather she spent half an hour showering, dried herself, then went back again, repeating the action four times. Windows were opened, her bed was stripped, and every piece of garment together with sheets, pillow cases and an accumulation of other laundry was taken to the launderette. That evening she caught up with the ironing, confirming to herself that she enjoyed folding, laying out and making everything look new. But creating order out of chaos did not signal the end of aftermath. The ironing had been slow and methodical but repetitive. She went over garments and linen again and again. Her pleasure in smoothing out creases was manic for she ironed out creases that were not there.

She began the next morning with a glass of vodka, and slowly throughout the day became drunk. She was not a natural drinker and was soon inebriated. Though helpless, she was aware. And she was frightened. She knew she had to be very careful – not move too quickly or suddenly, not carry more than one piece of crockery, or glass, or heavy object at a time. Certainly not handle a knife. All evening she played Elgar, and wept: the Cello Concerto, *The Dream of Gerontius*, *Sea Pictures* – Dame Janet Baker singing, Barbirolli conducting. Over the Introduction and Allegro she wept most.

Why am I weeping? I don't have the right to weep. I should have resisted more. My fucking curiosity! I don't have the right to be upset. All these self-indulgent tears! They weren't brutes, after all. I could tell from the start they weren't going to hurt me. Why didn't I resist more – kick, bite, scream, spit? I became resigned too soon. Slut! Peasant! I'm lumpen. Once a lumpen prole always a lumpen prole.

She whipped herself with words until sleep delivered her, and woke next morning with an aching head not knowing where she was. Nor did she care. She kept the curtains drawn, and sat around all day doing nothing, eating nothing, not even listening to music, just drinking water. Silence but for the sound of passing cars.

I don't know what I'm supposed to do. I don't know who I am – a pig-farmer's daughter, a university-educated young woman of the eighties, a Jew, a Gentile, a girlfriend, a mistress, a whore? Loss. Loss. I was of a piece, now I'm in pieces.

I should have scratched them, made them bleed, gone to the police with bits of their skin under my fingernails, taken the police to the barn, described what happened there, imitated their voices, painted a picture to help find them.

I feel empty, worthless, full of self-loathing. Will I ever recover? I don't know whether to stay in, go out, ring Manfred, ring

Tamara, take the phone off the hook or what. I feel hungry. I feel sick at the thought of food. Do I tell Manfred everything? Do I tell him nothing? If I tell him will he despise me? Will I seem unclean? Will he be angry – with them, with me? Will he understand? Will he urge me to seek them out? I won't. I don't want to. What will he think of that? What conclusions will he come to if I don't want to prosecute? Loss. Loss. I was of a piece, now I'm in pieces.

As the image of the barn came back to her she was filled with a desire to find it. She wanted to see it again as though returning to the scene would exorcise what had taken place.

I will do it. That's what I'll do. I think I can find my way there. I will not be cowed down. I will not.

Frank and Pearl were surprised to see her.

'But it's good you've come,' said Pearl, 'cos those two boys what give you a lift that night came and left a parcel for you. We was thinking of posting it but my, thaa's heavy. Cost a bomb to send. We was going to phone you.'

Beatie opened it at once. Inside were four miniature loaves of bread, each different, four scones, and four small pots of jam – two of strawberry, two of blackcurrant. And a note.

We are mortified by what we have done. We feel you will recover. You seem that kind of woman. Less so, us. This is the last thing we are doing together. Our friendship has come to an end. Best bread and scones in Norfolk. You'll have to find your own cream.

Each had signed their name with an X alongside.

I do not understand the meaning of things. I do not understand. There is no meaning, there is only purpose. I do not understand the meaning, only purpose. The question is not what is the meaning but what is the purpose. Not meaning. Purpose.

She did not drive to find the barn but instead visited the two cemeteries where her parents and Stan Mann were buried, laid flowers, talked a little to each, not much for she was consumed more by feelings than thoughts, and she drove the roads and lanes of the flat Norfolk countryside where she had driven her mother, listening again to Elgar, and weeping at the words of Cardinal Newman who had come face to face with the dark night of his soul:

I can no more; for now it comes again,
That sense of ruin, which is worse than pain,
That masterful negation and collapse
Of all that makes me man.

44

'I'm worried about her'

'I'm worried about her.' Manfred met Tamara for lunch in the café in Shepherd Market where all three of them had met at different times. 'It's not like her to be so distant.'

'Are you lovers?' Tamara was her usual upfront self.

'No,' replied Manfred honestly, 'but it doesn't stop me fearfully wondering if her distance is preparatory to an announcement.'

'Of what?'

'We want to be lovers, I know it. But we neither of us seems able to break through the age difference.'

'That's ridiculous.' Tamara's tone was defensive.

'I know *you* have a much younger lover but that works because you're still young.'

'So are you, Manfred. Come – look at yourself. Look how you behave. You have the air of a young man, the stance, the bright eyes, the energy...'

'None of which seems to matter. And so I fear she's preparing herself to end it all, and I would not have a single argument with which to hold her.'

'It could be that she's depressed because "yourideas.com" hasn't worked, and she doesn't know where to turn next. Perhaps she's taking time off to weigh up life's possibilities.'

'I'm in a position to relieve her of financial worries, she knows that.'

'But that's not Beatie.'

'Don't I know that's not Beatie.'

'She's taken herself through college without help and she wants to make her own mark without help.'

They ate in silence for a while.

Tamara asked: 'Does she ever talk to you about her future, her plans, her hopes?'

'Rarely.' Manfred thought a moment before adding: 'I think she's anxious that if she talks to me about aspirations I'll think they're veiled requests for help. You?'

'No. The only thing she used to talk about is her hobby for collecting and filing the parts of things. But even that she merely toyed with.'

'Do you think,' asked Manfred, 'that I should ignore her request to be left alone, and just turn up? I mean it's been going on for nearly three months. I miss her, dammit! She makes sense of my life. She's more than a companion, she completes me. Without her I drift. I don't want to do anything unless she shares it. I take no pleasure in anything I do. She's left a meaningless gap in my life.'

'Don't the bees fill it?' Tamara's tone was a gentle jibe.

'Bees have a limited life and hold limited interest,' confessed Manfred. 'I enjoy the keeping of them, and the honey is the best I've ever tasted, but I can't say I've discovered the purpose of my last years.'

'Don't talk like that, Manfred, you've got another twenty to go, at least.'

'Precisely! And I don't want to keep bees for the next twenty years, and do nothing else.'

'But there's mountaineering and trekking for your children's charities – doesn't that take up time?'

'Yes, but not my attention. There's a lot of me left unused. And besides, I'm in love.'

Manfred wanted to change the subject, he felt uncomfortable talking about himself. He asked Tamara why she thought 'yourideas.com' failed.

'Simple. It was a dud concept to begin with. Ideas fall into categories: those conceived by original minds capable of putting their ideas into practice without help, who just need encouragement, for which we can't charge. And those ideas – less daring – conceived by people incapable of putting them into practice even with all the help in the world. My boyfriend, Lee, is a whizz-kid sound and lighting engineer who always wanted to set up shop to provide services for film, TV, theatre and the pop music world. I've always wanted to make films, produce or direct – I'm not sure yet. And Beatie – well, because she's not sure I'm not sure what she wants.'

Before they parted Manfred asked: 'Do you think she wants to end it, our relationship?'

'Nah! Made for each other. She's never been so happy. Comes in glowing after an evening out with you.' Manfred was reassured but, paradoxically, even more anxious about her silence.

And then happened something that astounded them all.

45

Pay attention to the quiet ones

Pay attention to the quiet ones, I said. Didn't I always say it? The quiet ones. Pay attention to them. I always said it, and I was right. Natasha couldn't keep time, she lost watches, she seemed the least resourceful of the twins, the one who loved too much and didn't think things through, but I said – I always knew – still waters run deep. A cliché, I know, but a cliché is only wisdom grown old with too much telling. Whatever else Natasha didn't have she had an instinct for potential in others. She sensed something in her Greg-the-guitarist. I could kick him to kingdom come, to kingdom come! For abandoning her, for taking the money and running off to Australia I could kick him to kingdom come. But Natasha took him back when he returned, and not simply because he was the father of their child, my gorgeous grandson, but because she saw, she sensed, she intuited, something was rumbling there, behind those dull blue eyes, stirring. Something was stirring. Not too energetically, not too obviously, not too bubbly, just a little. Just a little bubbly. A talent. A little bubble of talent. Natasha didn't know what it was a talent *for*, she just knew there was something about the man. He didn't pluck complicated chords, his fingers were not dexterous, but he had a feeling for the melodies he played and sang written by other people. He added to them, seemed to find out how they were meant to be sung, created an atmosphere around them. That's why his busking was lucrative. People who never dropped coins for buskers dropped them for Greg. Many couldn't understand why he was busking. Some even stopped to tell him so.

One day, when he was singing the song he had composed to the lyric of the Scruffy Poet, a middle-aged man with a bald head, dressed in Armani casuals and carrying a very expensive-looking briefcase, stopped, threw a five-pound note in Greg's guitar case and asked him who wrote the song. Greg told him he'd written the melody, and related the story of the Scruffy Poet thrusting the lyric into his hands.

'You've got to find him,' said the bald-headed man, 'because I work for New Found Records, and I think that's a potential hit song, and I want to record it.'

Is that a fairytale story or not? I ask you. My daughter had picked a man who could compose hit songs. She knew. The quiet one, the one I said pay attention to, the one who lost watches, loved too much, and didn't think things through, she knew. Pay attention!

46

When Beatie came through the office door

When Beatie came through the office door looking like death warmed up I was on the phone listening to my excited sister.

'I didn't tell you in case nothing came of it,' she was saying, 'but it's gone through the roof. Number one in two weeks. "It's Me You Love" – you hear it everywhere. And Greg's so bloody modest about it. He says it's the orchestration that's made it a hit, and the lyric. We've got to find the Scruffy Poet. There's a lot of money waiting for him. Oh, Tamara, we're rich too. It only takes one song, just one. And they like Greg's other songs. At least the melodies, not the lyrics. They want the Scruffy Poet's lyrics so that's another reason we have to find him. But how do you start looking for a scruffy poet? I mean Greg can't go back to busking in the hope he'll turn up, and there aren't homes for scruffy poets where we could search him out . . .'

Perhaps my greatest joy was to hear the happiness bursting out of my sister. She was even developing a sense of humour. There were now two readjustments I had to make in my life: the collapse of 'yourideas.com', and an impecunious sister turned rich. How lives change. Without warning. In a flash.

And there before me was a deathly white Beatie Bryant.

'Sleepless nights,' she explained. 'Working out my future.'

'And have you worked it out?'

'I'm getting there.' But nothing followed.

'Well?' I asked.

'I'm not ready to talk about it. Remember what the wise priest said: 'If you want to make God laugh tell him your plans for tomorrow.''

I don't know about God but it made me laugh. Smile, at least. God would laugh because he knew it all – one long black comedy for him. I pressed Beatie.

'Just that? Worrying about the future? Nothing else?'

'Nothing else.' I was not sure I believed her.

'Everything all right between you and Manfred?'

'My rock.'

'He's very worried. Patient but worried. He feared you were going to break off with him.'

'I know. He told me.'

I couldn't contain myself.

'Beatie,' I dared, fearful of what I was about to say, 'you look melancholy. Would you be upset if I said I didn't believe you? If I said you looked as though you've been doing more than worrying about your future?'

'It's just that the death of my mother has caught up with me,' she replied. 'My mother and an old friend of the family called Stan Mann who I loved very dearly. Both gone. And I went back to their graves and talked with them, and wept a little. I'll be all right. Don't worry.' She brightened up but I still didn't believe her.

'Oh, my God!' I exclaimed. 'I haven't told you – the most wonderful news about my sister and her guitarist boyfriend. I've just heard. It was her I was speaking to when you walked in. We were all wrong about him. And her, too.' As I related the extraordinary events I could see even more colour spread over Beatie's cheeks, and a touch of the old glint re-entered her eyes.

'What a wonderful sequence of events. Your dad talking her out of the abortion, the return of Greg, the busking, the Scruffy Poet, the music producer. I love it when the parts come together like that.'

And I loved that her eyes were shining again. The shine remained even when she looked around our office now denuded of nearly all we had accumulated, from coffee cups and saucers to prints hanging on walls.

'It looks a sad old place with white spaces on the wall where prints hung,' she said.

'Change!' I exclaimed. 'Something new! Into the unknown! Challenges!'

'Women are supposed to be better than men at change,' said Beatie. 'I'm not sure I can be counted among them.'

'That's nonsense,' I cried, anxious that melancholy should not cloud the shine that had returned to her eyes. 'I don't know anyone who's lived with so many changes in her life. And stark ones, too. Pig-keeper's daughter to college undergraduate!'

'Maybe,' she said, unconvinced.

'Are you sure everything's all right with you and Manfred?' I dared again.

'My rock, my love,' she replied.

I had to believe her.

47

'Are you my rock, my love?'

'Are you my rock, my love?' she asked over the phone. The question unnerved me. Her tone was heavy. Her gaiety had gone. Paradoxically the question betokened recovery. Recovery from what, though? I was quick to answer.

'Yes, your love and your rock.'

'Will you take me out somewhere?' It was midafternoon.

'Now?' I asked. 'This instant?'

'It can't be this instant, silly. I'm not there.' The gentle sadness in her voice made me want her here, now, at my side, in my arms, on my lips – now!

'I've picked up the extension in the bee shed,' I explained. 'Come over. By the time you get here I'll be out of my space suit, we'll have a drink, look up *What's On*, decide where to go, then dinner afterwards. How does that sound?'

'Sounds wonderful. You'll look after me?' It was a strange request.

'Every minute of every day of every year,' I assured her.

'Just this evening will do.'

'Is that all you want?' I asked, unable to hide disappointment that she had failed to respond to the laying of my life at her feet.

'I didn't say that,' she said. 'I said, 'This evening will do for a start.'

'Ah!' I replied fearing I was about to be pedantic, 'you didn't say that. You didn't say, "This evening will do for a start", you said "*Just* this evening will do".'

'Couldn't you hear 'for a start' in my voice?' she pleaded.

'Beatie, I'm a lover. Lovers are alert and anxious about every detail in a relationship.'

'Are you a lover? Is that what you are? *My* lover? You can't be *my* lover because you've never made love to me.'

'Is a lover only a lover when he's made love? Isn't a lover someone who loves?'

'Listen to us,' she laughed. 'We must be made for each other, we're both such pedants.'

When she came through my front door the lover in me fled and I became her father she looked so drawn. After a long embrace in which she clung to me as though rescued from a nightmarish experience, she said:

'Don't tell me, I look awful. I know it. I've been without makeup for weeks so my skin is dry, but I've brought my box of tricks and if I can use your bathroom you'll see one woman enter and another come out.' I asked could I watch.

'I'm going to pee first, you can't watch that. We don't know one another well enough. But if you want to watch me makeup – why not? You'll just miss the drama of transformation, which personally I would prefer. But to please you? I feel in an accommodating mood, I want no differences of opinion, no conflict. My contentment is your contentment, my happiness is your happiness.' She gave a curtsey and bowed her head. 'Your wish is my command.'

I didn't want my wish to be her command. I left her alone to makeup, though watching women makeup is one of my pleasures. There is such confidence in the process, such understanding. When she makes up the woman is understanding her face in mysterious ways, she is revealing intimate secrets about who she is, or thinks she is. Watching her one is being allowed into an inner circle. All her different persona are there and she is deciding which one of them she is today, this evening.

But she is strange. I have never encountered *this* persona from her inner circle.

*It's true. I **am** strange. I can feel it. I am in the grip of a part of me I have never met — a mixture of anger, wildness, and love. I don't think I will be able to stay away from this male, this solid, mature, kind, concerned, intelligent, sensitive, courteous, generous male. He's a male to be cherished, hung on to, treated honestly. A male not to be played around with. He had said 'If we're going to be honest, you and me.' When we first met that's what he said. He **knew** we had a future together. Why am I calling him 'male'? Look at you. You've neglected yourself. You used to be able to look in the mirror and tell yourself you were beautiful. Not your body, just your face. Your body was lumpy, fleshy, Rubenesque. The kind of body men want either to bite into or fall asleep upon. Manfred has done neither. And he won't now because I'm no longer fleshy. Goodbye, Rubenesque. Christ! Look at me. My clothes are hanging on me. How can I dare contemplate being his partner? Hold on, Beatie Bryant, you've forgotten what you used to tell yourself — real beauty is shape combined with intelligence and character. And don't you trust the male, Manfred, to know these things? Your eyes, your eyes, look at your eyes, there is still intelligence in those eyes. Trust the male to see those intelligent eyes. Why, why, do I keep referring to him as 'male'? It's such a diminishing term. You don't want to diminish him, Beatie. Not this one. Not this one. Those males in the barn — let them go. I can't! You can! I can't! You can, you can, you **can**! Damn it, Beatie, they didn't enter you. You weren't **really** fucked. Let them go. Stupid boys, stupid experiments. It backfired on them. They'll walk around with their tails up their arse for the rest of their lives. Let them go! Go! Go! Let them go! I don't think I like that eye shadow, nor that colour lipstick. Rub it off. Start again.*

When she came out of the bathroom I gasped. This was not merely a woman transformed by makeup, this was a different woman. A defeated woman had left me, a triumphant woman returned to me.

'You are so, so beautiful,' I told her.' She said. ' Thank you. Can we eat before we go anywhere? *If* we go anywhere?'

I said of course we could, adding: 'What on earth happened in there? You did more than makeup before my mirror.'

'Yeap!' she replied enigmatically.

'And you're not going to tell me? Not about anything? Not about the last three months nor the last forty-two minutes?'

'When the time is ripe, darling. All is in the timing.'

'That's the first time you've called me "darling".'

'The timing was ripe!' She smiled. Her gaiety had returned.

It's true. I was a different woman. I had let go. The moment I realised it wasn't really rape I could let go. Offensive, a violation, humiliating to have been brought to orgasm against my will but they had not entered me. Is it a spurious distinction to make between entering and not entering? I don't know. Whether or not doesn't matter. It's what I feel. They had reached my doorstep, trodden down a few flowers, but they had not entered my house, my honey pot. I could let them go.

Astonishment glowed in Manfred's eyes. It gave me pleasure. I was back in control. We opened a bottle of white wine and luxuriated in the contemplation of food. Which country did we fancy? Thinking about what one wants to eat is almost as good as actually being there. Images and tastes come back. One can sit in one's lounge and visit Greece, Spain, Italy, China, Mexico and India smacking one's palate in an effort to detect the tastes one's taste buds crave. That's what one is hungry for, not food but tastes.

'Indian!' I said.

'There's no such food as Indian food,' said my pedantic partner, 'just as there's no such food as European food. Every Indian state has its own style from Hyderabad, Lucknow, Kerala, Rajasthan . . . Want me to go on?'

'There's more?'

'Gujarat, Goa, Kashmir . . .'

'I believe you!'

'*I know a restaurant that offers most of them.*'

'*I'm your man – er – woman.*' *I faltered a little. Manfred noticed. Had I got up too soon from my sickbed? Had I let go of something that still clung? I pretended I had made a funny. Manfred leaned over and kissed me gently on the lips. I made a second mistake and stiffened my lips. He felt it but stayed as though trying to reassure me everything was all right even though he didn't know what had been wrong. Slowly I relaxed and kissed him back. But still no tongue passed between us. He hung there a good minute – which doesn't sound long but minutes are always longer than they sound.*

I reached for *What's On*. 'It's still early,' I said. 'We can take in an exhibition before eating . . . Let's see . . . Good God! There's an exhibition of Carrier-Bag Art at the Hayward.' She asked what on earth that could be. 'Haven't you noticed,' I explained, 'the kind of imagination that goes into the outside of certain carrier bags these days? I had a client who collected them. Friends used to save him their carrier bags from their travels around the world. Paper, cloth, plastic – with shop names in stylish graphics, colourful logos, reproductions of the work of famous artists from da Vinci to Mondrian. He'd collected over ten thousand by the time we parted. I wonder if this is an exhibition of his collection? Shall we go?'

'Let's,' she agreed. 'And then Gujarat, Kashmir, Goa . . .'

'. . . Lucknow, Kerala, Hyderabad,' I echoed, and kissed her again. Gaiety and relief were spreading. I couldn't hold back the tip of my tongue, and felt the tip of her tongue creep towards mine. But a tip, a mere tip. 'I think,' I said, 'that with all this wine in us we need a little nibble before we go to the exhibition. I've got something in the fridge, chopped liver, egg and onion. We can have it on matzo. Interested?'

How could I not be?

When he left I reached for What's On *and idly ran through the categories: cinema, theatre, music recitals, poetry – poetry! What was happening in the world of poetry? Poets reading in pubs . . . in fringe-theatre venues . . . poetry and jazz . . . an all-day poetry marathon . . . I* *didn't think I could take a **whole** evening of poetry readings. Poets descended into hallowed voices when reading their own poetry, as though their words were handed down by God – which I suppose is what some of them would say happens. 'Not I, not I, but the wind that blows through me', wrote D. H. Lawrence. An unfortunate metaphor for Godly inspiration I've always thought. But one of the events caught my eye. 'Speak a Poem' – a competition sponsored by BP taking place at the Central School of Speech and Drama in Swiss Cottage, just down the road. It was the finalists evening, public invited. The aim, announced the advert, was to seek out anyone who could 'convey the poem to the listener'. The word 'poem' was emphasised, presumably to create a distinction between the teller and the tale. It appealed to me at once. I had a need to hear good poetry read for its own sake rather than for showing off the reciter's 'depth of feeling'. Then I remembered. And called out.*

She called out: 'Manfred! I forgot to tell you. Natasha is rich. Greg-the-guitarist has hit top of the pops. The Scruffy Poet is rich, too, only no one knows how or where to find him.' That was astonishing news.

'They'd better find him quick,' I said, coming through with a plate of broken matzos. 'Taste!' I invited her. 'Rich chopped liver, mashed into hard-boiled eggs and covered with lightly fried onion rings.'

'Why "quick"?' she asked.

'Because,' I explained from my experience, 'the recipient has to register in order to claim his due. The Performing Rights Society doesn't hold onto unclaimed royalties for ever.'

'That's unfair,' she protested. 'And don't tell me 'life's unfair'. My nerves can't stand clichés.' I wanted to ask a question. She cautioned me: 'Timing, it's all a question of timing.'

'OK,' I accepted, and handed her a ragged square of matzo. She held it in one hand and held another hand under her mouth to catch the bits that always fall off, and crunched into the crispy, unleavened bread heavily ladden with chopped liver.

It was delicious. Not too smooth, not too lumpy, and just nicely peppered. It reminded me of the liver Ronnie's mother, Sarah, used to make.

The taste, and the sound of her name in my head, brought memories of Ronnie flooding back, which in turn made me regard Manfred closely. Was he an older Ronnie? Was that his attraction for me, I wondered?

'Manfred,' I asked, 'did you ever want to be a writer?'

'Of course. Every Jew wants to be a writer. No matter what they're best at, even brilliant at, every Jew wants to write memorable poetry or the century's novel. The "word" is magical. The word is a wand you can wave and make people feel what they've never felt before, go where they've never been before, think thoughts they had never before thought. Abracadabra – you're a great lover. Abracadabra – you're a brave explorer. Abracadabra – you're a scientific genius. For as it is written: "In the beginning was the word".'

'Yes, but,' I reminded him, 'that's not from the Jewish book of Genesis, it's from the Gospel according to Saint John.'

'Who was Jewish!' trumped Manfred. 'Of course he'd think the world began with the word.'

'Why didn't Genesis begin with it?' I asked.

'I have a theory it did but it got lost, along with the story about Lilith being Adam's wife before Eve.'

'Did you actually write anything?' I asked.

'Dreadful poetry and unpublishable short stories. Just as there wasn't a melody in my throat so there wasn't a metaphor in my mind, either.'

'You realise we're going to have to spend time hanging around buskers in the underground? Tamara and I agreed. All of us – Natasha, Greg, Barney . . .'

'Barney?' Manfred asked in a tone suggesting Barney would never do any such thing.

'We have to find the Scruffy Poet,' I said. I reached for more chopped liver. 'This is so good, Manfred.'

'Don't tell me I would make someone a good wife. My nerves can't stand clichés.'

I choked on a matzo crumb and had to drink more wine.

48

I could not have made a better choice

I could not have made a better choice. I refer not to the Indian meal, which was a Moghul dish of meat cooked Tandoori style – the Moghuls, explained Manfred, conquered India in the sixteenth century and their influence is mainly felt in the north: Punjab, Haryana, Uttar Pradiesh. He knew such things because he had climbed in the region. No, it was the poetry event that captured me.

Contestants had not only to recite poems but talk about them. Each programme involved the contestant reciting by heart a poem from a given list, and another of their own choice. They could speak about their choices in any way they liked – explaining what the poem meant to them, or where the poem came in the poet's development; anything as long as it didn't last more than twenty minutes.

There were contestants from all walks of life – a *secretary* who I suspected wanted to be an actress and who, not having the training, was mannered. *A banker* whose view of poetry was that it could only ennoble; the communication of meaning or emotion played no part in his considerations, and thus he delivered ponderously. *A secondhand book-dealer* who delivered his choices as though he had written them, and thus was gloomy and sepulchral. *A housewife* who had recently thrown the last of her four children out of the house and was discovering new horizons in the arts so that her delivery was overstimulated, her voice in the high registers telling us: 'how beautifully I am reciting this'. A *miner* from South Wales whose singsong cadences and passion earned him third place. *A drama student* whose enunciation was too careful and thus boring for my taste, but sufficiently thoughtful to earn her second place. Finally the judges summed up and I was thrilled to hear them announce as the winner someone who I, too, considered way above the rest. Manfred agreed. He was *the manager* of an engineering works in Nottingham with a naturally mellifluous speaking voice and an accompanying intelligence that tempered the melody and gave each word its correct emotional and intellectual weight. He chose a Louis MacNeice poem, 'The Sunlight on the Garden', with which I was not familiar; and Sonnet 66, with which I was.

> *Tired with all these, for restful death I cry*

How tempting it would have been to swing on the word 'tired' thus giving tiredness to the word instead of letting the word 'tired' speak for itself, which he did. And when he came to the line

> *And right perfection wrongly disgraced*

he chose to avoid anger, and delivered the line with a weary laugh as though remembering his own 'right perfections' being dismissed as wrong ones. He drove the lines to a climax of incredulity at the stupidity of men.

> *And simple truth miscalled simplicity*
> *And captive good attending captive ill*

Here was a reader who linked the poet's words to his own life. Everything about him was persuasive: confidence not overbearing, modesty without obsequiousness, intelligence devoid of cockiness.

'They got it right, they got it right,' I said excitedly to Manfred, clutching his arm, 'the judges have got it right.'

'Makes a change,' he muttered, 'they usually get it wrong.'

'It's not a question of wrong.' I was in the mood to argue with him. '"Wrong" is not the issue. Judges offer opinions.'

'That's what an opinion is,' said Manfred, 'a declaration that other people are wrong.' The 'argument' was short-lived.

Nothing could dampen my excitement. As the evening progressed I was not only engrossed by the competition, I was seeing how the idea could be taken further. By the time it was over I knew 'Speak A Poem' would make a wonderful TV programme. I had to tell Tamara about it. First I worked out a three-page 'treatment' and then arranged to meet her for lunch in Shepherd Market to explain the set-up.

'It's a natural,' I said, excitedly. 'And you're the right person to put it together. It will not only help launch your career as a director, it could take off everywhere and also make money. The idea is the brainchild of a woman called Betty Minton who earns a living giving poetry recitals. I've written a draft treatment. Three pages. Read them now! Now! While we're waiting for the meal to come. They're slow here, you've got time.' She didn't have time, not for all three pages, just the first one.

Speak A Poem – idea for an ongoing weekly TV competition

Can be adopted in every country in the world.

Calls for an anchor man or woman (AP), contestants, film crew, four judges, a live audience.

At the end of a year there is a final competition for first, second and third prize, which will take place over two consecutive evenings.

The prizes are monetary of, say, £25,000, £10,000, and £5,000.

Aim

To promote the power and relevance of poetry.

Preamble

Poetry is the language of lovers, thinkers, romantic spirits and –
unfortunately – opportunistic politicians.

Most people have been touched by poetry at some time in
their life. They've been called upon to memorise or recite or,
driven by an emotional event, to write it; or they have had a
poem written for them by precocious offspring or ardent suit-
ors.

There is a poem for love, death, ambition, loss, greed, heroism – every basic human emotion or attribute. Even trite verse
considered 'poetic' by grannies seeking the right birthday card
is a response to a basic instinct to celebrate in rhythm and
rhyme.

Most people have passionate thoughts about what makes a
poem or how it should be recited. For this reason such a TV
series as here outlined will command a vast, curious and quar-
relsome public eager to pit their judgements against those of the
judges.

'That's all you need to read for now,' I said. 'The other two pages
are just suggested rules and a sample shooting script.'

'Hmm!' said Tamara, having read the first page.

'Is that all you can say? "Hmm"?' I was on the warpath.

'It was a cautionary "Hmm".'

'To hell with caution, Tamara!'

'What on earth has got into you?'

'I had a crisis. I fell apart. I want to put the parts together.'

'Humpty Dumpty!'

'I AM NOT HUMPTY DUMPTY,' I yelled. 'The parts *will*
come together again.'

'But this project is for *me*, you say?'

'Yes!'

'So how . . .?'

'Manfred took me out, our first time in an age. We went to an exhibition of carrier bags . . .'

'Carrier bags?'

'Yes.'

'You mean – *carrier* bags?'

'Yes, yes, yes – forget the carrier bags. And then we went to a restaurant selling different dishes from different parts of India and I learnt that there was no such thing as Indian food just as there's no such thing as European food, and then I looked at *What's On* to see if there was a film or theatre we wanted to see, and I stumbled upon this advert for "Speak A Poem" competition, and I could have chosen anything else but I didn't, I chose the poetry competition and we listened to all these different people reciting and there was this manager of an engineering factory who recited a Shakespeare sonnet and a poem by Louis MacNiece and he was so enthralling and I got so excited about what the judges would say and who they'd choose and why – and I could see it! I could see it on television. The parts came together, it was meant to be, I felt certain about it as about nothing before. And I could see all these people arguing and saying that's not how you recite poetry and oh wasn't he wonderful and wasn't she dreadful and sack the judges and what a glorious poem that was must read more of him or her and I could write better than that and suddenly everyone would be talking about poetry and there'd be competitions in schools and copycat versions in the local village hall and the bookshops would have special displays of poetry books in their windows and everyone would become an authority on poetry and there'd be quarrels in the bus queue and fights on street corners . . .'

It was then that Shepherd Market began spinning, and Tamara grabbed my hand.

'Beatie, you've gone pale.'

'I want to be sick,' I said standing up. She helped me to the loo, thankfully missing all those diners deep in their salads, soups and steaks. Tamara paid for our food, which we didn't eat, grabbed a sandwich, and took me to Manfred's house where they laid me out on a bed on which I slept for two hours. When I staggered back into the lounge I could tell they had been talking about me. Manfred felt my forehead.

'Well, it's not as hot as when you came in. What gave you a temperature, do you think?'

'Excitement,' I lied. Or part-lied for I was truly excited about the television programme. 'Excitement and the Tandoori dish, and being with you after so long, and the poetry, and the ideas it gave me. Too heady. All too much.'

'Do you want anything?' Manfred asked.

'Now I'm hungry. Got rid of my breakfast, missed my lunch, what's in the fridge?'

'More chopped liver?'

'Oh, yes. Tamara, you must try it. Thought any more about my idea?'

'Yes, and of course I love it. Only one problem. We don't have the money to make a pilot, and a pilot is what's needed because TV producers are frightened about anything new, and take a lot to be persuaded, and usually can't be, and poetry is not sex or violence or money games or the story of everyday folk up the road.'

'But what about those paragraphs where I point out how most people have been touched by poetry at some time in their life?'

'It's true. I agree. But I know the producer mentality. Few have visual imagination, and if they do they have no courage to take risks.'

'How much would a pilot cost?' Manfred asked.

'God knows,' said Tamara who should know but was too responsible to hazard guesses. 'It would need to be properly budgeted in order to come up with a reliable figure.'

'Guess,' urged Manfred. 'Round figures.'

'About five to seven thousand? Perhaps even ten. Hire of equipment, technicians, suitable space, production team, judges, assembling an audience . . .'

'What if I bankrolled it? Would I be considered an investor and in line to make a royalty?'

'You should know about such things better than I do,' Tamara told him.

'Why don't you budget it?' he suggested. 'As long as Beatie has a major role in it I'd be interested in the pilot.'

'Oh no,' I said. 'I'll take a small royalty for thinking of the idea but I have other plans.'

'Other plans? In the plural?' Manfred was surprised. 'Plans you've not shared with me?'

'A plan. Just one. I only thought about it last night.'

'Would you care to share it with me now?' Manfred looked hurt.

'Don't be hurt, Manfred. I want to think it through before testing it on you for your blessing.'

I was still not one hundred per cent recovered, but I felt the colour had returned to my cheeks, and I was on the way. What I held back from Manfred and Tamara was that my fever was also due to my 'plan', a plan that was giving me palpitations each time I thought about it. Listening to the poetry I became aware that poetry was made up of potent parts. Words, the meaning of words, their sounds; then rhythm of line, metaphor, image, rhyme, alliteration, spirit – or is 'spirit' too nebulous to be considered a 'part'?

When I returned home I looked for a book I remembered Ronnie giving me – a series of radio talks by the poet Ted Hughes for young people. *Poetry In The Making*. What would Hughes have to say about the 'spirit' of a poem? I skipped through the pages and was arrested by a passage that gave me another 'part' to a poem. The 'senses'. Hughes wrote:

*Words that live are those which we **hear**, like 'click' or 'chuckle', or words which we **see**, like 'freckled' or 'veined', or which we **taste**, like 'vinegar' or 'sugar', or **touch**, like 'prickle' or 'oily', or **smell**, like 'tar' or 'onion': words which belong directly to one of the five **senses**. Or words that act and seem to use their muscles, like 'flick' or 'balance'.*

I could never in a hundred years write a poem, nor would I dare, but observations like that excite me because suddenly I am made aware of something I was not aware of before. My 'plan' fell into place. No matter how much I had reasoned myself to 'let it go' I knew I had not. The two college boys lingered. What I had said to Tamara was accurate – I had fallen apart. '*They need to rub me out and draw me again,*' said a character in a play, I can't remember which one. I had been 'rubbed out', or parts of me had been rubbed out. I needed to join up the parts to be whole again, and the one way I could do that was to break down as much of the material world as possible into its parts. It had begun in order to satisfy my curiosity, had become a hobby, and now had grown into a need.

I would devote the next ten years of my life, or however long it took, to assemble an *Encyclopaedia of Parts*. I must find a publisher to fund it. I want to start at once.

I was not prepared for what followed.

49

Beatie was not prepared for what followed

Beatie was not prepared for what followed. Her life was to be held up for another six months.

She drew up a comprehensive list of publishers in the UK and the USA, and wrote to editors asking would they be interested to read a two-page synopsis of a publishing idea. Her reasoning was this: not to send the unsolicited synopsis but first to write a tempting letter evincing curiosity. If they were tempted then two things would have been achieved: *they* would have solicited the synopsis, and her name would have been twice before them. Her preliminary letter described her idea in low-key language: a long-term encyclopaedic venture with worldwide potential, as for example *Who's Who in the World* and *The Oxford Companion to English Literature*.

It was after she had finished drafting her introductory letter and drawn up her list that she involved Manfred. He declared it a brilliant concept and, as was their routine, suggested they talk about it over dinner. He took her to Lanagan's, a spacious restaurant very much in fashion. They could talk without fear of being overheard.

'Parts,' Manfred began, 'an encyclopaedia of parts. Why, one wonders, hasn't it been thought of ages ago? But,' he cautioned, 'I must tell you that my life is dotted with ventures I've thought surefire that have failed, and others I've dismissed that went on to make fortunes. Am I to be trusted? Is my judgement sound? *I* may think it's a brilliant idea but my approval may be the kiss of death.'

'You built up and sold for enormous profit an accountancy firm for the wealthy, the famous and the beautiful,' countered Beatie. 'Your judgement must have been sound somewhere along the line.'

'You don't need judgement to be an accountant, you just need to be familiar with the laws on tax, clever at devising ways to avoid paying it and bold enough to suggest it to your clients who in turn need courage to accept your suggestions.'

'Do you have any suggestions about my project?'

'Maybe. Let's order first.'

Beatie loved being taken out by Manfred. He was an old-fashioned man who stood when she entered a room, and opened the car door for her. He knew how to look after and reassure her and lay everything at her feet. She felt comfortable with him, unthreatened. He was neither combative nor competitive, and knew both how to take over and when to step back. Though he looked after her he didn't make her feel looked after, rather he behaved as though all was her due.

She chose chilled Vichyssoise followed by lamb korma and carrot rice. Manfred skipped the starter but ordered a Delmonico salad so that Beatie had company during her Vichyssoise, followed by paprika chicken with yoghurt on a bed of plain boiled rice. The headwaiter, to whom Manfred was known, suggested a 1983 Sancerre.

'Your comments?' Beatie was eager to talk about her encyclopaedia.

'Before I comment,' said Manfred, 'let me tell you about one of my ex-clients, a Canadian writer whose father came home from work every day with a new idea for making a fortune. He was Jewish, of course, and all his ideas were impractical. One day he returned from work with an idea for making a fortune by re-sharpening disused razor blades – we're talking nineteen-twenties here – and he bought a grinder, one where you turned the handle and held the blade over the revolving stone. It wasn't even a trea-dle mechanism. This writer described how he and his brothers ground their fingers as well as the blades. Crazy! Every idea was crazy. But one day, in his mid-seventies, this daft old anxious father, desperate to provide for his family after his death, came up with an idea for disposable plastic cigar holders. It made him a for-tune and gave him three heart attacks. I like such people. Driven crazies! Not to be rich but to provide for their families. And they don't stop. Day after day they plot and scheme and invent ways and means. Restless old men. Every time they turn their head in another direction they see another idea.'

'And you think I'm like that?'

'A bit.'

'Even though I'm not Jewish?'

'And you're not in line for heart attacks, either, thank God. Nor are you a crazy.'

'And I don't have a family to provide for. But you're right. Human ingenuity excites me. Have I said that before? There are people out there throbbing nonstop with ideas. Not only for making money but for doing good deeds – caring about the envi-ronment, the victims of famine, floods and tyrannies. It excites me. Reassures me. Unfortunately none of them came to "yourideas.com", understandably. Ingenuity like that is also resourceful.'

'Your letter is good, Beatie,' said Manfred. 'But I'd look at it carefully to see if you can cut out a few "verys" that you seem addicted to. And though ending a sentence with a preposition is charming in literature it sticks out like a sore thumb in letters applying for jobs. You might also look at your split infinitives.'

'How do you know all this about writing?'

'I wanted to be a writer, remember? Knowing too much about correct grammar is probably what inhibited me from becoming one.'

'And?'

'And what?'

'What about a comment on the idea itself?'

'None. I have none. Just a warning and a suggestion. It's a brilliant idea but it's wildly expensive. They will have to pay you an annual salary for – how long? Five years?'

'Probably. Five to seven.'

'With no return. And they'll probably have to cough up extra money for a research assistant.'

'Perhaps it can be a joint venture, between two publishers.'

'Perhaps. But investment is only the half of it. Selling the idea as viable is the other half. Who's your market?'

'Writers for a start,' said Beatie. 'Not only creative ones but non-fiction writers, too, to say nothing of those thousands who *imagine* they're writers and who probably constitute the largest market. Everyone uses *Roget's Thesaurus* – whether writing a novel, a thesis, a history or a love letter. The same people will either forget the parts of something they once knew or will want to know what they've not known before. Every university department will want a copy, and every reference library.'

'It will take years to recoup investment.' Manfred felt it his responsibility to be cautious. 'Few publishers will have the vision.'

'Couldn't they produce the book in stages?' Beatie asked. 'A volume every three years?'

'Are you suggesting a publisher should publish an incomplete book? A book that doesn't fulfil its promise? "Parts" but only the first part!'

'You're right, of course! I won't suggest it.'

'But here's what I think you ought to do.' Manfred was coming to his major suggestion, pride in which he could not hide. 'Let me pay for a graphics designer to design a stunning dust jacket, one that can be used as a logo on all the letters you send out. There's nothing more persuasive than printed material to convey a total concept. A dummy dust jacket would powerfully convey a sense of the final product.'

She thought it an imaginative idea. And a generous one. She took his hand, kissed it and thanked him. All this generosity and attention without ever having made love. How long could such a relationship last? Were they destined only ever to be friends? Nothing wrong with that. Great friendships are rare. Passion is intense but ephemeral; friendship roots deeply, and lasts.

And so Beatie began the long haul of trying to sell an idea to manuscript-drunk-and-bruised editors whose anxious heads, like all who work in the arts, were flicking glances back at the formulas that had made last year's successes. The chemistry that makes an idea spark for some and not others is one of life's mysteries, thought Beatie as she neatly filed away negative response after negative response. There were those who were not interested even to read the synopsis; those who read the synopsis but were not galvanised enough to want to meet with her and discuss it further; and those who met with her but finally declined.

What she was unprepared for took place one crisp autumn morning on her way back from meeting with a young editor who had been uncharacteristically enthusiastic. Mostly, those who invited her into their office were cool and cautious, not wishing to encourage hope. This young editor, a novice who had not yet learned how to be interested without appearing eager, or admiring without conveying promise, had sent her away on a high. The idea had great potential he said, he would place it before 'the powers that be because', he said, 'I'm just a fledgeling out of college. A brilliant fledgeling I might add but not yet one to be trusted with unilateral decisions.' Beatie warmed to him. He was fresh and had a sense of humour. For this reason she was travelling the underground in a light-hearted mood, and barely knew where she was or who was passing her by as she changed at King's Cross from Russell Square onto the Northern Line for Belsize Park.

Slowly moving down on the escalator, out of her self-absorp-
tion, from among the haze of faces gliding up, her attention
drifted toward a familiar face. It was the ashen face of a neatly
dressed man with prematurely greying hair and eyebrows. A face
that had once been beautiful. Suddenly she knew, and shouted
out.

'Ronnie!' The face slowly turned towards her. At first the eyes
held no recognition, then gradually as the face passed her it
smiled. A hand waved. The slow movement of the head turning,
the limp wave, the ashen face brought a rush of joy and sadness to
her heart. 'Wait for me!' she cried out. He did, and was there for
her hug when she rushed to the level she had just left.

Like a person drowning, her early years flashed past. Ah, those
first heady days of meeting a young personality of a kind she had
never met before nor, coming from farm-labouring stock, could
have imagined existed in the world. His prematurely aged face
distressed her, but his eyes, delighted to see her, shimmered into
life and health sufficient to remind her of the boy who had
grabbed her hand and announced he was taking her to see a play.
A play! She hardly knew what a play was, let alone had been taken
to one. Nor had it been an easy choice – Shakespeare's *Merchant of
Venice* directed by a young director, fresh out of university. She had
actually become agitated when it was Bassanio's turn to choose
the casket, and had gripped Ronnie's arm with excitement whispering, 'Will he choose the right one, will he, will he?' and had
kissed his cheek when he did. During the Court scene she had
averted her eyes when Shylock drew his knife to cut the forfeit of
a pound of Antonio's flesh. Heady days of seeing films she had
never seen, listening to music she had never heard and making
love to a softly spoken young Adonis who wrote poetry and read
to her from books. His one failing, she recalled, was a certain
physical gawkiness – he could not dance. She had taught him to
jitterbug in a pub on the river called the Blue Angel where a gay
singer extravagantly gyrated most evenings and kept the clientele
in a state of intoxicated movement. Once he had learnt, Ronnie

couldn't stop. Heady days, heady days! A glowing young man, someone for whom the world was opening its treasures and rewards, a golden boy of promise for whom everything from art to rainbows was a thrill, which thrill he had communicated to her, gloriously turning her world upside down.

What had happened? He could be only thirty-five years old but he looked nearly fifty. What had ravaged him? Who had stolen the promise?

'Have you got time for a coffee?' she asked.

'I've got time for everything,' he smiled. It astonished her that seeing him again after all these years her heart ached with the memory of past days of youth and innocence. She felt sadness, too, and had to fight hard to hide it. She knew life damaged and disappointed but this face carried something other than the pain of disappointment.

'If you've got time for everything, how about lunch?' He protested that he couldn't but in such a way that Beatie guessed he was holding onto pennies. 'Come,' she pressed, 'it's on me. I owe you so much.'

'You owe me nothing,' he replied. While Beatie held on to the halcyon memories Ronnie remembered only that it was he who had broken off their relationship. As he looked at her beauty and registered her confidence he could not, now, understand why. At her insistence he relented.

There was no decent restaurant around King's Cross but there was a clean worker's cafe where the food looked fresh and each order was cooked on demand. They ended up eating an all-day breakfast of two fried eggs on fried bread with bacon, two sausages, grilled tomatoes, over-flowing baked beans and a plate of chips between them. And they learned about each other's lives. Ronnie had written a novel that a reputable publisher had put out into the market but had abandoned.

'How did I miss it?'

'No back up. No marketing.'

'Still, I'd've seen the name Ronnie Kahn.'

'No you wouldn't! They insisted I call myself Ronald Kahn.'

'Reviews?'

'Not ecstatic and not many. Not 'here is a brilliant newcomer', but 'here is a young writer of promise'.'

'Well?'

'I became the enemy of my promise – as Mr Connolly warned. Succumbed to flattery, attended too many parties, smiled too much.'

'I've never understood why people feel threatened by smiles.'

'It denotes confidence and joy, and who do you think you are to be joyous?'

'Did they commission another?'

'Too risky.'

'Did you ever write another, commission or no commission?'

'I tried. But it seems I only had one novel in me.'

'That's nonsense, Ronnie. You're only thirty-five years old – you've got two more lifetimes to write a novel.' She could not have attempted a more wretched consolation. When it boomeranged she was stunned.

'I don't even have one lifetime, Beatie. I'm dying. Cancer. The liver.' She regarded him intently. How serious was he? 'I'm in remission but I've been in remission a long time now.' The truth was in his eyes. She found herself unable to breathe, stood up, and moved to the door. The cafe owner raised an arm to hold her back then realised her condition.

'Air,' she gasped. 'Coming back.' He also saw that her partner had remained sitting, though not for long. Ronnie soon followed to the cafe door. He reached out his hand.

'Come back in, Beatie. I'm sorry, but . . . I . . . I I'm sorry, come back in.'

'I need a hot cup of strong, sweet tea,' she ordered, returning to their table where she wept as silently as she could. It was not easy to hide her tears in such a confined space where the diners were brawny men who would only interpret her tears as tears of rejected love. Not that she cared, though God knows they were for that, too, and everything else rotten in this life of wasted talent, thoughtless experimenters, visionless middlemen, tyrants and crazies who buried their heads in sand and threw bombs at the innocent.

'Oh, Ronnie,' she wept. 'It can't be true.' But the pain in his voice confirmed it was.

'Forgive me. I had no right to shock you like that. We have no life together, no friendship even. I should just have said I was ill, gastric flu or something.'

'No life, no friendship, but a past. An intense past. And it was yesterday, as though nothing has happened in between.'

'But it has. Look at you. Look at me. Let's talk of other things.'

Beatie knew he was right. He had told her something that could only upset her and leave her helpless, unable either to assuage her distress or alleviate his pain. She chatted about her life, and asked about his family. Both Harry and Sarah, his parents, had died. 'Thank God.'

'Why "thank God"?'

'Really, Beatie. To watch your child die?'

'Of course.' She was in complete disarray. Having begun to put the parts of her life together she was now in pieces again. This life-torn man before her was once so full of hope and dynamism and gaiety. To come to this. Why? Punishment for falling victim to a young man's hubris? There will always be, she knew, a part of life that makes no sense, a part that she would never find for her encyclopaedia, like the one element the scientists couldn't identify in honey.

'And Ada and Dave?' she asked, still trying to be inconsequential. His sister and brother-in-law had kept their Norfolk cottage as a holiday home but had returned from their rural idyll to London and were flourishing, he reported, running a joinery factory in Hampstead. 'Hampstead? That's up the road from me. I've got a flat in Belsize Park.' So what? So fucking what? The first love of her life was dying.

'I'm so happy to have bumped into you, Beatie.' He, too, tried to distract them from his announcement. 'Really. Have you any idea how happy it makes me to hear that you worked your way back into education? And college! Got to Oxford! My dream! I dreamt it but you did it. You actually did it. It makes me feel very proud.'

'You should be,' said Beatie, 'if I hadn't met you I'd have married a butcher. Not even a kosher one!'

He smiled. She had made him smile.

'Good thing we didn't meet for the first time now, eh?' He smiled again. That smile, she had always loved it. However ravaged the features of his face nothing could take the mischievous gaiety out of his smile.

'Don't you write anything? Short stories? Poetry? What about journalism?'

'Freelance journalism is what pays the bills,' he said. 'I was going to say freelance journalism is what keeps me alive but . . .' That mischievous smile again.

'Stupid!' she said. 'How can you make jokes about it?'

'How can I not? I make jokes about it, I write failed stories about it, I write failed poems about it. I'm thinking of offering a newspaper the diary of my last days.'

'I hate to say it,' said Beatie, 'but that's a good idea. A bit macabre but I bet you could earn a lot of money for it.'

'As long as it's paid upfront and not on publication!' They exchanged smiles again. Beatie felt comfortable with him, loving the return of a familiarity belonging to an important period in her life.

'And then it could be a book,' she said. 'All that money!'

'As long as it's paid upfront and not on publication!' That mischievous smile again. 'My sister would inherit.'

'It happens.'

'In dreams it happens.'

'No, no!' Beatie insisted. 'In real life, sometimes.' And she told him the story of Greg-the-guitarist and the Scruffy Poet who had a fortune waiting for him if he could be found.

'What was the Scruffy Poet's song about?' Ronnie asked.

'Oh,' she replied, 'the usual thing. Love. You must have heard it. It's all over the place.'

'I don't listen to radio. Can you remember the first line?'

'Not at all.' She was aware of his steady gaze.

'If I related it would you recognise it?'

'How can you if you don't listen to radio?'

'Let me try.' A hunter's look had entered his eyes. The next seconds were strange. She could feel something coming, it promised to be wonderful but she was trying to deflect it in case she was wrong and it was not wonderful and Ronnie's gaze meant nothing. But no, it *was* true. Her intimations were correct. She had understood why his eyes had come ablaze. He quoted:

"*You surely know it's me, it's me you love, you surely know.*" Beatie followed with the next line.

"*Your pain will tell you, please don't go . . .*"

Ronnie continued: "*Remain with me, my love, you surely know.*"

'That's it! The first lines. Oh my God! Oh, Ronnie. Oh, my God, Ronnie, the money is yours. Is that what you're saying?'

'I don't know,' said a confused Ronnie. '*Is* that what I'm saying? I don't know what I'm saying. I don't understand what's happening. Lets go over it again.' She repeated the story of the Scruffy Poet who had thrust scraps of paper into a busker's hand and had suggested the busker compose music for it.

'That was me,' said Ronnie. 'The Scruffy Poet was me. I was doing the round of buskers and offering the sheets to whoever I thought had talent.'

'Why didn't you go back to see if anyone had picked you up on it?'

'I did. A couple of times. But when I heard nothing, or no one was where they had been before, I gave up. I mean I couldn't spend my days stalking buskers.' He smiled his smile. They were both silent, soaking up this life-changing development that had come too late to change a life, neither of them knowing what to say or how to behave. Beatie broke the silence.

'You shouldn't have ditched me, Ronnie.'

'I wanted to protect you against what I feared I might become.'

'What daft decisions we make in our youth about the rest of our life.'

'I know. We think we're thinking things through but in fact we're plotting fantasies.'

'And you had a fantasy about yourself that turned out wrong.'

'Did it?' That face was so unbearably sad.

'You're rich, for Christ's sake, Ronnie.'

'How much?'

'I don't know how much.'

'Bet it's not much.'

'It's lots. Lots and lots, and it's yours, all yours. Oh, my God!'

'I want to pay for this meal,' he said, smiling what was now an uncontrollable smile, 'but I don't have enough. Could you lend me a fiver?'

'This is surreal,' said Beattie, 'you know that, don't you? Surreal! But oh, how the parts have come together. There's a whole and sometimes the parts do come together.'

Ronnie never understood what Beatie had meant by that sentence. Nor had there been time to explore it. Within four weeks the first love of her life was dead. Beatie felt immensely gratified to have met him in time to have been able to nurse him through that last month.

It was a distressing ending. Ada and Dave had been with him most of the day. Beatie took over for the late evening, promising to phone when the end was close. He had become painfully thin, his eyes large and staring with terror.

'It's such a difficult journey to make, this one,' he had apologised; then countered it with a visual image. 'This cancer is running around doing what it likes.'

For the last hours he was drugged out of this world. She held his hand and listened to his heavy, pointless breathing through an oxygen mask sounding as though he was snoring a deep sleep.

Why don't they remove the mask and let him die? she wondered. He doesn't want this. She whispered to him:

'Let go, Ronnie, let go, darling.' But he wasn't ready. A memory returned to her. Ronnie had told her the story of how he had sat with his mother beside his dying father and had urged him: 'Hang on, Joe, keep breathing; breathe, Joe, hang on.' And here was she telling the son to let go.

Only once did he regain consciousness. His eyes told her that he knew she was there to say goodbye. He struggled to speak, however. She had to bend close.

'No last words,' he whispered. 'Can't think of any last dying words.' He smiled his mischievous smile, which broke her strength, and she wept. She felt him give a last reassuring squeeze of her hand before drifting away. An Irish male nurse came in to give him two more injections and reduce the oxygen in the mask.

'He didn't twitch,' the male nurse said, 'that means he feels no pain.' She asked him why it was taking so long. He took her aside and gently explained. 'Dying is a slow process, especially for one so young, like being born. Different parts of the body must cease functioning before another part can cease. It doesn't stop all at once. Hearing is the last to go, which is why I drew you aside. But he feels nothing. His breathing is instinctive rather than physical. It will get shallower and then slowly fade. I promise you.'

Beatie dozed off as the hours crept into early morning. Suddenly she leapt awake. Ronnie's breathing was now gentler, the phlegm had moved, the struggling seemed over. She sat counting the gaps between each breath. The last gasps had a count of five between them. She felt his forehead. It was hard and cold. It was as though he was really dead but had to catch up with his death. The last breath seemed not far away. There was a long silence. Then a heave, another long silence. Another heave, and it was over. At that moment Ada and Dave came through the door. The Irish male nurse had looked in while Beatie was dozing, realised from Ronnie's breathing that the end was soon, and had rung his sister. She was distressed not to have been there for the end. Beatie lied and said he had breathed his last breath the second after they arrived. It was 6.25 a.m. All three stood looking down as a kind of beauty returned to his face. They hugged and parted. Later, Ada asked Beatie to plan the cremation service. She did, but was not able to function properly for a month afterwards. Manfred understood, and with characteristic grace stepped back till she was ready to receive him again.

Ronnie was cremated at Golders Green cemetery, and his ashes planted beneath a magnolia tree in the Norfolk house of his sister. He bequeathed them and his nephews his late-flowering fortune, a collection of short stories for which a publisher was found and a hundred pages, handwritten, of a second novel that showed promise but for which no publisher could be found.

50

'All things tire of themselves'

'*All things tire of themselves*' had been the first line of one of Ronnie's poems. Grief, too, tires of itself, and one morning in the middle of a week in spring Beatie Bryant woke up feeling unaccountably energetic and eager to get on with her life. There is something in the nature of grief that, when its power diminishes, the griever feels the time spent grieving has been wasted. Rationally Beatie knew that she both wanted and had to grieve, so much had accumulated to grieve over: the death of her mother, Stan Mann, Ronnie and the loss of her innocence. But the clothes of her grief were now sodden with use. They needed to be cleansed, she needed to be refreshed. This time she went not into her bath but to a gym with a sauna in which her clogged pores could breathe. She wanted her limbs, all the parts of her, agile again, everything about herself opened up and spring-cleaned.

'I think,' she said to Manfred with whom she was in discussion over breakfast about John Major's "Back to Basics" theme announced at the current Conservative Party Conference, 'that he can't get back to basics after what Maggie has bequeathed him. And I do believe she was a romantic at heart. I think her heart genuinely believed she had released the free spirit of initiative and enterprise, but her head hadn't understood that instead she had released greed and frustration. What terrible years they were.' Beatie was in full flood, talking as though she had just emerged from a long vow of silence and was ravenous for intellectual exchange. 'Terrible, terrible years – a decline in artistic activity, demoralising unemployment, sharp divisions of wealth, civil liberties under threat . . .'

'And,' added Manfred, 'the fading of a sweet humanity that I've always felt was particularly English.'

'Right!' said Beatie. 'Violence, menace and aggressiveness – that's her legacy. What chance does poor Major stand calling for 'the old values of . . .' She reached for the *Guardian*. 'I quote: "of neighbourliness, decency, courtesy . . ."'

'That's what Jimmy Porter was looking back in anger about – the absence of neighbourliness, decency and courtesy.'

'Before my time,' said Beatie. 'I'm angry because the streets are littered with beer cans, cigarette boxes and Kentucky Fried Chicken containers. And to cap it all the public prosecutor was afraid to put on trial those lunatics who called for the death of Salman Rushdie. Good morning, world!'

'Welcome back,' said Manfred.

'I'm going to find a publisher for *Parts* if it kills me,' said the pig-keeper's daughter. 'I feel I can take on anyone.'

She had left off hustling where the uncharacteristically enthusiastic and naive young editor had told her that 'Parts' had great potential, and had sent her away on a high. It was the day she had seen Ronnie moving towards her on the escalator. Since then she had heard nothing. A long enough time had elapsed for her to prompt him. He replied apologetically, regretting that his superiors had not shared his enthusiasm for her project. *If it's any consolation,* he ended his letter, *had I been running my own enterprise I would have snapped it up. Persevere!* he had commanded, and she planned to do just that.

The dummy dust jacket Manfred had commissioned was a bold

and attractive, zany design that played with the word P A R T S, breaking it down into its five letters – its five parts – which floated like debris across the page as though exploded apart. She sent out, three at a time, the invitation to publishers to read her synopsis, each accompanied by a dust jacket. There was interest but no commitment. The letters of rejection all had about them an air in common. She couldn't identify it until one rejection of total honesty arrived and seemed to speak the truth on behalf of them all.

To be honest, this editor had written, *the prospect of undertaking such a huge and long-term project fills me with terror, and I'm afraid I command neither the resources nor the courage to take it on.* That was it, thought Beatie, they have no courage. Maggie Thatcher had taken courage and daring out of the country. Market forces are fierce. The armies of enterprise are creeping through the dark landscape eyeing each other with fear. Few dare plant anything new. Not even for the sweet-natured John Major.

Meanwhile, ploughing through submissions, and while waiting for responses, Beatie helped Tamara and Lee set up the pilot of *Speak A Poem.* Betty Minton had been involved in an advisory capacity. She had built up the lists of poems modern and classical for contestants to choose from, and had suggested names for possible judges. A well-known stage designer had been brought in who had created a set that was dramatic without being garish, and Lee had designed lighting that was gentle and lyrical to accompany the mood of the spoken, lyrical word. Tamara directed the whole in a way that created excited anticipation. Every contestant was made to appear a mixture of interesting and eccentric; she exploited the drama of: 'Who is next?' 'What profession or trade?' 'How will they sound?' 'What are the faces in the audience revealing?' 'What will the judges say?'

It was a brilliant pilot but no TV company would buy it. The team were told that the public was only interested in quiz shows and soap operas about themselves. Poetry was a turn-off. Joe Public wouldn't even give it a chance. But it earned Tamara the offer of a producer's chair from where she knew she could plan a life, perhaps even smuggle in *Speak A Poem* at a later date. Meanwhile Betty Minton returned to running her live competitions around the country and, because the pilot, though not picked up, had earned high praise, Beatie felt vindicated and more confident to pursue publishers for her *Encyclopaedia of Parts*.

Manfred climbed his mountains, strode his deserts and buzzed round his bees. When he was away Jack Newsom kept an eye on his hives while Beatie kept an eye on his house, often sleeping there to help take the edge off missing his presence. Missing him made her wonder – why? It was not that her flesh was feeling neglected, they were still not yet lovers. Skins sulk, she knew that, but this was not her condition. My love my rock. He was her rock, really and truly. Over the months she had come to feel safe and secure – a fortunate state in which to be, she knew – so of course she would miss him, especially now when publishers' rejections were beginning to lower her spirits and narrow the drive of her energy. It didn't help that she was determined, stubborn like her mother, relentless; she still needed Manfred around to reassure her that somewhere out there, as she had convinced herself, was a publisher who was right and ripe for her project. She might know it but she needed Manfred to say it to her. She wanted his voice in her ear. He returned to her tales of rejection.

'The world is divided,' she raged, 'between those who bought Van Gogh while he lived and those who waited for posterity to make him an investment.'

'Very good, very good,' he could be impatient sometimes, 'but that's the way of the world and it doesn't help.' Coupled with his encouragement he suggested that she rewrite the synopsis. At first she was reluctant but his argument was persuasive.

'You keep complaining,' he reminded her, 'that bloody publishers are congenitally unable to reinvent themselves, that they're stuck in Neolithic slime. Well, maybe you're similarly stuck with your first attempt. Just toy with something different, write something in a completely fresh spirit. Make a movie script out of it as though for a Disney cartoon. What can it harm? You can always tear it up.' Of course she did not write a movie script, that would have been foolish, but she did restructure her few pages, made them livelier, less portentous. It didn't help. Rejection still followed rejection.

There had been, creeping from the back of her mind to the front, an idea that finally took hold and had to be pursued. The one publisher she had avoided was Lindsey Shackleton, the senior editor of Solomon King, the witch of Fitzroy Square who had reduced her to tears by telling her she would not amount to much. Beatie had nearly been demolished. Now she was fantasising that, witch though she was, Lindsey Shackleton might have that spark of imagination, and perhaps even courage. Beatie would bring out Miss Shackleton's true nature, she would present her with *Parts* and awaken in her the dream for which she had been waiting – the sponsorship of a book that would enter the history of publishing as had *The Guinness Book of Records*. No home or business or university would be complete without *Parts* on its shelves. *Parts* would be the final part to make a book collection complete, and she, Lindsey Shackleton, would ensure that it was so. Beatie convinced herself of this. And so she wrote:

Dear Miss Shackleton,

I don't know if, among all the applicants for jobs you must meet, you will remember me, but I can't believe you say to each of them what you said to me. I remind you. 'You enter a room,' you told me, 'with the air of one who imagines that everyone in it is an idiot.'

The observation unnerved me as you can imagine, and perhaps would have damaged my self-confidence had you not also said something about literature that impressed me sufficiently to override the hurt. You observed that books were like people – you trust them or you don't, you believe them or you don't.

This is not why I write, however. That first paragraph was merely by way of reintroduction. I write because I have been working on a publishing project that I believe has worldwide commercial potential. Enclosed is a synopsis. I hope we can meet to discuss it.

Lindsey Shackleton did not write a reply, she phoned.

'I was harsh on you, I remember, but it was because you impressed me and I wanted to test your mettle, see if you'd survive and bounce back. You have done. The synopsis you sent intrigues me. Let's meet.'

They met in the Fitzroy Square office, where Beatie took her through her index files, samples of nouns she had already broken down into parts. The witch, who appeared less and less of a witch as the day progressed, invited her to lunch. She admired the project, thought it imaginative and useful. 'Even thrilling. An incautious word I would normally not use.' She would like to get behind the venture, she told Beatie, and, having discussed the synopsis with colleagues who agreed the idea of an encyclopaedia of parts was an exciting one, she was empowered to talk business and offer a deal. Solomon and King were prepared to pay fifteen thousand pounds a year for three years, payable – after an initial advance of five thousand pounds – in monthly instalments, plus up to five thousand pounds a year for research expenses – payable on presentation of receipts. It was a generous offer. Manfred went over the contract with a fine-tooth comb, checked certain details with a literary agent friend, and made one, cheeky suggestion that all sums be increased with the rise of inflation. It was resisted but finally accepted.

'I'm taking *you* out for dinner for a change,' Beatie informed him, and included Tamara, Lee and Barney to form a celebratory party.

'Celebratory' was hardly the word applicable to the evening itself, however.

Not everything in these past two years had gone well for everyone – Manfred had organised his retirement satisfactorily; television powers-that-be rejected *Speak A Poem* but it had led to Tamara being offered a producer's job. Beatie, too, was gratified. She had seen an idea come to life on the Underground. That man she had met on the train, Derek somebody or other, had picked up her idea for 'Quote of the Month', the kind of quote to set people thinking, even talking among themselves. Derek had changed it to 'Thoughts of the Month', which was better, she conceded. 'Quote of the Month' suggested someone had recently uttered it; 'Thoughts of the Month' allowed quotes to come from the past. But why the plural? The first poster she had seen was headed: 'Thoughts of the Month – 3'. Where were 1 and 2, perhaps 4 and 5? She copied it down. Later, in another part of the station and in other stations she came across 'Thoughts' 1, 2, 4, 5, 6 and 7. An odd number. Derek had gone to town it seemed; he had flooded the walls of the stations and trains with 'thoughts'. 'Thoughts' were buzzing all over the place. As she stopped to copy them she saw other people doing the same. The travelling public on the underground was being sent off in all directions with these 'thoughts' rumbling around in their head. One couple even entered an exchange of words about one of the quotes.

Over the course of a week travelling the Underground she had seen all seven '*Thoughts of the Month*'.

In Leicester Square she had seen and copied:

'I came to realise that what we call the freedom of the individual is not just the luxury of one intellectual to write what he likes to write, but his being a voice which can speak for those who are silent. And if he permits his freedom of expression to be abolished, then he has abolished their freedom to find in his voice a voice for their wrongs.'

Stephen Spender: The Thirties and After, Journals 1933/75

In Belsize Park she had copied:

'War is sweet to those who know it not'.

Erasmus 1498

In Green Park she had copied:

'Granted this fashion of argument,' Eduard replied, 'you

women would become invincible: first sensible, so that one
cannot contradict; affectionate, so that one is glad to give in;
sensitive, so that one doesn't want to hurt you; full of premo-
nitions, so that one is frightened.'

Goethe: Elective Affinities

In Kings Cross she had copied:

'Don't give us what we want, we must have deserved something better.'

Brikt Jensen – Norwegian intellectual

In Marble Arch she had copied:

The manner in which we conduct such dialogue is also important. And how should this be? In goodness, gentleness and
tolerance, the Koran says. Each must present his evidence, and
each must respect the right of the others not to accept it. 'Your
job is to pass the message along. Whether they believe or not is
none of your concern,' God said to His Messenger in the
Koran . . . What is important, and least emphasised, is the social
function of belief, the all-important earthly purpose of religion.
It is what you do with your belief that should concern one, not
the belief itself . . . The test of your beliefs, whatever they may
be, is in how you treat me . . .'

Dr Hesham el Essawy, head of the Islamic Society for the
Promotion of Religious Tolerance

As she was copying that one into her notebook a middle-aged
Arab from the wealthy Arab community that inhabited the area
around the Marble Arch end of the Edgware Road stood by her
and asked:

'Why are you copying?'

'Because it's a reassuring voice.'

'Reassuring? What you want to be reassured about?' Beatie

sensed she was in delicate territory. He saved her answering. 'You think all Islam is fanatic, perhaps?'

'I'm reassured by the voice of tolerance and reason coming from any religion.' She hoped he would accept that and move away. Then she thought – why do I want him to move away? The purpose of such "poster thoughts" is to stimulate discussion. Yes, but not here in the middle of an underground station, and over such a complex issue. He held out his hand.

'Glad to know you.' She shook it, smiled, and returned the sentiment.

'Glad to know you, too.'

In Liverpool Street she had copied:

'That's why women are so much more essential to men than the other way round. Women are more used to accepting the consequences of what they do and accepting their own failings, while men simply must have someone to blame.'
                    from 'Unexplained Laughter' by Alice Thomas Ellis

She saw a second 'thought' in Liverpool Street and copied it:

'A man may start by wishing for truth without going the right way to arrive at it, and may end by embracing falsehood till he cannot bear to part with it.'
Augustus Jessopp, DD. 'Introduction to The Life and Miracles
                              of St William of Norwich'

All this she related to her friends at the celebratory dinner to which she was taking them in Chinatown. Sitting at a large round table she commanded their indulgence as she read out all the 'thoughts'.

'What kind of a man was this Derek?' asked Barney in wonderment at the spectrum of the quotations chosen. 'Did he impress you as an intellect?'

'He didn't impress me as an intellect at all,' replied Beatie.

'He wasn't employed to be an intellect, was he?' observed Tamara. 'He was employed to find one, that's all. Heads of departments succeed if they've chosen the right team. Your Derek had an eye for what he wasn't, obviously.'

Lee thought the quotations a waste of time. 'They won't be remembered, and most people – this is England, don't forget – will be too embarrassed to start up a conversation over them.'

'That's cynical youth talking,' said Tamara who, she confessed to herself, was disappointed by her young lover's response.

'In fact,' said Tina, there's more than one thing disappointing you, isn't there?'

'Go away, Mother,' Tamara hissed through clenched teeth.

'Oh, no!' said Barney. 'Not you, Tina. This is a celebration, not a wake.'

'And you've got your own reasons for wanting me gone, haven't you?'

'It's all right,' said Barney, 'just ignore her. She'll soon get fed up and leave.'

'Of course I will,' said Tina. 'I know you all know that I know what I know, and I don't want to upset Beatie's party. Nice girl. Not a girl any longer, though. A woman. Nice young woman. Tell her not to be afraid of Manfred.'

'I can't tell her that, for God's sake. It's not my place to advise her on such things. Ask Tamara.'

'Ask Tamara what?' Tamara asked.

'Can I suggest you two stop this,' said Manfred. 'There are times when it ceases to be charming and becomes intrusive.' They acquiesced, and Tina floated off.

Thus it was that 'celebratory' was hardly the word applicable to the evening. They sort of enjoyed being together but Tina was right, lives were going wrong. Tamara could feel her ardent relationship with Lee was slipping away. It was not only that passion was being true to its familiar, ephemeral nature; a certain staidness was entering her boyfriend's personality. He was beginning to balk at her effervescence. The more she enthused the cooler he

became. The more she was tactile the more he stiffened. Also – he
was losing patience with a dead woman's interference, and though
Tina's interferences irritated her daughter, too, Tina was her
mother, and you don't touch my mother or else. Just as you can't
discuss children with their parents – you offend them where
they've placed their most cherished endeavour.

And what *were* those secret thoughts Tina knew were burden-
ing Barney? These: proud and delighted, to say nothing of
relieved, though he was that his two daughters had found their
way in life, yet a new, dispiriting angst had descended upon him.
Barney was regretting having given up his biography on
Marcantonio. Shame and defeat had overtaken him. So much of
his life had been devoted to it, why give up at this late stage?
When he revealed his regrets to the company Beatie asked just
that question.

'After all the time and research you put into it, why give up? I
was never persuaded by your explanation those months ago. What
was it you said? 'The heart must face the fact of inequality . . .''

Barney corrected her. 'The heart must face the unhappy fact of
unequal endowment, is what I said. And I remember it because it
wasn't original to me. I'd read it somewhere, wrote it down and
memorised it.'

'You said something else, too. Everyone has a good story to tell
but not everyone is capable of telling it.'

'Something like that. And it's true.'

'But how do you know you're not capable of telling it until you
tell it?'

'That's true also. And it's why I'm regretting giving up.'

'Can't you pick up where you left off?'

'No. Something's gone dead.' Barney paused significantly. 'I
think.'

And then there was Beatie and Manfred. Poor, confused souls –
confident about their separate entities, coy and bewildered about
their togetherness. By now they had done so much together,
shared a life for a couple of years without, as it were,

consummating it. The relationship was in danger of becoming the habit of friendship and nothing more. Friendship was fine, precious, it lasts when passion dies, but no passion had been explored. Manfred had found relief now and then with old girlfriends. Beatie had known about it, understood, but was – she had to admit – uncomfortable. Nor was Manfred left feeling other than shabby. There was no heart in those encounters. Beatie was his love. All else was grubby second best. Why could they not settle into the amorous relationship both, each knew, the other craved? They had talked about it and agreed that if it was to happen then it would happen when the time, the mood, the rhythm, all the parts fell into place, or would not; they would recognise it, for good or ill. Neither knew that time was not far off. Their cloud of uncertainty still hovered over them.

There they were, all gathered to celebrate, each shredded by the loose ends of their lives. Yet they did celebrate. Beatie bought one bottle of champagne, Manfred the other. Gaiety won the evening because all hearts hunger for joy, and this combination of personalities had difficulty standing still. They talked and argued nonstop, laughed a lot and drew great pleasure from one another's company. Barney thought he might, just might, open his notebook again; Beatie and Manfred exchanged cosy smiles, smiles they frequently smiled, relaxed and familiar with one another. But this evening something more informed their smiles, one in particular. Both were struck, at the same time, by a truth each had been frightened to acknowledge: the difference in their ages was not a deterrent to intimacy. The opposite was true, it was a stimulant. Manfred's age was an intoxicant for Beatie; and Beatie's ripe young womanhood excited Manfred. In this celebratory evening he understood what had held him back – a fear that sixty years rendered his sexual longings lewd, vulgar.

Tamara and Lee also exchanged smiles but not the smiles of two people with a future; rather smiles of resignation, forgiveness and gratitude for a time that was rich but over.

Postscript

51

I told Manfred

I told Manfred about the rape. He was hurt that I had not trusted him enough to share knowledge of the ordeal with him.

'I needed to live through it on my own,' I explained, 'and I'm glad I did. You would have confused me, urged me to prosecute, made a big hoohah about it.'

'Probably,' he said.

'And in the end I rather liked the boys.' Manfred was a little shocked to hear me say this.

'Liked them?'

'They were clever, considerate and mortified. And they apologised in a manner that was lyrical rather than abject.' He went silent. It was a testing moment. I prayed he would not ask: 'Did you enjoy it?' He did not.

We were walking through the Heath to Kenwood House. It was a Sunday morning at the height of summer. The open-air concert platforms were being set up. Kids were playing football, others were rolling down the incline in front of the mansion, the very old were sitting on benches 'dedicated to the memory of', still capable of wonderment.

Manfred said: 'This is where I meet people who have been my bread and butter for years but whose names I can't remember.' A football came his way. He forgot his age and kicked it violently, losing his balance and falling heavily on his back. I laughed.

'It's not funny,' he said. Nor was it. He was on his back for the next two weeks. I enjoyed looking after him, bringing him breakfast in bed, selecting news items to read from the *Guardian* and the *Telegraph*, discussing with him daily what he would like me to cook for dinner. In return he was a source of patient encouragement as I ploughed through noun after noun breaking them down into their parts. I had to spend a lot of time in reference libraries, and worried how he would manage with me not being around. I had no need. He was a resourceful and methodical man, mostly defiant. But sometimes stubborn – he thought that lying on his back would, with time, encourage all bones to settle back where they belonged. It took ten days of subtle nagging to allow me to engage a chiropractor who wrenched his back into place in an instant.

One morning, towards the end of the two weeks, after he had refused my help and made his own way to the bathroom to shave and gingerly shower, when lying on his back in bed, reading and looking handsome and independent, his strength and flexibility returned, I could no longer hold back. I stripped before his amazed, wide and appreciative eyes, slowly, though not attempting to gyrate like a stripper, which would have been embarrassing, and dived upon him smothering him all over with the kind of kisses we had not so far shared. I peeled off his pyjamas, caressed his strong chest, nibbled his nipples, took him in my mouth and drank him dry. He could not yet return the pleasure. But in time he would, I have my needs!

A start had been made. The time had been right. We became lovers at last. The parts came together.

52

No one should be this happy

No one should be this happy. I will surely die. A penalty will be
exacted. I will fall again. Next time it will be worse. How could
I have lived without her all these years? Beatie Bryant and her
parts? Oh, she was a woman of parts all right, glorious parts.
Every part – from her generous heart to the thick bush between
her legs – was a feast and a blessing. How could it have happened?
A mistake had been made. Surely this voluptuous creature
smelling of strawberries and cider apples, devouring me as though
I was an Adonis of five and twenty, was not intended for me.
Love's postman had landed her at the wrong address. I had not
earned such joy. I'm a puritan, I believe everything should be
earned, few things are a right and those that are must also be
earned. How did I earn her, this Beatie, this chance encounter in
Shepherd Market? I didn't. She is a gift. Bestowed by herself. I
will devote every moment of the rest of my life plotting to make
her happy. Every day will be a surprise whether of an exquisite
chocolate or an exquisite pearl, an exotic print or an exotic holiday, a ballet, a homemade meal by candlelight, a body massage,
flowers for each room. A ring. A ring. I will marry her. A ring!
Every day I will think about her. Will I oppress her? No – because
she has her work and I have mine. She must put parts together and
I must climb mountains. God give me strength to enjoy her for
years to come. There is such madness looming in the world. Let
me have years, let the joy last. Years, years. Let me have years.

53

I will look after them all

I will look after them all. Barney, Tamara, Natasha, even Greg. Though I can't speak to Greg. He was not around for me to get into his head. I'll get to him through Tamara's head.

Barney will write his book – he'll have to get it published himself but I'll guide him to the last page. I'll even guide him to a new companion. It won't be passion. At his age how could it be? But it will be comfort, a body to cuddle at nights. Everybody needs a body to cuddle at nights.

And Tamara will make her first film. About me! The voice in their heads. A film about the voices we carry in our heads.

Natasha will need me most of all because she will go into business – for which she really has no talent – trying to obtain a licence to create and run one of the new radio stations for which everyone is vying. God knows why. The airwaves are cluttered with the same music and the same nonsense from listeners airing views on topics they know nothing about, and possessing scant intelligence to comment wisely even when they do. But there you are – she wants to create 'Radio Chanson' to offer singers like Piaf, Reggiani, Brel, Demarcyk, Farandouri, and the American greats like Jane Olivor, Barbra Streisand, Frank Sinatra, Mahelia Jackson, Nina Simone and Ray Charles et al. And of course her Greg.

'Call it "Radio Oldies",' I say.

'Go away, Mother,' she says.

But I won't. I can't. And I don't think they want me to. They want me in their head. That's how we live on in each other. Which is how it should be. And if it shouldn't be – that's how it is.